CONTACT: THE BATTLE FOR AMERICA,
BOOK ONE

COMING OF THE STORM

W. MICHAEL GEAR AND KATHLEEN O'NEAL GEAR

KENNEBEC LARGE PRINT
A part of Gale, Cengage Learning

GALE
CENGAGE Learning

Detroit • New York • San Francisco • New Haven, Conn • Waterville, Maine • London

GALE
CENGAGE Learning

LIBRARY OF CONGRESS CATALOGING-IN-PUBLICATION DATA

Gear, Kathleen O'Neal.
    Coming of the storm / by W. Michael Gear and Kathleen O'Neal Gear.
        p. cm. — (Kennebec Large Print superior collection)
    (Contact : the battle for America ; bk. 1)
    ISBN-13: 978-1-4104-2842-4
    ISBN-10: 1-4104-2842-7
    1. Southern States—Discovery and exploration—Spanish—Fiction. 2. Indians of North America—Fiction. 3. Soto, Hernando de, ca. 1500–1542—Relations with Indians—Fiction. 4. Large type books. I. Gear, Kathleen O'Neal. II. Title.
PS3557.E19C66 2010b
813'.54—dc22   2010016834

Published in 2010 by arrangement with Gallery Books, a division of Simon & Schuster, Inc.

COMING OF THE STORM

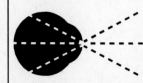

To our delightful Sheltie
Shannon

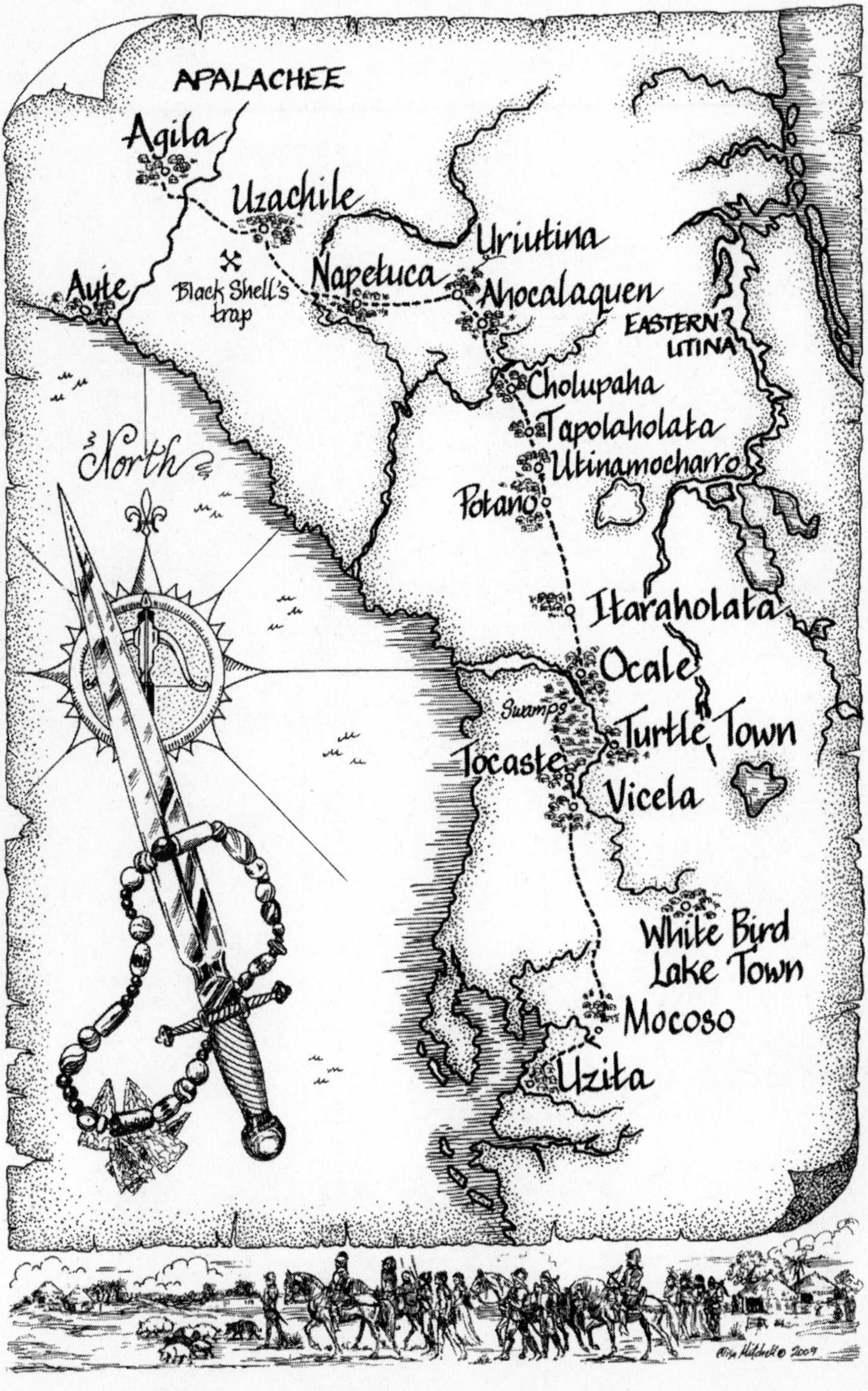

APALACHEE

Agila

Uzachile

Ayte

✗✗ Black Shell's
trap

Napetuca

Uriutina

Ahocalaquen

EASTERN
UTINA?

Cholupaha

Tapolaholata

Utinamocharro

Potano

North

Itaraholata

Ocale

Swamps

Turtle Town

Tocaste

Vicela

White Bird
Lake Town

Mocoso

Uzita

Lisa Mitchell © 2009

FOREWORD

Since the inception of the People books, we have been asked by readers to write Contact period novels. Previously we'd shied away. After all, unlike the archaeological cultures we normally write about, the information is readily available in the form of written historical journals and reports from people who were there. Some Contact period history is actually taught by the public schools. Or was.

Then one of our good friends — he jokes that he's got some white blood in his ancestry, too — remarked, "Man, why is it that except for Custer, we never won?"

The truth is, even after the Europeans finally figured out where the Americas were — it only took them fifteen thousand years longer than the PaleoIndians — it was anything but a slam dunk to colonize. Nor were most indigenous peoples opposed to having the strange white folk living down the road. Everyone was as happy then to exploit their neighbors, red or white, as they are now, and the Native peoples were never the innocent victims modern mythology would have us believe.

But where to begin? Which of the myths of Contact should we attack head-on?

In all the annals of American history, we can think of no individual who has been as undeservedly whitewashed with glory as Hernando de Soto. Counties throughout the American South are named in his honor. His statue stands in numerous city and state parks. Historical societies have lovingly placed markers alongside public highways, celebrating the route of his army. An American automobile was manufactured with de Soto's name on the hood and his likeness on the chrome emblem dominating the steering wheel.

Hernando de Soto is an American icon.

Perhaps we should be grateful that most people have heard of him. At least they realize that American history dates to 1539. That's a start. But de Soto wasn't the first European to land in Florida. Juan Ponce de León, Diego Miruelo, Francisco Hernandez de Córdoba, Alonzo Álvarez de Pineda, and Pánfilo de Narváez all sailed to Florida before de Soto, the most noteworthy of these being Narváez's 1528 expedition. It ended in spectacular disaster among the Apalachee of northwest Florida.

When de Soto landed at Tampa Bay in 1539, he brought with him a small army estimated at six- to seven-hundred soldiers, another hundred and sixty personal guards, pages, secretaries, lawyers, herdsmen, blacksmiths, carpenters, engineers, and numerous domestic servants. Two of the nobles even dragged their wives along to oversee their household staffs.

Not all in the expedition were so lofty. The dirty work — lifting, toting, and carrying — would fall initially to a corps of several hundred Caribbean slaves and occasional Africans. De Soto figured he could replenish and swell their ranks as they were brutally worked to death. Enough women and girls — captured in the Caribbean — were included to cook during the day, tend fires, and of course service the troops at night.

Estimates of de Soto's total complement — depending on the source — range from seven hundred and thirty to slightly over a thousand. Then we have the animals. Two hundred and fifty warhorses and an unknown number of personal mounts, packhorses, and mules were unloaded at Tampa Bay. The number of war dogs is undisclosed. And — last but not least — somewhere near three hundred pigs were brought ashore.

With this force de Soto would begin his trek across the American South and earn his place in history books, municipal parks, auto designs, and roadside markers. One wonders if five hundred years from now future generations will do the same for Adolf Hitler, Joseph Stalin, or Pol Pot.

For the most part de Soto's forces didn't stay in one place long enough to really commit full-scale genocide. Nor can we really get a good handle on the number of Native people he and his troops murdered. More were captured, chained, and worked to death than died in battle at places like Napetuca, Mabila, Chicaza, and elsewhere. The records left by his chroniclers, Rodrigo Rangel, The Gentleman of Elvas, Luis Hernandez de Biedma, and Garcilaso de la Vega, are full of martial accounts. The impact of de Soto's *entrada* is supported in the archaeological record at places like Tatham Mound (see Dale L. Hutchinson, *Tatham Mound and the Bioarchaeology of European Contact,* University Press of Florida, 2006).

With no apology to the local historical societies who have enshrined him, Hernando de Soto was a monster. We refer the reader to David Ewing Duncan's comprehensive biography: *Hernando de Soto.* De Soto got off to an early start — in his teens he burned his first man alive: a Panamanian chief who couldn't offer up enough gold. While murdering and pillaging his way across parts of Central and South America, he acquired skills that would have chilled a Nazi SS officer. During the Inca campaign with Francisco Pizarro, de Soto mastered the art of butchery and obtained stunning wealth.

Thus it was that when de Soto headed north through Florida in 1539 he rode at the head of the world's most advanced military, outfitted with the latest weaponry, and using tactics honed from years of combat against the Aztec, Maya, and Inca. He and his soldiers knew how to kill native peoples. The great irony is that, despite the odds, Southeastern Indians destroyed this monster. It's a classic struggle of good against evil. Yet, through the injustice of history, it is de Soto's name that is remembered with reverence.

Here then, is the other side of the story. The conflict was long, lasting four years. It was fought from Florida to the Carolinas, through Tennessee, Alabama, Mississippi, and Arkansas, all the way to Texas, and back. No single indigenous nation led the struggle, and no one people landed the fatal blow. The defenders didn't even think of themselves as on the same side. But all could recognize the monster when it came into their midst.

The arrival of Europeans in North America has been condensed into a single "conquest": as if one inevitable steamroller event followed another. That is myth. The fact — as de Soto's fate illustrates — is that the home team won most of the opening rounds.

Black Shell, Pearl Hand, and other characters in this narrative are of course fictional. Native nations, leaders, peoples, and towns, however, are real. With the transition into the Battle for America series, we must defer to written records. Hence, you will find Timucua names like Irriparacoxi, Uzachile, and Ahocalaquen. Dear reader, you cope with names like Albuquerque, Talladega, Minneapolis, and Pensacola every day. You can learn these, too.

The name Timucua was created by the French and copied by the Spanish to refer to speakers of the "Timucua" language. These original inhabitants of Northern Florida and Southern Georgia organized their societies into chieftainships of fluid and varying complexity. At the time of de Soto's arrival they were happily raiding one another, living off the land, worshipping the ancestors they buried in earthen mounds, occasionally sacrificing a notable captive to the sun, carving magnificent woodwork, and generally creating their own drama.

Some, like the Uzachile, organized into paramount chiefdoms — equivalent to contemporaneous divine-right kingdoms in Europe.

De Soto would slice his way through the Southern Timucua as if they were stalks of wheat. After reaching the organized and fierce Uzachile, we can only wonder how it would

14

have turned out had an informant not whispered in de Soto's ear. To learn more about these remarkable people, we recommend Jerald T. Milanich's *The Timucua,* Blackwell Publishers, Cambridge, Mass., and Oxford, UK.

For those who wish to follow along with actual historical sources, we recommend *The De Soto Chronicles,* Volumes I and II, Clayton, Knight, and Moore, eds., University of Alabama Press, 1993. A bibliography is included for those who seek additional information.

DREAMS

The Dream carried one of her souls away last night, or so she believed. The images her Dream soul saw were so vivid, fresh, and bright, that she might have relived them — exactly as she had on that long-ago day. The details, unmarred by the passing of time, remained as sharply defined in her memory as freshly chipped obsidian. The earthy, humid odors of soil, freshly cut palm fronds, and spring flowers came unbidden to her nostrils. The angle of the light, splashes of newly burst flowers in yellow, pink, blue, and red, dotted the green tangles of vine, brush, and tall grass.

The sun beat down from a haze-milky sky as she sawed at thick palmetto stems with a sharp clamshell. A stray bead of sweat trickled from her armpit, down around the swell of her bare right breast. The frond drooped, allowing her to sever the remaining fibers. She placed it atop the others she'd cut from the palmetto and straightened, grateful to relieve the strain in her lower back.

Once again he and his dogs came striding down the trail, fluid muscles flexing beneath moist, sun-darkened skin. White heron feathers, three of them, fluttered from the crook of his trader's staff, and a thick alligator-hide quiver rode crossways on his back. His face was smooth, angular, with a firm jaw and straight nose. She'd liked the look of his wide cheekbones and the half smile on his thin-lipped mouth. Oddly, for a man of his age, his face was undecorated by either paint or tattoo. His black hair grew fully from his head, pulled back into a bun at the rear and pinned with a bone skewer.

She remembered the rippling muscle in his arms, the thick spread of his shoulders, and the travel-stained fabric apron that hung down front and back from a breech-cloth tied about his narrow waist. His five pack dogs were walking ahead of him, and of course they saw her first.

She froze the image, staring up at the soot-thick thatch roof rising over her head. *What if I hadn't met his eyes? What if I hadn't felt that thrill as our souls touched across time and space?*

What if she'd just ducked down, crouched over her severed palm fronds? Sometimes the smallest decisions led to the most tumultuous events.

Don't look him in the eyes, girl. Just let him pass.

But their eyes had locked. Now, a lifetime

18

later, she relived that instant. Her heart picked up, blood quickening in her old veins. Her lungs expanded, and her loins tickled with anticipation.

She coughed, placing a withered hand to her mouth, and glanced around the dark room where she lay.

Would it have made any difference? Really? She shook her head, smiling up at the dark recesses of the roof.

"How were we to know?"

And if I had known? Had I let him pass, could I have saved the world? Would anything have been different? She grinned at the absurdity of the notion. No, even now, if she could go back — just like she had in the Dream — she'd do it all again.

She closed her eyes in surrender, summoning that day again, and pulling it around her like a wrapping. She breathed the moist warm air, felt the faint breeze, and ran her fingers over the stacked palm fronds. The ache tightened in her back, and her young heart beat with renewed vigor. Her skin was smooth and silky, her breasts firm and round.

He's coming, just as I had hoped.

Boldly, she lifted her head and stared him straight in the eyes.

The jolt was still powerful — relived as his sharp gaze met hers. Once again she saw his surprise melt into curiosity, the smile curling his lips. Something in his eyes, a reflection of his souls, challenged yet reassured her. A warmth built deep in the pit of her loins.

Wait, fool. Use your head for once. Men had always been her downfall — as they had been her mother's. *He may just be another man. Discover the depth of the water before you jump.*

She watched him stop and signal his dogs. All the while she stared into his eyes.

"Greetings!" he called in Timucua.

She straightened, rising to her feet. At the sight of her, he seemed oddly starved for breath. The change in his eyes as he took in her high breasts, narrow waist, and long legs was as predictable as sunrise.

Oh, yes. I've got him, assuming I decide I want him.

"Forget it," she said, mouthing those same words she'd said so many years ago.

Forget it? How?

As tears slipped past her tightly pressed eyelids and trickled down her wrinkled cheeks, the world she'd once known began to die all over again.

ONE

I am Black Shell, of the Chief Clan, of the Hickory Moiety, of the Chicaza Nation. But then, truth be told, ten long years have passed since I ventured out from my people. You see, in their eyes I am *akeohoosa.* It means "dead and lost" in the Mos'kogee tongue. A more precise term would be "outcast." When I was driven from my country long ago, I thought it a divinely bitter irony. The notion of being akeohoosa would have killed a lesser man. At least, that's what I tell myself. It has killed others, generally from despair, loneliness, and guilt.

My people, the Chicaza, have fostered the myth that they are somehow superior, that they hold themselves to a higher standard.

Such notions have served them well. By cultivating a code of honor, piety, and nobility, they have had fewer scruples about conquest or manufacturing a reason for war over some perceived slight or insult.

Only when I was finally an outsider did I gain any understanding of the strengths and weaknesses of such a system. You see, most other nations don't like the Chicaza. They think we're rather prickly and arrogant prudes. At the same time, people fear us because the only thing the Chicaza do better than preening, slapping each other on the back, and lying about our innate superiority, is make war. No one takes warfare with the Chicaza lightly.

That curious mixture of awe and dislike has served me well during my years as an akeohoosa. I'm not fond of my people, either.

That fateful day when all the trouble started, I heard the voice of Horned Serpent. It was that terrible Spirit Being — the great winged snake who flies up into the summer sky — who told me to run from my first battle. My clan called me a liar when I insisted that Horned Serpent spoke to me. Since the day I was banished, anger has run along my veins like hot liquid. It has spurred me in my wanderings.

What does an exile do? If he's of the Chicaza's Chief Clan — as I am — he trades and gambles. The things I trade consist of luxury goods: pieces of precious copper; polished white shell; buffalo wool, medicine herbs and Spirit plants; brightly colored feathers, and unusual carvings or artwork.

As to gambling, I have a facility for games like stickball, chunkey, or akbatle. In addition to those skills, much of my life has been dedicated to mastering the bow. Warriors — no matter what their nation — are a proud lot and more than willing to wager just about anything on their ability to drive an arrow through the mouth of a narrow-necked jar at twenty paces. Their temptation really rises when the challenger is a rootless foreign braggart like me.

I travel with five pack dogs. A trader's dogs must be large, sturdy, and sure-footed. Over the years dogs have come and gone, but the ones I traveled south with were among the best I'd ever owned.

My favorite — and most beloved — was Fetch. He was more than just a dog, having a partly human soul. He kept my spirits up when things turned miserable. His greatest joy in life came from retrieving thrown sticks, hide balls, or even rocks. He'd been with me for eight long summers, and a better companion you will not find.

Skipper, another of my dogs, was named for his curious sideways gait, his butt traveling a hand's width to the right of his front as he trotted. He was light brown with short hair and an oddly blue left eye.

Bark, well, his name says it all. At command, he'd stay silent, mostly, but if one of the other dogs stole something from him, he'd just plop on his rear and bark his fool head off in indignation. He was charcoal black, with a thick head decorated by old scars. Bark had another talent: When it came to a dog fight, he was terror unleashed.

Squirm? He liked to wiggle out of his packs and had made a study of how to do it without me noticing. I swore he had extra joints in his legs and spine. His long hair was dark brown and sleek, serving to accent the white blaze on his face and the milky bib on his chest.

Gnaw no longer lived up to his name, but as a puppy, several times he almost ended up as stew after chewing off sections of pack leather. He was the fastest and strongest of my dogs. Consequently he carried the heaviest pack. I thought of him as a huge gray monster of a dog — the image only sullied by the cute white tip on his tail.

For several years my path had taken me south, away from the civilized lands of the Mos'kogee and the other great nations. It led me to the Apalachee, who first conjured my curiosity about the bearded and pale sea peoples. While at Apalachee, I visited the place they call Aute. There I saw with my own eyes the bleached skulls of great and terrifying animals larger than elk. Upon these are said to ride the mysterious hair-faced men from the sea.

Eleven winters past, the invaders — calling themselves *Kristianos* — arrived from the south under the leadership of their chief, Narvaez. The Apalachee had nothing but disdain for the Kristianos, having watched them struggle through the coastal swamps and tidal flats, sick and starving in a land of plenty. In the end the Kristianos built rafts, ate their great beasts, and floated down to the gulf. After that, they simply vanished into the sea.

I had walked among their curious constructions at Aute, and saw the great wooden crosses they hung in the trees. I viewed with awe the mysterious metal left behind, and held pieces of their cloth. I wondered at the remarkable, many-colored beads they had traded off during their stay. My curiosity grew with each new discovery.

The *mikko* — as the Apalachee call their high chief — is named Cafakke, or Great Soil. He has a Kristiano skull in his palace at the capital city of Anhaica. I've held it, studied the narrow bones of the face and nose, and wondered at the man whose souls once resided inside that fragile bone. It was then I decided to follow out the source of the legend. For — fool that I was — I anticipated making a fortune in trade if only I could

25

obtain a sample of their goods. The great chiefs in the north would barter fabulous wealth for such exotic oddities.

I need not bore you with the story of my route down through the Timucua lands, my time trading among the Uzachile towns, or the trouble I had with the *holata,* or chief, at Ocale town. In a sense this story begins one late afternoon when I approached White Bird Lake town. For those who have never traveled that way, it is a land of pine forests, occasional hardwoods, and palmettos. Open areas — sometimes cleared by wildfires — are lush in grass and the soils are sandy enough for the cornfields to produce. Settlements tend to be inland from either coast, away from the threat of storms, though occasional great tempests do flatten areas of forest as they roar across the peninsula from one body of water to another.

The peninsular people are warlike, as ready to fight with their cousins a half day's walk away as with the Calusa and Tequesta to the south or the Uzita to the west. Most of their towns are built around one or two low mounds that serve as supports for the chief's house, charnel house, or perhaps a temple. A log fortification is usually thrown up on an earthen embankment around the town's perimeter — just enough to allow the defenders to shoot between the gaps.

When I say the people are warlike, it's not

like among the great nations of the north, where trained armies are unleashed by a slighted minko over some perceived insult. Instead these villages and towns are in a state of constant intermittent raiding.

At times, however, some war chief — called a *paracusi* in the Southern Timucua tongue — will manage to defeat enough of his neighbors to create a loose sort of nation relying on tribute from conquered towns. Such chieftainships — if you can even call them that — are fragile, easily sundered, and generally in a constant state of flux. They rise and fall based upon the charisma and cunning of individual leaders.

Such was the case with a fellow by the name of Irriparacoxi, a newly risen leader among the mostly disorganized Southern Timucua villages.

When a man is made chief in these lands, he takes the name of the town where he rules. Thus, a man might be named Red Hawk, but he will be called Holata Ahocalaquen, or Chief Ahocalaquen, from the moment he is confirmed. I thought it was confusing, but that was how the Timucua did things.

Irriparacoxi, which would translate as something like "high war councilor and combat chief," had subjugated most of the towns south of Ocale territory and north of the Calusa and Tequesta. Controlling such a large block of land, he was happily earning tribute from his subject towns and — more important as far as I was concerned — very taken with himself. Like the puffer fish of the seas, petty chiefs can blow themselves up beyond their true importance and greatness.

Remember, I was born and raised Chicaza. I know all about created self-importance.

That day I was walking at the head of my pack dogs, my trader's staff in hand. The trail was wide, well-trodden, with palmettos, pines, and oaks on either side. Spring was in full flower, the air almost muggy. An afternoon sun was squatting in the western sky — the southeastern breeze perfectly scented with honeysuckle, gallberry, phlox, and firebush, all in bloom. The very air seemed to buzz and vibrate with the hum of insects.

Overhead, flocks of herons were winging north, their trilling hoots floating down over the land. Mockingbirds called in lilting voices from the brush. I could see an osprey circling over a marsh off to the west. I took a deep breath, and the damp musk of vegetation and rich soil filled my nostrils.

The pack dogs heard her first, pricking their ears, tails rising as they inspected the brush off to the side. Then low growls broke out as the woman raised her head from where she used a sharpened clamshell to cut palmetto fronds.

At my hand sign, the dogs went quiet, panting as they watched the woman. Squirm tried, as usual, to shake his way out of his pack. I snapped my fingers in rebuke, and Squirm shot me a "you caught me" look.

"Greetings," I called out in my halting Timucua.

The woman straightened, and what a sight she was: tall, with raven-black hair falling down past her hips. Her broad shoulders reminded me of a swimmer's, and her arms were smoothly muscled. Some men might have thought her round breasts too full, but on her tall frame they just seemed perfect. A brown skirt hung from a thin waist, held in place by a knotted rope. Gleaming thighs and shapely calves made her long legs the stuff of any man's dreams.

Then her eyes met mine. Dark — like a midnight sun — they pierced me as if reading my very souls. A slight smile curved her lips, and a knowing eyebrow lifted. Evidently she was used to be being stared at by men.

Wryly, she said, "Forget it. I belong to the Irriparacoxi. He's a very jealous man."

I had a little trouble with her accent, but responded, "What makes you think I'm interested in you?"

She gestured at the panting dogs resting under their heavy packs. "Your tongue's hanging out farther than theirs. What's the matter? No women where you come from, Trader?"

None like you. In defense I said, "Women

29

enough." Gods, she was marvelous. I watched her bend down with a lithe movement to pluck up the armful of fronds she'd cut. She gave me an irritated scowl as she picked her way through the grass to the trail. She looked even better up close, with a triangular face and a curiously delicate and straight nose; her firm chin balanced soft lips and wide cheekbones. My obvious infatuation filled her with a dancing amusement.

"So you're the famous northern trader," she stated skeptically.

"You knew I was coming?"

"Word came down a couple of days ago. We heard that the Ocale chief didn't think much of you."

"He had the silly notion that I was a Potano spy."

"Are you?"

"No." I indicated my trader's staff with the white feathers dangling from its top. "I'm a trader . . . doing what traders do. I haven't even been in Potano country. They live over by the east coast. I followed the central trail south."

"Why?"

Was she being insufferable on purpose? "Because I've never been down here before. I've got northern goods to trade for things like spoonbill feathers, Taino tobacco, and sea turtle shell. Goods they don't have up north." Time to take the offensive. "So, why are you out here all alone?"

She was giving me a thoughtful appraisal, as though I were a deer haunch. "I came to discover what sort of man you are."

That threw me. "Why would you care?"

I kept trying not to stare at her breasts, or that narrow waist, or the way her skirt hung on those rounded hips. Was she a sorceress casting a spell on my souls? What would it feel like to run my fingers down her cheek, to see her smile at me?

"We all have our reasons," she whispered absently.

It took all my control to keep from gaping like a fool. What man wouldn't?

"You travel alone?" she asked.

"For the time being."

"Where's your woman?"

"I don't have one."

"Are you that difficult to get along with?"

"No. I've just never found the right woman. Most don't like leaving family, clan, and home. Trading can be a lonely business, never long with the same people." I shrugged. "It takes a certain sense of adventure to be a trader's wife. You've got to be footloose." I smiled. "Free."

"And you don't think a woman wants to be free?" Her head cocked, as if something important balanced on my answer.

I gave that some thought before replying, "Trading just isn't for women. Traders spend a lot of cold nights sleeping on the ground in the rain. There are days with poor food, or an empty belly. What I own is carried on my back or by the dogs."

"But you are beholden to no man."

"Only myself and the Power of trade," I agreed, then smiled. "Fortunately, having only myself to talk to, I win all the arguments."

"Is that important to you? Winning arguments?"

"I was making a joke. I do that. Make jokes at my expense. It keeps me from taking myself too seriously."

"Why?" It was as if she were trying to see right down inside my guts, as if somehow sitting in judgment. Judgment for what?

"Let's just say that if you get slapped around a lot by life, it's better to have a sense of humor," I grinned. "And believe me, life does have a habit of hitting you when you're not looking."

Her lips curled into a knowing smile. But thoughts churned behind her eyes — masked by a long-practiced control? Why did she keep looking at me that way? Not that I minded. A woman like her could turn her attention my way anytime. The fantasies she ignited started following their own path . . . to a snug bed.

"Forget it," she repeated. "I'm the Irriparacoxi's."

"Wife?" I asked, gesturing the dogs to follow as she started down the trail and I matched her pace.

She shot me a scathing glance and made a disgusted sound. "Luckily, no. But then, were I a wife, I could at least divorce him. As a bound woman, I'm his to do with as he pleases." A pause. "And he'd kill you just for looking at me wrong, let alone for trying anything else."

That explained a great deal. She was property. Bound women had only a slightly higher status than slaves. I could guess what her life had been like. "You've been around the wrong kind of men for too long."

"And you're different? I'd wipe the drool off my chin before walking into Irriparacoxi's great hall and announcing myself."

"He'd kill me just for drooling?"

"When it comes to me, yes."

"Then I'll drool carefully."

"Most men do."

I gave her another sidelong inspection. She was shooting similar looks my way, as if weighing something.

"You have a name, I take it?"

She smiled. "I've had lots of them."

"How are you known to Irriparacoxi?"

"In Timucua it translates as Pearl Hand. In private Irriparacoxi calls me . . . other things."

"I am pleased to know you, Pearl Hand. Among the traders I am known as Black Shell. A man of the far distant Chicaza."

"Yes, I know. You have something of a reputation, Black Shell. Even here we have heard of your legendary feats. They say you're quite a gambler."

I shrugged. "Sometimes I get lucky at a chunkey game." I reached back and patted the pack on my back. My chunkey lances and bow were protruding from the alligator-hide case I carried. "And on occasion an arrow goes where it's supposed to. Other than that, it's just talk."

I watched the muscles tighten in her delicate jaw. "Irriparacoxi fancies himself as a warrior. While chunkey is not a game played around here, his ability with a bow is seldom bettered by any of his warriors. Is that why you have come? To challenge him?"

I gave her a noncommittal grin. "Not particularly. Here, on the peninsula, if one will go south, he must pass through the Irriparacoxi's country. Unless, of course, he wants to wade through the swamps off to the west in the Uzita lands."

"But you will trade?"

I shot her a glance. "If Irriparacoxi has anything I want."

Pearl Hand couldn't quite hide the calculation behind her controlled expression. She shifted her load of fronds. "What's in the south?"

"Rumors. Stories about bearded pale-skinned men. I've seen the metals, the beads, and the magnificent cloth. Some of the stories are as fantastic as the stories we tell at home to frighten little children. I've heard that these strange men ride giant beasts. Among the Apalachee, I've even seen the alleged skulls of such. The way it's told in the north, the strangers have great floating palaces that ride upon the waves, and their war armor is made of magical metal. I want to see if these stories are true."

"Then you're a fool."

"A fool?"

Her level gaze met mine. "Trader, the stories are true. But the last thing you want is to meet the Kristianos. Unless, that is, you wish to spend the rest of your suddenly short life as a slave. They raid for captives along the coast. Those they take are herded into the floating palaces and sailed out to sea. In all of my life, I have never heard of anyone returning. The rumors are that most slaves are worked to death within a single season."

"Where? I mean, they can't have that much work in the floating palaces."

She gave me the same look she'd give an idiot. "They have great islands out in the sea. The slaves there work cutting down trees, clearing fields, mining, growing things, and building huge earthworks. Some of the stories I've heard make no sense, but on one point, no one disagrees: These are brutal men with terrible ways."

"I still want to see them."

With a note of exasperation she asked, "Why? So you can become a slave?"

"I'm protected by the Power of trade."

"They obey no laws or rules, Black Shell. And they have no respect for Spirit Power, at least as far as any of us can see. Walk up to them expecting them to honor the Power of trade, and they'll either kill you for the sport of it, or clap one of their metal collars around your neck and lead you off by a metal chain."

"Everyone believes in the Power of trade."

She gave me a pitying look. "Not the Kristianos."

"You seem to know a lot about them."

"When I was a little girl they tried to build a town. My mother went to them, searching for my father."

"I don't understand."

She threw her head back in a most provocative manner, her long hair swaying. "I'm Chicora. Does that mean anything to you?"

I nodded slowly, remembering the stories. "From along the coast up north. The bearded white men have been there twice over the years."

She continued giving me that look, as if I were remarkably dim.

I tried to understand. "They took your father . . . stole him for a slave? And your mother went looking for him?"

Her expression hardened, her mouth thin-

36

ning with irritation. "My father took my mother from Chicora, kept her until they had filled their great boat with slaves. But on that last night — in the confusion as they were packing — she escaped. When her family discovered she was carrying a bearded brat, they disowned her. For reasons beyond my understanding, she went back looking for the man when the Kristianos landed a few years later. I was very small then, having but five summers. The Kristianos didn't do very well building their town. Some of the things they do are inexplicably stupid. They were starving to death surrounded by food: things they wouldn't think to eat. Finally they loaded up and sailed off into the sea."

She was kind enough to ignore my gaping stare as I studied her face, the thin nose, the line of her jaw.

She gave me a humored glance. "You want to see one? A Kristiano? Holata Mocoso has one just over west of here. White men show up every so often; their big boats get wrecked by storms. The survivors, the ones Mother Sea doesn't suck under and drown, wash ashore. Usually in a pathetic state."

"Yes, I would like very much to see one. I have so many questions."

The look she gave me sent a shiver down my spine. "They are evil, Black Shell. By ones and twos, they even seem likable. But if they come in groups, run. Hide, for if they capture you, it's worse than dying on a square."

She referred to the log square onto which captives were tied and slowly tortured to death. Could they really be that bad?

"And you?" I couldn't help but ask, "You're one? Or at least half of one! Is this really true?"

She turned those gleaming midnight eyes on mine. "Oh, yes, Trader." Then she performed a saucy sway of her hips. "So, if they're completely evil, what does that make me?"

"Enticing," I said in Mos'kogee.

To my shocked surprise she smiled as though coming to a decision, and replied in precise Mos'kogee, "And just what would you do with me?"

I gaped at her, suddenly speechless.

Fully aware of my fluster, she added, "Just what I'd expect from a man."

I glanced down at my packs, calculating. What would it take to persuade Irriparacoxi to trade for this woman?

Reading my expression, she laughed in a cunning way. "More than you've got, Trader."

We'd see.

Two

White Bird Lake town was a typical settlement in the region. The town itself covered a hammock — or hump of raised ground — on the banks of one of the many freshwater lakes that abound in the central peninsula. A low earthen berm sporting a ragged wooden palisade rose above a ditch fed by lake water.

The ditch is, of course, defensive, but also serves as a garden for yellow lotus, cattail, spatterdock, and other aquatic plants cultivated by the people. Children learn to harpoon fish along its muddy banks.

Inside the fortification, a single charnel house perched atop a low mound on the west, just inside the gate. Irriparacoxi's palace dominated a higher mound on the eastern side. The two were built in a direct line with the equinox sunrise.

Through the rickety palisade I could see the houses were thatch-roofed, supported by a wooden frame, and floored with matting, but open sided — the climate being conducive to such designs, especially in the summer.

When trash and shell piles grew large enough, soil would be carted in by the basketload to make a raised floor for a new house, thereby ensuring the structure stood above high water in the rainy season.

Let me tell you about the Southern Timucua: Farming is a part-time occupation. As a person travels south, the soils become less and less suited to the cultivation of corn, beans, and squash. Being part-time farmers, Irriparacoxi's people rely on hunting, fishing, collecting, and trapping as the basis for survival, and their land is rich enough in such resources to support them. Constant low-level warfare — and the high death rate for newborn children — keeps their numbers low enough that, unlike those of us in the north, they are not as dependent on raised crops to feed a large population.

As Pearl Hand and I left the forest and entered the fields skirting the town, a shout went up. I held my trader's staff high at first, ensuring that no one misinterpreted my arrival as threatening. The staff also proved useful for beating off the town dogs that came running and barking, ready to pick a fight.

Despite being infatuated with Pearl Hand, the job at hand was to keep my dogs together, announce myself, and ensure that I was received with the respect and honor due a trader of my stature. Sometimes this included playing my little cane flute as I approached. Walking at Pearl Hand's side, the flute seemed unnecessary. Besides, I'm not that good at music.

Pearl Hand did her part superbly, stepping inside the gate and calling out, "A trader, the legendary Black Shell, comes from the north. Notify the Irriparacoxi and the priests! Someone prepare food! We are honored to host such a renowned man."

I arched an eyebrow and gave an appreciative nod. Meanwhile women and children were headed my way from across the fields, and with them came the dogs. It's tough to make a grand entrance through the palisade gate when you're jabbing at dogs to keep them away from the trade pack. Fortunately, the local kids seemed to catch on, driving their mutts back with sticks and other thrown debris.

Bark looked on with anticipation, but no fight came his way. Gnaw wagged his tail, the white tip flipping back and forth. Squirm sat and tried to scratch his pack off.

41

A wizened old man, white-haired and fragile-looking, came walking down the gate passage. He glanced at Pearl Hand with her load of fronds, and then at me. The look he gave Pearl Hand intrigued me; it smoldered with a reserved hostility.

"You are the trader known as Black Shell?" he asked, his hands forming the appropriate signs as he spoke. Unlike spoken languages which can be mutually unintelligible from one town to the next, sign language is almost universal.

"I am so known," I replied in my clumsy Timucua, my hands signing the words. "Be it known to the people of this place that I come under the Power of trade, may it please the sun, the ancestors, and the great Irriparacoxi and his councilors."

"I, *Anacotima* Red Wing, first councilor of White Bird Lake town, bid you welcome in the name of the great Irriparacoxi and his people. We have heard stories of the trader called Black Shell. It is said that you bear many wondrous items in your packs and that you are most generous with your trade. You are said to be an honest man, one who does not take undue advantage of his hosts."

The old man rambled on without a breath. *Anacotima* is a term that can be thought of as something like a combination orator, councilor, palace overseer, and supervisor.

For my part, it was all I could do to keep

from craning my neck as Pearl Hand disappeared through the gate. I bit off a sigh, turning my attention back to the old man. His job, of course, was to stall me with endless monologue while the town headmen were run down and informed, the chief's house was made ready, and all the rulers and shakers had time to put on their best dress, drape their jewelry, and get their faces painted to perfection. Meanwhile several women were being delegated the job of gathering up whatever was cooking and delivering it to the chief's house. To do so created the illusion that superb feasts were a boringly common occurrence in Irriparacoxi's mound-top house.

Traders' rule of thumb: The more pompous the chief, the more elaborate the preparations.

While the old man rambled on about his town and chief, I watched the local women scurrying in from the fields. Most carried baskets, some braced on their hips, others hung from tumplines: colorful straps that went around the forehead, suspending the burden basket just above the hips. As they ducked past, they'd give me shy smiles, then hurry through the gate. They wore field dress, which consisted of a skirt of frond fiber, undecorated, and held at the waist with a rope. Most had their hair up, secured with bits of carved shell or tied with decorated string. The children appeared healthy, but in this country, if you made it past five, it was due to a tough constitution. The Timucua lands weren't for the frail of mind or body.

Old Red Wing was droning on about the fertility of Irriparacoxi's lands — and how it had given his warriors the strength to conquer all of the surrounding towns — when a delegation of warriors and headmen appeared in the gate behind him.

One of the painted warriors leaned close, whispered in the old man's ear, and stepped back. I gave the fellow a casual inspection. He had a string of dried human ears hung around his neck. Trophies from raids, no doubt. When he looked my way and our gazes met, I knew just who he was: the completely arrogant and slightly bitter subchief, the one who reeked of ambition and thought himself superior to everyone but the high chief. It was in the way the man stood, in his flexed shoulders and smirky expression. He looked at me as if I were just some foreign fisherman come to trade.

As much as I hated guys like him, my job was to trade. And maybe steal Pearl Hand.

The old man took a deep breath, raising his hands. "Great Trader Black Shell, *Iniha* Stalks the Mist has just informed me that all is prepared. We welcome you to White Bird Lake town in the name of the Irriparacoxi. Come to this place, in the sight of the sun and ancestral spirits, and join us in sharing the Irriparacoxi's hospitality."

Red Wing bowed, then turned, leading the way. From behind the houses, the hollow blaring of conch horns announced our entry. I signaled my dogs to stay close and dutifully followed the old orator while warriors lined up on either side of us.

Smoke rose from evening fires that had been built in shallow pits before the open-sided houses, and people crowded around, anxious to see the trader. Irriparacoxi no doubt received a great many visitors and delegations — such things came with the conqueror's exalted chair — but strange traders were always a novelty.

We marched past the charnel house on its mound. The distinctive and cloying smell caused my nose to quiver. Like most peoples, the peninsular Timucua carry their freshly deceased to the charnel house. There, with great ceremony, the corpse is washed and cared for. Among some people the bones are immediately fleshed; among others the body is allowed to slowly decompose.

No matter what the process, this is all accomplished with precise rituals and great humility to reassure the souls of the dead that they are still loved and valued. Why?

Among the Timucua it is believed that — with the proper incentive — a dead person's souls will join the ranks of the ancestors who forever buzz around the living like some sort of Spirit bees. These ancestral ghosts do good work by repulsing witchcraft or illness and deflecting evil influences from the Spirit world. Sometimes they can appear in a person's dreams and offer sage advice.

And me? Among my Chicaza it was believed that people had five souls. The most important of these is the life soul that travels westward to the edge of the world. There, the soul encounters a cliff, a sheer drop over an abyss. Only in early spring does the Seeing Hand constellation appear just across the way. In the center of the hand is a dark opening, or eye. The soul of the dead must leap through, and only then can it seek the Path of the Dead.

I've always been sensitive about charnel houses — probably because my body isn't likely to end up in one. Exiles such as myself rarely meet kind fates.

Nevertheless, I touched my forehead as I passed the charnel house. The Timucua, like anyone else, appreciate strangers respectful of their traditions.

Towns have unmistakable odors: woodsmoke from cook fires, the charnel house, the delightful aroma of latrines and garbage piles, and of course the musk of so many humans. Each town is unique when entered, then seems to blend in with the memories of so many others. White Bird Lake town reminded me of musty, rotting cattails.

The Southern Timucuans excel in wood carving. As I passed, I admired the lifelike renderings of pelicans, deer, raccoons, anhingas, and various fish. One house was supported by posts carved into the shapes of leaping dolphins; the roof itself perched on their noses. Inside the open verandas I could see detailed reliefs showing birds, hunters, and deer. These had been painted with great care and would have demanded a high minko's ransom in trade up north.

I followed my escort across a small plaza. Unlike our great plazas in the north, this was little more than an oblong space between the houses. Irriparacoxi's palace stood atop a long flat earthen mound on the eastern edge of town. A dirt ramp led up to the building's front. Two exquisitely carved cougars with elongated bodies stood as guardians at the ramp top. Each had been carved from a single piece of wood, the cats rendered in a sitting position, their heads high, mouths open as if roaring. Their eyes had been inlaid with polished shell.

Behind them the palace was a grand building with an open front. Each of the poles that supported the roof had been carved to represent different animals at the base, the upper portion of the pole seeming to rise from their heads.

The man I took to be Irriparacoxi stood in

the center. His broad shoulders, thick chest, and belly showed the effects of too many feasts and not enough days on the war trail. Tattoos of sunbursts and dotted lines decorated his broad face and did little to ameliorate his cunning, dark eyes. The man's skin was liberally greased, not only for protection against the mosquitoes, but to accent his fading tattoos. Greased hair had been pulled high atop his head and tied into a bun. What must have been half of the white swan feathers in the southern peninsula had been stuck into it to create a starburst effect. A loose-fitting apron — into which a panther design had been woven — hung from his thick hips. Sunlight gleamed on the white shell gorget that dangled down over his chest, and another twenty or thirty strings of shell beads obscured his neck. He gave me a casual inspection as I walked up the ramp and stopped before him. At my signal, my dogs dropped onto their bellies, happy to rest under their packs.

To Irriparacoxi's right were two old men and an absolutely ancient old woman. Each had skin that consisted of little more than sagging wrinkles and faded tattoos. Their white hair barely held the few colorful feathers atop their heads. Given their undershot jaws, I doubt there was a single tooth left between the three of them.

On the right stood the warriors: four muscular men, arms tattooed with rings, stars, and what looked like bird heads. Starbursts were done in dark blue, black, and red dye over each breast. Ornate wooden war clubs rested easily atop their crossed arms. The thin-faced Stalks the Mist, with his necklace of dried human ears, took his place just in front of them. As a subchief, or *iniha,* he was subordinate to Irriparacoxi.

Anacotima Red Wing retreated to the side and cried out, "I present Black Shell, a trader of the Chicaza from the far north. He comes under the Power of trade and would share the great Irriparacoxi's hospitality."

In the flat, at the foot of the mound, a crowd had gathered. People were talking among themselves, waiting to see what happened.

"He is welcome," Irriparacoxi said with great ceremony. "Let it be known to all that Black Shell can walk freely in the Irriparacoxi's lands, and that no ill may befall him as long as he behaves by the Power of trade."

All eyes fixed on me. "I thank the Irriparacoxi for his warm welcome. My purpose here is to trade, and then to pass through the Irriparacoxi's lands causing no harm. I welcome your warm hospitality and in return shall regale you with stories of wondrous things that I have seen in my travels, and such news as may be of interest to you and your people. This I give freely in return for your kind reception."

Irriparacoxi clapped his hands then, calling, "Bring food!" In a lower voice he added, "I regret, good trader, that we had no word of your coming. Had we, a feast such as you have never enjoyed would have been laid before you. As it is, we pray that you will not judge us to be base and callous hosts; but we have only modest fare to set before you on such short notice."

"A starving man never complains, great Irriparacoxi." I smiled.

"Then we shall see to your hollow belly first thing," he continued most graciously.

Over the years I've developed a sense for men. Irriparacoxi was watching me the way a kestrel did a meadow vole. That set my teeth on edge. He should have been mildly curious, intrigued at the arrival of a noted trader, and hoping for an evening of diversion from the usual. Why, then, was I getting this rapacious look?

Arrangements were made for the dogs and my packs. A great fire was laid and lit. Steaming pots appeared from all over, women bearing them up the ramp like offerings, having wrapped them in old garments, or carrying them on litters made of sticks to keep from burning their hands. Someone had surrendered half of a deep-pit-roasted deer, and breads made of cattail and smilax root appeared as from thin air. Arriving at supper-time is an old trader's trick.

And then *she* appeared. In the growing gloom she emerged from the back of the chief's house. Gone was the drab dress. Her freshly washed hair was decorated with white feathers and bits of polished shell that accented those raven locks. Shell bracelets made a clattering as she moved her arms. No less than twenty necklaces of shell, bone, and colored wooden beads hung from her slim neck. A striking white skirt clung to her hips and swayed suggestively with each step.

Every eye in town was fixed on her as she walked so elegantly up to the great fire. For protection against the evening mosquitoes, Pearl Hand had greased her skin with a combination of puccoon and other herbs that discouraged the vicious little bloodsuckers. The perhaps unintended result was that every curve of her marvelous body reflected the fire's light.

When I managed to tear my gaze from her, it was to see Irriparacoxi staring almost breathlessly. The man's pulse was jetting in his neck, his eyes dilated, mouth hanging in a soft O. He wasn't the only one. Only the ancient priestess seemed unaware.

Pearl Hand glanced around, flashing a knowing smile. Then she fixed her liquid dark gaze on me, an eyebrow arching in challenge, as if to say, "Well, do you really think he'll part with me?"

THREE

Trade is a sacred concept, revered among all peoples in our part of the world. Through it, articles move from people to people, but there is more: the Spiritual aspect. Everything is born of Power, derived from the ripples of creativity that Breath Giver exhaled into the world.

When something is made — say, a copper pendant — the craftsman takes a bit of raw copper and meticulously pounds it flat. He places the copper on a carved wooden mold, then uses bone or antler dowels to carefully press the copper down over the mold. This must be done ever so slowly lest the thin metal tear or ripple.

Or perhaps it is a shell carver who laboriously cuts a large round piece from a whelk or conch shell. His concentration, creativity, and ability all go into the piece as he meticulously engraves a revered design or depicts a scene from one of the sacred stories. Power has gifted him with this skill, and part of that gift is imprinted into the piece he creates. So, too, is a reflection of an artisan's souls, imbuing his work with a bit of himself.

I've seen wood-carvers, in the final act of carving, physically breathe life into their creations. Anything made flows from Spirit Power, from Breath Giver's exhalation. Hence, trade is about the movement of Spirit between peoples, not just the meaningless exchange of pretty trinkets.

And then there's the unique relationship between the trader and the party he's dealing with. Relationships are the basis of life, whether it is with other nations, between people, with the Spirit world, or even with the plants and animals we rely on for survival. A shell carver up on the Tanasee River cannot practice his craft without the movement of whelk and conch north from the gulf. A healer among the Calusa can't cure certain diseases without medicinal plants from far inland. Trade can be likened to the blood flow of creation.

The result is that trade, too, is an art. How many times have I talked to young boys, wild with the dream of running off to become a trader? In their imaginations they see the adventure and excitement, but not the reality. Trade doesn't just happen; it must be orchestrated and is best considered as a grand game of strategy. I didn't just walk into a strange town and exchange a Mos'kogee pot for a Calusa carving. It was never that simple. Instead an intricate game of hawk and mouse had to be played. Sometimes I had to barter for days, exchanging a bag of corn for two sacks of clamshells. I traded them in turn for heron feathers, that I exchanged for an Apalachee pot, that I traded for *two* bags of corn. See where this is going?

Hoping to wrap Pearl Hand into my bed soonest, I laid all of my trade out for Irriparacoxi's inspection the morning after the feast. Fact was, I didn't think it would take much. When it came to trade, I was a rich man. The copper alone should have been worth any captive woman's value — even if she were a Chief Clan matron. Add the carved shell, the buffalo wool, the Spirit plants and dyes from up north, the furs, and the wooden carvings . . . well, I should have been able to buy the whole town.

The day was partly cloudy with a breeze blowing in from the south. Irriparacoxi, as was his right, inspected my trade, saying nothing, though his eyes lingered on the skeins of buffalo wool. Then he made a gesture with his hand, and people, one by one, according to rank and status, came up to see what I had.

While trade was brisk all morning — mostly trinkets in return for the usual bags of corn, dried turkey meat, colorful feathers, paint pigments, and so forth — Irriparacoxi just observed. You'd think he was a Mos'kogee high minko instead of a petty Southern Timucua war chief.

Every time he'd walk over and look at one of the more valuable pieces, Pearl Hand would scoff, saying something like, "That gorget, great one? I've seen them in the north. Most of the outlying farmers wear them as tokens to call rain to parched fields."

Of course, the peninsula needed no more rain that year. Worse, it was a bald lie, and she knew it. The piece in question was of Yuchi design, their most sacred image of the Sky World, and only the elite in the Chief Clan could wear it.

Why are you doing this, woman? Do you seriously want *to stay with this oversized, two-legged windbag?*

I ground my teeth, struggling to keep my expression in check. *Blood and pus, she's playing with me!*

Red Wing rose to his feet as two sweaty young men came trotting across the plaza, then climbed the ramp. They both dropped

55

to their knees just short of the porch, heads down.

Red Wing, ever the immaculate anacotima, strode over and bent toward them, listening as they spoke. He nodded, making a gesture with the flat of his hand to order them to stay, then hurried to Irriparacoxi, whispering in his ear.

The man made a face, muttered back to Red Wing, and strolled over to his raised bench. There he sat, arranged his apron, preened his hair, and with a gesture, signaled Red Wing.

I watched the two runners scurry up to kneel at the feet of their great leader. It was the opportunity I'd been waiting for.

"What are you doing?" I asked Pearl Hand. For the moment there was no one within earshot.

I couldn't read the thoughts behind her pensive eyes. "Trader, how badly do you want me?"

"So much it makes my heart ache."

"But the question is: Do I want you?"

"But I thought —"

"What? That I'd allow myself to be traded off for a few trinkets? Is that all I'm worth to you?"

I sputtered, unable to respond.

She sniffed in disdain. "Oh no, Black Shell, if you want to lie with me — even for a night or two — you'll pay what I think I'm worth."

"Do you really want to stay with *him?*"

"Do I want to go off with some scruffy trader and his flea-bitten dogs? Absolutely not. But I will go with a smart and cunning man who values me as a challenging and capable partner."

"Partner?" That set me back.

Her eyes seemed to enlarge as she stared into mine. For a moment I thought I was drowning. "Are you that man, Black Shell? I could be of great service to you and your trade if you're smart enough to meet me halfway."

Her lips parted the slightest bit, as if in invitation. Lost in her gaze, I'd forgotten to breathe.

Partner? I must have been gaping like an idiot. She just gave me that challenging arch of her eyebrow in reply, then walked over to stretch out on a shaded mat. She stared at me, eyes measuring. She didn't even glance over at where Irriparacoxi was ranting at the two hapless runners. Whatever news they'd brought wasn't making Irriparacoxi's day pleasant.

Partner? Was she serious? The idea was outlandish. Among my people, women and men were prescribed to specific roles. Different, and anything but equal. Men could be partners. But a man and a woman?

I was still trying to get my head around that — and my heartbeat back to normal — when the Irriparacoxi stomped back. His lips were set in a pout, then he growled, "Fools! Do they want me to go down there with a war party and break a few heads?"

"Do you play chunkey?" I asked hoarsely, ignoring his frustration. Pearl Hand had me that flustered.

"No, Trader. I make war on idiot subchiefs who refuse to follow my instructions. For the moment the idiot in question seems to be the *paracusi* in Sand Hill town. His tribute is half what it should be. *Half!* The fool thinks that just because a whirlwind flattened his town, he's not responsible for the shell beads he promised me."

"Some say you're very good with a bow." I pointed to a small wooden statue of his. "Perhaps we should shoot at marks for that piece you have. My trade certainly doesn't seem to excite you."

Pearl Hand watched this with subtle amusement. She was lounging like a great cat, her sinuous body stretched out on the cattail mat. A slight breeze fingered her glossy black hair.

Irriparacoxi shot another glance at the skeins of buffalo wool. For the most part, buffalo hair had to be imported from the north. While buffalo had once ranged all the way down the peninsula, their numbers always reflect population: More people means more hunting pressure, means less buffalo.

Irriparacoxi gave me a slight smile. "I have

something you might trade for."

"Oh, I'm sure you do," I answered with a smile, hoping he didn't see my triumphant glance at Pearl Hand.

To my surprise, he walked back into the recesses of the chief's house, appearing moments later with a long, leather-wrapped item. At the sight of it, Pearl Hand's eyebrow arched; then she turned speculatively to watch my reaction.

Irriparacoxi dropped to his knees and slowly unwound the leather from a long metal sword. Among my people, we make swords of stone. These are very rare and valuable and owned by the *high minkos, tishu minkos,* and *hopaye,* or holy men. Chipped of a single piece of flawless chert, only the finest flint knappers can craft one. Such swords, almost as long as a man's arm, have only one use: the ritual sacrifice of prisoners.

The sword Irriparacoxi presented was unlike anything I had ever seen. The handle was leather, wrapped with a metal wire. The blade, a muddy brown in color, was clearly metal of some sort, but the crosspiece that made the handguard was silver. I'd seen silver before. Little nuggets of it are still traded down from the far north.

"It's Kristiano," Irriparacoxi told me. "Taken from one who was shipwrecked among the Tequesta. Their chief sacrificed the man to Mother Sun a couple of years back and sent this to me as a token of his respect."

I took the blade, marveling at the light weight and how the handle seemed to fit the hand. I ran my fingers along the weapon's gritty but still sharp edge. Then I ran a thumbnail along the flat, fascinated by the slight ringing noise it made. If they could make something like this, what other marvels did the Kristianos possess?

"It's so light," I whispered.

"Not so light a Kristiano can't slice your arm off with it," Pearl Hand said dryly. "It's stronger than you'd think. Almost impossible to break. The Kristianos keep them polished and oiled." She cast a dismissive glance at Irriparacoxi. "A wise man would take better care of such a fine blade."

Irriparacoxi's backhanded blow caught Pearl Hand by complete surprise, rocking her head back. The slap of it made me jump.

"The Irriparacoxi doesn't need a stupid woman to tell him his business!" he roared. Pearl Hand averted her eyes as she raised a hand to her cheek.

In that instant I could have run him through with the blade and seen just how effective the Kristiano weapon was. Perhaps, several years before, I might have. That I'd lived this long proved I'd picked up a little sense and experience.

I was bound under the Power of trade. One

doesn't murder one's host under the Power. Particularly when said host is disciplining his own property. And there was the practical aspect: I wouldn't have made it off the chief's mound alive. Every warrior in the town would have felt honor bound to kill me on the spot.

No, this was a thing for clever minds. Pearl Hand's humiliation and rage were apparent, but I forced myself to ignore it and concentrated on how to work the trade.

Irriparacoxi was reading every twist my plotting brain was taking. The knowing smile on his fat lips was beginning to irritate me.

He said, "If you leave all of your trade here and come back later, with just as much, I might let you have that sword."

I snorted, as if at a ridiculous notion. He'd entered the game. "No, for such a silly trinket as this" — I hefted the sword — "you ask too much."

"Then what is enough?" he countered.

"That gorget Pearl Hand thinks is so common, and perhaps your choice of three of my copper pieces, and several of the pouches of medicine plants . . ." I paused, as though pained, ". . . and I'll throw in that buffalo wool."

He threw his head back and laughed. "And you think *my* offer is ridiculous?"

"Well, what would I do with a Kristiano's sword? You can't call it any kind of a practical weapon. It's certainly no use for hunting deer, and it won't give a man any more advantage in single combat than a war club. Why, me, I'd take a good bow and carefully fletched arrows any day."

"You won't trade any bow for that blade," he muttered.

"My bow's not for trade." I paused thoughtfully. "Of all my possessions, I'd never part with it."

He glanced mildly at me. "And why is that?"

"Because the bow is special. It has a unique Spirit Power. If I call on the Power of the bow, I cannot be beaten in a contest, no matter how skilled an opponent may be." I gestured at my trade. "What would the wealth of the world be against that?"

Pearl Hand's expression had changed from seething anger to blatant amazement. She was giving me the kind of look she'd give a raving maniac.

Irriparacoxi continued laughing from down deep in his gut. "You expect me to believe that you've never lost a competition?"

"Not since I obtained that bow."

"And where did you get it?"

"I stole it from a tie snake's lair under the bank of the Albaamaha River," I lied. Actually I'd traded for it with a Caddo from way out west. "But, by the Power of the bow, I must tell you the truth: There is one man the

62

bow will not let me beat."

"One man?" he asked. "Who?"

"I don't know yet."

Irriparacoxi narrowed his eyes skeptically. "You don't know?"

"I'm told that the man who finally out-shoots me will be the greatest warrior who ever lived. His life will be the stuff of legends. Young men will sing his praises for generations after he is finally dead of old age."

Irriparacoxi cocked his head. "I think you spin stories like an old woman spins cord: out of anything around. You're playing me, Trader. Sorry, you're not fooling me with your fantastic creations."

I stiffened, sniffing in mock disdain. "I create nothing."

"Really?" He was on the verge of rising, taking back the sword, and leaving.

"All of my trade," I said firmly. "I'll wager all of it that my words are true. My skill with the bow against yours. The best of five shots to determine the winner. Your reputation as an archer is known as far north as Ahocalaquen town." I hesitated until he opened his mouth to speak, and quickly added, "But I understand if you won't take the challenge. It wouldn't be a fair contest, you against me. Not while I use my bow."

"Not fair?" A sly appraisal hid behind his eyes.

"Well, not worth losing your reputation

over. Not that people would speak ill of you. It's a thing of Power."

He was remembering the part of the story where I'd mentioned the world's greatest warrior would beat me. He had to ask, "And what if you win?"

I tapped the sword flat with my knuckles. "I keep this . . . and Pearl Hand."

I could feel her interest, but kept my eyes locked with Irriparacoxi's.

"The sword," he said softly. "But not the woman."

"As you wish, Great Chief. That being the case, I'll take my trade and continue on my way south in the morning. I'm sorry that we'll never know. It would have been a great contest between us."

He'd expected any response but this one. "The stakes are too high for you?"

I shook my head. "Too low. You see, it's a failing among us Chicaza that goes back to the way we perceive Power, the forces that underlie the very Creation of the earth by Breath Giver. You ask me to wager everything, years' worth of trade, while you will wager only a small part of your wealth. Were I to accept, Power would perceive me a fool and ensure that I lost."

He nodded, considering my words. Even this far south people understood the Mos'kogee principles of red and white Power.

He glanced thoughtfully out at two large

herons flying along the palisade. Beyond, several canoes bobbed on the lake as fishermen pulled in lengths of netting. Sunlight cast sparkles on the water, and in the distance, the lumpy green horizon of trees contrasted with low fluffy clouds.

Irriparacoxi said, "There is no man among my warriors better with a bow than I. I understand your reluctance to damage your Power." But it was the disappointment on his face that filled me with joy. Sometimes the willingness to walk away from a trade is the most important incentive of all.

Oh yes, I had him.

Four

All through my early years I had been trained to observe and study how people think and act. That said, to be a successful trader one has to entice another person to one's point of view. Trading is like warfare in many ways; the goal is to obtain something. In a trader's case — as in a war chief's — strategy and tactics are employed. A trader must understand the basics of behavior, especially those of a high chief's.

The following morning, just after breakfast, I left my packs under the Irriparacoxi's guard, took my bow and bird arrows, and called my dogs to me. Leaving the packs was a calculated risk on my part. I know my trade: how many pieces of shell, how the knots are tied on the medicine sacks, and the precise count of bone beads and feathers. I would indeed be the wiser should one or two pieces be missing, or even if a pinch of herb had been removed from a sack.

The disadvantage would be if half of my goods were missing when I returned, especially if Irriparacoxi swore on the sacred honor of his ancestors that no one had touched the trade. Does a single trader dare call a prickly chief a thief? Not if he wishes to tell the tale.

My advantage, and what made it worth the risk, was that Irriparacoxi was probably bound by the Power of trade. Second — and what I was counting on — was that he couldn't resist the temptation to finger through the packs. Then he'd spend a hand's time obsessed by the wealth. Greed is a wonderful thing. Traders live off it.

The dogs and I proceeded out through the gate as though we had no concern in the world. I'd wave, calling a cheery greeting to the people we passed. I acted like a man without a care, interested only in a morning hunt. The way led through the scanty corn-fields and past the stands of cultivated goose-foot, corn, and sabal palm.

Off to the right stood a series of raised wooden boxes surrounded by colored poles decorated with feathers. Such sights are common among the peoples of the peninsula. I've already told how when someone dies, the corpse is taken to the charnel house. Among the Southern Timucua, I had learned, family and friends hold vigil for four days, pray, and make offerings to the souls of the dead. After the fourth day the priest cuts off the limbs and head, removes the entrails, heart, and other organs. These latter are taken out and offered to the vultures and crows. The still-fleshed bones are stripped of meat and then placed in a large jar of water until the last of the flesh comes loose. After the bones are completely cleaned, they are taken out and placed in these raised plank boxes.

There they will wait until the winter solstice, when they are collected and, at the height of the ceremony, buried in the town's burial mound. The purpose of this is to ensure that the souls of the dead remain happy and close to the living. If all is done correctly, the Spirits will return in dreams and visions, sharing their wisdom from the afterlife. Hopefully they will also protect the living from witchery, curses, and evil that might cause havoc.

Should a trader like me die while in the town's proximity, his body will be dumped in the nearest river. You never know about a stranger's ghost. Better to leave his souls unmourned and conveniently disoriented so that they go off to haunt somewhere else.

I headed north up the trail I had traveled with Pearl Hand. With the dogs coursing ahead I broke into a trot, my bow in hand, the alligator-hide quiver bouncing on my back. The way led into the trees, and I was just catching my wind, grateful for the exercise.

The dogs enjoyed the chance to crash through the brush, seeking rabbits, voles, and squirrels. I was giving them the opportunity to run free, and they relished every moment.

The sun hadn't moved a finger's distance across the sky before I stopped, inspecting a trail that led off into the brush. Then I glanced back surreptitiously, seeing a lone man trotting along some distance behind me. He seemed to be staring absently at something off to his left. I recognized him: Stalks the Mist, the guy with the necklace of dried human ears. Maybe they helped his hearing?

Slapping a hand to my thigh to call the dogs, I trotted off down the side trail, then backtracked, leaped off to the right and into a thick patch of grass. I then zigzagged, using a halfhearted attempt at hiding my trail. Of course, with five dogs bashing their way through the underbrush, it wasn't much of a serious endeavor.

I finally found what I was looking for: a small clearing bounded by low brush grown through with grass. Just the thing to absorb an arrow's impact without damaging it.

The grass at my feet gave a ripping sound as I tore it loose and twisted it into a small loop about the circumference of my fist. Stepping off twenty paces, I tied it onto brush stems and returned to my mark before pulling out my bow and stringing it.

Bird arrows must be perfectly crafted, absolutely straight, and fly with perfection. Most birds, after all, are small targets. Bird arrows don't have stone heads but are blunt dowels of wood, meant to break bones and knock a bird flat so it can't fly away. Mine had provided many a meal while on the trail.

Drawing the arrow, I nocked it, drew back, and picked out my target circle of grass. Sighting over the blunt head, I released and watched it sail dead center through the grass circle.

The dogs were chasing around, creating a ruckus, and I called them to me. They burst through the brush, tails wagging, tongues lolling, with the look of sheer delight in their eyes.

"You come lie down now," I ordered, giving them the signal to drop flat. Bark and Skipper, always thinking of their comfort first, found shade and flopped down. The others just lay down where they were, taking time to scratch and watch me with lazy eyes.

I took another couple of shots until I heard Squirm growl. He had his head fixed on a patch of palmettos a little more than a hundred paces away. Bark, always ready to live up to his name, rolled onto his stomach, his thick head craning as he searched for the trouble.

"Quiet," I said softly. "No barks. No growls. Understand?"

I drew back, aimed slightly to the right of the grass ring, and watched my shot skim harmlessly past. I shook my head slowly, then went to retrieve my arrow.

Just before making the next shot, I noticed a big black beetle crawling along beneath the target and pulped him with a center hit. I shook my head again, plodding dejectedly over to stare down and kick at the unoffending grass with an irritated foot.

Squirm, bless his little canine heart, remained fixed on the distant palmettos, as if he'd seen a deer or quail. I pretended to ignore him.

Enjoying myself, I drove the next three shots through the target center, chortling happily as I retrieved my arrows. The next shot I aimed at a snail on a blade of grass that stood to one side. The broad point blasted him to oblivion, but I cursed loudly under my breath as I walked out and propped my hand disgustedly on my hip. Finding my arrow, I left the circle of grass hanging from the bush and did nothing to disguise the gashes my "misses" had made in the damp soil.

"Come on, dogs," I hollered just loud enough. "The way I keep missing, you'd think someone witched the arrow."

I never allowed myself so much as a glance at that patch of palmettos before I stomped out of the clearing, my movements those of an unhappy man.

On the way back, I went slowly, stopping once in the trail to pull out my bird arrows, and one by one, glance along their perfectly straight shafts. I made an effort of double-checking the fletching. I muttered to myself, shaking my head before replacing them in the alligator-hide quiver.

As I strolled into Irriparacoxi's town, people were polite, nodding and smiling. I trotted up the ramp, seeing Irriparacoxi on his veranda, a cluster of his subchiefs gathered around in a circle. A huge whelk-shell cup that contained black drink sat to one side. Black drink is the sacred tea made from a certain variety of holly leaves. It is only used on special occasions involving state business, religious observances, and sacred ceremonies. The presence of black drink meant Irriparacoxi was doing official business.

A quick inspection of my packs proved satisfying. They'd been gone through, as I'd hoped. But everything seemed to be present, though I didn't individually count the feathers. It would have looked bad since Irriparacoxi was shooting evaluative glances my way.

Pearl Hand stepped out of the back, and I fought the desire to grin. She looked stunning, her long black hair hanging down her back, a bright yellow skirt knotted at her slim waist. Pearl Hand glanced at Irriparacoxi and his council, then turned her evaluative eyes my way. As she walked over, her bare feet whispered on the woven floor mats.

I pulled out a carved wooden sculpture — a rendering of an eagle on a flat piece of wood that I had obtained in Ocale. Then I straightened. "I've got to go find food for my dogs. Want to come?"

She glanced at the council, her lips quirking in a curious way, her expression oddly amused. "I would. Doing so will infuriate Irriparacoxi. Payment for that slap he gave me."

"He might just give you another one, or worse."

"Not if I tell him I used the time to discover if you were determined to take all of your trade away. Besides, it will be a chance to see a master trader at work." A pause. "You didn't do so well with the Irriparacoxi today."

"I did well enough."

After ordering the dogs to stay and guard the packs, we started down the ramp. I could feel Irriparacoxi's eyes on me, could almost sense his irritation that I was with Pearl Hand. As we reached the bottom, Iniha Stalks the Mist passed, giving me a slight nod. Did he ever go anywhere without his necklace of human ears? The man's face wore a curious expression, as if he knew something I didn't. Then his gaze fixed on Pearl Hand's high breasts, and that irritating smirk bent his lips. He was still staring even after we'd passed.

"Who is that warrior, the iniha?"

Her voice was filled with distaste. "Most everyone just calls him 'Ears.' "

"I take it you don't like him?"

"He thinks that when Irriparacoxi finally tires of me, I'll be gifted to him."

"You have my sympathy."

"Then you really will leave without me?" Pearl Hand said ironically.

"Possibly. Irriparacoxi doesn't appear tempted by my trade."

"He was full of himself last night." She nodded back toward Irriparacoxi's council. "He lays the fact that you wouldn't wager against him to his prowess with a bow. According to him, word of his abilities has traveled long and far."

" 'Long and far' mean different things to different people in different places."

As we passed the houses, I was taking note of where game was strung up on racks to smoke. Most consisted of ducks, fish, and other treats. Traders who valued their dogs tried to keep them from eating fowl, especially cooked. The bones splintered in the gut, and it wasn't a pleasant way for a valued animal to die.

"And where were you off to this morning?" Pearl Hand asked. "It was a topic of considerable speculation."

"And, if I know your chief, no little suspicion."

"He gets wary about strangers wandering off into the forest."

"I was looking for birds, but didn't find any. And I needed a little target practice. Just to keep the edge. You know . . . if Irriparacoxi decided to change his mind."

"How did you do?"

"I'm glad the man turned me down. Somehow, Power didn't seem to favor my skills. Losing a whole load of trade like that, it would take months to recover. Not to mention what it would do to my reputation."

"But your bow is blessed, remember? You can only be beaten by the greatest warrior alive."

"And fortunately for me, if he's the chief here, he wasn't interested in proving the fact. I'll keep my mouth shut in the future."

I finally found what I was looking for in the form of a deer quarter, freshly skinned, hanging from a door frame.

"Greetings," I called, and a middle-aged woman emerged from around the corner of her house.

She nodded pleasantly, then her expression

dropped as she realized who accompanied me. Pearl Hand seemed to have that effect on the locals. Well, with all of them but Ears.

"Greetings yourself, Trader." The woman turned her attention back to me, but she crossed her arms defensively. "How can I help?"

I produced the little carving. "I just happened to have this, obtained from Ocale town. It's a masterful work, and I wondered if you would trade for that deer quarter."

She took the piece, glancing distastefully at Pearl Hand, and inspected the carving. "From Ocale, you say?"

"Like your people, they revere Eagle and the virtue he can bestow on a household. Generally these are placed above house doors to invoke good luck."

She held the flat piece of wood up to the light, inspecting it. "Fine workmanship, excellent attention to detail. Almost as good as we make here."

"The man who made it said that he used wood from a tree where eagles nest." I tapped it with a fingernail. "Over time, it is said, such wood absorbs the bird's Power."

She nodded, shot an evaluative look at the deer haunch, and added, "I've got a marriage to attend in a couple of days. It would make a good gift."

Within moments I had the deer quarter and

76

we turned our steps back toward the chief's mound.

"She didn't seem to like you," I noted.

"Most consider me a foreign woman with too much influence on their chief." The dry way she said it brought a smile to my lips.

"Do you?"

"Do I what?"

"Have too much influence?"

Her laughter hinted of mockery. "Trader, I've been all over. The sprawling and insignificant empire Irriparacoxi has built exists only because no one else would want this country, let alone the squalid little towns he has managed to cow into paying tribute. Look at the soil: With the exception of a few fields, it's wrong for growing corn. Mostly these people hunt and fish, collect roots, and scramble around for food. If they had anything of real value, someone like the Calusa down south would have crushed them and taken it away."

"How did you get here?"

She shrugged. "To save you the long story, I was running away from a man . . . and charged full into one of Irriparacoxi's deer hunts. You know, a surround where all the hunters form a circle and close in? I just happened to be in the middle of it. By the time I was caught, my pursuer, a Jororo subchief from over east by the coast, caught up. He wasn't properly deferential to Irriparacoxi."

"Poor man."

"His skull still hangs above Irriparacoxi's bed." The lines at the corners of her lips tightened. "I reach up and pat him every so often. A reminder of old times."

"I'll try to stay on your good side."

"Sometimes I wonder if Power isn't punishing me for being who I am. Maybe it's my father's blood." She gave me a searching look that went all the way to my soul. "Some say I bring bad luck. Traders live on luck, don't they?"

"We live mostly on tricks, patience, and skill," I replied, slowing our pace to enjoy every moment with her.

She made a gesture with her slender arm, the fingers birdlike and delicate. "You could have any woman in the town for the right trade. Why are you fixed on me?"

"Sometimes it just happens, Pearl Hand. It was the moment I first saw you beside the trail." I shook my head. "You already know you're a beautiful woman. But there's something about you . . . a quality of soul that fascinates me."

"A quality of soul?" she repeated softly, stepping slowly, her hair swaying. "Trader, these souls have been battered and scarred. But you're free to make up any fantasies you like." A somber pause. "I'm used to being the stuff of men's fantasies."

"Maybe you should just have the chance to be yourself for a while."

"And who is that?" she wondered. "I wouldn't know if I encountered her . . . And I'm not sure I'd like her if I did."

"That's a hard attitude to take."

She gave me another of those suspicious glances. "You're a hard man yourself. What drove you, a Chicaza in good health, to forego your own people? I can see it in your eyes, like a hard callus that's grown over the souls. You, too, are a bitter man in your own way."

I avoided her eyes, inspecting the heavy deer quarter. "My people and I . . . we had a little disagreement."

Amusement hid in her voice. "Oh, yes. Chicaza warriors can be so touchy about little disagreements. Tell me, it wasn't a matter of your silly Chicaza honor, was it? You people have the reputation for being much too preoccupied with putting on fronts, strutting around with all the pomp of mating turkeys, and believing yourselves superior to all others."

"You don't think I'm superior?" I cast it as a joke. I knew full well what other people thought of the Chicaza. They made jokes about how the Chicaza didn't learn to walk until a lance had been shoved up their rears. Many a riotous moment was had by mimicking Chicaza mating, generally with a wooden phallus the length of a man's leg strapped about the waist. The joke was that the man in the charade couldn't manage to lower himself

79

to his waiting woman without jamming it into the dirt and getting stuck halfway like an awkward tripod.

"It's too bad you won't reconsider," she said as we stepped onto the ramp. "I might have liked spending time in your company."

"Yes, well . . ."

"Trader!" Irriparacoxi bellowed from the veranda above. The council had apparently broken up. I strode up, dropping the deer quarter for the dogs to demolish. To my relief Bark didn't pick a fight when Fetch sank his teeth into the thick haunch.

Irriparacoxi came striding across the matting, a grin on his face. "I have given second thoughts to your challenge. I shall take your wager. The contents of your packs against the Kristiano sword and the woman here."

I caught sight of Ears standing back in the shadows. The fool wouldn't have been more obvious if he still had palmetto fronds stuck in his hair.

Pearl Hand glanced at Ears, then back at me, an amused smile playing at her lips.

Irriparacoxi missed it, his attention fixed on my packs. I could see the excitement in his eyes, as if he were already fingering his new property. He added, "Yes, things are indeed turning your way. While you will not win my sword, word has just come that the Kristianos have arrived in the big bay several days' march west of here. A great many of their

80

floating palaces are just off the Uzita coast. Some of the smaller vessels have entered the harbor, and the large ones are off-loading to obtain a shallow draft to pass the harbor entrance. Perhaps, after you lose everything to me, you can start over by stealing from them." His grin went tight. "Assuming they don't catch you and make a slave out of you."

To set the hook, I shook my head. "I'm not so sure that I want to shoot against you. That was yesterday. No, better that I —"

"The *woman* and the Kristiano sword, Black Shell." His grin widened. "Surely your blessed bow won't let you lose. Or was that just the silly tale I thought it was?"

I gave him a pained expression. "I suppose if I don't gamble against you, the story will be all over the peninsula?"

"Tales have feet of their own. They go where they will."

I sighed. "All right, but only half of my —"

"All of it," he growled. "As you said yesterday. Or do you mock the Power of trade and go back on your word?"

I glanced at Pearl Hand, aware that her large eyes had taken on a strange gleam. I fought the urge to reach out and run my fingers along her smooth cheek.

"Very well, Irriparacoxi. Let's see which of us Power favors."

EVALUATION

She sat on the high minko's raised dais, at the far right, just at the edge. To be placed there was always symbolic of the honor bestowed upon her. To her relief they seemed to ignore her failing bladder, the constant cough, and infirmities of bones and joints. They cared not that her legendary beauty had degenerated into the wrinkled mass of loose skin, the curious dark brown spots, and stringy gray-white hair. Loose teeth had fallen out one by one as if to mark the passing of her few dreams, until her pink gums were as featureless as the aspirations she no longer clung to.

She blinked to clear the haze from her vision, but it never helped these days. Things remained clouded and colorless.

From where she sat she could barely make out the *hopaye,* the high priest, who stood just to the high minko's right. The hopaye raised his hands, the clatter of his thick shell necklaces carried to her ears. Thankfully her hearing wasn't fading like the rest of her.

"We have to go back to the roots of our heritage," the hopaye cried, holding up two feather wands, one red, the other white. "Our world is interlaced with opposites: love and hate; peace and war; predator and prey; fire and water. Is there life without death? Light without darkness? Or pain without pleasure? We call this the sacred balance of existence. Why? Because these opposites lie at the very heart of Creation.

"Yes, in the Beginning Times, Breath Giver separated the Sky World from the Below World, and Sacred Crawfish dove to the depths and brought up mud. Giant Vulture flew across and flattened it with his wings, forming the mountains and plains. The great Horned Serpents crawled down from the heights, and where they went, the waters followed, creating the rivers.

"And binding this all together are the two Powers: the red, and the white. Equal and opposite, they weave through time itself. The red is that of creativity, reproduction, cunning, and innovation. And when unleased, it loosens chaos, war, and suffering. The red Power motivates us, fuels us with ambition, pride, and courage. It allows us to meet the struggle head-on, and to strive against adversity. Red Power drives the passion in life.

"And the white? There lies tranquility, peace, and goodwill toward others. Without the white Power we cannot appreciate harmony and contemplation. Compromise and understanding flow from it, as does knowledge, patience, virtue, and compassion. What, I ask you, is life without order? How can any achievement be appreciated?"

Pearl Hand jutted out her jaw in a grin. *Black Shell would have enjoyed this. Balancing the Power always obsessed him after Napetuca.*

As if he heard her, the hopaye cried out at the packed palace great room. "Breath Giver, in his wisdom, created the red and white to balance; and it is the act of balancing them that absorbs each of us throughout our lives. Without the red we fall into stagnation and sloth. Without the white, life becomes nothing more than a savage contest without satisfaction."

She was nodding, remembering, the hopaye's voice fading as she recalled the day Black Shell had gambled for her. Gods, that was so long ago. Nevertheless, the memory came rushing up from between her souls as though but a day had gone by.

"How clever you were," she whispered to him. "Already I was falling under your spell, daring to hope that you were more than just another man."

Her head bobbed as she recalled the way he'd looked at her. Wanting? Yes. In those days, what man didn't?

But Black Shell had seen her differently, with eyes that looked beyond her breasts, flat belly, and long legs.

"I thought it would fade. All the ones before

84

you . . . they just wanted what they saw on the outside." She grunted derisively. "But what did I know of real men? To those others, I was just a toy, a plaything."

Pearl Hand shook her head, feeling the bones in her neck grinding softly. "What fools we were, Black Shell and me. He actually bought that crap I dangled in front of him. Oh, yes, become a partner. Equals, you and I. And you swallowed it, like a fish takes a baited hook."

She rubbed her face, aware that her chin was wet from a trickle of drool. "That was the line that would tow me out of that fat Irriparacoxi's grasp. And then I'd be away, leaving you with empty blankets to find your fate among the Kristianos."

She wiped her chin, then dried her hand on the corner of her white-fabric dress. Such things were presented to her with great regularity. Honors for a woman such as herself. People were just as silly as Black Shell had been.

"Oh, yes," she whispered. "It was just going to be a couple of nights, enduring your bed, and then, in the darkness, I'd lift some of your precious trade and be gone. No one the wiser but Pearl Hand."

She laughed at herself, rocking softly back and forth. "We danced with the red Power, Black Shell. Both of us for our own reasons. Cunning was our creed: crafty, plotting, and bold. And in the end, old lover, whose trap did we fall into?"

She smacked a gnarled fist into her bony palm. "Power had laid its snare, and while we wished desperately for the white, it was the red that slipped around us like a ghost. It played on our weakness, my beloved trader. Horned Serpent gave each of us the last thing we ever thought we'd get . . . and in the end it doomed us both."

She realized that the room had gone silent, and images of Black Shell, stringing his bow, faded as she opened her eyes to see the crowded palace great room. Ranks of seated people had fixed their gazes upon her. To her left, the high minko, the hopaye, tishu minko, and pakacha thlakko were all staring at her with reverent eyes.

"Sorry," she whispered. "Go on, Hopaye. You were talking about the balance between the Powers."

The hopaye, a young man of perhaps forty . . . well, young to her way of thinking, walked over, spreading his hands. "Reverend elder, what did Horned Serpent give you? We would hear, all of us, and learn."

She squinted at him with her rheumy eyes, then out at the audience. "He gave us our hidden desires, Hopaye. You know, the things you want so desperately that you can't even admit to yourself."

"What were yours and Black Shell's?" She heard the pleading in the hopaye's voice.

She snorted. "Black Shell? The fool wanted a

destiny. And me? Idiot that I was, I only wanted to be loved."

"Is that so bad?" the tishu minko, head chief of the Raccoon Clan, asked.

"Only if it comes at a price," she murmured.

FIVE

Irriparacoxi made me wait until the sun was low on the western horizon. Rarely do I ever chafe, but this was one of those times. I was told to go down into the village to wait, so I asked a man I had traded with the day before if the dogs and I could rest under his ramada.

It might have been early spring up north, but down in the peninsula things got downright hot. I lounged around, sweating in the muggy hot air, and sipped from a gourd water bottle. Fetch used the opportunity for a prolonged game of stick. I flipped his evermore-slobbery stick as far as the next house. He brought it back, a look of adoration filling his eyes. Finally the heat got to him and he trotted off to gulp water at the palisade ditch. Then he returned to flop onto his belly and began the laborious task of turning his stick into splinters.

Around me, people continued with their daily routine. The woman across from me was weaving a new skirt on a backstrap loom. She kept glancing my way as she fished sabal palm fibers from a pile beside her.

Over by the palisade I could just see two men using a hafted whelk shell to shape a section of log. I couldn't tell what sort of image they were carving, but the steady *chop, chop* of the sharpened shell made a reassuring rhythm. They didn't have greenstone axes as we did in the north. Down here carving is done with sharpened shell and, believe it or not, sharks' teeth.

When the breeze came just right, I could smell coontie-root bread baking. After having seen the young woman four houses over draining water from the pounded roots, I imagined it was hers.

Meanwhile people kept walking by, casting me appraising glances as word spread of my coming contest with Irriparacoxi. With each passing finger of time, the number of people "just strolling past" increased. Some grinned knowingly, as if already savoring my defeat.

The sun continued to slip across the sky. I began to pace, anxious to have this over and have Pearl Hand and the Kristiano sword in my possession. Only after I spotted several of the priests leaving the chief's house and scurrying back and forth to the temple, did I understand why Irriparacoxi postponed our contest. These were what the Timucua called *yaba,* shaman conjurors who tried to wield Power to their own designs.

"Hey kids," I called to the dogs. They cast me lazy glances where they lay sprawled in the shade next to the packs. "We're being witched."

The dogs didn't seem to care that each of the old buzzards was carrying a hide bag and looking furtively in my direction. The two old yaba hurried up the ramp to the veranda and ducked inside. Irriparacoxi had called them to make medicine, or Power. Their incantations, sacrifices, etc., were to bless his bow and arrows. Only after being imbued with Power would he trust himself against me.

Meanwhile the dogs had flopped onto their sides in the shade, eyes closed. That or the wizened yaba had succeeded in placing a sleeping curse on them. If so, it was strong medicine indeed.

At the same time, I noticed another of the old men peering at me from behind the charnel house. The yaba was dressed in his best white apron, his face and chest painted in blue, white, and green pigments. Only when he thought I wasn't noticing did he shake buzzard feathers my direction, and spray what looked like urine out of an old bladder.

Given the stakes, any chief worth his spit would have tried conjuring. They're a silly bunch of geese down in the peninsula. Me, I'm Chicaza, born of Breath Giver's chosen people. And this wasn't my first gambling match. As a countermeasure, I opened my medicine pouch, removed my blessed shell gorget, and placed it around my neck to ward off any of their paltry spells. To be sure, I used a sprig of dried bald cypress leaves and pelted my head, chest, and back. Finally I rubbed an ointment made from alligator oil, beaver castoreum, and deer's gall onto my arms to ensure that Power maintained their strength and skill.

Pearl Hand appeared, strolling toward the ramada where I made my preparations. She stopped short as I finished rubbing on the ointment. "He's up there conjuring, you know."

"Of course. He thinks he's going to win."

A sparkle was dancing in her eyes. "He's been told you're only fair with a bow, and that the only way you'll win is by magic."

"The only way I will win, beautiful woman, is by outshooting him." I thumped my breast with a fist. "And any advantage I have is in here, down between my souls. My uncle started me on the bow when I was four. By the time I was six, I didn't get supper if I didn't hit ten for ten at twenty paces." I made a face. "It's that Chicaza preoccupation with honor, you see. That and if a man can't hit the mark, he'll be a laughingstock among the other warriors and nobles."

"Nobles?" she asked, that eyebrow rising again.

"We're Chicaza. If you ask us, we're all nobles. Even those peck-heads in Deer Clan."

She glanced back at the chief's house. Sunset was turning it a pleasing shade of yellow. A pale thread of smoke was rising from the roof eaves. Then her measuring eyes turned back to me. "Black Shell, can you really win this?"

At the seriousness in her voice, I nodded. "Let's put it this way: If I can't take an overblown peninsular war chief, my uncles would track me down and smear my face with fresh bear shit to add to the insult. He's a high war chief with a growing gut. How often does he shoot, Pearl Hand? Once or twice a week? And when he does, who does he shoot against?"

"His subchiefs."

"Oh, yes. The fawning subordinates who agree to never make the great man look bad. I do this for a living."

She stepped closer, lacing a firm arm around the ramada pole. Would that arm ever wrap so intimately around me? "If you win, he's going to be upset. The Power of trade?

Well, it's a nice policy as long as it doesn't involve Irriparacoxi's prestige, his Kristiano sword, and his trophy woman."

I met her earnest eyes and shared a slight nod of the head. "In other words, we'd better be out of here in the middle of the night."

"And long down the trail come morning."

I took a moment to study her. I'd known a lot of women. Where did that sultry quality come from? She should have been broken, given the trials she'd endured. Instead, when I looked into those eyes, I saw a steely resilience. It gave her catlike body an added attraction.

I asked suddenly, "What makes you think I'm the man to go with?"

She gave a slight shrug. "Maybe you're not. But back on the trail that day, when you looked me in the eyes, I saw your souls." A faint smile graced those marvelous lips. "If you are who I think you are, it might not be so bad. A trader's woman would have a freedom found nowhere else."

"You know what freedom is?"

"Since the day my mother . . . I'm just a possession." She glanced back at the chief's house. "You've never been owned by anyone, passed from slobbering man to slobbering man." I saw her close her eyes.

I could imagine. "I've already told you: Freedom means cold, wet trails, bad food, endless travel, and sleeping in the mud."

"Two sleeping in the mud is warmer than one," she shot back. "Besides, wherever you're going, it's away from here."

"I'm an exile, a man without status. My people would spit on me."

"Then we are alike." Her smooth brown shoulder rose in a casual shrug. "And we might get along. I've seen the desire in your eyes. You want me. And, if you win this thing, you'll have your full measure. Provided, that is, that I come to your bed as an equal."

"Ah, we're back to the partner thing?"

A soft laugh broke from her throat. "A cunning woman could help your trade. She hears things from other women that you, as a man, never will. Such knowledge could give you an advantage. Men like to talk to a beautiful woman. They can't help it. I can drop a word on occasion, mislead and manipulate."

Could it really work that way? Could I really throw out that crap my people had pounded into my souls about the roles of women?

I tried not to stare at the way her hip was thrust suggestively against the ramada pole. A tingle of anticipation ran through me. "Of course, if I turn out to be as bad as the rest, you can just slip away some night. It's easy to elude one lone man on the trail. It's not like here, where Irriparacoxi can send all of his hunters and trackers out to drag you back."

I watched that hit home, gaining even more respect for her. Oh, yes, she'd already thought that idea through. Then I added, "On the other hand, what if I'm different from other men?"

"Different how?"

"I've thought a great deal about your offer of a partnership. It goes against everything a Chicaza man is taught . . . which makes it exotically appealing to me. Would you be willing to stay with me for a while? Try it?"

Her brow lined as she studied me. "Maybe. If you can win this thing."

A conch horn blew, and I turned my head to see the trumpeter at the corner of the chief's house veranda. Irriparacoxi emerged and started down the ramp, his priests and a collection of warriors following behind.

"Time," I said. "You want to help me carry the packs over?"

She grabbed up two, and I admired the toned muscles in her arms. Calling the dogs, we carried my trade to the edge of the small plaza. All right, so it was only a trampled opening in the center of the town below the chief's house. Among the great nations to the north, such a place would have been constructed of packed clay, smooth, and perfectly surveyed.

Irriparacoxi gave me a look of anticipation as he stopped short, his retinue behind him. Ears carried the Kristiano sword. He was grinning like the contest had already been won by his august leader. The priests hovered behind in a knot, waving eagle fans, singing softly as they called Power. People were coming from all over. It wasn't every day their chief played a renowned trader for such high stakes.

"My people!" Irriparacoxi began. "The trader known as Black Shell has challenged me to a contest. He wagers all of his trade goods, his dogs, and packs."

What the . . . ? *My dogs?* But there was no time to object, and he had neatly boxed me. Changing the wager now would make me look petty and small.

"In return," Irriparacoxi continued, "I wager the Kristiano sword and the woman, Pearl Hand." Then he lifted his face to the sky, arms out. "Hear me, Mother Sun. Hear me, my ancestors. Grant me strength and skill! In your name, I represent our people. Make my eye keen and my heart stout. Steady my hand and guide my arrows true!" And on it went. Long enough that I should have gone off to take a nap.

Pearl Hand's face might have been carved from walnut. She just stared flatly at Irriparacoxi. I stared at her, and wondered what it would be like to untie the knot that held her skirt around those provocative hips. I imagined the cloth floating loose, sliding down the length of her long legs.

Finally, after having recited an endless list of ancestors and invoking aid from each, Irriparacoxi rolled on to a grand finish and made a gesture.

Two of his warriors stepped out twenty long paces and twisted two sticks into the dirt. Then, to my surprise, they produced the same grass circle target I'd used that morning. It had been sewn onto a piece of matting that they tied to the sticks.

I glanced at Irriparacoxi, and he was grinning back.

You scheming clever weasel. You mock me, fool?

To turn the tables, I bent my head back and laughed from deep in my gut. Ah, the games we play.

"Five shots each," Irriparacoxi cried. "And should we tie, we will play until one misses and the other doesn't."

"Done!" I agreed. "You first."

He stepped to the mark as one of his warriors walked up and offered him his bow. The polished wood rested on a cougar skin along with five cane-shaft arrows, all dewed with some liquid from the conjuring. Probably black drink. I took another look at the man. Please, tell me he'd quaffed a whole shell filled with the stuff. It gave a man the shakes.

Irriparacoxi reached for his bow, capably strung it, and retrieved an arrow. Taking his stance, he drew back, and the crowd went silent. His release was perfect, the arrow whistling down and passing just inside the lower edge of the circle. Shouts, whistles, and stomping feet demonstrated the crowd's pleasure.

I took my place, nocked an arrow, and felt a sudden nervousness. For several heartbeats I stilled my souls, remembering Uncle's long-gone lectures on the bow, found my target and released, watching the arrow lance the matting beside Irriparacoxi's hole. The crowd didn't whistle, stomp, and carry on for me. Who would have thought?

Irriparacoxi's next shot was nearer to center. I kept mine just within the ring. And so it went, one for one, until we had worked up to fifteen. Now the crowd was silent. I glanced at Pearl Hand. Her posture had grown stiff, and I could see worry each time I stepped up to the mark.

So, beautiful woman, you really are dedicated to this.

At eighteen each, we'd shot away the matting inside the target. Irriparacoxi's nineteenth arrow sliced the grass circle, leaving a hanging U shape.

"That counts as a hit!" Irriparacoxi cried.

"Agreed." I shrugged, walking to the line.

I took my time, breathing deeply, charging my muscles. My arrow sliced through the center of the ring. When I looked at Irriparacoxi, a gleam of sweat gave his tattooed skin a dull sheen in the growing twilight. He was pacing, clearly anxious.

Too much black drink. And it was becoming apparent that he might lose. How long had it been, I wondered, since he'd lost at anything?

His next shot shaved grass from the broken loop. Had the circle been whole, it would have been a miss.

"I take that as a hit," I called. "If it touches the grass, we shall call it good." And then I drove an arrow through the empty center of the target.

Irriparacoxi began muttering under his breath, calling on his ancestors. The sun had sunk below the palisade, sending shadows across the plaza, marking the target in gloom. He took his mark, and I could see the tremors in his arms, the beaded sweat on his forehead. Pulling the arrow back, the man seemed to tense. At the release, the arrow sailed just outside the grass loop.

A low moan went up from the crowd.

Pearl Hand was working her jaws, as if her mouth were dry. A sudden desperate hope shone in her eyes.

I took my mark, knowing that I had prepared all my life for this moment. I drew back, took a breath, let half of it out, and drove my arrow straight through the center of the target.

The crowd was silent, shocked.

I raised my hands high. "Praise the Irriparacoxi! He has shot a most excellent game!

What other man here could have done so well?"

A cheer went up from the crowd. They stomped and whistled, some breaking out in yodeling while others sang.

It was a nice try, but when I walked up and offered my hand, Irriparacoxi hissed, "Witchery," and stalked off.

I stepped over and retrieved the Kristiano sword from Ears. The look in his eyes was seething, like a pot at full boil. Then he turned, back stiff, and stomped away.

Maybe he should change his official name to He Who Stalks in Anger?

I turned to Pearl Hand. By blood and pus, she was mine. All mine. *You shall have your full measure.* The words thundered between my souls.

She waited until the others had walked off before saying, "I suppose this means we're not invited to a feast?"

"That would be my thought." I cocked my head, trying to read the expression on her face. Once more she was the property of yet another man. I couldn't tell if she was pleased or not.

"Come," she said, bending down for the packs. "The smart thing is to go back to the ramada. It's close to the gate." She paused. "He really thought he was going to beat you. He had a man spying while you were out practicing."

"I just wasn't at my best out there. Maybe it was the lack of a crowd."

The studious look she gave me was almost unnerving. "You planned it all, didn't you?"

"What do you think? That you're the only clever one?"

At least that brought a slight smile to her lips.

"My question," I continued, "is how do we keep someone from sneaking up and cracking my skull in the night? And how do we keep you from being dragged back to Irriparacoxi's house up on that dirt pile?"

She gave me a level glance. "After dark, the guard at the gate will have to empty his bladder sometime."

"And we'll be out before he can get back."

Then, to my surprise, she reached down and took my hand. Her touch sent a jolt through my system. She gave me a squeeze, saying, "That would be smart."

"I like smart. It's a whole lot more fun than stupid."

From beneath the ramada roof, we watched night settle over Irriparacoxi's town. I rested on my stomach, propped on my elbows, the Kristiano sword held in my hands. I just liked the feel of the thing, let alone its incredible value. In the Nations up north, such a weapon would be worth more exotic trade than I could carry.

Pearl Hand had laced up the packs, and

they were ready to be loaded onto the dogs as soon as the darkness was complete. Her glances were speculative, perhaps trying to decide if she'd really made the right decision.

I smiled to myself in anticipation.

The guard at the gate was lounging around, looking bored. On a hunch, I had Pearl Hand take him a gourd full of tea I obtained from an old lady two houses down.

Water in, water out?

The chief's house, up atop its mound, was silent and dark. The two old yaba, both looking shaken, burst from the veranda and hurried down the ramp for the safety of their temple. They were covered with some gray powdery substance that wafted after them to mark their passage.

"The ultimate humiliation, he doused them with ashes from the fire pit. Gods, he must be in a foul mood," Pearl Hand said as she came and settled beside me. She was fixed on Irriparacoxi's high dwelling. "This is one night I'm glad I'm not up there. He's blaming me, too, you know."

"Regretting your freedom already?"

She flipped that raven wealth of hair back. "Not yet. But maybe soon if he's so mouth-foaming mad he charges out of there with a pack of warriors to recover his property."

"He'd do that? Offend the Power of trade?"

"He might . . . by claiming sorcery. As far as he's concerned, that's the only way you

102

could beat him."

"It would ruin his reputation. Chiefs don't spit on the Power of trade. Once other traders hear about it, they'll steer clear of his towns."

"You're not in the north anymore, Black Shell. Trade here . . . it's different. If he comes for us, it will be in the middle of the night, when there are no witnesses. These people are backward and ignorant. You're used to the great Nations where old traditions dictate how people behave. You won't understand until you get it out of your system and start thinking like a dumb fisherman."

"Do you use this tone with all of your men?"

"You're not 'all of my men.' Most would have crawled between my legs by now, pawed my breasts black and blue, grunted themselves to satisfaction, and fallen asleep."

"We're going to have to find you a better class of men."

Her teeth flashed in the gloom. "I like what I see so far."

"Just wait. I still have time to disappoint you."

She reached over and laid a cool hand on my shoulder. "Partners? That still holds?"

"For as long as you want." I took a moment to study her shadowed face. "If, after a couple of weeks, we'd rather go separate ways, we'll do so."

"Why?" She sounded suspicious. "You could claim me just like you do that sword."

"You've run before, and you could again. I'm a lone trader on the move. I can no more own you than I could the wind. Besides, what good is a partner you don't want to be with?"

"Why should I trust you?" Her suspicions were growing. "We will eventually go through a large town with another chief like Irriparacoxi. You could sell me to him when you finally get tired of me. My chance to run would be long gone."

"I could. But stop just thinking about yourself for once. Here's the thing: I liked what you said about trade. You know, about how you'd hear things from women that they'd never say around a man? I may be an exile, but I'm not stupid." I paused, turning my attention back to Irriparacoxi's dark palace. "And, to tell the truth, Pearl Hand, I'm tired of being alone."

She, too, turned her attention back to Irriparacoxi's, the silence lengthening between us. Finally she said, "It's dark enough to load the packs on the dogs. That tea should be running its course through the guard."

A half hand of time later, we crept over toward the gate, only to discover the guard slumped against the palisade, his chin on his chest, sleeping soundly.

I whispered into her ear. "I thought he was supposed to go pee."

"Maybe he had a very long day," she mouthed, and added a shrug.

On tiptoes, we eased through the opening, and Pearl Hand laid fingers on my arm, leaning close to whisper, "If we follow one of the trails, pursuing warriors will be on us by midday. Old Rand's canoe is beached next to the palisade. I say we take it and cross the lake. They won't expect that."

"Who's Old Rand?"

"He's gone to Ocale for Irriparacoxi. No one will miss his canoe in the morning."

Smart woman.

I followed her down to the lake where she located a dugout that we dragged down to the water. The dogs, of course, clambered in without hesitation. In the north we traveled up and down the rivers in canoes all the time. A pointed paddle lay in the bottom, and I pushed us off, sending us south, across the lake.

Pearl Hand pointed from the bow. "There, to the right. You see those tall trees? That's a good landing, and there are rushes off to the side where we can hide the canoe."

Really smart woman.

Once off-loaded, the canoe hidden, we took a faint trail south. A hand of time later, we slipped off into a tree-thick hammock and wound our way through the pines and palmettos. It was a difficult business, walking through forest in the dark. I have to say: Pearl

105

Hand was motivated! She pushed herself to the limit, almost running. Given the frantic pace she set, I could begin to understand her desperation to get away from Irriparacoxi.

We were constantly muttering as we bungled into spiderwebs, tripped over deadfall, and speared ourselves with palmetto. The patter of the dogs' feet, plus our own blundering, made enough racket that even the water moccasins slithered away.

In the first light of dawn, Pearl Hand's face was smudged, her hair tacky with gray strands of web and accented with bits of leaves and pine needles. She had scratches all over her normally sleek skin, and her skirt was caked with mud. But that smile on her weary face was like sunlight through rain: gorgeous.

"Do you need a rest?" I asked.

In reply, she looked back over her shoulder — desperation returning — and shook her head. "Let's keep heading south. I'm going until I drop. Meanwhile he'll be scouring for our trail to the west. He knows you want to see the Kristianos. He'll expect you to head in that direction."

That was true. I did want to see them, to know they were real. At the same time I wanted even more to avoid any run-in with Irriparacoxi's warriors. "South it is."

Finally it was the dogs that determined our need to camp. They were literally staggering under their packs. Bark's white-tipped tail drooped. Skipper was limping. Fetch had taken to stumbling over his own feet. Even Pearl Hand could see they had nothing left.

Sunrise shot orange and yellow across the underbelly of threatening clouds. I watched them coast eastward in silent majesty across the sky. They kept the sun's heat from sapping us even further, while the low light shot rainbows through the coming storm. With the first spatters of rain, I led us to a copse of pine, gumbo-limbo, and poisonwood. Then we stopped, surveying the needle-strewn ground.

"This will do for now." I slipped the quiver from my shoulder. "We've got to rest the dogs, get them something to eat."

I bent to the packs as the heavens opened. While I cared for the dogs, she walked to the edge of the trees. Dropping her skirt, she used the rain to wash her smudged skin and wring out her hair. I pulled the packs and shook cornmeal from a fabric sack into the dogs' bowl. Then I joined her in the rain, untying my apron and scrubbing the mud and mire from my hide.

She was just standing there, naked, her head back, rain beating on her face. I watched the water streaming down her sleek brown skin. It beaded on the hard brown nipples jutting from her breasts and trickled in writhing paths down her muscular belly and thighs. Had mortal woman ever looked so marvelous?

She smiled, raindrops pattering on her lips, and slicked water from her face. Then she turned to me, dark eyes meeting mine. Instead of the fatigue I expected, a glorious peace filled them. Her smile grew as she walked over and used her palms to wipe the rain from my skin. The feel of her hands running over my arms, chest, and belly can't be described. I grasped her shoulders, reveling in the solid feel of her bone and muscle. I closed my eyes as she continued to run her hands over me, to conjure sensations no woman ever had.

With a hip, she playfully bumped my straining erection. "Come. If you're not too tired, let's see what your earnings have won you."

Six

We slept hard. The mat of pine needles insulated us from the mud. An unguent of grease mixed with datura, pine resin, and gumweed kept the biting insects at bay. And she was proven right again. Two sleeping in the rain was warmer than one.

I awoke a hand of time before dawn. I was on my side, chest to her back, her round bottom cushioning my groin. The darkness was complete. Life, I thought, couldn't be better than this.

Memories kept replaying in the eye of my souls. She had played my body the way a master musician did a flute. Each time the melody would rise to that last final note, she'd back off, only to take me higher the next time. And when she finally brought me to the peak . . .

My shaft hardened until I feared it would wake her. It did. She stirred and shifted, reaching around to grasp me. I groaned at the squeeze she gave me.

"Don't you ever sleep?" she asked gently.

"Are you a sorceress?"

She shifted onto her back, maintaining her distracting hold. "Where, by the Spirits, did that come from? A sorceress?"

"I feel enchanted."

"You were supposed to."

"Why?"

She paused for a moment. "I think, for the first time, I wanted to share myself. You don't just take, Black Shell."

"I don't understand."

"Out there in the rain, what would you have done if I hadn't wanted to lie with you?"

"I would have thought you were as exhausted as I was, and we'd have gone to sleep."

"Why?"

"Huh? Because you needed sleep."

"That's the reason I gave you so much."

"Did someone hit you in the head real hard when you were a little girl?"

"It's because you cared about me, Black Shell. That's a new thing for me. The men I've belonged to . . ."

When the silence stretched, I added, "Most women would have concluded that all men were the same by now."

"I'm not most women. And I've known some very good men." She growled irritably. "I just haven't belonged to them."

"You don't belong to me. Like I said, if we don't like each other, we can split trails any time."

"I'm still having trouble believing that."

"I gave you my promise. When a Chicaza gives his word —"

"Blood and pus, spare me a lecture on Chicaza and their ever-so-holy honor."

"Gladly."

She raised herself on an elbow, trying to read my souls. "I really could just walk away? Just like that?"

"Just like that."

My answer seemed to perplex her, and she lay back, staring up at the pine boughs overhead.

"How are we doing so far?" I asked.

She softly asked, "You're really Chicaza, right? Your people, they have peculiar notions about women and who they couple with. Does it bother you that I've had so many?"

Unwanted images arose to torture my souls. I couldn't help but think of her, naked like this, beside the likes of Irriparacoxi. "A little. But I'm not just another Chicaza. Pearl Hand, I haven't been among my people in years. Meanwhile I've been everywhere else. Who knows the ways of Power? Maybe I was cast out to learn a broader way of life? For now I'll just be me, and you be you." I shrugged. "I'm not perfect, so I'm asking that you tell me if I do things to irritate you."

"I usually get hit if I criticize."

"That sounds like a sure way to ensure I wake up alone the next morning."

She laughed. "Probably true." A pause. "Most likely you'll grow tired of my ways, and it will be me who wakes up alone."

I followed her gaze to the branches overhead, savoring the moment. "So far, Partner, I'm pretty satisfied. But I meant what I said: I don't want to be like the other men you've known."

"You're not." She looked slightly confused. "Gods, if I didn't know better, I'd say you were conjured from my dreams."

That made me feel warm inside. "Thank you. I could say the same. Some of the things you did to me, I thought my skull would explode."

"Those skills kept me alive and living well instead of working my life away bent double under loads of firewood, fleshing hides, and pounding corn as a common slave."

"I wasn't born a trader, either. That skill, too, had to be learned, along with the art of the bow, and chunkey, and all the different languages. You wait, you'll see."

112

"We haven't even scratched the surface when it comes to things I can do to a man . . . but you keep waking the dogs."

Then she proceeded to show me. I think I woke the dogs again.

Two days later, having seen no sign of Irriparacoxi's warriors, and having skirted several villages, we headed west toward the coast. Taking time to hunt, we managed to kill a deer, most of which the hungry dogs devoured, and several ducks fell to my bird arrows. Along the way, cattail root, yellow lotus, and smilax root provided stock for evening stews.

The more time I spent with Pearl Hand, the happier I became. She showed me how to polish the Kristiano sword to a silver sheen, to grease it, and with a sandstone paint palette from my trade collection, how to grind the edge to sharpness.

One bright morning I was sitting on the trunk of a fallen pond cypress overlooking a small forest lake. A whirlwind several years earlier had felled most of the trees, several having fallen into the water. New growth was already sprouted, saplings reaching fresh leaves toward the sky. Water lily and duckweed floated near shore.

I had the sword cradled on my lap and Fetch perched beside me, a partially chewed stick at his feet. He was giving me that desperate look, but my arm was almost worn out. Even the strongest arm can only throw a stick so many times. Mosquitoes were humming over us in a tall column, repelled by the last of my unguent.

Pearl Hand strode out from the elderberries and honeysuckle that shrouded the downed trees. As she sat beside me, Fetch took the opportunity to spit his stick at her feet. She obligingly tossed it out into the brush.

"What are you doing?" she asked.

With the sword I pointed at two lumps that protruded from the film of duckweed just down the bank. "Watching."

She spotted it immediately. "Alligator. Maybe as long as my leg, right?"

"Right. I'm hoping he comes close enough that I can spear him with this sword. It should go right through an alligator that small."

"And then?"

"Then we render the fat for grease to make more mosquito repellant, roast some of the meat, and feed the rest to the dogs."

She nodded. "Whatever you do, don't put too much bend on that sword. They're strong, but can't take a lot of weight sideways. Once bent, you can't straighten it."

I considered that — having worked with copper — and could understand her point. Maybe hunting alligator with the sword wasn't such a good idea. In our short time together, I'd come to appreciate her knowledge.

"How many peoples have you lived among?" I asked on impulse.

She dropped her chin onto her palms, staring thoughtfully at the water. "I've lost count."

We'd been talking in Mos'kogean. I switched to Coosa. "You speak most of the languages?"

In fluent Coosa dialect she answered, "Most of the eastern ones."

"And Kristiano?"

"Sí. Un poquito."

"Which means?"

"Yes, a little."

"Very well, then, beautiful woman, what shall we do when we get close to the bearded Kristianos?"

"Stay well away from them, Partner. They aren't very good at sneaking around in the forest. They clank, talk loudly, and bash their way through the brush. If we're smart, and leave the dogs behind, we'll have ample warning of their coming. Just take a peek at them, and let's get away."

I could hear the concern in her voice. I just couldn't believe it, so I asked, "They really don't honor the Power of trade?"

The wariness in her eyes left no doubt about her sincerity. "Black Shell, you simply must trust me on this. Will you?"

I nodded slowly. "I will."

"They are not like other men. They don't abide by the rules that govern us here. Accept that they are vicious and remorseless." She raised her hands and let them slap to her sides. "I know I can't talk you out of this, but I wish you'd let us head north, into the great Nations. The Kristianos bring nothing but misery and death."

I dropped my gaze, saying doggedly, "I just want to see them. I've heard so many stories, things I can't believe. Don't you understand? To see is to know, Pearl Hand."

"You promise? You just want to see them. That's all?"

"I do." But I didn't like it. I really wanted to see one up close, look him over like one did a strange and unique animal. Too many of the stories that were told stretched a man's belief. Could they really build floating palaces that moved like magic? It was said that they tied white clouds to trees in the middle of their large boats.

"I take your promise and your word, upon your honor."

Honor? She certainly knew how to bind a Chicaza.

At that moment two anhingas surfaced, one with a lump in its long neck as an unlucky fish slid down to become breakfast. The wary anhingas eyed the alligator and launched themselves to the safety of one of the fallen pond cypress logs. There they spread their wings to the sun, perching like worshipping lords. The male jerked his spearlike beak in our direction, as if pointing us out to his brow-throated mate.

"I've swam with them," I offered, indicating the anhingas. "They fly underwater like birds do through the air. It's a magical thing, seeing them down there. Then they fly out and spread their wings, worshipping Breath Giver. They are so like us in that regard."

"They have great Power," she added reverently. "They travel between all the worlds."

Both of the anhingas craned their long skinny necks to watch us. It was an eerie sensation, as if they were studying us, listening in. I shifted uncomfortably as a third anhinga appeared from the depths, splashed out of the water, and settled on another of the fallen logs across from its brethren. Water dripped from its feathers as it spread its wings to the sun.

"Why were you outcast?" she asked. "You let the sacred fire go out or something?"

Among the Mos'kogee people, the sacred fire was kept continually burning in our *Tchkofa,* or council house. To let it go out was to bring disaster down on the people. "That's a boy's job."

"Your face isn't tattooed. They do that when a boy becomes a man. Even I know that."

"I didn't quite make it to manhood. And that's all I'm going to say."

"We're partners. You and me. Do partners keep secrets?"

"Will you tell me everything that ever happened to you? Things you're ashamed of?"

She laughed, the sound of it bitter. "Oh yes, Partner. I've lived with shame for so long it fits me like a well-worn dress. But tell me, what is your clan?"

"Chief Clan."

"Ah, one of the nobles? So you were raised to be a high minko, a supreme chief?"

"I was." I glanced nervously at the anhingas. Pearl Hand was getting too close to sensitive issues. Even the anhingas seemed to be waiting for the answer.

"I hear the tone in your voice. Don't be so defensive."

"Why are you asking these things?"

"To know you, Black Shell." She threw a glance over her shoulder where Fetch was searching the brush for his stick. "Isn't that what partners do? Know each other? You have a handle on me, like that on a prize water jar. But you, you keep slipping out of my grasp. What would a man like you be doing, passing your life as a lowly trader when you could sit atop the high minko's mound in a great palace?"

Another anhinga shot up from the water, to perch beside the others. This one, too, turned

118

its dark brown eyes in my direction.

I thought about that long-gone day, when Horned Serpent's voice whispered in my ear, *"Run!"* The sibilant tones echoed across time and memory.

"Well" — I cleared my throat — "for one thing, I'd never have won you away from Irriparacoxi. I'd never have shared your bed. Instead I'd be locked up atop a mound, fretting my stomach into a burn over clan politics, sleepless, wondering who was plotting to undermine my rule. Sounds like great fun, doesn't it?"

She chuckled. "Great fun indeed. But you can't change who you are. You're a plotter, Black Shell. You knew that Irriparacoxi would send a spy to watch you practice with your bow. You played him like a fish on a line, didn't you?"

"He's a very predictable sort. I had to let his greed get the better of him."

She looked at me and winked. "That's what I like about you. You're a clever man, but one with so many layers. Knowing you is like peeling a wild onion. With each layer, the scent grows stronger."

"You're saying I'm stinky?"

"No, you're Chicaza. You've been trained to bathe every day. The Kristianos now, they stink. They think bathing makes a person sick."

"How do they stand each other?"

"By pouring water scented with flowers and such on their bodies."

I made a face. That sounded ridiculous. Why not take a bath and get it over with?

"Black Shell," she said seriously. "I'll get you your look at the Kristianos, but that's it. You understand, don't you? I won't take the chance that they'd capture me. I'll die first, even if it means driving that sword through my heart."

"Gods, you mean that?"

"As I have never meant anything before. If you do anything foolish, try and meet with them, or get captured, no matter how much I like you, I'm gone."

I nodded. But then, just a look? What would that hurt?

The anhingas were watching me with eyes that reminded me of obsidian beads. Gods, why were they studying me so? Yet another emerged from the water, shaking and extending its wings. When it, too, turned to study us, I felt a shiver filter through my souls.

For five days we traveled west, avoiding towns, hunting and fishing, making camp in glades, and enjoying the night fires. We would talk of places we had been, people we had known, and then retire to the blankets, where Pearl Hand and I explored the wonders of our bodies. I thought my life blessed for the first time since that fateful day when the voice of Horned Serpent forever ruined my life among the Chicaza.

I managed to spear a small alligator, answering my questions about the Kristiano sword. It would definitely do the job, but a barbed wooden spear would have served better. In camp we rendered his fat. Into this we mixed pine needles and gumweed to create an insect repellent. We kept a roast; the dogs enjoyed the rest.

Still avoiding villages — and the chance that our appearance would cause word to be sent back to Irriparacoxi — we followed winding trails. On one such trail we wound our way through clumps of saw palmetto and sable palm, avoiding the pointed leaves. Bark began to growl. I signaled for quiet as the other dogs stiffened, low growls deep in their throats.

A party of people rounded the bend a bowshot ahead. At sight of us, they stopped short, eyes wide, expressions tense. They looked, for all the world, like a bunch of rabbits ready to break. The women had tied their hair back, and heavy packs hung from their shoulders. The man carried a long spear tipped with wooden prongs, the sort of thing meant for fishing, not war. He immediately brandished it, as if for defense. He was a skinny specimen, nothing more than brown skin over ropy muscle. His belly, however, protruded, as if he were full of intestinal worms.

I held my trader's staff high, calling out in

Timucua, "Greetings!"

The man stepped forward, clearly nervous, and spoke in a language I didn't understand. Nor could I place the zigzag tattoos that ran down his cheeks. When I glanced at Pearl Hand, she just shook her head.

Resorting to signs, I signaled, "We come to trade."

The man signaled back: "Run! Bad works behind us."

"Bad works how?" I signed.

"Kristianos," he shouted. With that, they pushed off into the pointed palm barbs, heedless of the discomfort. The women followed, shooting frightened glances our way. Circling wide around us, they returned to the trail and headed inland at a dogtrot.

Skipper cocked his head, watching them go with his blue eyes. Bark used a paw to peel spiderweb off his scarred muzzle.

Pearl Hand, however, cast nervous glances down the now foreboding trail. "If they're running, Kristianos are somewhere nearby."

"I have to get close to see one."

"You have to get close to get captured or killed," she growled, backing warily down the trail.

"Listen, let's find a place to stash the packs and work up through the brush. You yourself said they weren't any good at sneaking through the forest."

She gave me a look that pulled at my heart.

"Black Shell, no good is going to come of this."

"We will be careful," I told her. "I promised. Just a look. Don't you understand what this means for me?"

She closed her eyes, almost reeling in defeat. "A look. And then we leave . . . no matter what. You promise that?"

"I do. I have. I promise it again."

"If this goes wrong, so help me . . . Like smoke through the trees, I'm gone. If we're spotted and separated, don't bother looking for me. I mean it, Black Shell."

I stepped close, taking her hand, meeting her worried eyes. "If anything goes wrong, head for the deepest forest, and then . . . well, it's your life. May luck grace your feet and souls."

She shook her head, as if annoyed. "What is it about you? Why am I *doing* this?"

"Come on. Let's find a place to leave the packs and dogs. Then I'll get my peek, and we'll be off." I turned, ducking through the palmettos, trying to thread a trail. "Besides, with my luck, we'll get to the beach, and they'll be gone. These raids don't last long, do they? A couple of days to a half moon? That's what I've heard."

"Sometimes they stay. Remember how I got here? They wanted to build a town."

"The venture failed. Like us, they probably learn from their mistakes."

"You're an idiot."

"Then why haven't you fled with those others?"

"Maybe I want to see you get caught. It will bring me satisfaction when I'm an old woman, sitting in the sun, remembering the great fools in my life." She sounded angry, and scared.

In a clearing we found a place where lightning had blasted an oak, splintering the tree and burning out the underbrush. "This will do. Help me with the dogs."

She'd become fond of my little pack, and quickly helped remove their harnesses and packs. Then we fed them long strips of dried alligator, and I gave the order for them to stay. Squirm and Fetch promptly lay down by the packs, tongues lolling. Bark gave me that searching look, as if he didn't quite understand.

"They won't leave?" she asked.

"Not until hunger or thirst drives them away." I left my trader's staff but took my bow and arrows. Just in case. Then I carefully laid the oiled Kristiano blade atop one of my packs. The thing would just get in the way in the brush, and I wasn't sure how one used it anyway — unless, of course, the opponent was a small alligator.

Leaving the clearing behind, we picked our way carefully, both of us studying the trail we would use to return to the spot. In places I broke branches and left scuff marks and other clues.

Night was falling as the trees thinned; I could smell the dank odor of salt water in mangroves. So much the better. Not even Kristianos could see in the dark.

Crouching down, we crept forward until we could see the water. The surface of the bay seemed to gleam a copper color as the setting sun glowed molten off the low swells. The beach here was nothing more than a tangle of mangroves, and for the most part impenetrable.

After several attempts and lots of backtracking, we found a trail that paralleled the shore, heading westward.

"The Uzita have several towns off to the west." Pearl Hand wiped a spiderweb from her face and scowled down where a banded water snake slithered under the leaf mat. "Kristianos don't like work. They'd rather take a town someone else built so shelter is ready-made."

A fork in the trail led toward the water, and we hurried down it to find a slender section of beach, white with shell. Stepping out, I looked past the screening mangroves and caught my breath.

To the west, silhouetted by sunset, I could actually see the floating palaces. I counted nine of them, rounded hulls with pointed bows, and what looked like winter-bare trees rising from inside them. How could such trees grow? Were the insides filled with dirt? And how were they watered, just by the rains? Or did the Kristianos' trees live off salt water like the mangroves?

"They are magical, those trees," I whispered in awe.

"Idiot. They're just tree trunks with the crosspieces tied to them. Then they hang big squares of fabric to catch the wind. That's what moves them. Like holding up a sheet in a canoe when the wind blows."

I felt slightly humiliated, but couldn't tear my gaze away.

"Gods, Black Shell, you're hopeless! They're just men, and nasty ones at that."

I don't know how long I stood there, watching as the sun's orange globe sank behind the far horizon of trees that marked the western perimeter of the bay. As the light faded I could see little lights on the distant vessels. Judging distance, we were only a couple of hand's time to the east.

As the light faded I reluctantly followed Pearl Hand back to the trail. "Does this lead to Uzita?" I wondered.

"You've seen them. Let's go."

"Only the floating palaces. I want to see the men and their great beasts. And no, don't say it. I don't want to meet them. Just spy from the trees."

She was shaking her head, and I could see

the fear and resistance. "If I ask you, will you come away with me? Please? I'll do anything. Be your woman, serve you. Black Shell, you don't know what you're risking."

I turned, placing a gentle hand on her shoulder. "You know the way back to the dogs. Go on. I'll be there by tomorrow night. I promise."

She nodded wearily, defeat in the slump of her shoulders. "It figures. The first man I ever care for, and he's going to go get himself made a slave." Her voice turned bitter. "Go on! Ruin your life. Just don't expect me to ruin mine."

Then she turned, starting back down the trail. She didn't even look back. Not once.

SEVEN

My heart dropped in my chest, and I took a couple of steps after her. Then I stopped, glancing back down the dark trail toward the Kristianos. She'd at least seen them. But me, what would I say for the rest of my life? That I was this close and just walked away?

Grudgingly I turned my steps west, working through the gloom. If I hid at the edge of the clearing, I could see them in the morning, get my fill, and slip back into the forest. I'd be back to Pearl Hand by midafternoon at the latest. Of all the names I could be called, "coward" was the one that sent my souls into a quivering rage.

"You're a fool!" I was surprised as Pearl

Hand's shadowy figure loomed in the dark trail behind me. She stalked past, fists clenched.

"Come on," she said through gritted teeth. "Let's get this over with. Maybe, the gods willing, I can keep you from doing anything too stupid."

The sensation of elation and joy that burst in my chest came as a complete surprise. I wanted to leap after her and crush her to me. But, well, I'm still enough Chicaza to have my pride.

A partial moon shining through puffy clouds provided a little relief as we made our way along the trail. I caught the faint reek of something and almost stepped on dark splotches in the trail. Slowing, I bent and picked one up. The thing was partially dry, a ball of something. I lifted it to my nose and sniffed at the sharp odor.

"What's this?"

Pearl Hand leaned close, taking it and sniffing. "Dung, my foolish lover. Pus and blood, I never wanted to smell that again. It's left by the animals they ride. Kristianos call them *cabayos.* They treat the animals better than they do their slaves. If you feel in the damp places, you'll find cabayo tracks. Once you see one, you'll never forget it."

Where a stream ran through I bent down, tracing the rounded impressions. They were huge, like a buffalo's track, but from a single rounded hoof.

By midnight we had forded several more streams and followed the trail to an open clearing. I knew we were getting close to a town: All the easily collectable firewood had been scavenged, and occasional stumps from cut saplings could be seen in the moonlight.

At the clearing, I eased along the fringe of trees and honeysuckle. I could see the village now, a palisaded thing with a surrounding ditch. Around its perimeter, some kind of conical fabric shelters had been set up. Fires winked, and I could see distant people moving among them.

I stared, amazed. So many people? Just how big were those floating palaces? There had to be hundreds in the camp, not to mention the ones inside the palisade!

The hollow sound of chopping, faint human voices, and laughter carried across the calm night. Metal made a distinct ringing sound I'd never heard before. Someone shouted in a language I couldn't understand.

"This is no slave raid," Pearl Hand whispered. "There are more than even landed at Chicora."

Something made a snuffling sound in the distance, and peering through the moonlight I could see a herd of giant animals off to the right. One seemed to have an unnatural protrusion in the middle of its back. I hissed, and pointed it out to Pearl Hand.

She squinted across the distance and said, "It's a person, a rider on the creature's back. What they call a *cabayero*. He's the night guard to keep the herd safe. There, you've seen them. Let's go."

"You need to work on your languages. There are more words than 'let's go.' Come on. Let's find a place to hide and you can explain everything to me."

"You've seen them. Let's go."

I pointed at the black forest behind us. "Through that? I say we wait for first light. We'll get back quicker, and without breaking a leg or stepping on a water moccasin."

A large fire could be seen inside the palisade. Kristianos were there, feeding it. "They're real," I whispered in amazement.

Pearl Hand only shook her head in weary acceptance.

The middle of the night isn't the best time to find a hiding place, but I located a stand of dogwood overgrown with nightshade and we wiggled under the stems.

"Come first light" — she gripped my hand, squeezing hard — "once you've taken a good look, we leave, right? No argument. No discussion."

"I promise."

"Gods, I'm betting my life on Chicaza honor."

"There are worse things to bet on."

"Like a Kristiano slave collar? They're

metal. The same stuff as your sword. You can't cut them."

I was filled with questions, but each time I asked, she just shook her head. In the end she burrowed down in the leaves and went to sleep.

I kept staring at the large camp and the Uzita town the Kristianos had captured. Beyond the flicker of the great fire, only the thatch roofs could be seen above the palisade. I looked at the cabayo herd, and noticed that the guard kept circling his mount around and around them. As they grazed closer, I caught the faint sound of singing. With a shock, I realized the man was singing to the cabayos, and the melody was unlike anything I'd ever heard. It reminded me of a mother crooning to an infant.

They sing to the animals? Traders never sang to their dogs. What was the point? A dog just flopped on his side and went to sleep. Then the breeze off the bay carried the scent to me, a slightly acrid odor new to my nostrils.

Sometime in the night I dozed off.

A slight nudge to the ribs awakened me. Morning light was gleaming in the east, sending orange rays across the high clouds in the sky. Pearl Hand poked me again, and gestured silently.

Shifting and pulling myself up, I peered through the leaves to see the cabayo herd, now no more than a bowshot away.

At first I thought they were all cow elk, but they came in so many colors: black, white, brown, and splotched. The males had no horns. Then I got a good look at the night guard. He wasn't more than a youth. A silver plate with arm holes was fitted over his chest. His legs were clad in a pale cloth, and his shirt was similar. Light brown hair hung down over his collar. Something about his face reminded me of a wedge — thin, with a straight nose like an adz edge. At first I thought his face was dirty, only to realize that straggles of hair had sprouted on his chin and cheeks.

"You've seen one," Pearl Hand whispered next to my ear. "Now, let's go." She gave my arm a no-nonsense tug and began crawling back through the brush. I took a moment longer, fixing the sight in my memory and carefully began crawling behind her. Within moments we were under the spreading oaks and trotting eastward.

"He sang to the animals all through the night," I said in wonder. "Do cabayos actually listen?"

"It keeps them calm," she said, casting nervous glances at the forest as we circled to pick up the trail. "I'm such a fool! I forgot how the cabayos can smell. It's luck, Black Shell, sheer luck that the wind held. If it had blown the other way, the cabayos would have smelled us. The guard would have known we were out there."

We hit the trail and Pearl Hand dropped into a distance-eating jog. Running behind her, my souls replayed everything I'd seen: the floating palaces; the cabayos; the man astride one of the great beasts, moving as one with the animal.

"For years I will talk of this," I almost cried with joy. "I've seen them! In the north, people will listen with awe."

"They'll listen, all right." Pearl Hand was shaking her head. "And if your Breath Giver is kind, the Kristianos will just keep to the coasts."

"They'd better," I replied. "If they were to go seeking slaves among the nations, the warriors would put a quick stop to it. It would be the Kristianos who ended up as slaves."

"You've never seen them fight," Pearl Hand growled over her shoulder. "And you wouldn't want to."

"You keep telling me they are men. Men can always be beaten."

"These can't. Not in a stand-up fight."

"And you know a lot about war?"

"About their kind, yes. A little."

She was getting angry, so I kept my own counsel, remembering the massed ranks of Chicaza warriors. No one could stand before a Chicaza assault, not the Chaktaw, the Coosa, the Yuchi, or the Tuskaloosa. No one.

Pearl Hand didn't know what she was talking about.

The sun had just crested the trees, and we had almost reached the fork in the trail that would take us back to the little clearing and the dogs when I heard an odd staccato behind us. For a moment I was puzzled, then I shouted, "Buffalo! Behind us. A large herd."

Pearl Hand's panic registered on her face. "Cabayos! *Run!*"

We sprinted full out, reached the fork in the trail, and pounded along. I was faster than she, and urged her onward.

I could hear the animals stop at the fork behind us, buying us valuable time. Then faint shouts came, and I heard the cabayos crashing through brush, turning our way.

"They must have seen our tracks," I panted. "How could they have come so fast?"

"You've never seen a cabayo run. If they have dogs, too, we're done." And she ran even harder.

Behind us I heard branches snapping and the odd snuffling sound made by the cabayos. "If they're that fast, we have to hide. Maybe they'll pass by. Quick. Off the trail. Take to the forest."

She darted through a hole in the sumac and palmettos, wiggling through vines. I crashed along behind her, hoping we weren't leaving a trail.

We broke into a grove of live oaks, darting

135

between their trunks and low branches. Then we were in pines, stumbling along, gasping for breath. Beyond them lay a stretch of open grass and tangles of briar, probably an old burn. Running here was impossible, our feet tangling in vines, the footing treacherous over old rotting logs. Honeysuckle and nightshade seemed like snares, and sawgrass raked our legs. We just reached the sumac and dogwood at the other side, bashing into the brush, clawing our way through.

I heard a shout behind us and saw a rider push his cabayo into the mess. The big animal shied and pranced, the man sawing at the straps running to its mouth.

"Run," I said as I gritted my teeth, pounding away under an open canopy of gum, live oak, and pines.

This gave way to swampy ground, thick with palmettos, gum, and occasional water hickory. Vines tangled the ground and wove a web through which we ducked and dodged. Each step sank in the black mud, sucking as we pulled our feet free.

How long did we stagger and stumble through that mess until we reached firmer footing on the other side? I don't know, but the sun was several hands above the horizon when we hobbled out into a stand of live oak and pine.

Pearl Hand wobbled along on trembling legs, and as winded as I was, I knew she'd

pushed herself to the limit. Onward we
pressed, powered by terror. We had to have
lost them. Those big cabayos just couldn't
follow us. I was sure of it.

"Rest for a moment," I called between
heaving gasps. "Then we'll head east, back
toward the dogs."

She dropped to her knees, chest heaving,
sweat running down her scratched and muck-
smeared skin. "You're . . . sure?"

"Cabayos would sink in that swamp. If they
want us that badly, they'll have to find a way
around. Meanwhile we can't run much farther. Not this winded."

I flopped down beside her, panting, my
heart racing. Beads of sweat trickled down
my face. "Gods, how did they find us?"

"Tracks," she whispered. "We should have
kept to the forest."

I nodded, feeling like a fool.

"Happy?" she asked. "Glad you've seen the
Kristianos?"

"Never again."

"At least you learn." She shivered then, eyes
closed. "That was too close." Then she gave
me a pleading look. "Promise. If it looks like
they'll catch us, shoot me. Drive an arrow
right through my heart."

I blinked from the sweat running into my
eyes. "You mean that?"

"Like I have never meant anything before."

"It won't come to that." I rose wearily to

my feet, giving her my hand. "Come on. Let's walk. Too much rest will make us stiff."

I tugged her to her feet and we plodded wearily eastward, my eyes searching for some sign of our trail back toward the packs. The thoughts running through my souls were sobering. When had I ever been that scared? Even that fateful day, when Horned Serpent's insidious voice ruined my life, had been nothing like this.

For a hand of time, we worked our way east through thickets of plum, buckthorn, and titis, then wound through pine and palmetto stands. My empty belly felt like a hole. At a small creek we dropped, slaking our thirst, and proceeded.

We crossed a trail, and I bent down, seeing in daylight the round imprints of cabayos. A chill frosted my souls. They were bigger than my palm, and fresh, made within the last hand of time.

Glancing up, I saw a lightning-riven oak, a familiar tree. We had come down this trail yesterday. Raising a hand for silence, I listened to the birdsong and whirring chatter of insects.

"You said the Kristianos clank when they travel?"

She nodded, panic so bright in her eyes they seemed glassy.

"The trail is that way." I pointed the direction the cabayos had gone. "It's not far. If we

138

stay behind them, we'll find the cutoff. But walk quietly. If we hear them clanking, we ease off without leaving sign, and take to the forest."

"And if they see us?"

"You hide." I placed a hand on her shoulder, staring into those eyes I had come to love. "I'll lead them away and lose them in the swamps. You wait for a day or two. If I don't return, the packs and dogs are yours."

"Why would you do this? Sacrifice yourself for a woman?"

I hesitated, hurt at the disbelief in her words. "For you, yes. You understand why, don't you?"

She nodded, a veiled expression, something I couldn't read, on her dirty face. Then a single tear slipped from the corner of one eye.

Weaving with fatigue, we set off. A finger's time later, I saw more of the distinctive round droppings left by the cabayos. This time I had no interest in inspecting them beyond a touch. Still warm. We weren't that far behind them.

Where was our trail? It had to be close. I kept searching for the broken limb I'd left to mark the route.

Finally, there it was! I almost dropped to my knees and wept with relief, but shot Pearl Hand a warm smile and eased off the trail. We were going to make it. I was almost shivering with joy.

Carefully, I retraced our route, eyes searching the forest. We were back from the bay, the ground dryer, more open under the trees.

Get me out of this, Breath Giver, and I swear, I'll head north and never visit these lands again.

"There," Pearl Hand said, pointing. "You left that branch on the ground to mark the way. We're almost there."

My souls were singing. We'd rest until dark, eat, and restore our strength. Then, with nightfall, we'd head east, and away from these terrible men.

Pearl Hand was staggering along, stumbling over her own feet. She had used up all of her reserves. We were just going to reach camp before she collapsed.

I remembered the trail we'd crossed the day before. Dimpled with deer tracks, we hadn't taken it because it ran east-west. Pearl Hand plodded wearily across it and into the brush on the other side, scraping through the palmettos, and disappeared into the brush. She'd fixed doggedly on our hidden camp, her only concern being to reach it.

I stopped, just long enough to make sure the soil wasn't marked by cabayos. Only the deer tracks marred the ground. In relief, I took a moment, just a couple of heartbeats to catch my breath. As I was about to follow Pearl Hand, I shot a glance back down the trail — just in time to see the rider pull up his cabayo. We weren't more than two bow-shots apart.

The scene is embedded in my souls: him sitting there, holding the straps, the cabayo stopped short, staring at me with pricked ears. Dappled sunlight was gleaming on the man's breastplate, and he wore puffed-out sleeves on his blue-striped shirt. A black beard graced his cheeks and went to a point below his chin. His eyes, like polished stone, met mine. They seemed so dark, unlike the shining metal hat on his head.

Time stood still, an eternity measured in heartbeats. Then it broke — shattered by his shout. He pounded his heels against the animal. I could see other riders coming behind him. How many?

"Kristianos!" I shouted as I raised a fist at the rider. "I'll meet you at Ocale town!"

Then I turned and ran with all the strength I had left.

The cabayos are incredibly fast, like stampeding bison; they can be on you in less time than it takes to draw a deep breath. I was just about to leap to the side when something hit me from behind. The impact lifted me off my feet, slamming me into the ground. I lost hold of my bow. My body bounced, and bounced again. After that . . . nothing but blackness.

THE GAMBLE

"What do you think? That heroes are just sprung from nothing? Popped out like pots out of a mold?"

She lifted her head, hearing the joints grind in her neck. The warm sunshine had soothed her aching body, allowed her to drift off into shallow dreams where faces of the long dead floated against a hazy backdrop, like images overlaying morning mist.

She blinked, hearing the old man's voice, and glanced off to the right. Yes, it was Throws-His-Fist, so named for the time when a Kristiano sword lopped off the man's hand. The hand, and the war club it held, had flown off to disappear in the middle of a fight. Now the grizzled elder sternly lectured his wife's grandson, pointing with his left index finger to emphasize his points.

The old man had his bony butt planted on a log, while the wide-eyed boy — all of eight summers of age — stared up worshipfully.

"Of course Power can influence the world, but

that's the point: Influence. Decisions, you see, lie within the hearts of men, creatures, and chance. Men can only be set on the path. After that, Power gambles."

Ah, yes, she thought as she closed her eyes, leaned her head back against the clay-plastered wall, and turned her wrinkled face up to the midday sun. *Power made a gamble. Perhaps an informed one, but an uncertain gamble nevertheless.*

Kristianos don't believe that god gambles. She smiled at the notion, remembering Black Shell and how he'd struggled to understand the incomprehensible Kristiano god.

Her passionate voice came from memory. "But, Black Shell, you have to think deeper. If that's the case . . . if god controls everything, even knowing the fate of men not yet born, what is the point of Creation? And worse, what does that say about the nature of god? He must be bored stiff!

"Power *must* gamble with men's lives. God cannot know the outcome. Otherwise the universe has no reason to exist."

She smiled at the memory of Black Shell's perplexed expression. Even back then, smack in the middle of it, he'd been blind to the very wind that blew him toward destiny.

Oh, blind, all right. Just as blind as I was. She chuckled at herself and coughed, thankful for the sunlight beating down on her withered body.

Memories of the day Black Shell was captured

143

rose to play behind her sun-reddened eyelids, the image unfaded. She remembered Black Shell's cry of warning, and she'd thrown herself to the ground, crawling like a snake into a thick tangle of grape. There she'd cowered, panting for breath, sweat trickling down her face. She'd heard the pounding of hooves, a triumphant cry, and then voices. The old familiar cadence of the language had stirred a latent terror deep inside her.

For moments she'd lain frozen, as desperate as a deer hearing the soft padding of a passing cougar.

Oh, how foolish I was. Her toothless grin spread, heedless of who might see and wonder. *Power made its gamble, all right. And all along, I thought it was Black Shell upon whose fate the gaming pieces had been cast.*

But in the end, she'd forced herself to raise her head, to see his limp body being bound to the cabayo's saddle. After they had ridden off, she had managed to rise, to stagger back to the camp, and throw her arms around the anxious dogs.

Only then had she been able to bury her face in Bark's fight-scarred neck and sob her terror.

Eight

For what seemed an eternity, my souls twisted sickly, colors of black and red swimming before my eyes. The pain in my head cannot be described short of a burst skull. My first conscious memory was of my gut heaving and bile filling my mouth.

When I blinked my eyes open, it was to see the ground passing just below my head. That reek in my nose came from cabayo, and my body seemed to be bobbing like a stick on rough water: jerking up and down. My gut cramped again, pumping more bile into my mouth. I was too weak to spit.

Periodically branches and saplings slapped my head or feet and my gut ached in minor sympathy to my cracked head. I'd never known such misery. Finally the realization sank in that I was strapped across the back of a cabayo, my head hanging down. No amount of effort would move my arms or feet.

A cheery voice spoke to me in a language I could not understand, and a fist smashed into my side. The mocking voice continued, the language rising and falling — finally ending in a laugh that sent a quake through my souls.

Shades of light darkened and grew blood-red behind my throbbing eyes.

I drifted away into memories of my boyhood, of running with friends, learning stickball — a long-gone racquet in my hands. Images of warriors returning from battle, walking through the palisade gate in bright sunshine, drifted behind my eyes. I could see them so clearly. White feathers filled their greased hair; their shining faces were painted in the colors of war: black and red. White teeth gleamed behind smiles as they marched in a double line. Three times they circled the Tchkofa council house, parading in the opposite direction of the sun.

Then my mother's face rose from the mist, her eyes dancing as she told me what a great high minko I would make. I could see firelight reflecting on her proud cheeks, hear the hope in her voice as she told me how I would meld the clans into the greatest of nations and conquer many enemies.

Then, from nowhere, came the voice of Horned Serpent, just as it had those many years ago: *"Run!"* Sibilant and terrible, it forced its way through the sounds of battle. The force of it stilled the clacking of war clubs against shields. Hissing arrows fell silent, and the cries of wounded men, the shrieks of rage and defiance, ebbed into silence.

"Run! Or you will die here."

Then I was running, tearing through forest, leaping roots, my feet pounding on the leaf mat as I pelted off through the dim light, shadowed by a thousand great oaks, hickory, and maple.

"Run!" Horned Serpent's voice goaded me to panic.

Voices intruded and ate their way into my sick pain. Real or dreamed? I blinked, forcing my neck to crane.

What I saw was horribly real. We were in a clearing, and I recognized the palisade from the night before: Uzita. Kristianos were walking up, all sizes and shapes of them. Their voices sent spears of terror and hopelessness, like needles through my souls. Then they were around me. One, a pale-haired man, lifted my head by the hair, staring into my eyes. His were blue, the color of a spring sky, and behind them coiled a violence that threatened to lash out like slivers of chert.

A rope was loosened around my gut and I

tumbled off the cabayo like a limp sack, slamming into the ground. I heard the grunt from my lungs as if it came from a great distance. Exhausted, I lay there, a ringing in my ears.

Kristianos were bending over me, their fingers picking at the rope that bound me. Rudely, they ripped them from under me, burning my skin.

Someone shouted an order I could not understand. Then I was kicked. The order was repeated, and I looked up. Kristianos surrounded me, repeating the order, gesturing with their hands that I stand up. More kicks followed, and I finally got my hands under my chest, heaving. With my right leg, I pushed up, only to topple as it collapsed under me.

The kicking continued, each stab of pain growing more and more distant. I began to float, and a gray haze settled over me, soft and comforting as it grew darker and I drifted away . . .

I remember dreams of Pearl Hand. We were young, living among my native Chicaza. She was smiling, handing me raspberry tea. Then her soft hands were stroking my skin. And over us crouched the mighty form of Horned Serpent.

He looked exactly as he had the day of that fateful battle. Sunlight glistened in tiny rainbows from the scales that armored his skull. The horns that jutted from his head were forked and might have been made of translucent red jasper that almost glowed. Awesome crystalline eyes stared down at me in glittering splendor, like faceted quartz. And in their gaze resonated a Power that sent its waves through my souls. Chevrons, dots, and dark-centered circles decorated the length of his huge body. Each consisted of a symbol from the first days, drawn upon his hide by Breath Giver during the Creation. And finally, those mighty wings rose from the center of Horned Serpent's back and spread above us, large patterned feathers almost transparent in the sunlight. Despite their immense spread, I was drawn back to the great serpent's eyes. Under their intoxicating stare I was frozen, stiff with fear.

"Why?" my voice croaked, as if the words were forced of their own volition.

"You are about to find out, Black Shell, of the Chicaza . . ."

The dream shattered when someone placed water to my lips. A ceramic cup grated against my teeth. Liquid splashed into my mouth, and I coughed, blinking my eyes open. I hurt all over, and couldn't make sense of what I was seeing: a man's face, bearded, looking concerned. He spoke, the words nothing more than a babble. Then he tried again, using language after language.

Finally, in Timucua, he said, "Drink."

This time, when he placed the cup to my

lips, I greedily sucked down the precious fluid, feeling it run cool in my belly. The cup empty, he dipped more from a wooden bucket. Time after time I emptied the cup.

From a sack, he removed bread, placing it to my lips. "Eat."

I took a bite of the bread, chewing, wondering at a sweet taste different from any bread I'd ever eaten.

"Who you?" he asked.

"Black Shell. A trader of the Chicaza. I come under the Power of trade," I replied in my native Chicaza dialect.

He shook his head. "Who you?" His hands formed the sign "name."

"Black Shell," I repeated, and finally gathered enough sense to look past him.

I was inside the Uzita palisade; houses were scattered here and there, and around them were placed great round wooden containers banded by metal. Boxes were stacked, and occasional cabayos stood tied off from the palisade just down from me. I could see Kristianos walking around, some chopping at wood, others passing with heavy boxes on their shoulders. At the far end of the town, cabayos stood hitched below the chief's house atop its mound. A large gathering of men, apparently at conference, were talking and gesturing. Then I sniffed, smelling woodsmoke, cooking, and the now offensive odor of cabayos.

"Where?" the man said, making the hand sign for the word.

Where? What kind of question was that? "Uzita?" I guessed.

He spoke in some foreign tongue.

At my lack of comprehension, he added, "You not Uzita" in Timucua.

"Chicaza," I told him, finally getting his meaning.

He shook his head. "Don't know." Then he pointed to himself. "Ortiz."

I made the signs with my hands. "Was I captured alone?"

He studied them, and nodded. "Only you."

I started to rise, only to hear clanking and feel a tightening around my neck. Reaching up I fingered a thick metal collar around my neck. Craning my head, I could see it was attached to a series of metal links that had been fastened to the palisade by means of some sort of heavy-looking loop.

Ortiz grinned at me, then signed: "Where you from?"

"Chicaza," I replied once again. Then I pointed, saying in Timucua, "North. Far."

"Oro?"

At my incomprehension, he asked in Timucua, "Metal there?"

"Not like this." I pointed at the collar and shook my head.

"Yellow metal there?"

Did he mean copper? "Yes."

He nodded, grinning, "You take us to metal in Chicaza?"

Why go that far just to find copper? I shrugged, then nodded. If he was fool enough to march on Chicaza, I'd be happy to watch his accursed Kristianos mowed down like summer grass before ranks of disciplined warriors.

"I come under the Power of trade," I told him. "Remove this." I pointed at the collar. "Do you understand? Power of trade? I am protected by Power. A trader."

"You work. For us."

"I'm a trader, protected under the Power of trade. Take me to your chief."

With that Ortiz gave me the sort of look he might have given a rock. He handed me the rest of the bread, picked up the bucket and sack, and walked off toward the council.

I tried to stand again, realizing the short length of metal loops wouldn't allow it. Having nothing else to do, I inspected the Kristiano chain, running the sun-hot rings through my fingers. I pulled hard and didn't see them stretch in the slightest. Then I fingered the collar, realizing it was sealed by two metal buttons.

One look at the palisade post was enough to convince me I wasn't going to pull that down.

So I sat there, eating the bread, looking out at the great floating palaces on the bay

152

beyond the houses, and studying the Kristianos as they passed.

I didn't want to see them this close. And then it came crashing down on me: *Gods, they've made me a slave!*

When I glanced out at the floating palaces, a new sickness deepened in my belly. Pearl Hand's words echoed between my souls. *"Kristiano slaves die within a season. No one has ever come back."*

Hearing the clanking of metal, I stared through the palisade to see a long line of slaves, native peoples, approaching from along a forest path. Each one bore a heavy box on his or her shoulders, and they were tied together at the neck with a chain. On they came, more than a hundred, walking past in a shuffling gait. From their tattoos, the shapes of their faces, and the cut of their hair, they were from no people I'd ever seen before. A handful, I noticed with amazement, had skin the color of charcoal, with broad noses and skull-tight curly hair.

The Kristianos must have brought them in the floating palaces. Large islands lay to the south, far out on the sea, and periodically they traded with the Tequesta and Colusa peoples. Maybe the Kristianos had captured some of those? I watched them deposit their loads while the Kristianos shouted orders, and then they shuffled off, back down the trail.

What really horrified me was the lack of expression in their eyes, as though their bodies had been left soulless, empty, and gutted by despair.

I lost track of the time — watching the arrival and departure of the slave line — drowning in a cold and bottomless sea of despair. Oh, how I knew that soul-sick sense of disbelief. It cores a person out, leaving him as hollow as a worm-chewed acorn. I'd lived it for days after my banishment from Chicaza.

But you survived. The words formed deep down inside me.

Yes, I had. I blinked, looking around. And maybe there was a way of surviving this? *Think, Black Shell.*

It came to me: What did they want with copper when they had metals like the stuff binding me to the post? Take them to Chicaza? The idea was foolish nonsense. If the Kristianos wanted copper, all they had to do was offer their metals in trade and they'd have every high minko, chief, priest, and trader in the Nations beating a path to Uzita. To obtain the copper, they'd scour towns and relatives, and raid others for every scrap to trade for Kristiano goods. Within a year's trade, the Kristianos would have piles of copper heavy enough to scuttle their floating palaces.

It just didn't make sense.

Figure this out, Black Shell. Do that, and perhaps you can win your freedom.

So I sat there for the rest of the day, watching the Kristianos. How do I explain them to normal people? Their hair comes in black, brown, tan, yellow, and even red. Their eyes range in color from black, to brown, to greenish, to sky blue. They like heavy moccasins that rise to the knee but are much stiffer than ours.

Their clothing, ah, now there's a marvel of weaving, cut, and dyeing. They have a stouter cloth than we do — much more durable. We can make colors just as bright, but theirs do not fade as quickly. The quality of their leather is superior to ours, and stronger.

They brought women with them, obviously slaves. These wore tattoos I had never seen before, and went about cooking, tending fires, and other menial tasks. None of them looked the least bit happy.

Then I saw my first Kristiano woman. Her skin was pale like theirs, her black hair done up in a style I had never seen before. She walked from one house to another, at the edge of my vision. To my amazement, she wore a full dress with a tight collar, sleeves to the wrist, the hem dragging the ground — despite the heat. It looked terribly uncomfortable. And, no, she didn't have a beard.

The next marvel announced itself with a curious grunting. I peered through the gaps in the palisade to see a herd of most peculiar animals. These things were round-bodied, long, with thick triangular heads, flapping ears, and no hair. They had flat noses and tiny curling tails. The legs were short, leaving the beasts close to the ground. The result was a bouncy gait. I watched in amazement as perhaps a hundred of the pink and black-splotched animals were herded past the palisade. They were so close I could see their little beady eyes and watch their splayed feet as boys used long poles to keep them moving.

I shook my head at the grunting and squeals, trying to place the creatures. What on earth were they here for? And for the life of me, I couldn't figure out how such a beast could survive without hair. They looked completely incapable of defense. On first glance, you couldn't help but think that a bear or cougar would shred one to pieces.

"They won't last long," I muttered to myself. But then, would I?

I leaned back, trying to find a comfortable position. Fear was returning to settle around my bones. The only good news — if there were any — was that by now Pearl Hand and the dogs were headed east.

"At least I saved you," I whispered, remembering my words to her on the trail. I closed my eyes, thinking back to the time I'd spent with Pearl Hand. A smile came to my lips. If only I could go back, turn my stupid steps to the north. I could have lived the rest of my life with Pearl Hand.

In anger I looked around, watching the Kristianos. That's when another long line of slaves appeared behind the palisade. These, too, were chained together at the neck, each with a heavy box on his shoulders. Guards walked along, armed with curious bows mounted sideways on wooden handles. Some carried whips that they used to keep the line moving. They had dogs with them. Big things with long muzzles. I wondered what they needed dogs for when they had cabayos to pack with. I called once, but the dog didn't cast me more than a glance.

The sweating slaves labored under their burdens as they entered the palisade and began stacking yet another pile of boxes. I looked at their chains, then at my own, giving it a vicious tug.

Pus and blood, Black Shell; you're a fool.

At sunset came another group on cabayos. They drove a collection of four men and five women before them. I watched with interest as these were taken one by one to an over-turned wooden pestle. A Kristiano used a metal-headed hammer to fasten the buttons on the collars. It was an interesting process, watching them kneel while the buttons were driven through. This was for the men. The women were taken to a hut, where, one by one, the Kristianos entered, and from the sounds, what they were doing with the women was obvious.

You got away, Pearl Hand. May Breath Giver grant your feet speed as you make your way north.

The men were brought over, a length of the metal chain was passed through their collars, and they were fastened to the palisade posts next to mine. The thing that locked them in place was a lump of metal, the loop of which clicked shut and couldn't be opened again.

I inspected mine again, seeing a little slot on the side with a round opening in the top.

"Greetings," I called.

The men looked broken, staring at the ground. None bothered to return my welcome. We just sat, all of us despondent.

I kept dreaming of Pearl Hand, remembering how she'd pushed herself to get away from Irriparacoxi. "Breath Giver, tell me she's far away, and gaining distance by the moment."

Run, girl. Run.

As evening fell, my thoughts were interrupted by the clanging of metal. For the first time, I watched men fight with Kristiano swords. Well, practice, actually. I was trained to the war club, having learned to parry, dance, and swing. Compared to a Kristiano sword, a war club is a slow and brutal weapon. For the first time I began to appreciate the brilliance of the sword's design. Light and fast, it could block, cut, parry, and stab. I watched, and marveled. Then came a terrible thought: *How can warriors with clubs stand against swordsmen such as these?*

It was a miserable night, sleeping there. The mosquitoes found us just at dusk and hummed in huge columns as I slapped them by the hundreds. The other captives didn't even bother, perhaps figuring if the little beasts drained them dry, they'd simply fade away and die.

Is that what you want, Black Shell?

I wasn't sure.

NINE

The following morning Ortiz arrived again with his bucket and sack of bread. He fed us one by one, and then, from a pocket, removed a thin piece of metal and inserted it into the slot in the lock. It clicked and sprang open. I was amazed.

I stood up, looking around as he freed the others. Did I dare take a chance and run for it?

Ortiz clapped his hands to get our attention. He spoke with the other captives, then looked at me, saying in Timucua, "Work." With hand signs, he added, "Do not run. Dogs hunt." And he pointed to a man who walked over with three of the big dogs trotting behind him.

So that was why they had dogs.

"Ortiz," I tried to sound as reasonable as I could, "I'm a trader, and come under the Power of trade."

"Work," he stated simply, almost dumbly.

A length of the heavy chain was run through my collar, leaving me a little more than an arm's length from the man ahead. I followed as a Kristiano gestured for us to move. The way led out through the palisade gate and along a beaten trail that paralleled the shore. Ortiz followed along behind.

"Do any of you speak Timucua?" I asked my fellow captives, but I might have been speaking Mos'kogee for all the comprehension in their eyes. I tried hand signs, and only got a shrug from one. These were locals, probably Uzita, ignorant fishermen and hunters who hadn't had the need to learn the sign language of the trade routes.

We arrived at the mouth of a small river, and what a sight. Boxes, the round wooden containers, and piles of goods covered with stiff fabric blankets were everywhere. Wide boats, manned by ten men plying curious flat-bottomed oars, were unloading yet more boxes and wading ashore with them. What wealth of trade did they contain?

Ortiz stepped past the dogs, speaking to the locals; then, to me, he added, "Work. Pack." Then he imitated the motions of lifting the heavy boxes. The local Uzita caught on first, one of the men bending and lifting a box to his shoulders.

I shook my head, refusing.

At a sign from Ortiz, one of the dog handlers brought the beasts forward, and with a single command, he pointed at me. The dogs began snarling, snapping with their powerful jaws.

I grabbed a box.

I still have nightmares about those dogs. I watched a woman run from the hut where the Kristianos bedded them. Evidently she'd had enough of filthy men between her legs. She barely made it past the palisade gate before the dogs were loosed on her. Her screams still fill my nightmares.

Then, to my astonishment, the funny little grunting animals were turned on her corpse. Within a finger's time, they'd stripped the bones. It was a horrifying lesson to us all.

"Puercos," Ortiz had told us, observing our shock and disbelief.

"What are they for?" I asked in Timucua.

"To eat," he answered.

Eat? I stared at the now despicable creatures. Eat the dead? Or what? Surely not even a Kristiano would eat such a vile beast as a *puerco.*

For three days I carried boxes — all heavy — from the landing to Uzita. The collar on my neck wore through the skin, and blood began to leak down onto my shoulders. The heavy chain jingled and clanked as it hung down my back, making the thought of running even more unreasonable.

The dog handlers had added a whip to their assortment of threats, and if we didn't move fast enough, it would come curling out to snap welts in our backs and sides.

Each day more men were brought in by the cabayos. Every morning and night we were given bread and water. They did let us drink from the side of the river between loads.

"I am a trader!" I called out once as Ortiz passed. "Do you understand? I am protected by Power."

That brought a snicker from one of the men down the chain line. He was a recent addition to our line, having been brought in the night before.

As I met his eyes, he made a dismissive gesture, saying, "Ortiz was Chief Mocoso's captive for ten years. He speaks only a little Timucua, a smattering of Calusa, and knows even less of your laws of Power. He barely understands the ways of our own Uzita."

"But doesn't he understand that Power will turn on the Kristianos if they ignore it?"

The man dropped his eyes as one of the guards walked past. "These people spit on your Power. Why then, do they exist at all, eh?"

And then we were ordered back to labor.

The world shrank, becoming the trail, the heavy load, and the endless plodding of our feet. I still hear the shouts, cringe at the feel of the whips. It comes back to me at moments when the souls wander.

I could feel my strength waning, dimming, as I stumbled along.

Our burdens varied. Once it was a collection of curious wooden things, padded with fabric. They were beautifully made, the wood intricately carved, the fabric decorated in little designs of incredibly bright colors. Upon delivering them to the plaza below the chief's house, we were amazed to see one of the Kristiano leaders cry out with delight, hurry over, and plop his bottom into what turned out to be a chair.

I stared in amazement. They'd brought chairs, of all things? Just to sit in?

Then we were ordered away, and by the time we made the return trip, the chairs had all vanished, evidently into the Uzita houses, where the new occupants could now sit to their pleasure.

Another oddity was the heavy collection of metal parts that we toiled under. Moving the pieces from the landing to town took more than a hand of time. Parts were so heavy we had to shuffle along, sidestepping just to carry them. We left the pieces at one end of the plaza where a muscular Kristiano with a big smile clapped his hands and chattered on cheerfully as he inspected the pieces.

By the time we were locked to the palisade that night, the contraption had been assembled, and a fire had been stoked inside. We watched that night as the smiling Kristiano and two younger men tended the fire, inserting bits of metal until they glowed red. These in turn were hammered on another lump of metal. I'd seen copper worked, but never hot like they did the *hierro* metal.

On the fourth day, one of the Uzita fell, dragging the rest of us down with him. Broken, he refused to get up. They turned the dogs on him. If you've never seen such a thing, hope that you never do. I pulled back to the length of my chain, horrified, as the dogs literally ripped the man apart. They went for the throat and face first, then his belly. One great black dog tore the man's side open, hooked his guts, and backed away, pulling living intestine from the wound. Then the others were on it, grabbing, pulling, emptying the screaming man's body of its contents.

What manner of monsters are these?

The guards were laughing, slapping their sides. I watched them howl with delight and, but for the dogs between us, would have leaped for their throats.

When it was done, one of the guards removed a great metal knife from his belt and called the dogs off. I watched in disbelief as he severed what was left of the ravaged corpse's neck, kicked the head off to the side of the trail, and ordered us to drag the body next to it. For the rest of the day, the empty blood-blackened collar hung on its chain, sliding back and forth to remind us of our fate should our strength give out.

Breath Giver, I would kill them all.

The morning of the sixth day the numbers in my gang had grown to nearly sixty, all bound along the palisade. The new captives looked like startled quail, having no idea what was in store for them. Ortiz arrived with his bread and water. We wolfed the meal like starving creatures, then washed it down.

At that point the Kristianos began to assemble before the chief's house. A wooden cross had been erected there, and I watched — a dull hatred twining around my souls — as the Kristianos knelt in lines. Several robed men walked out, taking a position before the cross. They spoke in soft tones that barely carried to where the line of us captives watched. I had figured the robed men were priests of some sort, and now they touched their foreheads, bellies, and each breast. The priest droned on, calling out on occasion, to be answered by the kneeling men. Then, one by one, the Kristianos rose and went forward, drinking something from a gleaming gold cup and taking a bit of food.

I fixed on that golden cup. We had the metal, of course, but just in little, mostly worthless nuggets. I didn't know it could be used like copper.

When Ortiz returned, the guards were in tow.

I called out in Timucua. "Ortiz, I am a trader."

He glanced at me, and gave a shrug. "What?"

"I'm a trader. From the far north." I pointed to emphasize my point. "What you are doing, it's against the Power of trade."

He gave me blank stare. "Power? Trade? I don't understand."

"Traders are not to be treated this way. Doing so offends the Spirits. It's a way that —"

"*Cállate!* We care not for your magic. A new way has come. We serve the true god. You are but an animal.

"Work," came the order.

I stared in disbelief, and was jerked into motion by the chain.

That day it rained, making footing treacherous. In the afternoon, another of the Uzita collapsed, and again the dogs did their vicious business. This time I looked away.

All of my concentration went into the task of staying upright. At midday a terrible pounding had started inside my skull. But an irritant at first, it grew to a throbbing, as if someone were stabbing giant cactus spines into my head.

When we passed one of the headless corpses

by the trail, the smell of it made my stomach lurch, and I kept from vomiting by will alone.

Gods, when would this day be over? It seemed hotter, and my nose was running. When my muscles began to fail, I reached down inside, and pulled up hate.

Oh, yes, wonderful hate. It can burn like a fire, and rouse the muscles. Used as a distraction, I could imagine myself sliding my Kristiano sword deep into the guard's guts, and watching his insides spill like a load of eels onto the ground.

I wasn't feeling right, something more than a lack of food. A different fatigue had left me weak and hot, desperate for water. A sudden shiver ran through me.

You're sick, Black Shell. Perhaps witched, some terrible evil inflicted by the Kristianos.

And then I tripped, falling, jerking the rest of the line down with me. For a terrified second I lay there, stunned, and then struggled to my feet. The others were staring at me in horror as I grabbed with mud-slick fingers for the box I'd been carrying. Lifting it, we all managed to scramble to our feet.

The whip cracked along my back, almost sending me tumbling into the mud again, but somehow, through brute will, I kept my footing.

When I glanced at the guards, they were watching me, anticipation in their eyes. The dogs were poised, tails out, anxious for the order to attack.

Grinding my teeth, tears leaking out from my eyes, I managed to bull my way forward on wobbly legs.

Concentrate! Think! Hate! Another slip, and they wouldn't hesitate. The sensation of teeth ripping my flesh sent a live terror through my bones.

By dint of will alone, I made the last three trips of the day, collapsing against the palisade as they fastened me for the night. Had I ever felt this hot? Sweat was beading on my skin one moment, and the next, I began to shiver, as if in the deepest of winter.

I wolfed my piece of bread, drank my water, and lay wearily, panting. *When have I ever been this sick? How will I survive tomorrow?*

I wouldn't. The dull knowledge lay deep in my souls. I recalled Ortiz saying they would keep me, perhaps as a guide to the Chicaza. That simple hope now lay dead. But for that last surge of fear, my gutted corpse would already be lying beside my severed head along the trail: food only for the seagulls and crabs that scuttled ashore with the darkness. I didn't dare think about the *puercos*.

I was feeling oddly light-headed. My vision wavering — like staring across a hot swamp at the height of summer when the air grows wavy. And, oh, was I thirsty. Shivers, ever more violent, continued to run down my arms and legs, first hot, and then cold.

I glanced up at the dark Sky World, seeking the familiar patterns of stars, but an inky darkness was my only reward. As light as I felt, I could firmly believe that without the collar, I could have floated up there, past the clouds, to the Path of the Dead.

Blinking my eyes, I watched the murky clouds turn watery. They seemed to melt and run across the sky. In the shimmering, I saw a large wooden square raised upright. A man was tied, wrists and ankles, at each corner. His head hung down over his chest. Angry patches of skin showed where lit torches had been pressed against his flesh. Dried blood traced lines down his naked arms and legs, the cuts still open and clotted. Dark bruises marred his ribs and face.

My uncle was standing beside me, and I remembered the time: I had just passed my seventh winter. The captive had been taken in a raid against the Choctaw, who lived south of us.

"Do you understand what is happening here?" Uncle had asked. He was my mother's brother, high minko of the Chief Clan, and the most important man in the world.

"We are bringing Power back into balance," I replied. "Warriors from his town raided us last fall. We retaliated, and he was captured in battle."

"That is correct." Uncle then walked forward, lifting the prisoner's head to look him in the eyes. "How are you feeling?"

"Fine," the hanging Choctaw managed, though his voice was scratchy. "Dogs like you know nothing of courage." Then the man twisted his head away, staring up at the stars, his eyes glittering.

A low song rose in his throat, the sound of it weak from the pressure on his lungs. It wasn't easy to breathe hanging like that. The pain had to be unbearable. The words were slurred to the point I couldn't understand them.

Uncle walked back, kneeling to look me in the eyes. "This man is a warrior, nephew. Tomorrow, at high sun, I will cut his heart out and set his souls free. By his courage, he has earned an honorable death." He paused. "Do you understand the lesson here?"

I remember nodding. "By attacking us, the Choctaw upset the balance between the red and white Power. One of our people was killed. The dead man's souls cry out for revenge. By setting this man's souls free, the balance and harmony are maintained."

"That's right." Uncle clapped his hand to my shoulder. "After this is done, we will send emissaries to the Choctaw under the White Arrow."

"The White Arrow is the gesture of peace," I replied.

"That's right." Uncle smiled at me. "Together, with the Choctaw, we will return the balance. Each of us has been tested, and each of us has proven our strength. Red Power was loosed, and now it must be brought back into harmony with the white."

I remember how Uncle walked out the next day, a long stone sword in his hand. Around us, the people watched; the hopaye and the lesser priests were singing. The warriors, in solid ranks, stood between the prisoner and the rest of the people. Uncle was resplendent in his fine white apron, a gleaming copper pin holding his tightly curled hair. My little brother and I stood just behind him to the right; the war chief and tishu minko to the left.

I watched sunlight flash on the long chert sword blade as Uncle held it high, calling the blessings of Breath Giver and the Powers of the Sky World.

The Choctaw had pulled himself up as straight as his weak muscles would allow. His broken voice was still singing as Uncle deftly drove the sword into his chest and cut the man's heart from his body.

Honor. A true man died with honor, even surrounded by enemies. It had been beaten into my young souls. Now, those same souls were floating, drifting in and out with each breath from my hot and sweat-streaked body.

I will die without honor. Pulled apart by dogs.

What did it matter? My people considered me a coward. I wouldn't even have the chance to die as the Choctaw did that day. I wasn't even being given the opportunity to measure my souls against fate. Where would my souls go? How would they find their way to the west, to the edge of the world?

We were taught that the life souls of the dead traveled westward, where the earth ended in a mighty cliff. There they were judged, and those found worthy made the leap, passing through the Seeing Hand's great eye, to land in the Sky World.

Those judged unworthy hesitated at the last instant, their doubts sapping their muscles enough that they fell short, as they did in life. The endless fall was only interrupted by water cougars or tie snakes reaching out from caves in the Underworld to snatch them.

And, assuming my souls didn't hesitate, would the great Seeing Hand snap shut as it judged them? Would they slam against the hard knuckles, only to fall?

Tears began to leak out of my hot eyes, trickling to cool on my sweat-damp cheeks.

Breath Maker? How can you allow these Kristianos to even set foot on your land?

I was so engrossed in despair I almost missed what happened next.

The woman who appeared out of the night wouldn't have drawn my attention, except that she dropped a bundle on the ground and spoke with the guard.

"Eres la guardia?"

"Sí," he replied. *"Tienes un nombre, mujer?"*

"María de Lopez. Conoces Miguel de Lopez? Es mi hombre."

"Qué haces aquí?"

"Es tu cumpleaños, no? Yo soy tu regalo."

"Qué?"

She pressed herself against him, running her hands over his body. Within moments they were on the ground. Some of the newer captives watched this with interest.

Then I heard him grunt, and a rattling came from his throat. I glanced over, seeing the woman fingering through his pockets. She rose like a wraith, picked up her bundle, and hurried along the line of captives, calling in Mos'kogee, "Black Shell?"

In my growing delirium, I asked, "Mother?"

"Idiot," she muttered, placing a hand to my face. Then she drew back. "You're sick."

"Pearl Hand?" My thoughts were reeling as she reached over my shoulder and inserted the thing Kristianos call a *llave* into the lock. I heard it click open. This was a dream, and what a wonderful one it was.

"Come," she said in Mos'kogee.

The captive next to me called something.

Pearl Hand hissed, *"Cállate! Hijo de gusano!"*

We all knew *cállate.* Kristiano for "shut up."

She pulled me up, only to have me almost collapse. Glancing warily back at the Kristiano houses, she unfolded the bundle. I was hardly helpful as she pulled a long-sleeved

174

fabric shirt over my arms and around my shoulders. It was the sort of thing a Kristiano would have worn. Then she was yanking white-fabric pants onto my weak legs, belting them at my waist.

"Why are you . . . ?"

"Shhh!" she warned.

Lacing my arm over her shoulder, she struggled to get me upright. I wobbled, the world spinning and wavering in my sight. The skin on my legs, arms, and torso tickled, irritated by the fabric rubbing against it.

"Why am I in these clothes?"

"So you look like a house slave," she growled.

A what? We started down between the houses, my weight staggering her. My legs had turned oddly rubbery, bending and folding beneath me.

The dress she wore felt damp and oddly sticky. I wondered where she'd managed to get into such tacky liquid. I tried to smell it, but my nose was thick and running.

A Kristiano coming toward us asked, *"Qué pasa aquí?"*

"Manuel es muy borracho," Pearl Hand replied to the dark figure and hurried us past. She had her hand on the chain to keep it from clanking.

"Es muy malo por un indio," the man mut-

tered. *"Dios lo ayuda cuando el jefe lo descubre."*

"Sí," Pearl Hand replied in a fear-tight voice.

The man followed for a couple of steps, then shook his head and continued on his way.

But for the clouds, he might have managed a better look and seen the collar and chain. As it was, we were just two figures passing in the night.

At the shore, Pearl Hand more dropped than lowered me into a dugout; then she struggled to shove it out. I heard her sloshing as she scrambled in, climbed over me, and paddled us out into the night.

"I'm dead, aren't I?" I whispered. "This is a dream."

"A dream? I could only wish," she muttered as she threw a quick glance over her shoulder and drove us out into the bay.

To the west, I could see the floating palaces, their little yellow lights flickering. And to think, I'd once thought them pretty.

Then I drifted off, happy to float on the swells. My souls rising and falling with the waves, while fantastic dreams unwound like a magical spiral . . .

TEN

I walked in the twilight below a giant forest. This was old growth, perhaps dating back to the Beginning Times — the boles as big around as a Mos'kogee's house. Looking up into the great interlaced branches, the tops of the trees seemed to vanish in an infinity of leaves. Giant roots, gnarled and thick as a man's torso, wound through the rotting leaf mat like great snakes that dove into the soil.

Overhead, birds flitted back and forth, and the angry calls of squirrels could be heard. As I went, I kicked moldy walnuts and hickory shells before me.

I could see deer peering at me from behind great trunks that six men would need to circle, fingertip to fingertip, were they to have any success at girdling them.

A soft melody, born of birdsong and the whirring of insects, carried to my ears. As I proceeded through the cavernous depths, I came to the realization that a faint trail marked the route I followed, as if thousands of airy feet had trodden there before me.

Here and there forest snakes lay, their colors blending with the leaves as they marked my passing with shining eyes.

"Where do you go, man?" a voice asked.

I stopped short, staring around, to discover a thin green snake perched atop a mushroom as big around as my head.

"That way." I motioned down the faint trail.

"To do what?" the small green snake asked.

"I'm not sure."

"Neither are we," the little serpent replied. "Have you decided that the time has come?"

"For what?"

"To surrender the price of life."

I puzzled at his words. *The price of life?*

"It must be paid by all." The little snake uncurled. "There is work to be done yet. Go. Make your choice."

I nodded, continuing on my way. Some memory — a thing that haunted me — lay just beyond my souls' ability to grasp. I puzzled over it as I continued, aware that the forest had a slight rise to it, the going ever harder.

Ahead I could see patterns of light shooting rays between the great trunks, and only as I approached did it become apparent that I had reached the edge of a mighty cliff. I stopped at the precipice, staring out into a vastness of stars. They seemed to twinkle against the velvet blackness, and looking down, I could see no bottom.

Across from me, a familiar constellation beckoned: the great Seeing Hand of my people. The gateway to the Land of the Dead.

I studied the familiar pattern of stars, so close I could almost reach out and touch them. The wrist was made from a line of three stars, the outline of fingers and thumb easily determined. In the center was the "eye" that observed those who leaped for its center.

It was said that those dead souls who brought Power with them and attempted to do with sorcery what they could not through worth, would be identified in midleap and slapped into the abyss. Those who passed through the portal would find themselves safely on the other side. According to the story, in the Beginning Times, one of the Hero Twins made the leap, battling with the sky god who guarded the entrance to the Sky World. After slaying the god, he hung the severed hand to mark the way for those who followed.

The leap, however, was just the first test. Only on the other side did the dead souls find the Path of the Dead, that hazy band of light that stretched across the night sky. At its base, during the summer months, lurked Horned Serpent.

Each spring he spread his wings and flew up from the Underworlds to guard the entry to the path.

Did I dare jump? I swallowed hard, thinking back on my life, on my exile so many winters past. What had I ever done that would be worthy?

Lost in indecision, I heard a grating sound from just below the cliff's edge, I started to peer over when a giant bird's head reared over the dropoff's lip.

Crying in terror, I backpedaled, lost my footing, and fell hard on my rump. I scrambled back like some awkward crab, staring down the length of an incredibly huge pale beak. A woodpecker's, to be more precise.

The point of it, a mere hand's length away, seemed to fill my vision, and looking down its length, I found two brown eyes taking my measure. A high crest of feathers lifted, giving the creature an even more fearsome appearance.

"Don't hurt me!" The cry was torn from my throat.

"Black Shell, of the Chicaza," the bird said in a hissing voice. "Come to measure his souls."

"No. I . . . I mean . . ."

"Are you dead, or aren't you?"

Mildly I squeaked, "I don't know. What . . . who are you?"

The great ivory-billed woodpecker leaned his head back, and laughter, like thunder, shook

180

the world. "I am the West Wind."

I watched as huge wings unfurled and stretched across the horizon as far as I could see. The West Wind? Well I could believe it. With one mighty beat those wings could have flattened even the mighty forest through which I'd just passed.

My mouth had gone dry. It was believed among my people that a great woodpecker guarded each of the cardinal directions, hovering at the edge of the earth, battling forever with the giant water panthers of the Underworld. The beatings of the Winds' gargantuan wings powered the gales that shook and rattled roofs and toppled trees.

The giant turned to inspect me with one fierce eye. "But, if you are not dead, what do you do here, Black Shell? You are Horned Serpent's creature. The smell of him is all over you."

"It is?" I didn't dare sniff, afraid of what such a terrible Spirit Creature would do to me.

The head tilted, as if in thought. "The great battle is joined, isn't it?"

"Great battle?"

"For the hearts and souls of the people." The beak opened and snapped shut with a crack that deafened. "Though why Horned Serpent would choose you, I have no idea. You aren't much of a hero. Turned your back on your own people."

I clamped my eyes shut, a terrible fear deep inside. "He called me, told me to run."

"Yes, a clever story, I'm sure."

I began to shake, aware that alone and unarmed, I had no chance against such a Powerful creature.

"Your answer doesn't lie here. Try the south next time. Horned Serpent rises in the night sky, guarding the southern entrance to the Path of the Dead. Perhaps he'll talk to you, give you meaning . . . or take it away." The last was said with scorn. "Go on. On your feet."

I pushed up with my feet, almost scrambling against the bulk of the tree, my fingernails eating into the bark.

"Now," the great bird hissed, "run!"

I dodged sideways as that long beak opened and darted in my direction. The sharp points slashed two great gouges in the old tree's bark where I had been. Turning, I ran as I had once run from the Kristianos. Glancing back, I saw the immense head dart at me, the beak snapping but a hand's length from my back.

Then I was in the trees, and laughter rang out, turning to thunder that shook the earth beneath my feet . . .

"Black Shell?"

I cried out, gasping, my legs thrashing.

"Black Shell?" At the same time I felt hands gripping my shoulders.

"No!" My voice came as a distant croaking sound.

Again thunder boomed — farther away this

time — and I blinked my eyes open. I felt hot and gulped cool air into my lungs.

"Black Shell, it's a dream. You're safe. It's Pearl Hand. Do you hear me?"

I kept blinking my eyes, but they didn't seem to focus, as though I were seeing through water. "What? Who?"

"It's Pearl Hand. You're safe."

I flinched when thunder rolled across the land, and sat up. I was in a small clearing, and a dark evening sky was filled with brooding thunderheads. Distant lightning flashed white through the clouds.

Pearl Hand? I raised a weak hand and rubbed my rheumy eyes. She was clearer now.

A small fire was burned down to coals, the grass around it mashed flat. My dogs, Skipper, Bark, Fetch, Gnaw, and Squirm, were lying beside the packs, watching me with soft brown eyes. Squirm wagged his tail when my eyes met his. Fetch immediately picked up a chewed stick, tail wagging as he dropped it suggestively behind Pearl Hand.

To one side I saw my bow and arrow quiver, evidently recovered from where the Kristianos ran me down. After all, what use did they have for a bow and arrows? My trader's staff rested beside them.

The presence of my weapons was oddly reassuring, though I didn't have the faintest notion — given the way I felt — where I'd get the strength to use them.

"Where am I?"

"A camp. We're just a little inland from the bay, far from the trails. It's higher here, surrounded by swamps. The Kristianos won't come here. Not unless we give them a reason, like you shouting at the top of your lungs."

"What about the West Wind?"

She bent down, lifting a water gourd to my lips. "You're sick. Fevered. Half out of your head."

I drank the gourd dry, then sank back onto a blanket, no strength left in my arms. In the process the collar chafed my neck and the metal links rattled. It took several attempts before I could identify the dark stain on her cloth dress: dried blood.

I tried to think back past the Spirit dream. "It was dark. You came. The guard . . . Where did your dress get bloody?"

Pearl Hand lifted a little stick of metal, what the Kristianos called a *llave*. "I needed this to unlock you." Then she produced a large knife made of the metal Kristianos called *hierro*. "They are so predictable. They lose any sense when a woman like me will lie with them."

"You killed him?" I wondered, seeing the world begin to shimmer. My body had grown light and seemed to be floating.

"Would you rather I hadn't?" she asked drily.

"No." I was having trouble keeping my eyes focused. "I thought you were far away. Run-

184

ning . . ." Images of fleeing the West Wind wove themselves into my souls. "Running . . ." But I couldn't seem to keep my thoughts centered.

"I am Horned Serpent's creature. In the south . . . south . . ."

The world began to fade, my souls floating lightly as thunder banged somewhere off to the west and a sudden gust of wind roared out of the night . . .

The country consisted of broken hills and ridges, outcrops of crumbling sandstone protruding from just below the ridge crests. The forest here consisted of patches of hickory, black walnut, red and black oaks, with pines and red cedar interspersed. Sassafras, plum, and firebush grew in the bottoms. The way proved difficult with grape, prickly greenbriar, and thorny smilax weaving an impenetrable maze.

With my trader's staff, I pressed the smaller vines out of the way, the older ones were as thick as a man's leg. Panting for breath, I paused, my gaze following the great vines up into the forest heights. Daylight gave the canopy above a light green glow, and I could see birds up on the distant branches, staring down, watching my progress as they leaned their heads close to each other. Their chirped comments rose in lilting melodies.

Resuming my way, I clambered over roots,

my feet sinking in the spongy leaf mat that carpeted the forest floor. A damp, mellow odor from the rotting leaves filled my nostrils. The question of what I was doing, or where I was headed, didn't seem important. I just had to get there . . . wherever "there" was.

As I proceeded, I could again make out a faint trail that wound through the forest, following the path of least resistance. It led me along the steep-sided ridge, and traced a sinuous route around the old gray sandstone boulders, all covered with moss and lichens. Water stains had left black streaks down the stone.

I noticed raccoons peeking around the boles of trees, their hairy little hands grasping the thick roots that shielded them. Curiosity filled their dark and gleaming eyes, as if they'd rarely seen a human like me. A copperhead watched from its lair in a cracked rock, the eyes seeming to gleam as its tongue flicked in and out.

Near the bottom of the forest, great beech trees rose from the soil, their smooth white bark almost pearlescent in the forest twilight. High overhead, leaves rattled with the soft breeze, and I could hear cicadas rasping. Occasional flower petals fell from on high, drifting down and sweetening the air.

The trail clung to the ravine side, following just under the sandstone outcropping. Deep inside the overhangs, I could see carvings pecked into the stone, and in other places, painted pictographs of Eagle Man, Water

Panther, Buzzard, and large renderings of Rattlesnake. The glyphs were old, weathered, and sometimes spotted with moss; but the Spirit Beast effigies seemed to watch me with living eyes.

Through the trees, I caught glimpses across the ravine, and realized it was narrowing. The way became steeper, the bottom closing until I reached a dead end. There the thick layer of weather-gray sandstone created an overhang, the interior of which was obscured by an inky blackness.

I could hear water trickling and became acutely aware of great thirst. My dry tongue rubbed dully over my teeth and scraped the roof of my mouth.

Desperate for a drink, I stumbled forward, crushing mayapple and holly, pushing through thorny raspberry and currants, until I passed under the overhanging stone.

I would have run right over the top of the slick-sided serpent, but some trick of the light shining on those polished scales gave me just enough warning to slide to a stop.

Gods! What if I'd awakened the monstrous snake? I'd never seen a snake like this. The thing was as big around as a canoe! In the dim light, patterns of chevrons could be made out, and as my eyes adjusted I could see they were black, red, white, and blue, the sacred colors of the cardinal directions.

I couldn't swallow down my parched throat,

and the sound of splashing water within the cave was likely to drive me mad. Frantic with fear, driven by thirst, I hesitated, then slowly took a step back.

The great serpent shifted slightly, and the head rose in eerie silence. "There is no going back." The words it uttered were sibilant, as if hissed from deep inside the monstrous reptile.

"I'm sorry," I croaked. "I'm just so thirsty." I took another step back, and the triangular head poised behind a coil. I gaped in disbelief. The thing's head was as wide as my leg is long. A forked tongue shot out, and I could feel the breeze it created as it flipped back and forth, then was withdrawn between those plated jaws.

Snakes can swallow things three or four times the size of their heads. My body wasn't even a snack, let alone a challenge.

"I'm sorry I bothered you." I lifted my foot to take another step back.

The head drew back to strike, vertically slitted eyes locking with mine.

"Don't," the thing hissed. "The only way left to you is forward. Choose. Ahead of you lies life. One more step back, and you're mine."

"Yours?"

"Oh yes. That is my Power. I've been given the ones who surrender to fear. I survive on those who flee. Run, Black Shell. Turn tail and make just one more step toward escape. Listen to your fear, skinny man. Give in to it. *Run!*"

I couldn't have moved had I wanted. Terror

had locked my muscles. The head moved closer, and I flinched as the arm-thick tongue lashed out, flicking along my shivering flesh.

I'm going to die. The realization was shouted between my souls. Best to make it quick.

With all my resolve, I stepped forward, eyes closed to avoid the sight of that mouth opening. Nothing. Not even the flickering tongue. I blinked, staring uncertainly. The head had drawn back, but the slit-pupiled eyes remained fixed on mine.

I took another step, right up to that hide, the scales large enough to use for plates. The snake's hiss reverberated inside the cavern. My leg was shaking as I reached out and started to clamber over the cold thickness of its body. The hiss grew louder. And then I was over, every muscle in my body trembling.

"Yes," the hissing voice said at last. "You may pass. I guard the way, and it can be followed, only through me."

"The way?"

I could see the water now, a crystal pool of it bubbling up from the rock. If I bent and drank, would that be the signal for the giant snake to strike? Cautiously I took a step to the water and eased down, eyes locked with the snake's.

Then it moved, the head drifting to the right; the monstrous jaws split, then opened. All the while I was fixed on that midnight slit of a pupil as it watched me. But to my surprise, the head slipped over to where the bulbous tail rested on dark stone. The mouth opened and slowly engulfed the tail, button by button, until it closed on smooth hide above the rattles.

A snake eating its own tail? The story was told to children everywhere. Yet here I was, seeing it with my own eyes.

Drink! Now! While you can. I bent down over the water, shocked to see light rising from beneath. Placing my lips to it, I sucked draught after draught. Did I lose my balance, or was I pushed? Water, cool and pleasing, closed around me, and I was swimming, striking this way and that, seeking the surface. But no surface could be found.

Panic left me thrashing, turning and twisting, desperate for the surface and life-giving air. In the tumult, I lost my trader's staff.

Drowning! My souls screamed in realization.

When the end came, I sucked frantically for air. I coughed as I drew a lungful of water, chest spasming, pulling water, expelling it.

But the gray mantle of death didn't darken my vision. Instead I slowly sank into the light, as though descending through a hole.

Things began to grow clear around me, a different world unfolding. Instead of sky I could see roots slipping down from the rocks overhead, and my feet settled on a floor covered with waving mosses and water grass. Fish darted this way and that, and to one side the biggest snapping turtle I'd ever seen lay half buried in mud, its round eye giving me a thoughtful look.

"This can't be happening," I muttered.

"Oh, but it is." The voice was deep, and came from behind me.

I turned.

My people draw images of Water Panther, the *Piasa,* and we fear him for his Power in the Underworld. This one was as tall as I. Feathered wings rose from the beast's back, speckled with brown and black bands. All four legs ended in scaled bird's feet, the claws sinking into the mud. While the body and head were that of a cougar, the long whipping tail was that of a large snake, scaled and marked by dark circles with white centers. Adding to the fearsome appearance, long canines could be seen protruding from beneath the upper lip.

I backed slowly away, wary of where Snapping Turtle waited in his mud lair.

"What do you want from the Underworld, Black Shell?" Water Panther asked. "You are a man of the middle world, not ours."

"I don't know why I'm here," I told the beast truthfully. "I was captured by the Kristianos. And then . . ." I frowned, having vague memories of Pearl Hand and waking in a camp with my dogs. But was that real? Or dream?

I clapped my hands to my head, suddenly unsure of anything: Horned Serpent, the West Wind, the great tie snake guarding the portal to the Underworld, even the Kristianos — were any of them real?

191

Movement caught the corner of my eye, and I turned, ready for some new threat. Instead, Anhinga — the snake bird — flew down through the water, wings flapping gracefully as it pulled up, seeming to float just off to Water Panther's left.

I'd swum with anhingas, seen them fly beneath the waves in the pursuit of fish and crawfish. Not so long ago I'd watched them, Pearl Hand at my side.

The bird cocked its head, inspecting me with a knowing eye. To Water Panther, it said, "Last I heard he was bothering the West Wind on the edge of the world. He wouldn't make the leap to the Seeing Hand. We're not sure if he's dead or alive, or just hanging in between. Now he's here."

"He mentions the Kristianos," Water Panther replied, his gaze never leaving mine. "Says he was a captive."

"Look at his neck; the wound is still there." Anhinga pointed with a wing. "Smell him. He reeks of their captivity. The West Wind says he's Horned Serpent's creature. But why would he choose a man like this? Surely better warriors than this common trader can be found."

Water Panther took a step forward, sniffing, lines of whiskers quivering behind the pink nose. "He smells of Kristiano metals and disease, but beneath it is Horned Serpent's musk." He seemed to consider. "Anhinga makes a good point: What sort of warrior are you?"

"Warrior?" I muttered in confusion.

Anhinga barely stroked with his wings. "In the middle world, he is known as a trader, an exile from the Chicaza. We watched him with his woman one day. We weren't impressed."

I stared warily at Anhinga. All peoples considered anhingas to be exceptional Power beings. Like ducks, they soared in the sky, walked the earth, and dove into the Underworld. To share Power between all three worlds made such creatures incredibly unpredictable, and at the same time, marvelous.

"A Chicaza?" Water Panther mused. "Great warriors, but this one hasn't the tattoos, and doesn't introduce himself with the name of Mankiller, the mark of a blooded warrior."

"I don't understand any of this," I said slowly, wishing to be anywhere but here. But to escape? Where? All around me was water, rock, and endless passages.

"He must have courage," Water Panther said reluctantly. "Otherwise the tie snake guarding the portal would be digesting his bones as we speak."

I nodded, hoping the notion of being courageous was worth something. "I'm just a trader."

Water Panther's head rose at the admission. "And what have you brought to trade?"

I looked down at my body, naked but for a breechcloth. "My trade is back with my packs."

"We don't want your middle world trinkets." Water Panther stalked closer. "Although copper has a certain value here. What do you have to trade?"

"Trade for what?"

"Your souls, Black Shell. Only the greatest healers, dreamers, sorcerers, and shamans make the journey here, but they come prepared, having learned the ways of Power in order to pass without being devoured by Spirit Creatures like me. You come alone, and in ignorance. What have you to trade for your souls?"

I tried misdirection. "But West Wind says Horned Serpent —"

"He's not here." Water Panther watched me with the same intent a cougar did a cottontail. "Horned Serpent has flown up into the southern sky, guarding the Path of the Dead where it leads up into the Sky World. He'll be there for several moons. You, however, are here now, and unprotected. Seemingly without trade to give for your souls."

"I have to return for my packs. I'll have something to trade. Perhaps a Kristiano sword made of —"

"That metal corrodes here, turns brown and flakes away. Most ugly." Water Panther reached up with a bird-claw foot. I tried to twist away, but the cold, taloned foot grasped me like an osprey did a fish.

"I can crush you with just a squeeze," Water Panther said softly. "It's not painless, but it's quick. You won't be around to feel what it's like to be eaten."

"I give you my word. I'll do anything —"

"Taken."

As quickly I was free, Water Panther staring at me, the black pupils like dark pools in those yellow orbs.

I staggered back, coughing after the restriction to my lungs. A bone-deep fear clung to my bones like old spiderwebs.

"I have your word," Water Panther repeated. "You'll do anything when I finally ask it of you. Now, go."

I felt myself being thrust backward, my body rising as I thrashed, suddenly aware that I was suffocating, unable to breathe . . .

Then a great pressure bore down on me. A crushing weight that felt sure to snap my ribs . . .

"Black Shell? Breathe!"

The weight vanished, my chest expanding.

I tried to cough, water blocking my windpipe.

The weight crashed down on me again, and I felt my guts being squeezed. Water Panther! He was crushing the souls out of my body.

"Black Shell?" came the frantic cry. "Please, breathe!"

The weight went away, the blockage in my throat loosened. I coughed, feeling something slimy and foul in the back of my mouth.

I spit it out, coughing and coughing, the very act of it shredding my throat.

My eyes fluttered open, and I lay gasping desperately for air. Above, a night sky was partially lit by a low moon. The stars looked as pale as scattered patches of frost. The Path of the Dead, like a band of hazy smoke, arched above. A small fire gave just enough light to see the dogs watching anxiously. My cheek rested on cool grass.

"Blessed gods," Pearl Hand muttered, climbing up from where she straddled me. "Blow your nose."

I did, my throat still tickling from the violent coughing. Mucus filled my fingers. I wiped them on the grass.

"Water Panther," I whispered. "He tried to drown me."

Pearl Hand sidled over, her face shadowed by night. I could tell she was inspecting me carefully. "Water Panther? First the West Wind . . . and now Water Panther?"

Her shoulders drooped. "You're fevered, Black Shell. It's a wonder you've hung on this long. Your lungs are making more fluid than you can expel. I've seen it before. People drown in their own phlegm."

"I was in the Underworld."

"You were almost dead. The only thing I could think of was to roll you onto the ground and jump on your back." She looked at the slimy wad on the grass. "I guess it worked."

Pearl Hand looked exhausted and sad, so I

asked, "Why are you doing this?"

After a pause, she said, "Because I have to."

"You owe me nothing."

"No," she whispered. "But that's the point, isn't it?"

Gods, she made less sense than Water Panther.

For a while we were silent, except for my coughing and wheezing. I told her, "Whatever sickness this is, you could catch it."

She tipped her head back, long hair tumbling down past her shoulders. Moonlight illuminated her enchanting face. "I've had most of their diseases as a child. All but the pox. That's a horror I'd as soon avoid."

"Pox?" I'd never heard the word.

"Don't even say it. Some think just the mention will bring it upon them."

I spit again and gasped for breath. A watery rattle sounded from my lungs. "I was in the Underworld. Underwater. I thought I'd drown."

"You were here, Black Shell. Drown? The same as, I suppose. If you hadn't been thrashing so, I might have slept right through it." She ran nervous fingers through her hair. "I'd have awakened beside a corpse."

"Thirsty. So very thirsty."

She placed the gourd to my lips. At the odd angle some went down my windpipe. Unlike when I passed through the guardian serpent's portal, this was most unpleasant. I couldn't stop coughing, fear of drowning clawing at the back of my thoughts.

Later, after she'd gone to sleep, I lay spent on the ground, riding the waves of fever. As always, it was Fetch who came over and pawed at me, a soft whine in his throat. But I had no energy for a game of stick. Finally he lay down beside me, nose on his paws, watching me with worried brown eyes.

I've given Water Panther my word that I'll do anything.

But what did that mean? As if in answer, my entire body began to shake, my jaws clattering like hail on an ice-covered pond.

DECISIONS

A hacking cough brought her bolt awake. *Black Shell! Gods, is he all right?*

She sat up, wincing from the pain in her back and hips, and looked around, her heart racing. The fire pit, located in the center of the room, was marked by a pattern of red embers, and a roof blotted the sky she expected to be overhead.

Pearl Hand rubbed a callused hand over her withered face, hearing the rhythmic breathing of the others.

I was dreaming. Back there . . . in the camp with Black Shell. So long ago.

She sighed, grunting as she lowered herself to the pole bed where it jutted out of the wall. Rolling onto her side, she pulled the blanket up to her chin and stared at the glowing embers in the fire pit.

Pulling the blanket's thick weave across her fingers, she looked back over the years, rekindling the dream that had haunted her sleep, remembering.

199

A grunt of amazement marked her disbelief. *How did I ever conjure the courage to go into that town and get him out?*

The dogs . . . Seeing them, watching them, forever staring down the trail, waiting for Black Shell, that had been even worse than her own tortured indecision. Fetch had been the worst, his preoccupation with sticks forgotten. Bark had refused to eat, although Gnaw had been happy to gulp Bark's meal before she could stop him. And there had been something desperate expressed in Skipper's oddly blue left eye that had driven her half mad.

I did it for the dogs. Of course.

In the darkness, a smile curled her thin lips. The infinite ways in which a woman could lie to herself were an unending miracle.

"I couldn't admit, not even to myself, that the mighty Pearl Hand had come to love him. What a savage master pride is."

But given the choice, which master demanded more? Pride, or Power? At first she hadn't believed. Oh, no. He'd just been sick, fevered, his souls loose from his body, driven out by the witchery of Kristiano disease.

"The dreams, Black Shell. They changed our lives. Changed the very world."

The embers winked and flickered as a draft played across the floor mats and stirred patterns in the coals.

"When did I finally come to believe? Was it the glow of the Spirit World reflected in your eyes? Or was it that I could never conjure the courage to leave you?"

ELEVEN

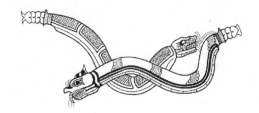

I awakened to an early morning sun that peered through gaps in a cloud-puffed blue sky. I still lay on the trampled grass, a blanket wrapped loosely around my body. I could see mangroves — thick with waxy green leaves — in every direction. The remains of a fire smoldered in its pit; sticks of driftwood had been piled nearby. One of the Kristianos' metal pots lay on its side near the fire, and behind it my packs rested in a line.

Of the dogs or Pearl Hand, there was no sign. My eyes seemed to have trouble focusing, being rheumy and crusted. Breathing through my hot, plugged nose was impossible. I tried to sit up, and only did so by the greatest effort. A quaking tremble ran through

202

my arms as I propped myself up.

A terrible thirst burned in my dry throat. I peered around for the drinking gourd and spotted it just beyond arm's length. The simple act of crawling over to it drained my body of any reserves. Despite the shakes, I managed to get most of the liquid into my mouth and reveled at the cool sensation rolling through my gut.

After emptying the gourd, I flopped on the ground, panting, hating the shimmering at the edge of my vision. For the time being I was happy to just watch the clouds floating across the sky and listen to the birds and insects. A flock of seagulls in flight came wheeling over, glancing down at the camp with curious eyes before drifting away on the breeze.

At least my weapons were close. I reached out, laying a hand on the bow stave where it protruded from its alligator-hide quiver.

Squirm, his white blaze and bib shining, and Gnaw, with tipped tail slashing, came crashing up the trail. Tongues lolling, they paused at the edge of the clearing just long enough to see me before charging over and mauling me with their mud-spattered paws. I enjoyed the sensation of their hot sloppy tongues as they licked me on the face, hands, and arms.

Then the rest of the pack appeared, Bark bellowing his pleasure before leaping full onto my belly. Pearl Hand walked behind, the hem of her skirt wet, a net bag of something over her shoulder. She caught sight of me under the pouncing dogs and called them off with a word. To my astonishment, they obeyed her perfectly, trotting over and plopping down at her feet to look up with adoring eyes. Only Fetch kept throwing me longing glances.

"You're awake," she greeted, and slung the bag down. I could see fish, crabs, and a couple of swamp rabbits, the latter looking a little worse for wear beneath the cording.

"I've never been this weak in my life." I rolled my head to one side, the collar chafing my neck. How would we ever get the accursed thing off?

"You're lucky to be breathing." She walked over and lifted the flap of blanket that covered my hips. From the relief on her face, I assumed I hadn't fouled myself.

"We were out of food," she remarked. "The dogs and I went hunting. That and I managed to sneak a look at the Kristianos."

"And?"

"Most of them have left. Perhaps four tens of cabayeros and maybe six tens of foot warriors remain. Most of the floating palaces have gone, too, but for some of the small ones anchored off-shore. The rest of the army has headed inland."

"Which means?"

"Pity Chief Mocoso. I think they've gone

his way. All but a handful of the slaves are gone, carrying the supplies and food for the *Adelantado*'s army."

"*Adelantado?*" I asked.

"That's what they call the Kristiano chief. His true name is Hernando de Soto. I learned that the night I sneaked into their camp to rescue you. They thought I was a slave woman, property of one of the nobles, because I spoke their language."

My souls were firmly enough anchored in my body to ask, "Why did you do that? Come back for me?"

She poked at the fire, adding sticks, bending down to blow the coals into flames. Then she glanced at me. "Because I'm an idiot, Black Shell."

"Who? My Pearl Hand? Not a chance."

"You have no idea how much I wanted to run." She gave the smoking fire a distant look. "Had you ever asked, I'd have told you I'd risk myself for no man." She shook her head. "I never understood what women ever saw in men, or why they did the foolish things they did. And then you came along. Maybe it was in your eyes, or the way you talked to me." She shrugged. "Maybe it was the way you held me . . . as though I were something precious. Whatever it was, I couldn't bear the thought of leaving you behind. Especially when you gave yourself to save me."

"I'd do it again." I let my gaze linger on

her. "Even now, knowing what being captured by Kristianos really means."

She smiled shyly. "Good. Because after what I've been through caring for you, you *owe* me."

"Owe you what?"

"More than you can ever pay, Trader."

"I'll make good on it." The world was starting to shimmer again and I pressed my eyes shut, as if to make it go away.

"Well, you got to see your Kristianos." She was grinning when I cleared my vision enough to look her way. "What do you think now?"

"I'd rather face Spirit Beasts." Which got me to thinking about West Wind and Water Panther. "We're not alone in this, you know."

"Oh, really? You got a Chicaza army hidden around here that I don't know about?" She began pulling animals from the net bag, laying them out. Big old Gnaw had begun to drool at the prospects.

"I've been having Spirit dreams." I glanced down at my hand, seeing something under the nails. Weak as I was, it took a couple of tries to clean my fingernails — and was surprised to find bark wedged under one.

I stared at it stupidly, remembering how West Wind backed me against the tree, and how I clawed at the bark in an effort to escape.

"Your souls have been drifting in and out

of your body. You cried out a lot." She frowned. "Things I didn't understand about great serpents, Water Panther . . . Odd things that frightened me."

"If just hearing about them frightened you, you should have been in the dream." I shook my head, which made the metal collar clink against the links. Fetch took it as an opportunity to bring a stick and drop it before me. I gave it a halfhearted toss, barely worth the effort, but it was all I had.

"What do you think it means?" She had busied herself pulling the hides off the rabbits. I could tell by the look of them that the dogs had run them down. It was enough to distract Fetch from his slobbery stick.

"I don't know yet." I swallowed hard, wishing for more water. "Somehow I've always believed, but never really *believed.* Does that make sense? Everywhere I go people have Spirit Helpers, guardians, ghosts, something not of this world. Once, a long time ago, I thought I saw and heard Horned Serpent." I made a face. "It didn't end well for me, and I was never really sure after that. Now all these Spirit Creatures in my dreams are saying I'm somehow tied to Horned Serpent."

She had the fire crackling and placed the fish down in the coals to cook. The dogs were paying close attention to her every move. Squirm caught the rabbit skin she flung in his direction. A small melee burst out as the rest of the pack tried to take it away.

"Horned Serpent," she mused. Then she glanced absently at the mangroves that blocked the view to the south. "It's early summer. He's flown into the sky, just above the southern horizon."

"To guard the Path of the Dead," I added, haunted by memories of the dreams. "Do you know what my people believe happens after death?"

"That the dead travel westward to the edge of the earth and make a leap through the Seeing Hand?"

"I made that journey."

"But not the leap?" Pearl Hand arched an inquisitive eyebrow. Gods, she was beautiful when she did that.

"I wasn't worthy." I looked down at where I'd scraped the bark from under my fingernail. "Maybe that's why I'm still alive. The West Wind told me there was more to do, that the battle had been joined. Then he chased me away." I stared uneasily at the little sliver of bark. "And then I went to the Underworld. I had to pass by a tie snake that swallowed its tail."

She was watching me with sober eyes. "It is said that tie snakes guard springs, passageways to the Underworld. When they devour their tails, they make an opening through which only the greatest holy men can pass."

"I did. But I'm not holy."

"No argument there," she muttered. "And that's when you met Water Panther?"

I nodded. "It seemed so real."

She finished gutting the rabbit, throwing the entrails to the dogs. Then she propped the pink carcasses over the fire and turned her attention to the crabs. "I have to go to the stream for water to cook these in. I'll refill the drinking gourd at the same time. I need to think about this."

That said, she picked up the Kristiano pot and dropped the empty gourd into it before strolling toward the rear of the camp. "Don't let the dogs get those rabbits," she called. Then she was gone.

I waited for a couple of fingers of time, my vision wavering, not sure if I were floating or not. Somehow I just couldn't keep myself focused — let alone the world around me. Periodically it wavered and turned glassy. The dogs could have made off with the entire meal, for as much attention as I paid them.

I didn't see Pearl Hand return. She was just there, talking, halfway through a statement I hadn't heard.

"What?" I cried in surprise.

"I said I think you need to tell these dreams to a priest. What do you Chicaza call them? Hopaye?"

"Why?"

She was dropping crabs into the Kristiano

pot, but paused long enough to give me a knowing stare. "Because you are being called, Black Shell."

"Called for what?" I mumbled, trying to keep my souls from floating off.

"Did you see that cross the Kristianos put up in Uzita?"

"I watched them kneel before it. They did something with a gold cup and bits of food."

She was thinking, her forehead lined. "Where they go, they take murder, death, and misery with them. In their wake they leave corpses and sickness. We don't see the world as they do, Black Shell. We think in terms of order and chaos, each trying to balance the other. Nothing in our world is truly evil."

"Kristianos are," I replied wearily. "I saw nothing good in anything they did. Only misery. Only death."

"Which is why we have to stop them," she said softly. "That is why Power has called to you. It's up to us. You and me. Otherwise they are going to come and ruin our world."

I was drifting, my body floating again, waves of heat seeking to burn the souls from my body, only to be chilled to the bone a finger's time later.

I barely remembered Pearl Hand spooning food into my mouth, or the cooling taste of water. After that my world turned silver and watery, warm, as my body began to float away . . .

■ ■ ■ ■

Once again I was walking in the dream. The difference was: This time I knew I was dreaming.

My path followed the banks of a great river. The water to my left flowed clear and dark, the surface swirling, welling, and sucking down in little whirlpools. Along the bank grew giant stands of cane, patches of willows, and berry-dotted currants. Great bald cypress trees with thick red trunks rose from leaf-crusted ground, and here and there gum trees and water oak lent darker colors to the forest. Hanging moss draped from the branches like triangular beards. Vines of grape and greenbriar rose up the trunks in thick ropes, and blossoms shot specks of color.

White herons floated magically over the water, glancing my way as they passed, and from the forest depths I could see bears watching from the shadows. At my approach, turtles raised their heads above the water, and fish splashed before diving into the depths.

The trail bent inland, and I walked beneath the shadows, smelling damp leaves, honeyed flowers, and the sweet perfume of a living forest.

A bobcat eased out of the gloom, paralleling my path on silent feet. The normally shy forest hunter kept giving me knowing glances, its yellow eyes gleaming.

A bit farther, the way wound along a levee that cloaked a backswamp filled with bald cypress and tupelo, the large boles of the trees ringed by water. An occasional heron or anhinga perched on the cypress knees, observing my passage as if they were guardians of the place. I shot the anhingas a nervous nod of recognition.

Leaving the swamp behind, I made my way up a steep terrace and stepped out from beneath red and black oaks to find a small clearing. The grass had been neatly cut, as if grazed by bison. Across from me stood a small house, the walls plastered and painted a bright white. Thick amber-colored thatch rose in a steeply pitched roof, and around the eaves smoke drifted in tendrils of indulgent blue.

I walked into bright sunlight and slowly approached the house. A great bear poked his head around from behind the structure, and through light brown eyes, followed my approach.

I could smell the most delicious odors of roasting hominy and beans as I stopped before the door, calling, "Greetings! Is anyone here?"

"A moment," came a scratchy response.

As I waited, I stared at the bear staring back at me. From the animal's demeanor, I couldn't tell if it was about to attack, or run.

The door hanging — made of old hide — had been painted in designs once; now they were faded ghosts of themselves. The hanging moved, and an old woman ducked out. Age had curved her back into a crescent, and endless seasons had engraved deep wrinkles into her sagging skin. Her nose might have been a mushroom pasted over an undershot and toothless mouth. Whiter than snow, her hair fell over her rounded shoulders. I could see a little green snake woven through her locks. It peered intently at me, then seemed to whisper something into her shriveled ear.

When I met her eyes, a shock ran through my very bones. The effect was like staring into all the ages of the earth: dark, deep, and endless. I blinked to keep my souls from being drawn into those hollow depths.

"Black Shell of the Chicaza," she said softly, and her voice reminded me of winter wind among the branches.

"Who are you?" I wondered.

"I have had many names among many peoples." Her eyes seemed to grow in her head, as if swollen from the memories. "Most are forgotten. Spoken by peoples long vanished, and in tongues no human can remember. Names have Power, Black Shell. But like seasons, they come, flourish, and fade away. I have heard my names uttered from the lips of the great and inconsequential, all imploring, seeking, and vain in their hopes for love, revenge, authority, or salvation." She shook her head slowly. "Fools, every last one. What care I

213

for a high minko's lust for conquest, or a whimpering youth's desire to see a pretty young woman's affection turned his way? In the end, no matter how many peoples he conquers, or how many prisoners he sacrifices to the sun, a high minko ends as crumbling bones. No matter how ripe a woman's body, or the bliss a man feels while shooting his seed into her young loins, in the end there is only age, infirmity, and fading memories extinguished by the darkening mantle of death."

"I am not here to ask anything of you," I replied warily. And then I knew her. "You are Old-Woman-Who-Never-Dies."

"First Woman," she agreed. "Very good, Black Shell. For a man who claims to have never really believed, you almost seem comfortable in my presence."

"I'm dreaming."

"And what is a dream? Real? Or just a fantasy of the souls?"

"I don't know."

"You are not alone." Then she raised a thin arm. "Come. Eat. We shall talk and then you shall rest. My daughter is here. She has always had a fondness for great men."

"Me? Great?"

She paused, halfway to the door, and shot another of those depthless looks my way. I felt blackness expanding, wavering, and fading, as she said, "That remains to be seen, doesn't it?"

A sudden anxiety — a weightless and falling

sensation in the gut — filled me as I ducked inside. I swallowed hard, aware of a terrible hunger, literally an ache in my gut.

Despite the gnawing desire for food, I looked around, seeing only the most rudimentary of furnishings. A simple pole bed had been built into the back wall. And there a woman reclined on elk hides. She raised herself on one arm, her full breasts like gleaming melons. I tried to ignore the way her hard brown nipples thrust up as if in invitation. Hair the color of raven wings fell in thick waves over her shoulders and matched her luminous eyes. She'd belted a short fawn-hide skirt at her thin waist that seemed molded around her hips and flat abdomen and emphasized her long and tanned legs.

Only Pearl Hand had ever reeked of such blatant sexuality.

I nodded politely, about to introduce myself, when First Woman gestured to the single mat that lay on the packed-dirt floor before the fire. "Sit," she cackled, a dark glow behind her eternal eyes. "I can feel your hunger, Black Shell. Eat. And listen while I talk."

I lowered myself to the mat, seeing the large ceramic pot that rested in a glowing bed of red coals.

First Woman used a cup to scoop hominy and bean gruel from the pot. Her hand trembled as she handed it to me. Our fingers touched for the briefest instant, and I felt dizzy. The sensation was as if a great gale blew through my belly, sucking my souls into separate whirlwinds. Quickly it passed, and I raised the delicious-smelling cup to my lips. Flavored with licorice root, sassafras, bumblebee honey, and mint, the hominy filled my mouth, sending a wondrous euphoria through my starving body.

Though I ate and ate, the cup never emptied.

"The Kristianos have come," First Woman said softly. "But the people do not understand. They see only the glorious metals, the great cabayos with terrifying riders, and the fine fabrics dyed in so many colors. To be a high chief — lord of a nation — is to covet the Kristianos' wealth and strength. Our peoples are fools, Black Shell. The chiefs know only lust and greed, and would see it fall to them as allies of the Kristianos."

Between sips of the delightful mash, I said, "I know them differently." And reached up to finger the scab left by their hated collar.

"In our world red and white Power are balanced," she said, as if I'd never heard it before. "Order and chaos, ebbing and flowing. Neither is superior, and both are necessary for the survival of a people. Give the red Power dominion, and all is disorder. Give the white Power preeminence, and stagnation results. It is the way Breath Giver made our world."

"Why do you tell me this?"

"So that you can fully understand the Kristiano world. To them, everything is either good or evil. The struggle for balance is inconceivable to them, Black Shell. They claim their god is good but in his service commit only evil. Unlike our people, they live in hypocrisy: taking all in the name of their god, and leaving only wreckage, disease, and death in their wake. Some among them seek to convert a person's souls to their ways. Do you know what our people call such men?"

"Witches," I replied, feeling a cold shiver go down my spine. Only a witch would seek to use another man's souls for his own purposes. To do that involved the use of magic symbols, chants, and Powerful objects.

"They call it salvation. Among them, god can only be worshipped in one way. Any other is considered evil, no matter what the ultimate goal may be." She smiled. "To them, I am evil."

I shook my head. "But you gave birth to First Man and Corn Woman." I gestured to her daughter, who still reclined, watching me through oddly smoldering eyes. "Your daughter, Corn Woman, brought corn and beans to the people, and gave birth to the Hero Twins: Morning Star and the Orphan. They in turn fought the monsters from the Beginning Times. Before that Cannibal Turkey, Stone Man, and terrible sorcerers made the earth unsafe for people and animals."

She laughed harshly. "To the Kristianos, such things reek of heresy and devil worship. They think god created the earth in six days. But it grew evil. To make the world good again, he

217

created a son, and men slew him on a wooden cross. The Kristianos are the son's legacy to the world. Perhaps a divine irony." Her tooth-less smile gave her wrinkled face a crazy look. "For they have corrupted their own god."

"How do we fight them?"

"By stealth and planning, Black Shell. Massed, as they are now, no nation can stand against them. But through time and slow attrition, they can be brought low. This, you must remember: Your way will be difficult, and people you would help can only be made into allies when they discover the true nature of the Kristianos. But they can be destroyed and driven away." A pause. "For the time being."

"What do you mean, for the time being?"

"This battle for our world will take lifetimes. You can only fight for the present. There will be victories, and there will be defeats. In the end, it falls to people, not gods, to determine the ultimate victor."

I thought about that, remembering the weight of the Kristiano collar that still clung to my neck in a hidden camp outside the Uzita lands. Kristianos could be hunted, picked off one by one, and slowly weakened.

"The food you have just eaten will heal your souls of the Kristiano sickness. Now you must rest for the cure to take effect." First Woman pointed to where Corn Woman lounged on the bedding. "My daughter has made a place for you."

I set the cup aside and stood, feeling oddly weary. I nodded and walked over to the pole bed. Corn Woman smiled up at me, sliding to the rear and making room for me. I seated myself, and she reached up, her cool hands stroking my hot skin. Then I watched in amazement as she peeled the skirt from her hips and guided my hand to the springlike tangle of her pubic hair.

Her nimble fingers untied the breechcloth from around my waist, pulling it from my hips. I glanced over just in time to see First Woman waddle to the door on her age-bent legs. She paused as she pulled the hanging aside, and glanced back, eternity in her eyes. Then she was gone.

"What are you doing?" I asked Corn Woman as she pulled me onto her soft body. I stared down into her dark eyes as she smiled, spread her legs, and wrapped them around me. The sensation of her full breasts against my chest sent a thrill coursing through my tense body. Her cool fingers tightened around my straining shaft and guided me inside of her. She sighed as I entered, her hips rising to meet mine. In a moment of eternal clarity, I stared at her euphoric expression, knowing it matched my own.

Time began to stretch and flow, our bodies moving together, an endless floating dance. As the tingle built beneath my thrusting shaft, she tightened, arched, and waves of ecstasy rolled through us, shared as if from a single body, but with intensity unlike anything I'd ever known. Her soft cries added to the moment, my souls pulsing and exploding in response.

I remember lying, spent, atop her, cushioned by her soft body. Her black hair spread over the hides, wavering as if teased by a hidden breeze. For a time I floated, and felt her shift and slide from beneath me. Rolling onto my side, I watched her stand, refasten her skirt about her hips, and walk gracefully to the door.

Sleep, however, did not come. I thought about my conversation with First Woman, and how in the Beginning Times, Corn Woman had come to the people. It was said that during her moon, menstrual blood had leaked from her sheath, spotting the ground. That she had scooped it up with the dirt and carefully placed it in a pot. Then, ten months later, she had looked inside to discover the Orphan, as a baby boy. According to the story, she had raised him, taught him to hunt, and fed him corn and beans, though she would never tell him where they came from.

Finally, one day, the Orphan had lied about going hunting, sneaking back to peek through a crack in the wall. He'd seen Corn Woman straddling a dish. With a comb she had scratched her right thigh, and corn had trickled down out of her sheath. Then she scratched her left thigh, and beans had cascaded out of her.

Discovering Orphan's deceit, she had driven him away and sent him in search of other people. When he returned, three moons later, the clearing where she had lived was filled with corn and beans. But Corn Woman had never been seen again.

And now she had taken me to her bed. So, who does that make me? It was a terrible and important question, one that would plague me forever.

In a rush, I leaped to my feet, retied my breechcloth, and bolted for the door.

Outside, I turned, looking around the clearing. First Woman was nowhere to be seen. But off to the side, I noticed a tall green corn plant rising above the grass. Surely I could not have missed it when I had arrived.

Walking over, I found the soil turned, and in the middle of it stood the corn plant. For a moment I couldn't identify the form at the plant's base. An old woman lay on her back, arms and legs spread wide. Her aged skin was wrinkled, scabbed with old wounds; both breasts sagged flat on her chest.

My mouth dropped open, and I staggered to a stop, gasping. From deep in her sheath — the base of the stalk cupped by her vulva — the corn plant rose high, leaves drinking in the sunlight, full ears topped by fine brown silk.

Corn Woman's eyes met mine, and she opened a toothless, pink mouth to laugh . . . and laugh . . .

TWELVE

I jerked awake, every nerve in my body electric and afraid. A body moved against mine, and I froze, fearful I would open my eyes to Corn Woman's. Instead, it was Pearl Hand whose face rested opposite mine.

"Welcome back," she whispered, and I was aware of her slim brown arm resting on my shoulder. I lay on my side, facing her. The cold awkwardness of the collar and thick metal links bound me to the real world. Beyond Pearl Hand the familiar clearing could be seen in the moonlight. "Was it a pleasant dream?"

I shifted, my racing heart beginning to slow. "You wouldn't believe me if I told you."

Pearl Hand grinned, teeth flashing in the

moonlight. "I might. It was a delightful experience."

"W-What?" I stuttered in confusion.

She gave a slight shrug. "You were cold. When I snuggled against you" — she reached down, cool fingers wrapping around my shaft — "well, it was too good an opportunity to waste, even if you slept right through it."

I drew a deep breath of cool night air into my hot lungs. "That was you?"

"I hope you didn't think it was some other woman."

I swallowed drily. Gods, would I always be thirsty? "Corn Woman," I whispered softly. "I was with Corn Woman. Old-Woman-Who-Never-Dies offered me her daughter after she fed me and we discussed the Kristianos, and how to beat them."

"Corn Woman?" Pearl Hand raised herself on one elbow, studying me in the darkness, as if to read the truth in my souls. "You mean . . . *the* Corn Woman? From the Beginning Times?"

"Her." I sagged, body and souls drained. "But my body was here? With you?" Thoughts were reeling in my head. "I don't know what's real and what's dream anymore."

"It's the fever," she told me as she rearranged the blanket over us. "But if you can couple like that while dreaming of her, go ahead. I don't think I've ever felt such a delight. It rolled from my hips through my entire body. And it seemed to last half the night."

Parts of the dream were still replaying in my souls. At the memory of the endless hominy cup, my belly knotted with hunger. "In the dream, I ate and ate. It was so wonderful."

"You should be half starved." She crawled out from under the blanket, her naked body silvered by moonlight. "There's some fish, and I found cattail roots. They've been baking in the coals. Let me get you some. Then maybe you could dream of Corn Woman again and drive me half out of my body like you just did."

"Food would be good," I agreed. "But if you find any green shoots growing down there, I swear, I'm through forever with coupling."

The fever, it seems, had broken with the dream of First Woman, as if the soul food she fed me had indeed cured me. But for the next four days I was weaker than a sick puppy. Fetch took it as an opportunity for an endless, if uninspired, game of stick. Pearl Hand, bless her, went about hunting, fishing, and collecting, doing nothing but tending to my needs.

I watched her go about her duties, never complaining. When, I wondered, had there ever been a woman like this one? For hands of time, I needed do no more than toss Fetch's perpetually returning stick and watch her move about the camp.

"What are you doing?" she asked once, apparently nervous under my relentless stare.

"I'm looking at you."

She suddenly went self-conscious, pulling her hair around, checking it for sticks or leaves, then inspecting her front, as if something might have dribbled on her cloth dress.

I laughed. "No, nothing's wrong. I just like to watch you. It pleases me, and . . . well, it leaves me in wonder."

"How?" She gave me a suspicious look.

"Because you fill my souls with a joy I never knew a man could have. You are the most beautiful and wondrous woman to ever delight a man's life."

"Are you fevered again?"

"Oh, yes. All it takes is your smile, or the slightest touch, and I'm all dreamy inside."

She smiled at that. "You'd think you were in love."

In a voice laced with seriousness, I answered, "Very much so. I would have you forever."

She hesitated. "As a wife?"

"If you will have me. Yes."

She walked over then, taking my hand. "Are you serious, Chicaza? You know who I am . . . what I've been. Among your people I'd be —"

"Forget about my people. Not one of their high-born, clan-bred dainties is worthy to so much as wipe your feet." I squeezed her hand. "I've been a man long enough to know the difference, Pearl Hand. You are a woman worthy of far better than me. I wouldn't trade you for all the high minko's nieces in Chicaza . . . or anywhere else, for that matter."

She searched my eyes for a moment, reading my souls. "You've been chosen by Power, Black Shell. It frightens me . . . knowing that terrible times are coming. I can't see our future, but I know it's filled with blood and sorrow."

I nodded slightly, aware of the collar chafing my neck. "Things are happening to me. Things I don't understand yet. But it's not just me. It's you, too. We're fighting for our world, our peoples . . . all of them. I would do that with you at my side."

At her hesitation, I added, "But not if you would prefer another —"

"No." She shook her head. "That's not what worries me. It's that . . ."

"Yes?"

"I don't want to lose you."

I lifted her hand to my lips. "Nor I, you. But together, well, it makes sense that Power would choose us. You know the Kristianos, speak their language, and can pass among them. Who better than us — exiles versed in the ways of so many peoples — to find and use their weaknesses against them?"

She considered that, glancing down at the Kristiano knife lashed to the belt at her side. Thinking about the man she'd coupled with and killed to save me, no doubt. Kristiano blood was already on her hands.

She met my gaze, nodding slightly. "I will be your wife."

"And I will be your husband."

No family or clan was present to witness our joining. No great feasts, exchanges of gifts, races, or games marked the unification of our lives, but it was accomplished with a strength of purpose not even a high minko could command.

We left that little camp four days later, loading the dogs and packs into the canoe and paddling out from the rise in the mangroves. We paddled up the mouth of the Mocoso River just after dark lest any of Chief Mocoso's people spot us, but the village several bowshots up from the landing was dark and looked abandoned. The Kristianos, we learned later, had taken every man, woman, and child capable of bearing burdens, and marched them inland.

In crossing the river, the Kristianos had built two substantial bridges, and the passing of their army left a beaten trail for us to follow. The soil, even after this many days, was stippled with cabayo and *puerco* tracks, and the vegetation to either side was beaten flat.

I stood there, looking down the churned route taken by the Kristianos. "We need to be very careful. They may be days ahead of us, but we'd be foolish to take chances."

"At the first sound, even if it's ever so faint," she said, "we've got to get off the trail."

"No matter what, we both have to keep the dogs quiet." I met her sober gaze. "This might surprise you, but I don't want to see another one up close."

"So, you do learn?" she said scornfully. But there was a twinkle in her dark eyes.

By morning I was exhausted, having used up all of my frail reserves on the trail. That and the weight of the metal links dragged the collar down and pulled the skin raw on my neck. With each step the metal links clanked and swayed until I wrapped them like a perverted necklace to hang down over my chest.

I was staggering by the time we found a deer trail that led off into the scrubby brush. Under a stand of pines we made camp, fed the dogs what little we had, and ate dried fish.

The next day, armed with a rock and several hardwood dowels whittled from branches, Pearl Hand began the task of driving the metal buttons out of my accursed collar. The work was tedious, my position cramped as I knelt beside a lightning-riven stump. By midafternoon, and tens of dowels later, the final button parted. The collar swung free of my neck.

In celebration, I hugged Pearl Hand until her ribs almost cracked. The collar, with its metal chain, went into the packs. Somewhere it would bring good trade. Still, the chafed skin around my neck would take days to heal, despite the unguents Pearl Hand applied to my wound.

Thirteen

Three days later, I was walking in the lead, still trying to come to terms with what had happened to me. At night, sleep was plagued by nightmares, and I relived the horror of captivity. The dogs, the whips, all of it came back to replay among my wounded souls.

That day, as I led the way down a winding trail lined with tall grass, palmettos, and scrubby pines, I kept glancing down at my hands, legs, and feet.

Am I still the same man? Or had the Kristianos killed the old crafty Black Shell? Was I now nothing more than a walking husk?

We hadn't made particularly good time, having stopped to hunt, collect roots, and rob nests of their eggs. More than anything, I seemed eternally hungry, but my strength was rapidly returning. I had taken up my trader's staff again, but the old confidence hadn't returned.

I am afraid.

And more than anything, I hated myself for it.

In an instant, as if from thin air, two Kristiano war dogs were growling and snapping, leaping at me. Terror seized me, and I cried out, leaping back, my arms rising to defend my throat and face.

"Black Shell?" Pearl Hand called from behind, breaking the vision as surely as a bubble popped on a pond surface. "What is it? A snake?"

I gasped for air, staring in disbelief at the empty trail where the dogs had been, so clear and memorable.

"Nothing . . . just a . . . No, nothing." I reached up and wiped a hand over my face, desperate to control my breathing and heartbeat.

"Are you all right?" she pushed up next to me, concern in her eyes.

"Images, just ghosts of memory." I gave her a searching look. "Did they witch me? Cast some sorcerer's spell on my souls?"

She pursed her lips, watching me carefully — then reached up to press on my scabbed neck with a finger. "You will have a scar here.

231

This one you will be able to see. The ones they left on your souls, Black Shell, those you can only feel."

I took a deep breath, drawing the muggy hot air into my lungs. "What did they do to me? Why do I feel this way?"

"You have always been a proud man. It's who you are: Black Shell, of the Chicaza, born of the Chief Clan, bred to one day become high minko. No matter that you're exiled from your people, you've always had that to cling to. The Kristianos changed that."

"How?"

"They took away everything that you believed about yourself, robbed you of who you are. Nothing in our world could have prepared you for what they did. In our world, even enemies are someone. When prisoners are taken, even if they are tortured to death, it is to determine who they are. On the square, even the most despised enemies are tested for courage, endurance, cowardice, or fear, and we identify them accordingly. We see the people, animals, and plants around us as beings with souls. Even rocks are treated with respect.

"Kristianos are different, Black Shell. They committed the most terrible atrocity: They made you into nothing."

"Nothing?" I felt my souls drop, as if suddenly sick.

"Nothing," she insisted. "Don't you see? To

them you had no souls, no identity. You were simply a convenient thing to be used for labor, and completely meaningless to them." She arched an eyebrow. "What greater crime is there than to make a person meaningless . . . nothing."

I bowed my head, nodding. Blood and pus, she had figured it out. "So, what do I do?"

"Decide who you are, Black Shell. You have a unique opportunity to do what few people ever can. Think of it: You have been Black Shell of the Chicaza, both before and after you left your people. Spirit Power has spoken to you. The Kristianos then took everything from you and left you empty, sick, and dying."

"But Power carried my souls to the Spirit World."

"Perhaps because you were dying, your souls were prepared. Power has chosen you, Black Shell. You have a choice to make."

I frowned, trying to see the why of it.

"It's your decision. We don't have to fight the Kristianos. We can go away, just you and I. You know them now, know what they can do to you."

"Or I can follow the path that Power has laid out for me." I gave her a sidelong glance. "What if I do choose to run?"

She gave me a reassuring smile. "I'll go wherever you lead. We'll make a life together."

I glanced back to where the dogs had laid

down in the trail. Squirm was rolling his shoulders, trying the pack bindings to see if he could wiggle out from under the weight.

I exhaled and said, "It's so tempting. I'm afraid, Pearl Hand. Scared like I never have been. But that's the thing. If I give in now, surrender to the fear, it will never stop."

I reached out and laid my hand on her shoulder. "You understand that, don't you? If we don't go after them, fight them, they'll have won. It means I will have died in their chains, no matter how long this body lives."

I watched her smile widen, warmth growing behind her eyes. "Yes, you are still the man I fell in love with."

"But you'd have gone with me had I chosen to run?"

She shrugged, taking the lead and gesturing the dogs to their feet. "For a while. At least until I learned if they'd really broken you for good." She paused, then added, "One thing I've learned, husband: I need a man in my life. A real man. One who earns and deserves my respect."

I followed along behind her, emotions churning. Breath and thorns, yes, I was scared. Memories of captivity kept chewing at my courage, and fear lingered like webs at the margins of my souls. Then, I needed only glance at Pearl Hand's back, her provocative hips swaying with each step.

She'll never be a coward's woman — and you know it.

I grinned to myself, contemplating that she was right. I could choose as few men had ever been able to. Power had taken my souls to the edge of the earth, to the Underworld, and Corn Woman's bed. I'd married the most desirable woman in the world, so long as I was worthy of her.

What challenge was a terrible Kristiano army compared to that?

The following morning was hot, muggy, and sunny. We followed a trail off to the side of the main Kristiano route. The sky above was a dull blue, fading to white at the horizons. Not even a breath of breeze could be felt. The leaves hung, as though limp in the heat.

Perhaps half a bowshot ahead, three men and two women came trotting around a bend. They drew up in sudden fear. As they started to bolt back the way they had come, I cried out, "Wait! We come under the Power of trade!" I lifted my staff high.

For several heartbeats, they hesitated, talking among themselves. In Timucua, one man called, "Who are you?" As if a man, woman, and five pack dogs were a hostile raiding force.

"I am Pearl Hand," my wife called. "And this is the trader, Black Shell. We mean you no harm."

I walked easily forward, motioning the dogs back to decrease the threat.

The man who spoke stepped forward hesitantly. He was dressed in a breechcloth, carrying a short hunting bow. Scars covered the man's left arm as if it had been mauled by an alligator. His hair was greasy, unkempt, and littered with twigs and leaves. "You should be careful. Kristianos are all around the country. We ourselves are fleeing from them."

The other two men were easing back, a half step at a time. The expression in their round faces stated better than words that they'd bolt up the trail like rabbits at first sign of trouble. The older of the bare-breasted women noticed and gave them both a sour look.

"We would learn of them," I said easily, walking up to the man. "How are you called?"

"Most know me by the name of Sun Fish. These others are of Two Loon village." He pointed to the two women, ignoring the men, now a good ten paces back. The women stood uncertainly, both of them shooting worried glances our way. "The Kristianos were there four days ago. We survived by luck."

I nodded. "May your ancestors bless you, and may luck continue to walk with you. If you head south, there are more Kristianos around Uzita. Not all have gone ahead."

"Thank you." The man glanced uneasily at his comrades. "We'll keep to the east, but try not to blunder into Irriparacoxi's lands. He

236

might think we'd make good slaves, too."

"The Kristianos didn't go there?" Pearl Hand asked, curious.

"Some did. But after several days they were recalled to join the main body. They gave Irriparacoxi many wonderful things: wondrous beads, metal chisels, mirrors, and metal pots. In return they took many of Irriparacoxi's people with them. He ordered his iniha to take several hundred and serve the Kristianos. The poor fools, no sooner did they arrive than they were locked in collars and turned into slaves." He looked suspiciously at the pack dogs, and then us. "You follow the Kristianos' trail? On purpose?"

I nodded. "They made me a slave for a while. Somehow we will pay them back."

Sun Fish shook his head, obviously finding the notion ridiculous. "They won't be that hard to catch. They have taken local guides. The Kristianos don't know it, but they've been led into the swamps off to the west."

"Why not the trail to the east?" Pearl Hand asked. "With cabayos, the travel would be much easier."

"They know nothing of the country. Some of the ones who have escaped told us that a man named Ortiz translates for them. He speaks only a couple of the languages. So he asks someone who asks someone who asks someone who knows, then the answer goes back through all those people. Besides, I think the guides figure that if they lead the Kristianos into the swamp, there might be an opportunity to escape."

"Good thinking," I agreed and glanced at Pearl Hand. She, too, seemed to be mulling the idea. "So if we would avoid the swamp, where should we go?"

"The trail forks just north of Vicela village. The western trail runs straight to Tocaste, where the Kristianos have made camp. Bear off to the east. After crossing three creeks, you will see an old burned farmstead with a trail leading into the oaks. Take that one. If you do not, you'll be in Irriparacoxi's lands."

"We would avoid that," I agreed. "Do the Kristianos march unopposed?"

"They do not," Sun Fish said with a smile. "There are constant raids. Several soldiers and a couple of horses have been killed. But any time massed warriors try and attack them, the result is a disaster. Few of those who flee survive." Horror shadowed his face. "They have terrible dogs."

"Does anyone know where the Kristianos are headed?" Pearl Hand asked.

Sun Fish shrugged. "Given their direction, probably Ocale. They seem to travel from village to village. At each one they take all the food, spend the night, and march to the next one. Anyone who is asked will tell them that Ocale has more stored food than any place."

"Before you go" — I bent down and took a

couple pieces of shell from Bark's pack —
"this is in trade for your information."

"We thank you," Sun Fish said as he fingered the shells. "May the ancestors bless you and keep you safe."

"And you."

We watched them hurry past and disappear down the trail.

"So, do we try and beat them to Ocale?" I wondered. Then I remembered that trade didn't go so well the last time I was there: that pesky business about the holata believing I was a Potano spy.

"How do we know?" Pearl Hand asked. "Power has just chosen us to fight. It hasn't bothered to tell us how to do it."

Which, when I thought about it, set my nerves on end. De Soto was up there, ahead of us somewhere with his metal-clad army. And Pearl Hand and I were supposed to stop him?

The land Pearl Hand and I were marching into, meaning the central peninsula, was thickly populated. Villages tended to be a day's march apart, which, when you think about it, makes sense. People could extensively exploit the root grounds, hunting areas, and fisheries within a half day's walk in any direction. They knew them inside out and didn't have to infringe on anyone else's territory. A hunting party could still make it home

239

by night. Village sizes tended to reflect the quality and quantity of food resources available.

The country wasn't especially rich, considering that the people mostly relied on wild game, fish and turtle traps, clam beds, and — one of the regional favorites — snails. Most villages had huge trash mounds where generations had tossed the shells after extracting the clams and snails. They made a stew of snails that I'm not particularly fond of, but the locals like it.

Water fowl contribute to a large part of the diet, especially in winter when the ducks, geese, herons, and other birds migrate south. The killing of a deer, raccoon, or brace of rabbits is considered a delicacy. Hunting pressure has exterminated the bison, and it is the lucky animal that can pick its way down from the north without ending up in a deep-pit roasting oven.

For our part, we skirted the little villages of Guacozo and Luca, both of which were nothing more than tossed wrecks, looted clean by the Kristianos. It made for creative traveling since the trails all radiate out from town centers. Following deer paths is a tricky business — a well-worn trail tends to evaporate the farther along it one travels.

Two days later, north of Vicela village, we found the trail Sun Fish had mentioned. Just after the second creek crossing we encountered a body lying in the middle of the trail. Even as we approached, the telltale round imprints of cabayos could be seen in the sandy soil. The animals had circled a young man who lay facedown. In the center of his back was a gruesome wound already crawling with flies. Beside him were the marks of boot heels where a rider had dismounted and pulled something from the middle of the man's back.

I'd seen the crossbows during my captivity, but hadn't been able to convince myself they were any improvement over a normal bow. Imagine a short bow fixed crosswise on a handle that acts like an extension of the arm. The butt of it is placed in the shoulder, and the short arrow is aimed. A little lever releases the string lock, propelling the stubby arrow at great velocity.

Nor did I understand the firesticks the Kristianos carried. The weapon reminded me of the blowguns used by the forest hunters in the north. My people made blowguns from sections of cane, and they were excellent for hunting squirrels and small birds. Kristianos hunted men with theirs. The tube is made from metal, which is cradled in a wooden mount. To shoot it, a section of smoldering cord was touched to the powder, which — like a blowgun hunter's breath — expelled a lead ball faster than the eye could see. Smoke and fire erupted along with a crack like thunder.

The body before us had the classic signs of an arrow wound. I'd seen more than enough to know.

From the tracks it was easy to read the victim's last moments. He'd been running, the cabayos charging down behind him. Unlike the time when I'd been in a similar situation, they hadn't just knocked him down for a prisoner. Instead they had ridden close and shot him in the back. Under the hoofprints, the soil marked where he'd fallen and slid.

"What do you think?" Pearl Hand asked as I bent over the body and shooed the dogs away. They were sniffing unsurely, wary at the scent of death.

"I'm thinking a crossbow arrow," I replied, looking into the wound. "Something was pulled out. Here, you can see the boot heel imprints where the Kristiano leaned back as he pulled. Some of the tissue came with the shaft. Then the Kristiano remounted and the cabayos turned around and headed back from whence they'd come."

"How long?" Pearl Hand asked, indicating the body.

I grabbed an ankle and lifted, feeling the stiff joint. "Maybe this morning."

She glanced worriedly up the trail. "Well, we're warned. They're close."

I nodded, stood, and withdrew my bow and

a couple of hunting arrows before slipping the trader's staff into the alligator-hide case beside my chunkey lances.

"From here on we had better show more care."

"Travel at night?" she suggested.

"It would be safer." I glanced around the unfamiliar countryside. "But I think we'd spend so much time being lost and backtracking that it wouldn't be worth our time. Let alone the possibility of stepping on a water moccasin in the dark."

We proceeded slowly, taking our time, listening, keeping an eye on the trees, searching for any sign of Kristianos. Our ears sought any hint of clinking metal. Even the dogs seemed more alert.

After crossing the third creek, we almost missed the burned farmstead; honeysuckle had reclaimed all but two charred roof supports that protruded through the greenery.

For a half day we followed the trail northeast, only to have it end in a palmetto thicket beyond which was a marshy swamp filled with lotus, cattails, and reeds. Several pairs of alligator eyes were watching us from the water, and given the size of them, wading didn't seem an option.

We backtracked and located a trail running north through stands of oak, poisonwood, and palmetto, the hammocks dotted with pines. This, too, ended at water, but here, pulled up in the palmettos, were three small dugout canoes, paddles resting beneath the inverted hulls. From the bank I could see another landing across the way.

Borrowing the largest of the vessels, we loaded the dogs and crossed in a hand's time. Turning the canoe over, we placed the paddles beneath and continued. We hadn't made it three bowshots into the trees before a young man rose from the palmettos, an arrow at full draw in his bow. I looked into his eyes, reading terror and desperation. Only thin air lay between the bone-pointed arrow and my frantically beating heart.

Fourteen

"Wait!" I cried, holding up my bow. "We travel under the Power of trade." Gods, I hoped he spoke Timucua. At the same time, I was signing like a madman, the bow making my hands awkward.

I peered into the young warrior's hard eyes, saw him hesitate, and then lower his weapon. The arrow remained drawn, but no longer pointed at my chest.

"I am Black Shell," I said reasonably. "A trader."

"The one who took Irriparacoxi's woman?" he asked in accented Timucua.

"I'm the woman," Pearl Hand gave him a respectful smile. "News of Irriparacoxi's loss seems to have traveled."

The youth shrugged, as if it were no matter. "There are other concerns than Irriparacoxi's skill with a bow. You have heard of the Kristianos?"

"We're trying to avoid them," I replied, motioning the dogs to rest.

"They have taken Tocaste town, and our chief. No one knows what to do. We are guarding all of our trails. I thought about killing you as you landed, but decided that first I'd see how you acted. Thank you for replacing our canoe, even if it's on the wrong side of the crossing now."

"We only wished to cross. We thank the owner for the use of his vessel . . . and would offer trade in compensation." I hoped that sounded reasonable.

The youth nodded, then glanced worriedly back at the crossing. "I should get back to my post. The Kristianos could come at any time." He pointed up the trail. "Turtle Town is that way, less than two hands' journey. Tell them that Muskrat sent you. But expect no grand feasts, Trader. Many have been killed or captured. A number of the clan leaders are taken hostage. The healers have wounded to care for."

"We understand, Muskrat, and thank you."

He hesitated, then asked, "The Kristianos . . . I mean, the stories people tell about them, are they true?"

"Worse than you've heard," Pearl Hand said softly. "So much worse."

His expression pinched with concern, then he nodded sadly before hurrying down the trail to guard the crossing.

Turtle Town occupied an elevated sandy ridge, surrounded by small gardens of corn, squash, and beans that had been cleared of trees and brush. A rickety-looking palisade surrounded a collection of houses, a small plaza, and a mound topped by a thatch-roofed charnel house. The chief's house was the largest structure, open-sided and thickly thatched.

Four young warriors, little more than boys actually, came charging out the gate, bows at the ready.

I lifted my arms, calling, "We are traders and come in peace under the Power of trade. Muskrat has sent us."

The boys trotted to a stop, looking us over warily. Squirm started to growl, and I gestured him to silence.

An old man appeared in the gate behind the boys and called, "Enter, traders, and be welcome. Such as it is." Then he spoke to the boys who reluctantly lowered their bows.

"I am Black Shell, of the Chicaza" — it sounded good to believe it again — "and this is my wife, Pearl Hand, of the Chicora."

"Greetings." He bowed slightly. Gray had filled the hair on his head, his weathered face a leather of wrinkles and scars. Faded tattoos covered his cheeks and forehead, and his shoulders had been painted black with charcoal. "I am called Old Man Crawfish these days. Head elder of the Musselshell Clan. Come, our chief and many of our council are not here."

"Muskrat told us the Kristianos have them."

Crawfish nodded. "For the moment we have been spared. Our scouts tell us the Kristianos are headed north into the swamp. May the fools all drown in the attempt." He sighed. "It seems we can't be rid of them any other way."

"We have heard there has been fighting."

He nodded again. "Much to our regret. Seven are dead; more are wounded. The healer is doing his best in the chief's house."

Pearl Hand said, "We have some medicine plants."

Crawfish gave her a wistful look. "Alas, there is not much we can trade. At the order of our chief, Holata Caramaba, most of the food, jars, and pots were sent to Tocaste. The men and women who bore them have been made slaves. Well, but for a few who escaped with their lives. Others were run down like fleeing rabbits. They have terrible hunting dogs. And what they do to a person . . ."

"I've seen," I said bitterly.

"Then you are a lucky man, Trader. They didn't get you. Or does the Power of trade

248

protect you?"

"They spit on the Power of trade."

"In that case the Spirits of the ancestors will grow so incensed they will destroy them."

I held my tongue, thinking that only a seasoned army of Mos'kogee warriors might do the trick.

Most of the people we saw were either the very young or elders. At the chief's house I bade the dogs to lie down and unlaced the pack containing dried gumweed, tobacco, and mint leaves. I also took out some coneflower petals and pine resins. Brewed into tea, it was the best I could do for their wounded.

The healer was called Spotted Wing, an old woman past her bearing years. She nodded as Crawfish introduced us and listened as he spoke in a language I didn't understand. Evidently not all the residents understood Timucua.

Spotted Wing led us under the roof to where two men and a woman lay on cattail matting. First came the stench, then I got a really good look at what a metal sword could do to a human body. The woman had taken a cut across the thigh. The wound gaped like a great smile. Only the bone had stopped the blade from slicing clear through. The great artery — fortunately or not — hadn't been severed.

"We left it open," Crawfish said upon seeing my horror. "We tried sewing up Bat Fish's arm." He pointed to one of the men — the flesh on his upper arm stitched closed like a leather flap. Streams of yellow pus were leaking out along the length of the wound; his hideously swollen arm was blackened, greenish, and mottled looking. Fever burned beads of sweat out of his skin, and his eyes were rolled back in his head.

"They should have just cut his throat," Pearl Hand said in Mos'kogee. "It would have been kinder."

I turned my attention to the third man. A thick poultice had been applied to his belly, but from the smell of it, I knew his guts were punctured.

Crawfish turned pleading eyes on ours. "Do you have something that would heal them? Perhaps a medicine in your packs?"

I shook my head. "Nothing for wounds as festered as these. I'm sorry. But a tea made from the things I have brought would help."

Crawfish gratefully took what I offered. I walked back, stepping into the sunlight, Pearl Hand following. Outside I drew deeply of the sweet air.

"You look terrible," she noted.

"Arrow wounds are bad enough. Those people in there, they're flayed open like fish under an obsidian blade."

She glanced sidelong at me. "Seeing those people, are you still sure you want to pursue the Kristianos?"

I considered that as I glanced around the subdued village. People were watching us discreetly. Up on the high mound, I could see the charnel house. It soon would have at least three new additions to the number of rotting bodies tended by the priests. "Haven't we had this discussion already?"

Her beautiful face had taken on a sad expression. "Would it be so bad, just going somewhere out of the way? Just the two of us?"

"Changing your mind?"

"Seeing what's in that house? Well, it sobers the souls."

"It does indeed. But that day on the trail, when you told me to choose? I did. And it was the right choice. The dream visions I've had . . . I mean, I've gone places in Spirit form, seen the Seeing Hand at the end of the earth, and stared into the West Wind's eyes. I've traveled to the Underworld. I owe something to Water Panther. I've eaten in First Woman's house."

With a barbed remark, she interrupted, "Not to mention driven your peg into Corn Woman."

I ignored her. "They all say I've been chosen by Horned Serpent for something, and whatever it is, it involves the Kristianos." I paused, thinking back, replaying images of the dreams. "This is a war, Pearl Hand. We

251

have been chosen to fight."

But, like her, more than anything, I wished I could just turn tail and run. Maybe find a place to spend the rest of my days enjoying the sunshine and rain, lingering in Pearl Hand's arms, and growing old beside her.

You'd spend the rest of your life despising yourself.

Crawfish assigned Pearl Hand and me to an unoccupied house for the night. While the people did their best for us, the evening feast was a somber affair consisting of fish, boiled snails, fresh-water mussels, and palm berries.

Throughout, people constantly glanced back at the chief's house, from which low groans could be heard.

Muskrat arrived just after dark and went into council with several of the other boys. Later he came ambling over to where Pearl Hand and I sat on the matting of our open-sided house, tossing a deer-hide ball for Fetch. The rest of the dogs chased after him, trying to steal it. Frustrated at never getting the ball, Bark dropped on his butt, gave me a forlorn look, and began *arf-arf*ing in mournful tones.

Pearl Hand called him over and ruffled his ears, as much to shut him up as to comfort him. That brought Gnaw, his white-tipped tail slashing the gloom.

Muskrat squatted on his haunches off to our left and scratched behind Gnaw's ear.

252

The dog loved it. Fetch spit the soggy ball at our feet, ears pricked, ready for another chase. I propped a foot on it to keep Squirm from grabbing it away.

"No sign of the Kristianos?" I asked.

He gave a shrug. "A runner came just before dark. They're off to the north. The fools are trying to wade across the swamps. Sometimes they're in water up to their necks. Several of the cabayos have stuck in the mud and drowned in their panic."

He looked wistfully up at the cloudy night sky. Lightning flickered in the distance. "If we had all of Irriparacoxi's warriors we could paddle up in canoes and kill them one by one."

"And if turtles could fly, they'd snap all the mosquitoes out of the sky," I reminded. "But they can't, so we're plagued."

"I'm headed north in the morning," Muskrat said softly, poking a finger at the charcoal-stained earth beside Gnaw. "Taking a canoe to keep an eye on them in case they turn back south. If I had two more people to paddle, well, I'd drop you on the east side at a good trail head."

I glanced at Pearl Hand. She shrugged.

"Very well, Muskrat. We will accompany you. Besides, I would see the Kristianos wading up to their necks." Anything to enjoy their suffering for once, and this would be an opportunity to observe their order of march without having to worry about riders chasing us down.

"You're sure this is a good idea?" Pearl Hand asked after we'd retired to our bed.

"I'm not sure I ever have a good idea anymore. But if the Kristianos are floundering in the swamps, maybe we'll learn something we can put to use."

"You're an idiot, you know."

"Yes. And fortunately for me, you love idiots."

The next morning, just before dawn, we loaded packs and dogs into the large dugout canoe Muskrat had procured. I could tell by his actions that he wasn't overjoyed at the scouting task his people had ordered him to undertake.

Myself, I was preoccupied with the dreams I'd had during the night. In them, Water Panther prowled the depths, just below our canoe. All the while he contemplated the notion of switching his tail and dumping us in the swamps.

As we were preparing to push off, voices rose in song, the melody solemn. We looked back, just able to make out the shapes of people emerging from the chief's house. They carried a body borne on a litter.

"My cousin," Muskrat said sadly. "He died in the night. Relatives are carrying him to the charnel house."

254

"Shouldn't you be there?" Pearl Hand asked.

He gave her a flat, listless look. "These are not normal times."

We said no more as we loaded the dogs and packs, then pushed the canoe out into the calm waters. The three of us plied paddles to drive us through the bald cypress, tupelo, and water-oak-lined passages that led north. Fetch perched himself in the bow, surveying the water ahead as if he were a lord overlooking his domain.

Insects buzzed and hummed over the water, while birds of all kinds sang in the trees or flitted across the surface in search of prey. Anhingas perched on cypress knees, watching with their beady brown eyes. I waved at them and wondered what they'd tell Water Panther and Snapping Turtle. In backwaters choked with duckweed and yellow lotus, alligators peered with unblinking eyes and turtles sunned themselves on logs protruding from the murky water. Several manatees, like gray sentinels, paused in their feeding to watch us pass.

From the sun, I gauged the time to be nearing midday. How Muskrat found his way through the endless maze of channels, islands, shallows, and passages was beyond me. Pearl Hand and I were sweating. As badly as my shoulders ached after several moons away from a paddle, I could tell Pearl Hand suffered even more.

Fetch growled first, Bark and Squirm chiming in. Gnaw and Skipper's ears pricked, eyes alert. I hushed them with a single command.

"There! Hear it?" Muskrat asked from his position in the rear.

We coasted on the water, and I noticed the dogs were fixed on the channel ahead. Faintly, my ears picked up a distant shout. Then another. I snapped my fingers in rebuke as Fetch gave a low bark.

"Men," Pearl Hand said as we dipped the paddles and eased forward again.

"I'll keep us toward the east side," Muskrat said. "There is better cover in the channels. Safer to keep out of sight."

We proceeded for perhaps a hand of time, the shouts and occasional cries growing louder as we pursued a way through narrow channels, ducking strands of hanging moss.

One of the cabayos made that eerie braying they did when losing sight of companions. The sound came echoing over the water and sent a shiver down my spine.

"No barks!" I hissed at the dogs, getting reluctant looks in return.

Muskrat started us past a small island when Pearl Hand raised an arm in warning. The island was a low thing, covered in saw grass and brush, and as we cleared the vegetation I could see them, perhaps five bowshots distant across open water.

The Kristianos were in a long line, perhaps waist deep as they slogged through the shallows. They cursed and splashed along, ripples of water radiating from their passage. Each man bore his weapons in a pack on his back. It hit me that they looked like ugly snails crossing the water. Even over the distance I could tell their movements were labored, as if they were on the verge of exhaustion. Sunlight gleamed from the metal armor and helmets.

After every ten men came a line of captives, their bodies bent under great packs perched high on their backs. Some labored under those ridiculous chairs, others — in teams — carried wooden tables, and two struggled to bear some sort of boxy thing that stood on four legs.

My heart went out to the slaves, but as bad as my lot had been, I'd had solid footing for the most part. No straining of the ears was necessary to hear the clinking of the accursed chains.

Like an obscene caterpillar, the line of humans sloshed and slogged through the watery muck.

"Why cross this mess?" Pearl Hand wondered. "They needed but go further east and follow dry trails from town to town. This is madness."

I propped my elbow on a knee and rested my chin as I studied the struggling men. A line of cabayos came into sight, the animals tied together, led by a single man with a rope. The beasts — clearly unhappy — lurched and buck-jumped, muddy water sluicing from their hides.

"Because they don't know any better," I mused. "And here is the advantage we can exploit."

"Just because they get lost and stumble into a swamp doesn't make them easy to defeat," Pearl Hand countered. "What do you have in mind? Luring them into a marsh, then canoe up and shoot them down with arrows?"

"That might have possibilities." Then I tried to put words to my thoughts. "No, I was thinking more of their arrogance. I'm a trader, and I know I'm ignorant when I enter a new country or meet a new people. Not knowing the customs, I beg forbearance for the mistakes I will make, and ask politely about the manners, the country, the animals, and the trails. These Kristianos, they don't think they have anything to learn from us. To them we're little more than insects. But here, watching them, it's plain to see that such arrogance carries the roots of their final defeat."

She glanced at me, eyes thoughtful. "You've never seen them fight. Their armor, weapons, and discipline allow a small number to defeat a huge body of warriors." She shook her head. "To overwhelm them would take vast numbers of warriors. Probably more than any coalition that could be put together."

"I haven't seen them fight. But I've seen what their weapons do to a man's body. And, unlike them, I'm more than willing to take your word that to attack them head-on is suicide."

"Good. We'll live longer that way," she added grimly.

We'd been talking in Mos'kogee. Muskrat asked what we'd been saying.

I resettled myself, watching those miserable people out there in the water. "We're trying to figure out how to defeat them. It's too bad we don't have a thousand Chicaza warriors in canoes to paddle up and kill the Kristianos in deep water."

He shrugged. "Even then their armor might save them. I'm told one of my cousins shot one from right up close. His arrow hit center, and stopped cold. The man he shot killed him with a thunder stick and paused only long enough to brush the arrow off as if it were a blunted thorn. The ones wearing the cloth, they have padding with metal plates sewn inside. And arrows glance off the metal body armor like hail off a rock."

"So we must shoot for the face or neck," I mused. That kind of accuracy was difficult in the heat of combat when men were moving, ducking, and weaving.

I glanced at Muskrat's bow; it was nothing like mine, having a short and thin stave of local wood. In the peninsula, bows were made for hunting the local small deer, rabbits, and the like. In the north, among the Nations, bows were larger, stronger, with a tremendous pull meant to drive solid wood-shafted arrows right through a wooden shield. The light cane arrows of the southern hunters didn't come close to matching the penetration.

But against Kristiano armor? That I didn't know.

We watched another group of Kristianos come into view. At first I couldn't understand what I was seeing, and then, to my astonishment, realized it was the *puercos* swimming in a horde.

"Maybe this is a job for women," Pearl Hand remarked. "Lure them one by one into our beds and cut their throats. Kristianos have an ungoverned appetite when it comes to lying with women."

I countered, "Once they catch on, they won't take a woman to bed unless she's stripped naked." I paused. "No, this must be fought over time, by wearing them down." I thought of their great floating palaces, and how far they had come from their homes across the sea. "They're heading inland, up the peninsula."

"Which means?" Pearl Hand asked.

"They are getting farther and farther from any resupply." Which left the question: Just how far did the Kristianos plan to travel?

FIFTEEN

Muskrat dropped us on the eastern edge of the swamps at a trailhead that took us inland onto higher ground. We bid him the best of luck in the future and turned our steps to the east. The dogs, chafing under their packs, followed along behind.

We wound through scrubby palms, honeysuckle, and stands of live oak, the air perfumed with the scent of earth, spring flowers, and the damp must of vegetation. I watched a spiral of buzzards off to the north, wondering if the Kristianos had dispatched yet another unlucky soul to bloat in the sun.

That night we camped under a copse of live oaks. I'd cooked us a supper of smoked fish that we'd traded for at Turtle Town. As I scrubbed out the ceramic pot I'd used, Pearl Hand wore her arm out throwing Fetch's stick. She enjoyed the melee that followed as the other dogs tried to steal it.

Afterward I retrieved my pipe, loaded it with tobacco, and lit it from the fire. We sat side by side, backs to the trunk of an oak. I stared up at the gnarly branches as I exhaled a cloud of blue. Live oaks are wonderful, and I always see images in their intricately bent branches, sort of like how people see pictures in the stars.

"You've been preoccupied all day," Pearl Hand remarked as I passed her the pipe. She drew and blew the smoke up at the hovering column of mosquitoes. The vicious little beasts remained stymied by our greased unguent.

"I'm trying to understand what's happened to me. Seeing the Kristianos, realizing that my souls have traveled to the Spirit world, it's all starting to sink in." I took the pipe and drew the smoke in, letting Sister Tobacco ease my worry. "No matter what, nothing will ever be the same again."

"No," she whispered. "It won't."

"It's an eerie thing, to be called by Power. I've done what only the great dreamers have: stood face-to-face with Spirit Beings." I paused as she took the pipe, then asked, "Do you believe?"

"In Spirit Power?" She studied the pipe for a moment, her face pensive in the gloom. "All peoples believe in something, some Power, or ghosts, or gods." She handed the pipe back. "I've just never been this close to it before."

"I was . . . once. And it cost me everything." I sighed. "No one believed me. They thought I was lying to save myself." I paused. "And for a long time afterward, I wasn't sure they weren't right."

I gestured absently with the pipe. "Oh, I've attended to the forms, offering food in thanks, participating in the rituals. But these Spirit dreams, they were as real as I am, sitting here with you."

She glanced at me. "Why choose you? Why not some Powerful priest or dreamer, someone who has studied the ways and forms of Power? Or perhaps a great sorcerer who can call the winds, lightning, and storm to destroy the Kristianos?"

Like smacking an acorn with a hammer stone, she'd hit on the question that had been plaguing me. "In the dreams I was told that this is a fight among men. That we would decide."

"All right. But why leave it to people? Why can't Horned Serpent just dive out of the sky, snap off their wooden cross, and kill them all?"

I fingered the pipestem. "Maybe because our Power and the Power of the Kristianos is balanced. Somehow equal. Like red and white Power. Perhaps the ultimate way of it will be determined by what men decide to believe."

"Or who can conquer the other." She gestured her futility. "In that case, the Kristianos win."

"It's early to be saying that."

"I've seen them fight, Black Shell. I might have been little, but it's nothing you are ever likely to forget. Outnumbered and surrounded, I watched them break and destroy a huge mass of Chicora warriors. I'd never seen so many dead. The nightmare haunted my dreams for years."

I shrugged, remembering how the Chicaza fought. I had no idea how good her Chicora would have been. As for the Southern Timucua, they were part-time warriors who made war with puny arrows, as if it were an extension of a hunting party. Ten Chicaza would overwhelm fifty Timucua with no problem.

Then I brought up another consideration that had come to roost like a buzzard between my souls. "When Power asks, a man simply can't walk away. Not and expect to enjoy a happy and healthy life. You, however, aren't bound." I glanced at her. "The chances of me making it through this without —"

"I'm with you."

"Why? You're deathly afraid of the Kristianos." As if I wasn't! "You've got everything

264

to lose if they catch you. The way of this is going to be hard, dangerous, and will likely end in disaster for one or both of us."

She patted my knee. "Believe me, I know better than you do." Her grip on my knee tightened. "Black Shell, what if it were different? What if I'd had the Spirit dreams and you were still free to go? What if I were the one chosen to fight the Kristianos?"

"I don't understand."

"What would you do? Take off and leave me to my fate? Go off somewhere to safety and live the rest of your life without a second thought?"

I sighed in resignation. "I would rather take my chances, enjoying every second I had, just to be with you."

"And there, my lover and husband, you have my answer."

The following day, we immediately got lost. The trails along the edge of the swamp were a maze of deer traces; deer usually move from food source to food source before scattering.

By bearing east, we finally stumbled onto a main trail and headed north. Perhaps we'd traveled a hand's time through mixed grasses and trees when the dogs perked, ears forward, and low growls broke from their throats.

I signaled for silence and motioned off to the side, leading the way as Pearl Hand followed me and the dogs into the myrtle and buttonbush. We crouched as the faint clink of metal and the occasional snuffling of a cabayo could be heard.

I was trying to muzzle the dogs, all of whom weren't cooperating with being silent. Metal clanged, and I thumped Gnaw to keep him from barking.

Through the brush I could see the rider as his cabayo — sweat-streaked and mud-caked — clumped up the trail. That foul cabayo had either heard or scented us. It was on alert, looking this way and that, ears pricked. The Kristiano followed his mount's gaze, panicked eyes shifting to and fro. A metal helmet perched on his head, locks of dark hair hanging down just under the brim. Rust speckled his metal breastplate, and a crossbow rested across the pommel of his saddle.

That's when Fetch couldn't stand it anymore. He burst from where Pearl Hand was trying to hold him and charged, barking and snapping.

Then the unexpected happened. The man jerked the crossbow up and took aim. I heard the twang of the release, and Fetch squealed, literally under the cabayo's feet. The great animal began to buck and jump, its head down, back feet kicking high. The Kristiano stayed with the snorting beast until it tangled in the brush on the other side of the trail. Cabayo and rider crashed down. The animal immediately scrambled to its feet and bolted off down the trail.

I knocked an arrow and hurried forward. *In the name of Power, tell me Fetch is all right.*

The Kristiano jumped to his feet, looking dazed, and bent down to retrieve his crossbow, but then stopped short, desperation filling his eyes as he stared straight down my arrow.

"Pearl Hand?" I called. "Are any more coming?"

I heard her emerge from behind me to stare down the trail. "Not yet, but they don't like traveling alone." Then she asked something in the Kristiano language.

The youth answered, frozen in his tracks. Then his expression softened, and he said something else.

"He says he's lost." Pearl Hand's voice held an amused note. "He's thankful he found friendly Kristiano *indios* who speak proper language."

"Alto!" Pearl Hand called as he lowered his crossbow and placed a foot in the round loop just under its front. The Kristiano froze, panic returning to his eyes.

"How's Fetch?" I asked, unwilling to lower my aim.

She stepped over to Fetch, but I dared not take time to look. The Kristiano was watching me with fear-bright eyes.

"It isn't good," she said softly.

I felt my heart sink, and said to the Kristiano, "Then I'm afraid it isn't good for you, either, you *hoobuk wakse.*"

An instant before I drove my arrow though his right eye, Pearl Hand said, "Wait. He'll have information we can use."

I hesitated, desperate to loose my arrow. All of the abuse the Kristianos had heaped upon me came rolling back through my souls. I thought of how they'd worked men and women to death, then cut their heads off to free the collars. How the dogs had done their vicious work, and the misery of captivity. He read the tracks of my souls, and swallowed drily.

Oh, yes. I am your death.

Pearl Hand was chattering something harsh in Kristiano, and the young man nodded, dropping the crossbow, and lifting his hands high.

"What did you say?" I managed through gritted teeth.

"I told him you desperately wished to kill him, but that his life might be spared if he would answer a few questions. He has agreed."

I kept my arrow ready as he stepped slowly forward. Staring into his brown eyes, I read the fear, and savored it like a starving man does a fine elk roast.

I backed a step as Pearl Hand made him kneel in the trail, and after pulling some braided leather straps from one of the packs, she tied his hands behind him.

Only then did I release the tension and allow the arrow to ride forward. I bent to Fetch, and winced. The stubby Kristiano arrow had penetrated the length of his body. Blood was leaking out from Fetch's mouth and nose, his eyes gone glassy. And just that quickly, his souls fled.

I knelt beside him, my fingers tracing softly along his head. Carefully I smoothed the sleek brown hair on his muscular shoulders, and straightened his flexed front leg. How many camps had we shared, how many frugal meals? How many lands had we traversed? I remembered the time a pack of Coosa dogs had jumped him, and how for days I nursed him back to health. In lonely camps, it had been Fetch who would sense my despair and approach with a stick, dropping it suggestively on my foot.

"I pray they have a great many sticks in the Land of the Dead, old friend." And then I bent and unstrapped the pack from his back. The arrow had driven through the upper corner of one side, and Fetch's blood soaked the soft, tanned leather.

The other dogs were standing off, sniffing, eyes wary as they glanced from Fetch to me, then to the Kristiano, as though trying to understand. How could they, when I myself could not?

Pearl Hand walked over and picked up the

crossbow. Then she pulled the bloody arrow out of the earth beneath Fetch's body. Putting her foot through the loop, she took several tries before muscling back the string and locking it. Then she settled the bloody arrow in the groove, nocking it firmly.

The Kristiano watched her, trickles of sweat running down his face, his mouth working as he whispered words I didn't recognize.

"What's he doing?" I asked, eyes slitted, wishing only to reach over and strangle the life out of him.

"Praying to the Kristiano god."

"We have no golden cup here," I muttered as I carefully picked up Fetch's body and carried it into the grass. I left him, his bloody nose pointed west — the path to the Land of the Dead. Beside his head I placed food and would have left water for the journey ahead, but not having a source close, this he'd have to find on his own.

Then, squatting beside him, I called to his souls. "You are gone, old friend. Head west . . . to the edge of the world. There, after passing through a great forest, you will find the sheer cliff. Pay no attention to the West Wind, but jump with all of your might through the Seeing Hand. I know your heart, faithful friend. The Guardians will read the measure of your souls and let you pass. There, in the beyond, one day I will join you when all is finished here. Then, oh yes, we shall play fetch forever."

I gave him one last pat and stood.

"Come on," Pearl Hand called. "There may be others coming."

She had hung Fetch's pack around the Kristiano's neck. I took one last glance back at where my dog now rested, and glared at the Kristiano, violent murder in my heart. Pearl Hand walked a couple of steps behind him, the crossbow aimed at the middle of his back.

I called the rest of the pack and followed. They kept looking back, whining, then turning their questioning brown eyes to me for an explanation. No one could see the hot tears streaking down my cheeks.

Sixteen

Firelight illuminated our camp in the thicket of live oaks. While the screening of saw palmetto, thorny greenbriar, and poisonwood around the edges would ensure that no light could be seen from beyond, we didn't want reflection from the leaves. We kept the fire burning low.

Pearl Hand and I used an unguent against the swarms of mosquitoes. Remembering my treatment at the hands of the Kristianos — let alone what this one had done to Fetch — our captive didn't receive similar benefits. The vicious little beasts hovered over him in a humming column.

I chewed meat from a duck's thigh as I

watched the Kristiano, periodically tossing a piece to the four dogs who watched me with intent stares. It only added to the sense of loss that Fetch wasn't there to share.

Pearl Hand kept shooting me solicitous glances, knowing full well how Fetch's death affected me. She looked gorgeous in the firelight's golden glow, her long hair rippling down over her shoulder, and curled around the curve of her bare breast. Her dark eyes softened as she met my gaze.

Not all peoples shared my love of dogs. For many, a dog is just a replaceable commodity, and the source for an occasional meal. I'd been in villages where dogs are only kept to dispose of the trash, sound a warning in the event of an approaching enemy, and are easily replaceable from any local litter. Such doings, it seemed to me, reflected a poverty of the soul.

As is accepted among Mos'kogean beliefs, I tossed what was left of the duck into the fire, thanking the bird for its gift of food. The rising smoke would carry the prayer to the animal's soul. Since the Spirit dreams, I found myself adhering to the old ways with a newfound reverence.

The duck gone, Squirm had paced over to look out at our backtrail, waiting, watching. He shot me a glance, his white blaze contrasting to the shadows.

"Fetch isn't coming," I whispered and patted my leg, calling Squirm to lie beside me. Gnaw dropped his gray head on his paws, shooting questioning looks — as only a dog can — between Pearl Hand and myself. Always slow to pick up on a situation, Bark walked over to where Squirm had stood and waited expectantly, apparently sure that Fetch would be coming at any moment.

I tried to ignore him and turned my attention to the Kristiano. The source of my current misery was staring raptly at Pearl Hand's breasts. Granted, all women had breasts, but the way he was ogling Pearl Hand's would leave one to believe that Kristiano women were somehow woefully and inadequately endowed.

"Does this piece of two-legged filth have a name?" I asked.

Pearl Hand said something in Kristiano, and he tore his gaze from her chest. Chin up, he stated: "Antonio Ruiz y Gonzales." This he followed with a long explanation.

Pearl Hand translated, "He lists a bunch of ancestors and says he comes from the same town as *Adelantado* de Soto."

"You should have stayed home," I muttered. "Where are the Kristianos headed?"

After an exchange, Pearl Hand told me, "He says that they wished to winter in Ocale, but there is only enough food for a couple of weeks. Several parties are scouring the countryside for other villages to loot."

274

I considered that, giving the young man a narrow-eyed stare. "They'll have to head north. The Uzachile might have enough resources, but the nearest great nation is Apalachee. Only High Mikko Cafakke has the surplus to feed such a large force. The other option is to head north into the interior."

She spoke to Antonio and I caught the word "Apalachee."

"*Sí,*" came the response.

"Yes," Pearl Hand told me, though I'd picked up on *sí* during my captivity.

"What do they want?" I asked. "Why would they come here? What do they expect to get out of us? Land? Control?"

Pearl Hand spoke softly, and Antonio rattled off a vigorous response. She said, "They expect to get rich. They come in search of gold." Her mouth quirked. "And there's something about saving our souls for their god."

"Gold?" I shook my head. "What could they want with gold?"

Pearl Hand shrugged. "They value it the way our people value copper."

"Tell him there is very little gold up north."

Another exchange followed, and Pearl Hand replied, "He assures me we are liars. They have heard of much gold in the north. Captives have told the *Adelantado* that all gold comes from the north. The Kristianos have seen bits of it in the captured towns."

"Copper from the north? Yes," I agreed. "But most of the gold being traded around the peninsula comes from their wrecked ships along the shore. A few traders have tried carrying it up to the Nations, but they can't make much from it."

Pearl Hand gave me a wry smile. "I think I understand where this is coming from. Imagine you're the Uzita chief and these vermin march into your town. What are you going to tell them? That there is no gold in the north? If you do, what will the Kristianos do? Maybe burn your town in frustration, clap you into a collar, and perhaps even stay and take your lands? No, Black Shell, better to tell them anything that will encourage them to leave just as soon as possible. Tempt them into the north, and just maybe the Coosa, the Ockmulgee, or the Apalachee will destroy them once and for all."

That made sense. None of the fragmented chiefdoms in the peninsula could muster the kind of force necessary to destroy the Kristianos.

"I don't understand this business of saving our souls."

Pearl Hand turned to the Kristiano. He chattered on for some time, Pearl Hand frowning often as he spoke.

She finally turned to me. "It sounds crazy, but apparently they think our souls are lost,

276

somehow evil. They think we serve some evil Spirit named *el diablo,* and our souls will burn forever as a result."

"Breath Giver isn't evil. Nor are the Spirit Beasts. When we die, our souls go to the edge of the earth." I thumped my chest. "I've been there, stood on the edge of the cliff and seen the jump through the Seeing Hand that leads to the Path of the Dead."

She shrugged. "Antonio says that the only way to save our souls is to accept his god."

"Who is his god?"

At Pearl Hand's question, Antonio started off again.

Pearl Hand finally held up a slim hand to stop him. "He says his god is the true god, and his religious society, called *católicos,* and its leader, is the only way to god. Anything else is . . ." — she made a face — *"del diablo."*

I frowned, rubbing Gnaw behind his ear. "What does he believe? That we're all witches?"

I listened to them discuss this.

"That's what he believes," Pearl Hand replied. "He says we are all *perdido,* lost. Only by accepting his god will our souls live forever."

"Ask him if all the Kristianos have accepted this god."

At Antonio's insistent response, Pearl Hand told me, "He says the Kristianos are his god's warriors, that they carry the true cross. By

277

what they do here, they will all go to *paraíso,* which is a wonderful afterlife full of holy people who sing, and their god smiles at them."

"Let me get this straight: All the misery they are making here? And getting rich, too? This is in service of their god? So he will let them into this *paraíso?*" I made a face. "Would you want your soul to go there? Stuffed full of Kristianos who commit atrocities? Give me the Path of the Dead where I'll find my ancestors and dogs any day! What do they do? Raid each other and make war for eternity?"

Pearl Hand translated: "He says it is all peace, what he calls *tranquilo.* God will reward them for the good work they do while they are alive here."

I fingered the scabs on my neck, remembering "their good works here," like turning the dogs loose on unfortunates whose strength failed under their lash.

In a whisper I asked, "What kind of god do they serve?"

Pearl Hand didn't even take time to ask. "They say it is the one true god. He's called *Dios.* His son is *Jesús.* I'm not clear on this, but they appear to be one and the same. *Jesús* came to earth and enemies pinned him to a cross to die."

"That doesn't surprise me, given what I've learned of Kristianos."

278

"*Jesús* rose from his grave, went back to *paraíso,* and became one with god. And there's a sacred Spirit mixed up in it somehow. All this was done to save people's souls from being lost and sent to burn forever."

"Even if they are good people?"

At her question, Antonio responded in some length. Pearl Hand's smile was amused. "He says to be good, you must believe in the true god. If you do not, you are evil. And that's that. If we would save ourselves from an eternity of fire and torment, we will free him. He will then take us to one of his priests who will save our souls and send them to *paraíso.*"

"Sure we will. And I suppose Fetch will be waiting there, tail wagging, and happy to see us?"

I said it in jest, but Pearl Hand asked anyway.

"No," she told me, "animals don't have souls. His god didn't give them any. Only the souls of people inhabit *paraíso.*" Then she added, "And, unlike us, they think people only have *one* soul."

I just glared at him. His god didn't give souls to animals? Who'd want to spend eternity in a place without animals? Just what did they eat in their *paraíso* without deer, elk, and birds? What kind of foolishness was that? In the beginning, Breath Giver breathed life and souls into all creatures and plants. To

279

live was to have souls.

And the notion of only *one* soul? That was simply ridiculous! How did a body stay alive when the dream soul was out wandering about? Many people, like the Yuchi, thought you had as many as four souls. My Chicaza believed in five.

"Tell him he's a fool," I muttered.

At Antonio's reply, she said, "He says you are the fool. He has the truth, and serves the one god. You, he says, are *maldito,* cursed by god."

"Better cursed by his god," I growled, "than condemned to his *paraíso* full of murderers and thieves like him and his *Adelantado.*"

Antonio's words gave me a lot to chew on — especially in light of the warnings I'd heard in my Spirit dreams. The nature of the battle with the Kristianos began to come clear. This was not just a conflict between men. The Kristianos wanted us to become followers of their god and send our souls to *paraíso* to spend eternity being smiled at and singing, but without animals, hunting, campfires, and stories told by our ancestors. Where was the joy in that? And worse, what if they won in the end?

That night I was tormented by dreams. In them, I walked through a sterile *paraíso* where no animal souls provided company. I was alone, carrying a dog-chewed stick, with no Fetch to chase it. When I called for him, screamed for him to come, I found myself surrounded by Kristianos who chased me — driven on by a terrible god who laughed as innocents were clapped into collars and slain by sword-wielding bearded men.

I woke to a faint light dimming the eastern horizon. "Whatever the afterlife," I whispered, "Give me one where my souls are judged on who I am, not who I serve."

And in the meantime, I would do all I could to send as many Kristianos as I could to the terrible eternity of their *paraíso.*

Seventeen

"What do you think?" I asked, head cocked as I studied the pile of clothing on the ground. We were standing in our little clearing, the morning sun sending rays of light through the leaves while warblers, mockingbirds, and wrens sought to outdo the chirring insects with song. The fragrant smell of blossoms mixed with the scent of grass and faint whiffs of woodsmoke from our fire. Bark still stood at the trail, his scarred muzzle pointed back toward where we'd left Fetch.

I tried to ignore the hollow sense of loss.

"He's a skinny specimen," Pearl Hand replied as she studied the naked Kristiano. "I believe that but for his hair, you'd lose him completely in a snowbank."

I glanced at the Kristiano, still shocked by the whiteness of his hide. Somehow I couldn't help but think it couldn't be healthy to be that white. It made my skin crawl to see all the places he had hair. It matted in a shallow V on his chest and ran down in a line, thinning at the navel to thicken around his penis and testicles. It continued down his thighs and calves. Tufts of hair even could be seen on the knuckles of his toes. His frame was spare, ribs and shoulders sticking out. The ropy muscles belied the threat projected when he was dressed in armor. Up close, he had tiny brown spots on his arms, chest, and thighs. Bug bites made ugly red welts everywhere else, and the chiggers were feasting where the mosquitoes hadn't been able to. All in all, a naked Kristiano looked pretty pathetic.

"I was talking about his clothes," I countered, bending down to pluck up the metal breastplate. The thing reminded me of a beetle's shell. That it should be so light surprised me, and I admired the workmanship that could pound metal so thin and uniform. There was no way I'd ever buckle it around my chest and shoulders; the thing was too small.

I tapped it with a fingernail, listening to the now rusting metal sing. There had to be Power in that, but red or white, I couldn't tell. Maybe both, given the metal's now browning color. Power is drawn to color, and the speckled brown spreading on the silver didn't inspire me with awe. Or perhaps the Power faded if the metal wasn't polished every day. I'd learned that with the Kristiano sword.

Beneath the breastplate Antonio wore a fabric vest, layered, and into which had been sewn little squares of metal. Inspecting it carefully, I could see how the batting, mixed with metal, could stop arrows. The thing was worth a fortune for the small metal plates alone. They could be patiently hammered into beads, or sharpened and fixed to a staff to serve as an ax.

His shirt was of heavy cloth, white with blue stripes that would have defied the best weavers in the north. I liked the puffy sleeves that allowed free movement of the arms. For the moment it reeked of the Kristiano's sweat. The pants and undergarments also amazed me. Kristianos wore a lot of layers. His footwear was made of very durable leather unlike any I had ever seen, and the stitching? Well, remarkable is the only word to describe the workmanship. His helmet was also a thing of wonder — light and protective — good for rain with its brim; a man could parade around untouched in a hailstorm of stunning intensity. I began to see what Muskrat meant when he told of his cousin's arrow being as impotent as a mosquito bite.

The disadvantage was clear when I lifted the whole of it. No wonder they rode cabayos. This much weight wouldn't be debilitating in the morning, but after a long, hot day's march, it would sap any man's resources.

"Impressed?" Pearl Hand asked as she watched me sort through the belt and under-garments.

"Very." I lifted a little knife with a *hierro* blade and tested the sharp edge. "This alone would bring a chief's ransom in the north." I dropped it into one of my packs.

"You can see how difficult it is to kill them," Pearl Hand replied, glancing speculatively at Antonio. Uncomfortable under her gaze, he dropped his hands to hide his balls and penis.

I'd have been ashamed of them, too.

"Arrow placement is critical," I agreed. Then, on a whim, I carried the metal breast-plate over and leaned it against a palmetto. Stepping back to my bow, I strung it, nocked a war arrow, and from ten paces, shot. The arrow shattered in a ringing clatter, the breastplate bouncing and falling to the side. When I walked over, I was amazed to see that the *hierro* carapace was only dented. The discovery was worth the loss of the arrow.

Antonio had a smug look on his face, and I considered driving a second one through his now vulnerable and oh so pale chest.

And one day, Antonio, I will. When I do, I

285

promise, I'm sending your soul to the Land of the Dead, where you can serve Fetch the way your people made me serve them.

I ran a finger over the dimple my shot had made in the armor. "We make chest armor in the north," I mused. "Ours is crafted from wood, or perhaps woven cane. Nothing as good as this."

"That's why they make the crossbow," she told me. "Even though you turn your nose up at the short arrow, its iron head and the power of the bow will send it through armor like that."

I nodded. "Hence the undercoat, right? The outer metal slows the arrow, which the batting and plate can stop."

"That would seem to be the idea," she agreed. "The thunder sticks, though, will go through them both if fired from up close. I saw such a thing as a little girl."

"Then they would shoot right through anything our people wear." I thought of one of their heavy little lead balls and couldn't help but believe our best wooden armor would be as effective as grass when it came to stopping one.

"Thunder sticks have one shot," she reminded me. "It takes a long time to load them again. Until that happens, a thunder stick is just an awkward club."

"Provided you survive that first shot."

"That," she agreed, "is the problem. And

they tend to cover their shooters with archers and spears. The combination of those weapons is what makes them so terrible."

"Ask Antonio, Who is this *Adelantado?* We know he seeks gold and works for his god, but why did he come here?"

Pearl Hand carried on an exchange for a while, then explained: "The *Adelantado* has many exploits to his name in another country to the south. He was in an army that captured a great nation called Inca. He killed many people and took much gold and silver from the Inca. Doing so made him one of the richest men in his country, called Espanya. De Soto's high minko, called *el rey Carlos,* and a holy leader, called *Papa,* gave him all of this country as his own."

"Who? If this was a high minko's land to give, why have I never heard of him?"

Pearl Hand repeated the question, to which Antonio replied in length. She then said, "This is the way Antonio says it works: Kristianos believe that *Dios* created the world. This *Papa* is the leader of *Dios's* priests, the *católicos.* Since *Dios* created the world, the *católicos* can give it to whomever they wish."

"And where does this *rey Carlos* fit in?"

"The high minko rules by the will of *Dios,* but he appears to be under the command of the *Papa.* Somehow, it takes two of them, but they both agree to give the *Adelantado* any lands he captures."

I shook my head at the absurdity of it. "A high minko across the sea is giving away lands he's never even seen because he thinks his god created it?" The things I had been told in my Spirit dreams began to make an even more chilling sense.

Pearl Hand shrugged, missing my suddenly sober expression. "I told you long ago, they are arrogant."

"The worst is yet to come," I whispered, gaze fixed on the breastplate. "I've had three Spirit dreams."

"Yes, so?"

"The important one — the one all Spirit dreamers seek — is the fourth dream."

"You were sick last time. Your souls were wandering."

I nodded, glancing uneasily at Antonio. "But the fourth will come. I will dream again, and when I do, the stakes will become clear." I shivered at the thought.

She frowned, lines marking her smooth forehead. "And we're caught right in the middle of it?"

"You don't have to be."

As she shook her head, long locks of raven hair played down her back. "Power is counting on us. Both of us."

"Go somewhere. Be safe."

She said something to me in Kristiano tongue.

"What?"

"That's why I'm here, Black Shell. I know something of them, speak their language. Power needed me to rescue you, heal you of their disease. Power is working through me." She gestured toward Antonio, standing awkwardly, his hands cupping his genitals. "Power gave us the Kristiano. A captive so we might learn more. We're being prepared. Given a chance to learn things before we're thrown into the battle."

I nodded, staring at the dimple in the breastplate. "But there are just the two of us."

"Perhaps," she murmured softly. "For now. But there will be others."

Then she walked back to Antonio, gesturing for him to sit. He dropped, staring up at her. He had that look in his eyes again, as if he'd never seen a real woman before.

"What are you doing?" I asked as she began speaking in Kristiano.

"Refreshing my knowledge of their tongue," she replied between strings of Kristiano. "So that I am even better at knowing their souls."

I thought about that, and turned to my own study of the man's armor and clothing. What if we didn't have as much time as I thought? Suddenly, every heartbeat mattered.

We worked in shifts. I would leave one day — taking my bow and arrows — to go hunt. We had, after all, three human and four dog bellies to keep full.

The next day I would stay with the Kristiano, patiently trying to learn his language. For her part, Pearl Hand would take one of the dog packs and pick berries, dig roots, and collect seeds. She was also good at tickling fish, which involves reaching slowly under banks and carefully grasping whatever's hiding there. She caught turtles and snared rabbits.

My progress in the language — which Antonio informed me was called *español* — came slowly at first, being unrelated to any tongue I was familiar with. Then, at night, Pearl Hand would coach me while she practiced with the crossbow. In the beginning, I'd thought the design was silly. Maybe the Kristianos weren't the only ones who were arrogant. Seeing the power that device unleashed, I would never doubt a Kristiano weapon again.

We only had the one iron-tipped arrow. Antonio's others had vanished with his cabayo. That one was precious since we had figured out it would pierce Kristiano armor. I made her some practice arrows, which allowed her to learn to aim and shoot. She had a proficiency with the weapon that I certainly didn't.

Since we were experimenting, I took out the Kristiano sword, batting it around like a war club. Antonio laughed at my feeble efforts. It got to the point where he was grabbing his belly and making faces.

"If you're so smart, show me how it's done." I gave him a mocking look.

"Untie." He offered his bound wrists. He gave Pearl Hand a smug look, as if suddenly sure of himself.

Granted, I was smart enough not to let him have the real thing, but with Pearl Hand watching — the crossbow ready on her lap — I provided staves of the approximate shape. Antonio, to his immense satisfaction, started out battering me unmercifully; but, it turns out, a sword, while very different from a war club, uses many of the same principles.

"Watch his feet," Pearl Hand coached. "Left one in front. Forward and back, not dancing about like a girl at a round dance."

By this time I was covered with bruises and hadn't landed so much as a blow against his clothing. Yes, we'd let him dress, but I had pitched his boots into a swamp where they'd never be found. He didn't look like the kind who could go far barefoot.

Each time he'd whack me with the stave he'd grin stupidly at Pearl Hand, as if to impress her with his superiority. The next time he did, I used his preoccupation to rap him across the ribs. At that, his expression clouded and he was at me with redoubled fury.

War clubs are slower, with more bobbing

and weaving, jumping and swinging. The hardest part of the sword was the thrusting, until I remembered spear-training as a boy. By the time he was winded, I began to rap him across the ribs. The more he tired, the slower his movements. I was able to see how he did it.

I finally knocked his stave to one side, leaping forward in a thrust, driving the blunt end of my stave into his gut. He stumbled backward, chest heaving. Antonio's bitter burst of cursing caused me to retreat.

"He says he would have killed you many times over before you landed that blow." Pearl Hand didn't need to translate; the man's anger and hatred couldn't be missed.

"He would have," I puffed, catching my breath. "But if we keep at this, I will learn it."

"Why?" Pearl Hand wondered. "It's not like you'll be able to beat them at their own game. He's barely more than a boy. Put you up against a man who's practiced that all his life, and he'll gut you like a fish."

"I know." I winced as I prodded my ribs. "But our warriors will go up against them with war clubs. The sword is quicker, faster. If I learn it, perhaps the knowledge will be useful."

"How?"

I shrugged, tossing the stave to one side, staring down Antonio's hatred with my own.

"I don't know. But someday, perhaps it will make the difference." I pointed to Antonio. "You and me. Tomorrow. Again."

Pearl Hand stood, covering Antonio with the crossbow while I rebound his arms and legs. In the process Antonio chattered in *español.*

"He wants to know why we're keeping him prisoner. He says his father, Don Luis Ruiz, is a very rich man, a subchief of the *Adelantado.* Don Luis will pay ransom and make us both rich."

"I am rich enough," I muttered. "And just so there is no misunderstanding, you are only here to teach us how to defeat you."

Pearl Hand translated. Antonio, eyes slitted, rattled back.

"He says that as long as the Kristianos follow the true god, they cannot be defeated by any accursed agents of *el diablo.* But for you, Antonio says, he'll make an exception and send your damned souls straight to the fires of hell."

I bent down, glaring into his angry eyes. "What if I kill you first? How then will you manage this?"

Pearl Hand translated his reply. "He says his father will come for him at the head of many *soldados,* and he will laugh as he cuts your throat. In the meantime, he says he refuses to even talk to us, or eat our food. He is done polluting his soul with the agents of *el diablo.*"

I jerked the last of the knots tight. *"Prefieres muerto?"* I asked in my very bad *español.*

"Un día, te mataré. En el nombre del Dios, lo prometo." Antonio jerked his head in hot affirmation, as proving it to himself.

"He says —"

"I know." I waved down her translation. "He's going to kill me." I stared at the welts and scrapes left on my chest and belly by the staves. "But today is not that day."

I walked over, picking through Fetch's pack. There I found the hated collar and a length of sinew. These I pulled free, seeing Antonio's eyes widen.

Walking up to him, I dangled it, letting the half rings of the collar jangle and dance at the end of the chain. He tried to wiggle away as I bent down, but was no match for my muscle as I slapped the halves of the collar together around his neck, and sitting on him, tied it tight with sinew.

"How does it feel?" I asked, rising.

A passionately foul string of curses was my answer.

I watched him finger the collar, violent rage in his eyes. So I yanked up on the chain, tying it to a live oak branch. True, it could easily be defeated, but it made me feel good.

Pearl Hand's expression betrayed skeptical amusement, but she held her peace as I reached for my bow. The dogs came to immediate attention, as always, anxious to go along. I waved them down. "I'm going to see if I can drive an arrow through some unlucky furry creature by way of adding to the meal pot." I gestured. "Watch him."

She nodded. "Be careful. Antonio's been missing for a while. They will still be looking for him."

I used the bow to bend the poisonwood back and eased through the saw palmetto. Then I carefully picked my way through the grass. We didn't follow the same route twice, leery of creating any kind of trail.

Pearl Hand was right. I didn't want to try fighting Kristianos with their own weapons. But gaining a familiarity with the sword also gave me a healthy respect. Attacking swordsmen with war clubs would be disastrous. What other surprises did the Kristianos have for us? I thought about the thunder sticks, about the crossbow that was definitely more powerful than even the finest composite bow with which I was familiar.

And then they had those odd long spears, tipped with metal points as well as a large cutting blade that jutted out to the side. The things looked awkward and cumbersome. I was willing to wager a good shell gorget that they were anything but. Otherwise the Kristianos wouldn't be lugging them around.

When I reached the main trail I noticed the cabayo tracks first thing. They'd been through in the last hand of time. I carefully scouted up and down the length of trail but could see no sign of them.

I started back the other way. I was after deer, right? Just because it was in the general direction of Ocale town didn't mean I was looking for trouble.

The faint clink of metal was accompanied by a cabayo blowing. At first I wasn't sure which direction it had come from, so I just slipped into the grass, weaseling back away from the trail. A large copperhead ghosted off, disturbed by my presence.

Then I crouched down, obscured by the leaves of a sumac. Overhead an osprey winged by, a fish clutched lengthwise in its taloned feet.

Metal clanked again, and I heard a man's voice. A cabayo snuffled, and leather creaked. The first rider came into my limited view. He wore a helmet, this one polished to shine in the sunlight, and a lance was propped in a stirrup holder. Behind him came another, and yet another. Six in all, two with crossbows, the rest holding lances. Swords hung at their sides and shining metal shields covered their left arms.

After they passed, I crept out, smelling the acrid scent of cabayo. Carefully I eased along after them. The day was brutally hot, and I thought about all those layers of clothing they were sweating into. They should have drawn every mosquito within a day's walk, and flies, too.

For some time I trotted along, staying just far enough behind to hear them. From previous excursions, I knew the trail crossed a small creek that fed into the swamps. Beyond that, I figured it was too close to their camp at Ocale town to take chances. Pearl Hand might not come to get me again.

I could hear the cabayos splash into the water, and was on the point of turning back when a shout went up, followed by war cries. I hurried ahead, stopping when I could just see the crossing.

The cabayos were milling, splashing in the water, and even over the distance I could make out arrows clattering against the Kristianos' armor. Ocale warriors were dancing around, loosing shaft after shaft. The Kristianos, wheeling the cabayos in the water, formed up under shouted commands and charged, the lancers each catching a darting warrior. The two men with crossbows rode close before shooting down fleeing warriors. Then they drew their swords as the heavy cabayos crashed through vegetation in pursuit.

Within moments it was over. Shouted commands brought the riders together. Two men stepped down, walking over with their swords to kill the wounded. Then, as though the skirmish were nothing, the Kristianos re-

297

mounted, laughing, clanking their shields, and continued on across the creek.

I waited a full hand of time before sneaking up to view the carnage. It had been a well-planned ambush — the Kristianos completely surrounded — and had it been anyone but Kristianos, nothing would have saved them.

Shattered arrows lay on the ground, a couple in the churned mud of the crossing. I studied the dead; the lances had been most efficient, though a follow-up slash of the sword had made sure.

One of the warriors who had fled had been ridden down, his head split in two with a sword. Flies were already enjoying the feast.

One by one I counted the dead, finding sixteen. It was a small fight, the first I'd seen involving Kristianos, but it shook me to the core.

I squatted there, looking out at the muddy water. If six Kristianos could do this to sixteen Ocale warriors, what would it take to overwhelm the entire army in a frontal assault?

I shivered at the realization that no Nation, not even my bellicose Chicaza, would stand a chance.

And you want Pearl Hand and me to stop them?

I looked up at the blazing sun, seeking an answer, and finding none.

EIGHTEEN

Two days later, I was hunting. As I stalked along an overgrown deer trail, I should have been paying attention. I was out to kill a deer, turkey, opossum, anything for the pot. Instead the green palmettos, mulberries, and honeysuckle might have been a gray screen. My bow rested forgotten in my hand, the nocked arrow an abstract. I kept mulling over something Pearl Hand had told me the night before.

"Antonio has a high opinion of himself," she'd whispered as we lay in our bed. "He keeps telling me what a great man his father is, and how one day he, Antonio, will be a *don,* too."

"What's that?"

"Like a subchief."

"He's not going to live that long."

She tickled my ear. "You've seen the way he looks at me?"

"That might be one of the reasons he doesn't live that long. What's with him? Don't the Kristianos have women back where they come from? I saw two in Uzita while I was there."

"Antonio would like me to believe that if I take him back to his people, I could become a wife. He would shower me with great honors, fine dresses, and place me in charge of many servants in a very important family."

I turned in the blankets. "You're kidding?"

She chuckled softly. "Can you imagine it? Me, with that skinny little boy?"

"Imagine it? The very thought makes me want to throw up." I flipped the blanket back. "Maybe I'll go kill him now."

She pulled me back down, running a teasing finger around my ear. "Later. For the moment, I think I'd like to enjoy a real man."

Antonio — on top of being a Kristiano — had only proved himself to be an idiot. It was going to take a lot more than promises of riches and status to win her over to the Kristianos. She knew them for what they were.

Nevertheless, it bothered me. I was used to men admiring Pearl Hand, but the thought of a maggot like Antonio constantly gawking at *my* woman? Outside of the amusement it provided Pearl Hand, it only kindled rage between my souls.

And then — jerking back to where I was — I tightened my grip on my bow. *Fool! You're supposed to be hunting! What idiocy possessed you to . . .*

I heard voices coming from down the trail. I eased back, the arrow still nocked in my bow, and crouched in the tangle of grape and greenbriar, thorns from the latter raking my skin. I was no more than ten paces off the trail when a small group of men and women — burdened with baskets hung from tump-lines — passed.

Their expressions were glum, hair dirty and unkempt. Smudges could be seen on their bare legs, and the women's skirts looked as if they'd been sleeping in them. The man in the lead kept glancing uneasily back at his companions as if seeking reassurance by their very presence.

I could catch snatches of their conversation, their local dialect of Timucua almost incomprehensible.

As they passed, I rose, calling, "Wait! I am a trader, and approach under the Power of trade."

You'd have thought I was a wolf attacking a group of rabbits. The women screamed, throwing themselves to the ground, hands over their ears. The men whirled, bringing up bows, fear in their faces.

I held my bow off to the side, my right hand opened, fingers splayed. "I only want news. Do not shoot."

They hesitated for a moment, the men, licking their lips, clearly afraid. It was a younger man, muscular and tattooed with traditional starbursts on his cheeks and breast, who called, "Who are you?"

"Black Shell, a trader of the Chicaza. I come under the Power of trade. Under that Power, I give you my word: I mean you no harm."

The youth lowered his bow. "What news do you want?"

I sighed and stepped forward. "What is happening with the Kristianos? Have you heard anything?"

The older man finally lowered his bow and nodded. He was gray-haired, wrinkled, with a rounded stoop to his shoulders. His rheumy brown eyes kept casting warily about in case I was not alone. "They have left Ocale, heading north. They have run out of food, even after raiding Acura and all the surrounding villages. We heard this from one of our people who escaped just yesterday." He gestured toward Ocale. "We ran at their approach and have been hiding. Now we are going to see what is left."

"Not much, knowing the Kristianos. You'll

be lucky if they haven't burned everything to the ground."

He gave me a weak smile that exposed pink and toothless gums. "Then at least it will save us the effort. No one would live in a house the Kristianos have polluted. Not only do they destroy the Spirit Power in the house, they leave it full of disease. Anything left standing, we will burn anyway." He shook his head. "It will be a hard winter. Instead of eating our corn and squash, we're going to have to go out each day to gather roots, nuts, and fruits. From dawn to dusk we will have to fish and trap birds just to keep our bellies full. They've fouled the entire country with their stink."

"Such is their nature," I agreed.

"I remember you," the younger man said. "You came through several moons ago, heading south. I am Two Panthers. You stayed with us for a night."

"Your chief, Holata Ocale, thought I was a spy working for the Potano. Perhaps now he will understand I'm just a trader." Something about Two Panthers seemed familiar.

"You were asking about the Kristianos, weren't you?" the young Two Panthers asked, brow lined as he remembered.

"I was a fool." I pointed to the healing red welts on my neck. "I found them. They put one of those metal collars on me and made me work. Power was with me; I got away."

303

"What do you do now?" the old man asked.

"I watch them. Trying to figure out a way to destroy them."

"One man alone?" Two Panthers asked.

I gave him a shrug. "Power is with me."

"It was with our healer, too," the old man said wearily. "He went to fight their god, calling on all of his Powers. They sent great dogs to tear him to pieces." He scuffed the trail dirt. "Whatever their Power is, ours is no match."

"Wickedness," I answered. "That is their Power. That and, of course, their armor and weapons. But we have something else, something they can't beat."

The old man cocked his head, giving me a skeptical look. "What would that be, Trader?"

I gestured around. "We know the land . . . and have time."

The women had risen self-consciously to their feet, resetting the burden baskets over their hips. One now said, "And how will that work against them? Parties of our warriors have tried to ambush them, and most were killed. No one can stand against them."

I shrugged. "Not yet. But I saw the Kristianos suffer as they were crossing the swamps." I gestured around. "They have left Ocale. Out of food. Imagine that. Here, surrounded by things to eat, they are hungry. They may have eaten your stores, but at least you won't starve." I nodded to myself, putting it together. "No, we won't beat them, but the land will."

"You can carry on your fight," Two Panthers said. "We just want to be left alone, to care for our dead, and rebuild."

"You shall," I agreed. "But I think if you are smart, you won't replant or rebuild for a while. Without stores of food, they won't be tempted to come back."

The old man chuckled, clearly not amused. "How right you are. They've even eaten the seed corn. We have nothing to plant, but will have to trade for it."

The look Two Panthers gave me sent a shiver down my spine. Then he asked, "They've brought death, haven't they? Not just to our people, but to our world. Nothing will ever be the same, will it?"

I hitched up my belt, not knowing how to answer. The finality in his voice might have encompassed the entire world. Even the sun in the sky seemed to dim. "I must be going. Remember me to your chief. Tell him I really wasn't a spy."

Two Panthers gave me a dull look. "The Kristianos killed him in the first fight. If the clans agree, I shall be Holata Ocale now."

I remembered him, sitting in the chief's house, the youngest son. He'd been quiet, his skeptical father and older brothers asking barbed questions about my real reason for being there.

305

"You have my sympathy, Two Panthers. May the holata's souls rest peacefully and protect you from evil. And your mother, Sabal? She provided me with a wonderful feast of corn, palm heart, and fish mixed with elderberries." It was the only highlight from my time in Ocale.

"They took her. Captured her in a raid. The last I saw, she was being led off with a rope around her neck. If you should happen across her on your journey, tell my mother we will be waiting should she ever escape."

"And your brothers?" I remembered two others, older than this one.

"Dead." Two Panthers gave me a weak smile, as if that were the best to be hoped for. "May the Power of trade be with you, Black Shell of the Chicaza. You're going to need it." With that they all turned, walking stolidly up the trail to discover whatever wreckage remained of their lives.

When I returned to camp, it was to find Pearl Hand nursing a bruise on the side of her face, the dogs clustered around her. Antonio was nowhere to be seen.

"What happened?" I asked, hurrying over to her. I turned her face up, seeing the discoloration on her cheek.

"You didn't check his bindings this morning," she accused hotly.

"No, you did," I shot back.

"I told you to."

"But I thought you'd done it."

She jerked her head away. "This is pointless. He got loose and jumped me. Hit me hard and knocked me over. As I scrambled to my feet, he was leaping for the sword. That's when the dogs tore into him. By the time I got the sword, he was running headlong for the brush." She pointed at a hole torn in the vines, palmettos, and poisonwood. "He crashed through there, figuring the dogs wouldn't follow."

I glanced over, considering the direction he'd fled. That was east, and the Kristianos were headed north. Should we try to hunt him down?

Pearl Hand's crossbow now lay beside her, the bowstring locked and the war arrow nocked. She followed my gaze, saying, "Well, I thought he might come back."

"Why?"

"Because he was shouting that I would now be *his* woman."

I stood, looking around the little clearing. Antonio had been in such a rush he'd left behind his armor, fleeing barefoot in only his cloth pants and shirt. I climbed partway up one of the live oaks, staring out at the saw grass on the other side. The trail Antonio had left was clearly visible.

"I'll bet he's cut to ribbons, and the poisonwood will be doing its work about now."

307

"He'll be headed straight back to the Kristianos," she said softly. "We've got to leave. He'll bring them here."

"They left yesterday. He's going to be very disappointed." I told her what I'd learned from the Ocale.

She sighed, slapping her thighs, and stood. "Then we had better be after them. Who knows, we might track him down on the trail."

I thought about that. "He's alone, barefoot, and unarmed in country he doesn't know." I shook my head. "If a snake or alligator doesn't get him, the first hunter he runs into won't hesitate to drive an arrow through his heart . . . assuming he's lucky. If he's unlucky, they'll take him back and sacrifice him to the sun." It wouldn't be a happy death, given the anger and rage the Kristianos had kindled in local hearts.

"I'm afraid you lost your collar. It was still around his neck."

"Too bad we didn't have metal buttons to seal it fast."

"He hates you for that, you know. He said he'd pay you back more than once for the insult."

"I'll be waiting."

The dogs were happy to be on the trail again, and I began to realize, it was just as well that Antonio had escaped. We passed two parties of Ocale that day. All were headed home to see what was left. Antonio's future looked grim.

I said as much to Pearl Hand.

She mused for a moment, then asked, "Would it have bothered you, seeing him cut down?"

"Only slightly. He was our captive, after all. That, and he could be carrying this pack." I had Fetch's over my shoulder, doubling my load and inhibiting any movement.

She shook her head. "You'd be carrying it anyway. Not even claiming he was our slave would have saved his life. The Ocale would have just pushed us aside and cut him to pieces."

News in the backcountry, however, is often euphemistic. We hadn't covered a finger's travel before Two Panthers, the old man and women in tow, came hurrying down the trail.

"Two Panthers?" I called, reshuffling my load, raising my hand. It felt odd not to be greeting people with my trader's staff — resting as it was with the bow, arrows, sword, and my chunkey lances.

"They're still there!" I could see the churning anger in Two Panthers's face. "Only a part of them left. The others, like maggots, continue to infest us."

"Did they see you?" I asked, glancing back down the trail, half expecting to see Kristianos galloping our direction.

"No." His expression was irritated. "Not

309

even I am dumb enough to just charge out of the forest. I looked first, and saw a small herd of their cabayos and *puercos* chewing up what's left of our cornstalks. And guards in armor lounge by the palisade gates."

"So, what will you do?" Pearl Hand asked.

Two Panthers shrugged. "Back to the forests and swamps for now."

"Two more parties of your people are behind us. They'll need warning." I glanced back down the trail.

"And you, Black Shell?" Two Panthers asked, clearly concerned. "You are welcome to come with us. Another man good with a bow is always appreciated."

I glanced at Pearl Hand, and she arched a questioning eyebrow.

"They're split?" I paused, considering. "Then maybe some advantage can be had of this. Which way did they go?"

"North."

With the Kristianos still at Ocale, Antonio's fate was no longer sealed. He might even be on the verge of stumbling into the town as we spoke, provided he found the right trail and didn't find Ocale warriors in the process. One thing was certain: He'd have his cabayeros scouring the countryside for us.

To Two Panthers I said, "The Kristianos will be beating the country all around where you first met me. They will know where I camped. Keep all of your people clear of that area. Meanwhile, is there a trail Pearl Hand and I can take that will veer wide of Ocale? The last place they'll be searching for us is in the north."

"How would they know where your camp was?" Two Panthers asked. "Surely you don't trade with them?" His gaze fixed on the sword and pack of armor, old suspicions beginning to brew.

"We had a Kristiano as a slave for a while. He got away this morning." I pointed with a finger. "But he will be back, and probably with a large party in tow. You, and your people, don't want to be found."

Two Panthers gave me an incredulous look. "You actually managed to take a *Kristiano* for a slave?"

"And learned a great many things, but we're wasting time. You need to find a place to hide, and we need to get around Ocale without being butchered."

Two Panthers gave me a dubious look, then squatted in the trail, outlining the routes we could take around Ocale. Pearl Hand and I bent down, listening intently as Two Panthers explained the landmarks, directions, and turns. In trade, I gave him the metal breastplate that had been awkwardly strapped to Bark's pack. The big gray dog wagged his tail, as if happy to be rid of the thing.

Two Panthers immediately buckled it about his wiry frame and preened before the awed eyes of his companions.

"Be careful," I called as we parted.

"Go with Power, Trader." And then they were gone, hurrying down the trail.

"Power had better be with him, too," Pearl Hand noted. "He'll be too busy polishing that metal to outrun any Kristianos."

"But he'll make a very pretty holata, assuming he is confirmed," I added as I took the trail. For the moment, it was a race between us getting out of the area and whether or not Antonio managed to stumble into Ocale and turn the countryside upside down.

For two days we played hawk and mouse with cabayo-mounted patrols, easily fading into the underbrush at the first sound of their clanking armor. Maybe it was Fetch's demise, or perhaps the dogs were getting used to the game, but they'd developed a particular growl at the approach of cabayos. Nor did they need reminding to keep quiet while we were hiding.

Whatever the fate of Antonio, he didn't catch up to us.

Past Ocale, the trail of the Kristianos was easy to follow. Not only did the cabayos and the passage of so many feet churn the trail into a wallow, but every now and then we passed a dead body, the hapless man or woman literally worked to death. From the tattoos we could tell if they were Uzita, Mocoso, Tocaste, or one of Irriparacoxi's. The ones who had been in the collars had had their heads cut off; the others had been finished with a sword stroke when they'd finally collapsed.

The flies would lift in angry black columns, only to resettle on the feast as we passed. As the days wore on we could mark the direction of travel by spirals of buzzards overhead, and the distance they had on us by the swelling of the rotting carcasses.

Pearl Hand stared at one, a young woman who had been cut down from behind with a sword stroke. The buzzards had been at the wound. She'd been so young she might not have even been out of the women's house.

"Even the meaning of death is changing," Pearl Hand remarked. "There are so many, and it has grown so common. We forget that she had a name, was someone's daughter. That she had dreams, hopes, and perhaps even looked forward to marrying a special boy."

"Now she's just another nameless corpse." With a foot I rolled her over, wincing at the bite marks on her young breasts and the bruises on her thighs, partially hidden by the rumpled skirt.

Pearl Hand said nothing, but a hardness lay behind her smoldering eyes.

Then the rains came. We trudged onward,

water pelting down to turn the trail into muck.

We passed through Itaraholata, Potano town, and Utinamocharro, trading off bits of Antonio's armor to the disorganized, broken, and dispirited survivors, most of whom had fled to the woods. By these means we were also able to keep track of the Kristianos' location, now more than four days ahead of us.

The town of Tapolaholata we found gutted — and upon the ground lay no less than forty viciously chopped and hacked bodies, all placed in a line. One of the shocked survivors told us the tale. His name was *Yabi,* which translates to "get well" in the Timucua tongue. He was a round-faced man with a broad mouth that almost split his head in two.

In between bouts of crying over his wife's and son's bodies, Yabi related the following: "Five days ago, a family of the White Bird Clan was harvesting its corn patch when out of the forest came cabayos with riders. The White Bird family — men, women, and children — were quickly surrounded. Only one young boy got away. He ran in terror to warn the town. Our chief, Tapolaholata, called a warning, telling the people to flee to the forest. Meanwhile scouts watched as the Kristianos led the White Bird captives, roped at the neck, into the palisade.

"How did we get our people back? Tapolaholata devised a plan. One young man, kin to the captives, offered to deceive the Kristianos. He donned the holata's hat and took his sacred staff, and walked boldly up to the palisade gate, calling on the Kristianos that *he* was chief, and if they would surrender his people, he would guide them and serve them.

"The Kristianos were happy with this arrangement, and released the other captives. That night the false holata, knowing the plan, told the Kristianos many things — anything, in fact, that seemed to make them happy.

"Meanwhile Tapolaholata gathered all of his warriors, and even the women. Just after dawn we assembled beyond the palisade, almost three hundred of us. The plan was that we would frighten the Kristianos with our numbers. That was when our brave false holata led this de Soto out, telling him that if he could speak to us, we would do his bidding. This young man was a strong and fast warrior, and when he led de Soto close to us, he used his chief's staff, and struck the guards accompanying him. Then he ran, and to our surprise, the Kristianos were not frightened. Instead they sent a terrible dog to chase the fleeing warrior down. At the same time they came charging at us."

Yabi slowly shook his head. "We ran, all of us, fleeing through the forest. But they just kept coming. I, myself, crawled under a rotting log, and one of their great cabayos leaped

315

over it, those hooves pounding the dirt before my eyes.

"I hid for almost two days, and when I came out and made my way back, the dead were laid out just like this." Yabi pointed with a trembling finger. "Look at them. Men and women, little children. All butchered like deer from a forest surround. So many of our people, and we didn't manage to kill a single one of them. Not one."

Yabi swallowed hard, eyes begging the question. "Are they Spirit demons? Perhaps filled with evil sorcery?"

"They might as well be," Pearl Hand said through gritted teeth, her pained eyes on the line of corpses.

Yabi rose on uncertain legs, and wobbled over to the shredded remains of a man. The corpse had been gutted, the severed head stuffed down into the pelvis, as though to look out through a gaping cavity that had been cored out of the anus.

"This was the false holata, the deceiver." Yabi sadly shook his head. "This was the bravest man I have ever known. I cannot say his name now, for it would anger his souls and bring me misfortune. But could I say it, I would do so with great pride. For he, truly, was the best of us."

Pearl Hand and I looked down the row of dead, now tended by a handful of relatives. Then out at what remained of the town. The buildings had been burned, the palisade pulled over, and the posts piled and set on fire. Tendrils of blue smoke still rose over the charred remains.

"Where are the rest of your people?" Pearl Hand asked. "The other survivors?"

Yabi — tears leaking from the corners of his eyes — raised his round face in despair. "They will not come back here." He pointed again to a smoldering ruin on a small rise. "That was the House of the Dead. Where the ghosts of our ancestors have dwelt among us since the beginning. For four days, as is our custom, we will tend the dead. Then we will carry them there, to the burned charnel house, and then we, too, will leave."

"To go where?" I asked.

"East," Yabi confided. "We have kin there. And, who knows? The Kristianos may come back."

"They may indeed," I replied, contemplating the line of corpses. "And there are even more Kristianos down south at Ocale. If what we know of their plans is correct, you will not want to be here when they arrive."

Nineteen

The people of Cholupaha, one of the Uzachile frontier towns, fared better. They had
received news of Tapaloholata's fate a day's
march to their south. The Cholupaha holata
ordered that his people pack what belongings
they could, and all fled to the forest. The
happy Kristianos had looted the granaries
and gorged themselves on fresh stores of
corn.

Just beyond Cholupaha, as we slogged
through the rain, we found a great bridge —
another wonder created by the Kristianos.
This one spanned the rain-swollen Black
Duck River, just a little over two bowshots
across. Pearl Hand and I stopped, marveling

at the sight. The thing was built of timbers and freshly split planks lashed over cross-pieces. The wood, so neatly cut by the *hierro* axes, gleamed in the rain. To surface the span, earth had been carried and poured over the planks. We walked out on the soil, marred by the passing of cabayos, and stared over the edges at the swirling waters below.

The dogs, tails wagging, glanced over, too, as if curious at what we were seeing. Squirm gave me a questioning look, his white blaze accenting his mystification at our preoccupation with water. I ran my finger over the cut marks left by the Kristiano axes, musing at how they reminded me of the work of a giant beaver.

On the trip down, I'd had to hire a canoe to carry me across. This time Pearl Hand, the dogs, and I walked across, feet dry but for the rain-slashed mud. Then we followed the trace into virgin forest.

And straight into more trouble than we wanted.

Crossing the river put us firmly in territory controlled by the great Holata Uzachile, the most powerful Timucuan chieftain in the north. Not only did Uzachile's resources allow a larger population, but only a unified chieftainship could hold off the powerful Apalachee to the west and the Mos'kogean nations to the north.

This was thickly forested land with low rolling hills. You must put yourself in that place: an old forest of walnut, great oaks, hickory, and gum trees, the sky literally roofed with arching branches high overhead. Beneath that lofty canopy, the ground is open, matted with leaves so deep the foot sinks at every step. The sensation conjured by the massive tree trunks, the hanging vines, and the semi-darkness is one mindful of the Underworld, where little light penetrates. Here, the soul perceives a sense of age and grandeur.

The forest, however, is anything but quiet, with birds singing, squirrels chattering, and the distant breeze in the treetops. Night or day, the ear is regaled with the whirring and clicking of insects.

That day, while rain hammered the high leaves, we followed the chopped trail left by de Soto on his march north. The way wound around the great boles of the trees, and large drops of water collected on the leaves high overhead, then fell with soft plops onto the leaf mat. Or louder spats when they hit us.

Because of the sound-deadening rain, we had no warning. The wet soil, thick with leaves, muffled the sound of the approaching cabayos. Sodden leather didn't creak, and the misty droplets of water falling from the leaves absorbed any clink of metal.

The riders were coming at a trot, and I happened to look up just as they saw me. We both shouted a warning at the same time.

My only thought was defense, dropping Fetch's pack, throwing off my quiver, and pulling out my bow. I managed to get it strung and grabbed up the quiver as I scuttled off behind the thick bole of a walnut.

The dogs were barking, burdened by their packs, and Pearl Hand had run the other way, stopping only long enough to step into the crossbow's foot loop and pull the string back with both hands.

Then the riders were upon us. I fished out an arrow, not taking time to see what it was, and drew. I aimed the blunt shaft of one of my bird points. Too late to switch. I drew down on the black-bearded rider thundering toward me. He had a lance in his left hand, a round shield strapped to the forearm. His right held the reins that controlled his cabayo.

We weren't more than ten paces apart when I released, having taken the center of his bearded chin for my target. I watched the blunt tip of my arrow impact just below his right eye. Then I ducked back behind the tree.

I swear to this day, I could feel the impact of his lance through the thick bole. Then came the cracking of wood, and he was past, right hand to his face. The cabayo — uncontrolled — raced off down the path.

I fished for another arrow; it was a hunting shaft tipped with keenly flaked white chert. I drew, stepping around the tree, seeing five cabayos milling, two others following after my first opponent.

"Oyé! Aquí!" I cried, wondering where Pearl Hand had gotten to. My pack dogs were nipping at the cabayos, and I saw Gnaw get kicked; he yelped, flew, and tumbled, bits of trade bursting from his pack.

No! Not my dogs!

At my shout, the men turned, sawing at the reins of their panicked cabayos. I waited, unwilling to pick a target from the melee. One man got control of his beast, guiding it in my direction.

A feeling of peace seemed to settle on me, the old control of countless years of practice firming my hold on the bow. This rider had lowered his lance, spurring his horse. Again I waited, watching him close the distance. At my release, I caught the momentary widening of his eyes, and he tried to jerk away. It was enough to save his life, but not enough to keep the arrow from entering his right cheek. The impact of it twisted his head and he dropped the lance, pawing at the feathered shaft lodged deeply in his face. His cabayo hammered on, and until I die I will hear those grunting explosions of hot breath as the animal passed.

Bending for another arrow, I heard a cry, and looked past my tree. One of the riders was shouting, *"Fuera! Ahora! Fuera!"*

They laid spurs to their animals, pelting on down the trail. I stared in disbelief. My final wounded rider, his left hand still clapped to the arrow sticking out of his face, had recovered control of his mount and went charging after them. Curses carried in the still forest air. The pack dogs, but for Gnaw, ran barking in pursuit.

"Pearl Hand? Are you all right?"

She emerged from behind her tree, looking shaken and disheveled. "I'm all right. You?"

"Fine." Taking time only to grab up some arrows, I ran for Gnaw, who was cowering in the trail, his tail between his legs. I knelt down, took him by the head, and stared into his frightened brown eyes. The other dogs came hobbling up, panting, tails lashing, as if in great victory.

I quickly stripped the pack, seeing where the muddy cabayo hoof had struck it. Then I ran my hands over Gnaw's ribs, relieved to find none broken, though he whined when I pressed.

Relieved, I sat there in the mud and hugged him close, feeling my panic subside. Only when he began to squirm did I let him loose and turn to the mess littering the forest floor. Most of my trade had spilled from the packs and lay scattered about. Bark's pack had slid around until it hung from his belly. Squirm, delight in his soft brown eyes, was almost out of his. Figures.

A broken lance was embedded in the walnut, the shaft nothing more than white splintered wood. Pearl Hand walked up, almost casually leaning on the crossbow. "I didn't kill him."

"Who?"

"The first one I shot. The armor stopped the arrow, but I think he'll be hurting. You? Get any?"

"My first arrow was a bird shaft. I hit him just under the eye."

"Ouch," Pearl Hand muttered. "And the second?"

"Ran it through the side of his face. It probably cut along the side of the skull and stopped when it hit the inside of the helmet."

"He'll have a most wondrous scar."

"If infection doesn't kill him. Why did they just leave?"

She shook her head, staring back down the trail. "The leader ordered them away. That's what *fuera* means. They don't usually back off from a fight. Unless they're on a special task for the *Adelantado*."

"Let's get the trade picked up." I petted Gnaw's gray hide a final time and pulled myself wearily to my feet. "I'd as soon get out of here. What if that's just the advance guard?"

"I don't think so. They'd have gone back to the main party." She glanced thoughtfully to the north. "Maybe now that they're in Uzachile, the *Adelantado* has found more than he bargained on?"

"Let's hope."

I fought the urge to shiver as I went about picking up bits of shell, small flats of copper, beads, skeins of buffalo wool, pieces of Antonio's armor, and pouches of medicine herbs.

"Whatever's happened up ahead, I'd like to know sooner rather than later," I added, making a hasty job of packing.

"Me, too." Pearl Hand was tying Squirm's pack on. "But I've got a problem."

"Outside of hunting the most dangerous men on earth, what might that be?" I picked up the dropped lance, inspecting it with a critical eye.

"The arrow I took out of Fetch, it had that funny metal tip. It punched right through that cabayero's armor. The ones we've made of stone? They just splinter."

I inspected the lance. The tip was small, and square in cross section. I thought it lacked a good cutting edge, but it had been built for tough penetration. "We have those little metal plates in Antonio's armor. Maybe we can fix that."

She nodded, giving Squirm a pat on the head. Then she looked down the trail where the cabayeros had fled. "I hope so. We're going to have to do better in the future."

Yes, we would. But we were alive, and we'd learned. In the coming days, we would be learning a lot more. By definition, the future is an unknown. Ahocalaquen town, however, lay just ahead.

There is a reason Breath Giver keeps the future hidden to all but an unlucky few.

TWENTY

The town of Ahocalaquen — which means "like tempting fruit" in Timucua — had been smart enough to evacuate, like its southern ally Cholupaha. In the beginning only two locals were caught by the advancing Kristianos. Those unlucky souls told the Kristianos where the already harvested corn had been hastily cached. At least half of the harvest still remained on the stalk, and numerous corn and squash fields surrounded the town.

Adelantado de Soto, however, didn't just pass through as he had done in the south. After finding plentiful corn, beans, and squash buried in pits and under house floors, his raiders located more in outlying farm-steads. He decided to rest his forces.

More or less.

For one thing, his slaves were wearing out, and many were dying under his lash. For another, those taken from Irriparacoxi had come to the conclusion that cooperating and willfully helping would earn them a release from the collars and heavy chains. Many, so freed, had now cast their lot with the Kris-tianos. Having been in their place, I could understand. So far, no one had been able to bloody the Kristianos in their relentless march. Surely such strength had to have something going for it. Those who converted to the *Dios-Jesucristo* god — however that worked — were given extra rations and got to drink out of the gold cup. In their minds it gave them some of the Kristianos' Spirit Power. But why anyone would want to die and go to an afterlife like the Kristianos craved was beyond me. So now they could look forward to spending eternity serving their brutal masters?

What joy!

Myself, I wanted to spend time with my ancestors telling stories around campfires in the night sky and socializing. I would meet legends from among my people. Learn from our greatest hopaye and minkos who had gone before. Later, my children, and their children, and so forth, would all arrive, and

I'd learn how things had worked out for them. They'd want to hear about my fight against the Kristianos, going to the Underworld, and meeting First Woman and Corn Woman. We'd all play with our dogs, hunt the spirits of deer, elk, and buffalo.

Was there really a choice here? Or was I missing something important about the Kristianos?

A hand's time after the attack, Pearl Hand and I were traveling a couple of bowshots off the main trail. We kept just close enough to follow the trail, but back so that we could easily hide should more cabayeros come charging out of the gloom.

Skipper was the first to stop short, sniffing and growling, his ears pricked. Squirm and Gnaw immediately froze, wary. Bark — being as dim as the forest gloom we traveled through — slowed, growling himself, but unsure why.

"Greetings!" I called in Timucua. "I am Black Shell, of the Chicaza. I come under the Power of trade."

Silence.

I glanced around, head cocked. Pearl Hand slipped a toe into the crossbow loop, muscling the string to the latch.

I held out a warning hand before she dropped a stone-tipped arrow into the weapon's channel.

"I repeat: we come under the Power of trade."

Bark lived up to his namesake, and I gestured him to silence.

"From where?" an unexpected voice called.

"From the south."

"And what have you seen there?"

"Death . . . and too many Kristianos."

I caught movement, forms shifting from behind the trees.

"Then why are you following in their tracks and carrying their weapons?"

"Plunder from fights we've had with them. Perhaps we can use such weapons against them. Nothing else seems to penetrate that armor of theirs."

A man seemed to detach himself from a tree. I ordered the dogs to stay and walked forward. Bark tried to follow, growling. He was still in the mood to fight. Pearl Hand bent down and whacked him across the nose to get his attention. He gave her a surprised look, then meekly dropped to his belly.

The warrior was of medium height and stocky, tattooed with stars and zigzag lines, the sides of his head shaven. A central roach of hair was pulled up and tied like a pom. Red paint had been liberally applied to his square face. Despite the wet day he wore only a breech-cloth. Hard black eyes met mine, and I noticed that while his bow was lowered, it could be pulled back and released quickly.

"I have heard of Black Shell of the Chicaza. He came through our lands several moons ago." He gave a slight tilt of the head. "And the woman?"

"My wife, Pearl Hand." I indicated the dogs. "As you can see, they are pack animals. These days my trader's staff rides in my quiver. A bow, it seems, is the only badge of office the Kristianos respect. They are without honor."

For the first time he nodded, then made a signal. Warriors appeared from all directions, perhaps ten in all. "Lucky for you the Holata Uzachile and his people honor the Power of trade."

I took a deep breath, slightly relieved. "We had a fight with eight cabayeros a ways down the trail. They seemed to be in a hurry."

"The Kristiano chief sent them south this morning. Perhaps he wanted to save their lives? They won't be here when we kill the rest."

"Perhaps." I shifted my packs. "You have my name. I do not have yours."

"Blood Thorn. I am iniha of the Fish Clan, of the Uzachile Nation. I am the first son of Bit Woman, wife of Paracusi Eagle Fighter, war leader of Ahocalaquen. I am received in the Utina council of Holata Uzachile."

Iniha meant a subchief — and not just any subchief since he sat in council at Uzachile, the capital city off to the west. Beyond that,

331

his mother was married to the war chief, or *paracusi,* of Ahocalaquen town.

"Where are the Kristianos?" Pearl Hand asked.

Blood Thorn jerked his head toward the north. "They sit in Ahocalaquen, behind the palisade." His expression turned grim. "Through treachery they have taken our holata. Initially his niece was taken captive. Our holata went to meet with the Kristianos, promising to surrender his freedom for that of his niece and some of our people taken captive with her. The Kristianos agreed, but when Holata Ahocalaquen surrendered himself, they kept him and refused to let the others leave." He spat his disgust. "They are maggot men without honor, and their given word is no more sacred than dog shit."

Pearl Hand asked, "So they just stay in the fortified town?"

"No. They send out parties of cabayeros each day to raid. To stop this, only this morning we gathered in force — three hundred warriors in six squadrons — hoping to engage them in a great battle and destroy them." He snorted in disgust. "The cowards stayed behind the palisade. After a couple hands of time, eight riders burst out and fled. Like I said, we think they wished to save their lives."

"Oh, no," I told him seriously. "Just the opposite, Blood Thorn. To the south, in Ocale, are another eight hundred Kristianos. And

332

you can bet that as soon as those riders reach them, they'll be on their way here."

He gave me a hard-eyed look. "You know this?"

"We know this."

He glanced at Pearl Hand, who stood easily, almost arrogantly, her crossbow lowered but ready at hand. His very male inspection of her tall body ended at her defiant eyes, as if she dared him to say something.

To his credit, he gave her a slight nod, saying, "Perhaps you should come with us."

We followed him for a hand of time through what would have been trackless forest for me.

I figured we were getting close when Blood Thorn nodded to a warrior with a strung bow who hid in the root cavity of an old deadfall. Then, a couple of bowshots farther, we followed a trail through honeysuckle, myrtle, and greenbriar into a small clearing in the trees. There, perhaps three hundred men, women, and children waited in the misty rain.

Impromptu shelters had been raised, and the grass was beaten flat. Under a shaky ramada roofed with branches, several men and three women crouched. They were older — perhaps forty summers of age — each painted for war. The men wore their hair in the same fashion as Blood Thorn.

People watched us pass, pointing and talking under their hands as Blood Thorn led us to the ramada and announced our presence

in the flowery oratory of the Western Timucua. Then he told of our fight with the eight
cabayeros, and said that we brought information on the Kristianos.

One of the men stood, a wiry specimen, his
broad face painted red. Old scars crisscrossed
his hands, forearms, and shoulders. He
studied me, then Pearl Hand, smiling in a
way that irritated me as he took in the damp
dress clinging to her curves.

The man turned his attention back to me.
"I am Eagle Fighter, paracusi of the Ahocalaquen." Then he recounted his clan and
lineage, told stories of the battles he'd fought,
and finally offered his hand. The gesture was
that of a potential ally given to another.

I gripped his hand and nodded, saying, "We
thank you for your welcome, but wish it were
under different circumstances. We come from
the south, following the trail of the Kristianos."

"Then, as we call upon the blessing of
Mother Sun, our ancestors, and spirits,
perhaps you shall be here when we kill them
to the last man."

Pearl Hand softly said, "You will need more
than Spirit Power, Paracusi. We have followed
a trail of misery and death to reach this
place."

One of the women stood. "I am Bit Woman,
of the Fish Clan, daughter of White Fruit,
cousin of Holata Ahocalaquen, who is captive

in his own town. You raise my curiosity, Pearl Hand, of the Chicora. The warriors of the Uzachile Nation are nothing like those disorganized towns in the south. We have fought the Apalachee, and beaten them, sent their warriors scurrying home amid the wailing of widows and the crying of fatherless children. The Kristianos have seen nothing of the art of war. Our ancestors now rally, bringing Power from the realms of the dead. Our call for warriors has only now reached the outlying villages. Soon there shall be five hundred men and women, all ready to wreak our vengeance on the Kristianos, their dogs and cabayos. We have more than Spirit Power, we have the beating courage of our hearts."

"It won't be enough," Pearl Hand said in a respectful tone.

Eagle Fighter burst into laughter. "Oh, yes it will. We weren't prepared when they arrived. Only this morning we appeared in force. Unlike in the south, they saw disciplined ranks of warriors all marching in formation. They refused to fight, hiding behind the palisades. We might have taken them, but thought it better to await the arrival of kin and greater force."

I nodded appreciatively but said, "Those eight riders this morning? The ones that broke out? We met them on the trail. While we wounded three, they could have killed us both. Instead they were bent on making their way south. The reason is, yes, you did frighten the Kristianos. By riding their cabayos hard, those riders will reach Ocale tomorrow night. When they do, the main force will start north. With forced marches, they will arrive within the next six days."

"How many of them?" Bit Woman asked.

Pearl Hand said flatly, "Around eight hundred Kristianos and as many as five hundred captives who bear their equipment."

"Over a thousand?" Eagle Fighter asked incredulously.

I nodded. "All armored and looking for battle."

Bit Woman began to look worried, glancing uneasily at Eagle Fighter. "This is unforeseen."

"We must strike now," one of the other men said. He stood, crossing his arms. "Holata Ahocalaquen and the rest must take their chances. If we destroy the ninety here, we can ambush the trail as the others arrive. At the bridge they have built, we can gather and kill them as they try to cross."

"Don't," Pearl Hand and I said together.

"Why?" Bit Woman asked, skepticism in her eyes.

Pearl Hand stepped forward, grounding her crossbow. "Even with five hundred, you will not destroy all of the Kristianos in Ahocalaquen."

I added, "I have seen them survive terrible

ambushes, only to turn and destroy the attackers."

"Those were southerners." Eagle Fighter made a dismissive gesture with his hand. "Part-time warriors who would rather hunt. What do they know of war?"

"I am Chicaza," I replied evenly. "I know a great deal of war. I was trained to it. Among all Nations, the military might of the Chicaza is spoken of with awe. Believe me, if you attack the Kristianos head-on, you will lose."

Blood Thorn seemed to swell with indignation, as if we had attacked his very manhood. "And *you* know this, Trader?"

"Pearl Hand and I passed through the Tapolaholata, who also know how to fight. They attacked with three hundred warriors to free some of their captives. The Kristianos broke their formation and butchered nearly forty. Fortunately, the Tapolaholata were close to a forest and most managed to flee. The Kristianos then mutilated the bodies of the dead, laid them out like flayed fish, and destroyed the town. According to witnesses we talked with, not a single Kristiano died."

I looked into Blood Thorn's eyes. "Do you understand? Three hundred attacked, forty died, the captives remained in chains, and *not one Kristiano was killed.*"

"You are sure of this?" Eagle Fighter asked.

"On the Power of trade, I so swear." Beside me, Pearl Hand nodded.

"Then what?" the second old man asked belligerently. "Do you counsel us to just give up?"

"Crane asks a good question," Eagle Fighter added, nodding at the man. "Are you just here to dissuade us? Is that your intention?"

"No," Pearl Hand said adamantly. "Not to dissuade you . . . just to ask you to understand their strength. Harass them, grind away at them. Sneak close at night and kill their cabayos. Pick them off one by one through clever traps."

"There is no honor in that," Bit Woman scoffed. "We will place our trust in the goodwill of the Spirits and our ancestors, and in the strong hearts of our warriors. We are a pious people. Power will protect us."

The others were nodding, minds made up. I could see it in their eyes.

"The Kristianos are arrogant," Crane growled. "They do not honor the ways of war. Holata Ahocalaquen went to them to ask for the release of his daughter. They agreed, and then they went back on their word and *took* him. Like weasels, they made a mockery of honor. They are nothing more than filth on two feet. But for the safety of our captives, we would have destroyed them this morning."

I glanced at Pearl Hand. Kristianos, it seemed, had no exclusive claim to arrogance. There was more than enough of that to go around. What the Kristianos did have was the ability to steep their arrogance in the blood of others.

TWENTY-ONE

Pearl Hand and I made camp back in the trees where better protection from the rain could be had. Eagle Fighter had ordered that no fires be set. It made sense since the smell of smoke would have drawn the Kristianos had any cabayo patrols been about.

We put together a small lean-to — just enough to shelter us from a drenching should the dark skies open again. Our meal consisted of dried palm-heart cakes seasoned with elderberry and myrtle berries. The dogs shared a short meal of bear grease and dried fish that we'd looted from Cholupaha. The Kristianos apparently hadn't wanted it.

I asked. "Do you think the Uzachile heard

a single word we said? They're leaning toward war."

"They don't know what they are up against," Pearl Hand insisted for the fifth time. "Fools! Why won't they listen?"

"Did I?" I asked glumly.

She gave me a secret smile, ironically amused. "No, my love. But you learned."

"It would have been at the price of my life, but for you," I said, enjoying the way the firelight played in the hollows of her cheeks. I sighed at my luck and added, "It's just that the Kristianos are beyond belief. Nothing in our world has prepared us for the likes of them. They exist outside the conventions of men, knowing no bounds of proper behavior."

"They come from another world." She shivered slightly. "Blessed Spirits, what a terrible place it must be."

"No wonder they want our land. Even that *paraíso* Antonio was talking about sounds liked a grim place. After a couple of days here, who'd want to go back to this *España?*"

We glanced up as Blood Thorn approached and squatted; the muscles in his legs bulged, and he seemed hesitant. He took time to pet the dogs, which immediately raised him in my esteem.

"The council didn't end as you expected?" he asked softly, then grinned as he found Gnaw's favorite scratch place.

"We just know," Pearl Hand said woodenly.

"We've seen. That your council does not . . . well, perhaps it is only to be expected." Then she added, "Could we offer you a palm cake? We don't have much, but you are welcome to one."

"I would appreciate that." He took the cake, bit into it, and nodded. "Good. Thank you."

"Your people must think we're crazy," I added. "Here we come . . . strangers bearing what seem to be unbelievable tales of Kristiano invincibility."

Chewing, he said, "Any force can be defeated in battle."

"The Kristianos, too," I agreed, "but not by traditional means. They have changed the rules. Beneath their armor, and behind their weapons, they are only men. It's getting to the men beneath that makes the problem thorny."

"Tell me your story," he said. "Start at the beginning."

So Pearl Hand and I did. To his credit, he just listened, never displaying disbelief by even so much as a squinted eye. Instead he took it all in, considering everything we said.

"This is the armor we took from one." I showed him the metal helmet, the undercoat of cloth-covered metal plates, and the lance.

Finally, when we finished, he picked up the undercoat and asked, "This will really stop an arrow?"

"Even one driven from a Mos'kogee war

342

bow, like mine. We had a breastplate for a while. I shot it, and the impact only left a little dimple, like driving your thumb into hardening clay. It was a bother to carry so we traded it down south."

He glanced curiously at us. "Would you come with me? Spy on the Kristianos? Perhaps you could tell me what I'm seeing."

I glanced at Pearl Hand, who answered with that questioning arch of an eyebrow. I slapped my knees, saying, "Of course. But if we see any of them scouting with their war dogs, we've got to run. Fast."

We collected our weapons, commanded the dogs to stay, and followed Blood Thorn through the thickest of forest, following trails through brush, and finally, at his signal, crawled through a tunnel-like maze of grape, greenbriar, and honeysuckle.

"The children play here," he whispered as he elbowed up to a screen of greenery.

I looked around nervously at the incredible web of roots, stems, and vines. There would be no quick escape. I suddenly felt like a mouse in the bottom of a basket.

We elbowed along like snakes through the maze. I hadn't crawled like that in years. Finally we parted the leaves and could see the town. Before us was a patchwork of squash and bean fields. Ahocalaquen — perhaps five bowshots beyond — consisted of a ditch and palisade on the perimeter. The top of a burial mound could be seen protruding, along with the roof of a large council house. Through gaps in the palisade posts, we could discern houses, a temple, and a charnel house. Thankfully far away, across the cornfields, I could see the herd of cabayos, guarded by no less than ten riders. The gate was defended by another fifteen or twenty men on foot, the total difficult to determine as they kept coming and going. Other sentinels had been placed on platforms behind the palisade, all with eyes on the forest. Two groups of captives, each guarded by a Kristiano with a war dog, worked the cornfields, picking ears that they placed in large baskets.

"What are the sticks they carry?" Blood Thorn asked.

"Thunder sticks," Pearl Hand whispered. "They shoot a ball of lead that will penetrate a shield and the man behind it. In battle the thunder sticks are always protected."

"If we tried to rush the palisade from all sides, what would they do?"

I thought about that. "I think they would mass swordsmen and those long spear-axes at the gates. Crossbows and thunder sticks would shoot from between the palisade posts, moving around the perimeter anywhere a threat developed. Any of your arrows that made it through would be stopped cold by their armor."

I pointed at the cabayos. "Meanwhile the cabayeros, in full armor, would ride around in mass, crushing any formations before them. The riders carry deadly metal-tipped lances — like the one I showed you. They use swords the way you might use a sickle to mow down grass for thatch. The dogs will be working in conjunction with the cabayos, inciting panic, leaping among warriors you are trying to control. Once your formation breaks — and it will break — no one can outrun the cabayos. Anyone fleeing will be cut down from behind or knocked flat by the cabayo."

"But they can be shot off the cabayos with arrows, can't they?"

"Only if you hit them in the face." I made a gesture of futility. "Anywhere else and the arrow shatters on their armor. Think of throwing a cactus thorn at a turtle. The effect is exactly the same."

"You're not exactly inspiring me." Blood Thorn took a deep breath.

"Actually, I hope we are," Pearl Hand said. "Inspiring you *not* to try a frontal assault."

"Our warriors are proven," Blood Thorn insisted. "And the Kristianos have our holata through treachery. Knowing that will stiffen our resolve."

"Listen to me," Pearl Hand pleaded. "Hear my words, and take them to heart. It's not about the courage of your warriors. Yes, they are proven, but against the Apalachee and the Potano. People who fight like we do. Your warriors have never had to stand before a massed charge of cabayos. Or face men who shoot thunder sticks with fire and lightning."

I added, "If one hundred of your warriors close and shoot at one hundred Apalachee, ten or fifteen will be wounded in the first volley. If you shoot at one hundred Kristianos, maybe one will have to retire from a lucky hit. Think of the turtle and cactus thorn. The difference is that the Kristianos, unlike the Apalachee, will laugh off the attack as a mere annoyance. They'll just keep coming."

"And," Pearl Hand added, "their crossbow arrows will penetrate your wicker and wood shields and still go through a warrior's body."

Blood Thorn's jaw was working as he watched the Kristianos. "My holata . . . and his niece, Water Frond . . . are in there."

Even as he spoke a mounted patrol emerged from the forest trail, four captives, roped at the neck, following behind. We watched as they plodded toward the gate to cries of greeting. Riders dismounted, clapping hands together, chattering about the new slaves they had taken.

"But some have been killed in the south?" Blood Thorn asked hopefully.

"By ones and twos," Pearl Hand replied. "Warriors have sneaked close enough to drive an arrow into a head or neck, or under an armpit. Sometimes it is done at night, sneak-

346

ing up to a village and shooting a man as he defecates, or in the early morning before he puts on his armor." She paused. "As Black Shell says, they're just men underneath."

"One or two at a time," Blood Thorn whispered, as if to himself. "And you say there are almost a thousand of them? That could take years."

"Perhaps," I said longingly. "But it might be the only way we can finally win in the end."

TWENTY-TWO

For three days we camped, did a little trade, and managed to hunt enough to keep the dogs fed. Meanwhile, warriors and subchiefs came by, asking questions about the Kristianos, inspecting what was left of the armor. While we were not invited to the councils, no attack had been made.

Which is not to say that there wasn't skirmishing. Mounted patrols were shot at from ambush, and at least one war dog was killed. When the cabayeros crashed into the brush in pursuit, it was generally to find their elusive enemy had slipped away. If it did nothing else, it proved our claims about Kristiano armor were not fantasies.

Blood Thorn arrived just before dark on

the fourth day. He looked tired, but offered a couple of ducks a hunter had managed to down with bird arrows.

"Eagle Fighter has decided a few fires can be built with the coming of dusk," Blood Thorn said by way of greeting. Then he proceeded to pet the dogs, who were more interested in the ducks. "He asks that you cook and then cover your fire quickly so no smoke is in the air by morning. Enough warriors have arrived from the surrounding towns to provide a screen. We'll have plenty of warning should the Kristianos come this way."

I immediately set about plucking, asking, "And what is the news?"

Blood Thorn smiled. "Lest you think your words were in vain, the council has decided not to try a massed attack. Some of the other holata and paracusi have come in. You were right about the armor. We haven't managed to kill a single Kristiano. Either the arrows bounce off, or just the point sticks in their armor." He shook his head. "The turtle and the cactus thorn."

"What else was said?" Pearl Hand asked, using her metal knife to lever up the soft soil for a fire pit.

"Confusion," Blood Thorn admitted. "Some call for war, others think there must be a way to solve this. They want to send a delegation to the Kristianos in an attempt to

349

speak with Holata Ahocalaquen. I have offered to go with them."

I shook my head, rubbing duck feathers on the leaf mat. "Look what happened when your holata went to free his niece."

Blood Thorn smiled wistfully. "His sister's daughter."

"Yes," I agreed. "I understand your people trace descent through the mother as do mine." A man's responsibility was to his sister's children. His wife's children were of another clan, and while a father might be solicitous, decisions about their upbringing were none of his concern.

Blood Thorn gestured his frustration. "It's as if we can do nothing. They cannot bring the fight to us; we cannot take it to them. We just sit. Meanwhile, people slip away to hunt, collect berries, and fill their stomachs, and by ones and twos they are captured. The Kristianos wait inside our palisade and eat our corn and squash as it ripens. The whole thing is maddening."

"But better than dying . . . or worse, wearing one of their collars." I pointed to the fading red scars that would mark my neck forever.

"Some of their captives from down south have managed to escape when the Kristianos weren't looking. Our scouts picked them up and brought them in," Blood Thorn offered. "The chiefs questioned them for a day and then let them go. Those people just want to go home and see what's left."

"What did you learn?" Pearl Hand asked.

"That the Kristianos are waiting. Some riders came in yesterday on mud-spattered cabayos." He glanced at us. "You were right: The others are on the way. When they arrive, matters will only be worse."

"They can't stay forever," I remarked. "Once they've eaten everything — and with the majority of them coming up from the south, that will be sooner rather than later — they've got to go on and raid the Apalachee, or head north."

"Not back south?" he wondered. "You have told me they come in search of gold. We certainly don't have any here."

"They've already eaten everything in the south," Pearl Hand snorted in derision. "That or they will have to climb aboard their boats and sail back across the seas. Without wealth, the *Adelantado* would return to his people as a failure."

Pearl Hand placed kindling in the fire pit, then searched one of the packs for the fire bow and the little oiled pouch that held charred grass for starter.

"If there's wealth," Blood Thorn admitted, "we don't have it. There's gold up north, isn't there?"

"Little nuggets," I replied. "All the gold I've ever seen up north wouldn't make the rim on that cup I saw them drinking from. Generally when someone finds a gold nugget, they toss it back in the creek. It's useless."

"What filled Kristianos with such nonsense?"

"Somewhere to the distant south, across the sea, they found gold. Lots of it. Now they want more," Pearl Hand replied as she began sawing the small fire bow back and forth, spinning a hardwood dowel in its block. Smoke began to rise and she nudged some of the charred grass into the grooved base. When it began to smolder, she skillfully dumped it into the tinder and blew. A tiny flame rose.

As Pearl Hand fed twigs to the fire, I finished plucking the first duck and started on the second. A silver thread of drool leaked from the side of Skipper's mouth as he waited for a taste.

"What of you, Blood Thorn? Why are you here, sharing our fire, instead of at your wife's?"

"Not married." He made a gesture with his hand. "Not yet, anyway." He looked longingly off into the forest. "Water Frond is just coming of age."

"Water Frond?" I asked. "Your holata's niece?"

"I've been in love with her for years. Although the marriage will be in part political, neither she nor I would wish to have any other. She's Panther Clan. It is expected that we will marry. We would have, a couple of days ago, had the Kristianos not come. She just passed her initiation into the women's house."

I finished the second duck as the fire began to crackle and wiped my fingers clean. Then I reached into one of the packs, recovering a fine white shell, already drilled for suspension from a string. I handed it to Blood Thorn. "Here. Our gift to you for your marriage. Think of us when you wear it."

He took the piece, admiring it in the growing firelight. "I thank you. I shall string it from a beaded thong. It will be hanging from my neck when I take Water Frond as my wife, and after we are wed, I shall insist that she wear it."

And then a gloomy look expressed itself. "I hope."

"Hope?" Pearl Hand asked, taking the ducks and using a sharp piece of chert to gut them.

Blood Thorn shrugged. "Even as we speak she's in there." He nodded in the direction of the occupied town.

I nodded, understanding now why Blood Thorn was so desperate to be part of the delegation sent to see their chief.

After we had finished the ducks, Blood Thorn disappeared into the darkness, seeking his own bed. I walked the dogs, allowing them to evacuate away from camp, and returned to find our fire smothered and Pearl Hand awaiting me in the blankets.

I slipped out of my breechcloth and snuggled in beside her warm body.

"He really loves her," she said as she hugged me close. "He tried to hide it, but you could see it deep down in his eyes. Maybe that's why he's here so often, hoping that maybe some clue about how to free her can be found."

"We haven't told him what Kristianos do with the women they capture."

"And we shouldn't." She paused. "But as she's the chief's niece, perhaps the Kristianos have held back. It wouldn't do to deflower a virgin of such status when doing so could bring down the wrath of an entire nation."

"Do you really think the Kristianos fear the Uzachile nation?"

"Maybe for the moment they are acting with caution. But the main body of their force is still in the south."

"And if the *Adelantado* or one of his subchiefs has taken the girl?"

"That depends." She tightened her hold on me. "Timucua don't have the same concerns about a woman's virginity that you Chicaza do, but I think it would drive Blood Thorn into a rage if she was being handed about like a slave to warm just any man's shaft."

I nodded. "If that's the case, it could be the

354

spark that sets this whole mess on fire."

I felt her sigh. "Perhaps. Let us just hope that you and I don't get burned." She paused. "With all that's wrong in our world, with misery lurking behind every bush, I want to live for tonight as if all was well."

"And your meaning is . . . what?"

"We fight corrupted Power with good, or healing Power. Perhaps by just loving each other, we can cure some of the pain. We need to make the best of now, my love," she whispered as she straddled my body and slid onto my willing shaft.

Twenty-Three

When news of the Kristiano reinforcements came, Blood Thorn took us to the secret warren of tunnels that led through the maze of briars. Once again we crawled on our hands and knees to a place where we could see. There, peeking through the leaves, we watched as *Adelantado* de Soto's long army marched into Ahocalaquen.

Clumps of weary riders on sweat-soaked cabayos came first, emerging from the forest to our right. In their wake followed columns of footsore *soldados,* each group with their particular weapons: thunder sticks, crossbows, the long hatchetlike spears, and finally swords.

Interspersed between the groups staggered

long lines of slaves taken from the south. Many of these stumbled, and I winced as whip-wielding guards laid into some and turned the dogs loose on others. These were men, women, and older children, all naked, sweaty, and streaked with mud and grime. Many carried regular packs, others manhandled the awkward chairs, tables, pieces of the curious metal contraption for working iron, and other oddities, the purpose of which still eluded me.

One older woman tripped, spilling her load and dragging down the others chained to her collar. It took a moment to recognize her: Sabal, mother of Two Panthers, wife of the Ocale holata. The woman who had made such excellent food for me many moons back.

The guard was so infuriated, seeing the palisaded walls of his destination, that he didn't bother whipping Sabal. He just walked up and, with several strikes of his sword, cut her head off. Then he bellowed for the rest of the group to take up her burden along with their own and used the flat of his sword to keep them moving.

I stared, dumbfounded. Two Panthers's words came back: *If you should run across her . . . tell her we will be waiting.*

Two Panthers would wait a very long time.

At the palisade, a formation of Kristianos marched out and a curious horn sounded. A ragged shout rose from the line of newcomers as they continued to emerge from the forest — an obscene vomit of men and animals.

Colorful flags were unfurled and the *Adelantado*'s men from Ahocalaquen formed lines, weapons raised high, to welcome the newcomers as they plodded wearily forward. Just before the first arrived, the thunder sticks were raised, and a popping crackle could be heard as puffs of blue smoke shot toward the heavens.

How long did the procession take? Perhaps not a finger of time; it only seemed an eternity.

I watched as the bumping and snuffling horde of *puercos* brought up the rear. They seemed to ebb and flow, trotting ahead in their bouncy gait, ears flopping. The beasts immediately went to rooting around in the picked-over squash fields. Fortunately, they missed Sabal's body for the moment.

When the last had entered the gates, Ahocalaquen looked full to bursting. Then, by groups of ten, the weary cabayos — stripped of their equipment — were led out by young men in armor. We watched in amazement as the animals immediately began to roll in the cropped grass, as if to rid themselves of their master's scent the way a dog did. Then they would stand, legs apart, and shake.

Whistles, shouts, and the sound of revelry carried across the grass and the denuded corn and squash fields. No one tended the body of poor Sabal.

"So that is that," Blood Thorn said softly. "Now we must send a delegation to ask for the relief of our holata and the rest. But what will the price be?"

Pearl Hand said, "I heard that he needs people to carry the supplies." She gestured at the forlorn body no more than four bowshots from where we hid. "The *Adelantado* seems to be going through his at a furious pace."

"Do you think so?" Blood Thorn hissed passionately.

I glanced at him. "My friend, what I think is that you and your council have a decision to make. What is the ultimate value of your holata and the rest? What are you willing to endure for him?"

"For Water Frond, anything." Blood Thorn clenched a fist as a sign of his resolve. Then he shook his head. "I don't know. Seeing this, the number of them . . . Perhaps . . . perhaps if we accommodate them, carry their packs beyond our territory, they will free our people and leave us in peace."

"Perhaps," Pearl Hand agreed, without conviction.

We stayed for a hand of time, watching. The only activity was a line of slaves, chained at the neck, who were sent out under guard. They carried curious curved knives on the end of sticks almost as long as their bodies. These were put to work, swinging the odd blades into the grass. Only when I saw others gathering up the cut grass did I understand that this was a new, much more efficient-looking sickle. The line of cutters moved slowly across the distant grass, bundle after bundle being carried to the hungry cabayos.

When we had finally wiggled out of the briar tunnels, Blood Thorn had a somber look on his face. As we trotted back for the camps, his shoulders slumped.

We weren't the only ones, of course. Warriors had been hidden all along the route, watching from the shadows. That night they held a sober and cheerless meeting. Talk around the evening fires was low, and not once did we hear laughter.

Later, in our blankets, Pearl Hand asked, "What do you think the Uzachile will do?"

"I don't know," I told her as I held her hand, running my thumb over the back of hers. "Their decision now can only go two ways: They can do what the Kristianos demand, or refuse. One way they may save their chief and perhaps Blood Thorn's future wife. On the other, they may only save themselves."

"You don't think they'll try an attack?"

"Not anymore." I remembered the events of the day. "Not against so many." I paused. "Seeing the thunder sticks shoot wasn't very scary."

"Only because you weren't standing in front of them."

"How can loud popping and smoke be that dangerous?"

She heard the tone in my voice, propping herself on one elbow. "Listen to me. Don't act like the fool you were down at Uzita. Trust me on this. If you ever see a thunder stick pointed at you, run! Promise me that."

I heard the tone in her voice, too. "I give you my word."

"Good," she said softly, and lay back. "I have come to love you too much. Standing over your dead body would be like having my heart torn out of my chest."

"I'll be careful."

"Yes, you will. After all, it's not our fight."

But somehow, we managed to forget that.

For four days nothing happened. The skies poured rain. Making a fire at night was a chore. Wood collected from ever farther away had to be whittled to obtain dry shavings for tinder, and even when lit, it smoked and burned poorly.

The Timucua, like most people, didn't conduct either peace or war efforts in the rain. Ceremony had to be attended to for each endeavor, which meant dressing up, painting faces, and donning bright feathers, caped headdresses, and other fine regalia. One couldn't cut a dashing figure when even the finest grease-based paint was melting down one's cheeks and chin to drip onto one's chest. Nor did the brightest of feathers have the same impact when wilting around one's ears.

The Timucua had also adopted the curious affectation of preceding peace delegations with an offering of deer meat. Just prior to the arrival of the main Kristiano army, four — the sacred number — deer had been procured. Given the interruption, and then the rain, the deer ended up digesting in Timucua guts. As more were procured, and the rain continued, they, too, vanished into empty bellies. After all, one didn't offer spoiled, maggot-infested meat as a peace offering. Doing so just didn't create the right frame of mind among the recipients.

In addition, the proper rituals had to be attended to, including the appropriate prayers to solicit aid from the Spirit Powers and the ancestors. Black drink had to be brewed, the pipe had to be smoked, and the delegates ritually cleansed in smoke. All difficult in a downpour.

Lastly, like so many peoples, the Timucua had for generations played flutes to alert the other party that they came in peace. Such flutes were exquisitely crafted from hardwoods, the holes carefully drilled, and the final result blessed by proper ritual. In the current conditions they would produce more bubbles than fine music.

Don't think I'm being sarcastic. All the

peoples I was familiar with indulged in such preparations. My own Chicaza have stunningly elaborate ritual preparations for war and peace that are equally as cumbersome. It's just that after having traveled so much, and seen so many different approaches to propitiate such a variety of Spirits and deities, I wasn't sure that just barging in and shouting, "Hey, let's quit fighting!" wasn't equally as productive.

But then, most other people weren't outcast *akeohoosa*. So maybe I'm not the proper authority on such matters.

When the rain finally let up, Pearl Hand and I joined the collection around the council ramada, noticing that it had been remodeled with a much more substantial roof. Eagle Fighter, Bit Woman, and Crane were there, of course, as were a whole host of new people. Warriors had been trickling in during the lull in activity, and the camp looked like a small town, with lean-tos, and even some partial houses constructed. I'd estimate that at least six hundred had come to hear the deliberations.

Pearl Hand and I were standing at the rear when Blood Thorn found us and dragged us forward to the front row. He displaced a couple of grizzled-looking warriors and insisted that we sit.

The resulting reshuffling, due to status, war honors, kin affiliation, and so forth, caused no little consternation but was finally resolved.

Eagle Fighter called the invocation, prayers were offered, the pipe was smoked, and black drink was provided. Then the various iniha and paracusi elaborated on the problem of getting Holata Ahocalaquen away from the Kristianos. The new paracusi called for war; the various holata from surrounding towns called for negotiation. Eagle Fighter and Bit Woman argued that any mistake could be deadly for their captives.

Iniha Blue Sun Stone, a delegate from Holata Uzachile — their paramount chief — rose. Eagle Fighter gave him the speaker's staff, a length of wood painted blue and topped with mockingbird feathers. He was a tall and handsome man, with a serious expression that lent gravity to his straight posture and lanky frame.

Blue Sun Stone looked out at the crowd. "I come bearing the words of the great Holata Uzachile. He has heard of the treachery committed by the Kristianos.

"Know, however, that strangers can make mistakes when coming into a new land. Holata Uzachile, understanding that they may be unfamiliar with our ways, advises that we approach the Kristianos in peace. That we explain our ways to them and allow them to make restitution."

Grumbles rose from the Ahocalaquen warriors around us.

"Wait!" Blue Sun Stone cried. "Hear the words of the Great Holata. He asks you to entertain another consideration. If the Kristianos can be made into allies, they might be persuaded to join us."

Mutters of amazement could be heard.

"Oh, sure," I muttered. Pearl Hand had a look of incredulity.

"Were we to ally with the Kristianos, we could strike our ancient enemies, the Apalachee, a terrible blow. In gratitude, we could bestow Apalachee lands upon the Kristianos. It is good country, and they would do well farming fields now farmed by the Apalachee."

I shook my head in disbelief.

"Invite a pack of cougars to live just across the border?" Pearl Hand wondered. "Is this idiocy, or what?"

Blue Sun Stone raised the speaker's staff, reminding his audience he had the floor. "Let the Kristianos provide the buffer between us and the Koasati, Pensacola, Apalachee, Mos'kogee, and Albaamaha. In return, we will have access to their trade in wonderful weapons, looking glasses, and remarkable metals."

I slumped. It was the same old ploy that I had heard in so many places, so many times. Among the Nations, it actually worked on occasion, for a while, until something set someone off.

"The Kristianos are different," Blood Thorn said respectfully. "What does the Holata Uzachile say if they refuse?"

Blue Sun Stone nodded. "The Great Holata has hopes that we can accomplish his wishes. He also understands that with strangers, they may need some, shall we say, incentive? Holata Uzachile is no fool."

"Want to gamble on that?" Pearl Hand whispered drily.

Blue Sun Stone gestured with the speaker's staff. "He has sent his other iniha to gather warriors. If peace cannot be easily negotiated, we will provide a demonstration of the massed might of our warriors. Such a sight, Uzachile's strength unveiled, may well persuade when words will not."

Eagle Fighter asked the question that was plaguing my souls. "And if the Kristianos are unimpressed with Uzachile's might?"

Blue Sun Stone gave him an insatiable grin. "Then they will learn the error of their ways. We will take what we want from their dead warriors and allow the survivors to serve us."

"His feces will sprout wings and fly before that happens," Pearl Hand mumbled as she shook her head.

Blue Sun Stone then added, "But the Great Holata does not think it will come to that. As an added inducement to bring about the release of Holata Ahocalaquen, and broker a peace between our peoples, Uzachile is prepared to offer the Kristianos many fine gifts, an ample supply of food, guides, or any other encouragements they might need."

At that he handed the speaker's staff to Eagle Fighter.

I sat in shock, sharing a stunned disbelief with Pearl Hand. At that moment a runner came bursting into the clearing. He made his way through the knot of people and rushed up to the council, exclaiming, "The Kristianos! They're leaving!"

Pearl Hand leaned toward me. "They must have finally run out of food."

In the hubbub that followed, Eagle Fighter resorted to a conch horn, blowing it for silence. It worked.

"Where are they heading?"

"North, on the Uriutina trail," the runner reported. "We watched long enough to be sure. Holata Ahocalaquen and the others march with them. I saw them with my own eyes."

"We must follow," Blue Sun Stone cried so that everyone could hear. "The Kristianos must be made aware of Holata Uzachile's offer."

"Of course we'll follow," Bit Woman said sharply. "They've got our people."

Eagle Fighter asked one of the other chiefs, "Holata Uriutina, what of your people and town?"

"My scouts will ensure that the town is evacuated," the chief replied. "But we cannot move the corn. We have just about finished the harvest. The granaries are full."

"That is the least of our problems," Eagle Fighter said stiffly. "Maybe they'll just head on out of the country. Go bother someone else."

"They should be so lucky," I muttered to Pearl Hand.

Eagle Fighter raised his hands. "I want our scouts shadowing them. The rest of us shall follow. Warriors, I would speak with you as the others pack to leave. We will march in formation, ready should any attack develop. Any women with small children shall stay here. When we have proof the Kristianos are truly headed to Uriutina, you need to begin the cleanup of Ahocalaquen."

"That's a chore I'm happy to avoid," Pearl Hand added under her breath.

Blood Thorn stepped over to us. "You will come, of course?"

I nodded. "Oh, yes. The opportunity may present itself to kill a couple of Kristianos." I was thinking of poor dead Sabal left in the field. I wondered if anyone had ever attended to her body, or if they had just left her to the *puercos,* or simply to rot.

After packing the dogs, we marched with the warriors. Blood Thorn insisted that we accompany the chiefs. Our way led through

368

the abandoned town. A stack of dead captives had been placed off to one side, probably people worn down from the forced march up from Ocale. From the looks of the lower ones, the *puercos* had been at them.

At the sight, there were growls of rage from some of the warriors. The ones from Ahocalaquen just glanced at them, worry about their own people foremost in their minds.

We followed the cabayo-chopped trail north into the forest. At a rain-swollen river, the Kristianos had built another of their great bridges. The Timucua who had never seen one before were amazed, many bouncing up and down on the thick, dirt-covered timbers. Leaving that behind, some of the warriors started pitching the round dung balls left by the cabayos.

It lasted only until we encountered the first dog-savaged and decapitated body. After that the mood changed.

Our force camped in the forest, screened by a line of scouts, while the Kristianos occupied a small village. Or at least the leaders did. Most of the Kristianos slept in the open with the slaves.

"What did you think of Holata Uzachile's plan?" Blood Thorn asked that night as he warmed his hands at our fire. Above us the smoke dissipated through the branches of a great hickory tree. The dogs were sprawled on their sides, and I missed Fetch. He would have wanted to play stick with a piece of firewood.

"He's an idiot," Pearl Hand growled.

"He's our Great Holata," Blood Thorn said sharply. "Please, have the appropriate respect."

She gave him an apologetic look. "He doesn't understand the Kristianos. When they came among my people years ago, the Chicora, too, made alliances and went off to conquer territory from our enemies. But what the Kristianos conquered, they just added to their holdings, which included the Chicora. There is no equality when it comes to Kristianos, Blood Thorn; only domination."

In a more mollified tone, I added, "This *Adelantado* de Soto, he's a different kind of man than any we know. He acts from invincible strength and great cruelty. The Kristianos think of us as beings accursed by their god. Their cabayos and war dogs are treated better." I shook my head. "I was their slave. I felt their whips, and I talked to one — face-to-face — for several days. You must believe me. Anything they say is only for the moment. It can be taken back without any consequences."

Blood Thorn shook his head stubbornly. "There are always consequences. Holata Uzachile is assembling warriors. Even the Kristianos will have second thoughts. They did the day we appeared in force after they had taken our chief."

"Perhaps you are right," I said to keep the peace, and gestured for Pearl Hand to be still. "And with the promise of gifts from Holata Uzachile, it might be enough to convince them." But I doubted it.

Pearl Hand was giving me a knowing look; she didn't believe it either.

On the other hand, even the Kristianos would believe that letting a chief go and accepting presents would be better than walking through a hostile land fighting all the time, wouldn't they?

"I shall know tomorrow," Blood Thorn said quietly. "Blue Sun Stone has convinced the others that we should send a peace delegation into Uriutina when the Kristianos arrive there. I have volunteered to go with them."

"Be careful," I said softly. "I'd miss your company."

He smiled. "And I yours."

With that, he stood, bid us good night, and walked off toward where the chiefs were camped.

Pearl Hand watched him go, a curious sympathy in her eyes. "I wonder if that's the last time we'll see him?"

TWENTY-FOUR

We camped for two days in the forest southwest of Uriutina. During that time we didn't see Blood Thorn, although a steady stream of warriors came by to hear about Kristianos and see the armor, lance, and sword.

I had continued to pound out metal points from the pieces I cut out of Antonio's undercoat. For a piece of the cloth, a warrior traded me a bundle of straight ash-wood arrow shafts. These I cut to length for Pearl Hand's crossbow, and began fitting the crude metal tips.

On the last night a ruckus was heard, and we followed the rest to see the peace party returning, their flutes in hand, all dressed and painted. Blood Thorn walked behind Blue Sun Stone, and I could see from his expression that he was both irritated and perplexed.

At the sight of us, he gestured, motioning for the crowd of warriors to let us past.

"Come," he said. "I need you."

Glancing curiously at Pearl Hand, she gave me the familiar arched eyebrow. We followed to where the chiefs had established their camps in the center of the gathering. Warriors crowded around until Eagle Fighter ordered them back and told them to sit in rows.

Blood Thorn bade us follow him, actually taking my hand to ensure that we were included in the central circle.

"Well?" Bit Woman asked without bowing to the usual formalities.

Blue Sun Stone lifted his hands in frustration. "We're not sure what to say. We approached, and a captive came out with a big man with a black beard who speaks some of our language."

"Ortiz," I growled a bit too loud.

Blue Sun Stone and the others shot surprised looks my way. Blood Thorn asking, "You know him?"

"Oh, yes. Much to my sorrow. He was cast ashore when his floating palace ran aground. The *Adelantado* freed him from captivity and put him in charge of translations. He also has responsibility for the captives."

Blue Sun Stone jerked a quick nod and continued, "We told him we wanted to offer peace and Holata Uzachile's good will. Ortiz took us through the gates, and it was a sobering moment, walking into that mass of staring Kristianos. I would rather walk into a den of hungry bears than do that again."

"What of our people?" Bit Woman insisted.

Blue Sun Stone took a deep breath. "They apparently will not be freed." At the groan from those around us, he held up his hand. "At least, not yet."

Blood Thorn's jaw was working, indicative of the churning in his souls.

Blue Sun Stone continued. "We were taken to the *Adelantado*. This man, de Soto. He received us politely, heard what we had to say, and told us in return that he valued Holata Uzachile's friendship, the offer of gifts and food, and that he would welcome guides to the Apalachee border."

"Then why not release our people?" Eagle Fighter demanded.

"Because," Blue Sun Stone said stiffly, "he says he values their company. At that point, Holata Ahocalaquen was brought before us. He has been well treated, although our people have been made to carry heavy loads."

A rustle of unease went through the warriors.

Blue Sun Stone raised his hands to quiet

them. "The *Adelantado* is not opposed to peace, but he told us he needed assurances that we were not deceiving him. At that point Holata Ahocalaquen asked what the Kristianos needed. De Soto asked for people to help carry his supplies. Holata Ahocalaquen then ordered that some of his people volunteer to do this. As a matter of good faith."

There was stunned silence.

"In the collars?" I asked.

Blue Sun Stone shot me a look. "No. They are to be volunteers, not captives, who do this. From their behavior, if they do not run away or cause trouble, the Kristianos will judge our true motives."

"Don't do this," Pearl Hand grumbled. She tucked her long hair behind her ears and cocked her jaw defiantly.

Eagle Fighter asked, "But if we accede — provide the people to carry their equipment and supplies — our holata and the rest will be freed?"

"That is our understanding," Blue Sun Stone replied.

"Do you remember their words?" Pearl Hand asked. "Not what Ortiz said, but what they said in their language?"

"No!" Blood Thorn cried. "And that is the problem. We speak to Ortiz, Ortiz babbles in their turkey talk. Then all the Kristiano chiefs talk among themselves as if we are not there. Finally, after they have all had their say, de

Soto tells something to Ortiz, who tells us."
He clenched a fist. "And even I can tell from
their pale Kristiano faces that much is going
on that they don't tell us."

"The exact words," Pearl Hand repeated.
"Can you remember any?"

"It's babble," Blue Sun Stone said, arms
spread. "As incomprehensible as Mos'kogee
is to us."

"*Trampa? Engaño? Broma?*" Pearl Hand
asked. "Did you hear any of those words?"

At the same time, both Blood Thorn and
Blue Sun Stone nodded. "I think so, but it's
hard to tell."

"In Kristiano tongue, those words mean to
trick, or deceive, or joke," Pearl Hand said
hotly.

"Wait." I held up a hand. "They've already
said they were worried we were going to trick
them. How do we know how it was used?"

She shrugged. "We don't, but when it
comes to Kristianos, always assume the
worst."

"You *speak* their language?" Blood Thorn
asked in amazement.

All eyes fixed on Pearl Hand.

"Hold up a bit here," I said, raising a hand.
"I can see where this is going, but no. My
wife doesn't set foot in their lair."

No one seemed to be listening.

"Who are *indios?*" Blue Sun Stone asked.

"That's what they call us," I answered.

"We're not Chicaza or Uzachile, just *indios*. As if we were all one people lumped together."

"That's insulting," Bit Woman cried.

Blue Sun Stone glanced at me. "You speak some Kristiano, too?"

"Not much. Just what I learned among them and from a captive."

Eagle Fighter asked, "Blue Sun Stone, what else did you learn? Are they heading farther north, or planning on staying here?"

"They are turning west." Blue Sun Stone rubbed his hands together. "De Soto will accept Holata Uzachile's offer of hospitality, perhaps to broker a peace." He took a breath. "Holata Ahocalaquen will accompany him there."

"To ensure cooperation," Pearl Hand interjected.

"No," Eagle Fighter stated flatly. "Trust must go two ways. The Kristianos must release our people first." He glanced at me. "Otherwise, what is to keep him from refusing to release them when he marches on to wherever he's going?"

"I agree," Blood Thorn added. "I think we should provide the porters to carry his load. That will be our gesture of faith. He, in turn, after he sees our goodwill, must free our holata, Water Frond, and the other captives. If he does this, we will continue to bear his supplies as far as Uzachile town."

"And if he doesn't?" Bit Woman asked.

Blue Sun Stone, expression hard, replied, "Then we have our warriors waiting somewhere in the west. Let us say Napetuca. That is time enough for both parties to understand the will of the other."

"Napetuca," Eagle Fighter agreed. Then he asked Blue Sun Stone, "You will send a runner to Holata Uzachile? Have him assemble his forces there?"

"It would make sense," Blood Thorn interjected. "If the Kristianos plan on treachery, we can provide an" — he glanced at Blue Sun Stone — "inducement?"

Blue Sun Stone nodded. "A runner will be sent. I agree. At Napetuca we will know if *Adelantado* de Soto plays us for fools, or if he really will honor an alliance."

"And what if he doesn't?" I asked softly.

"Then he will pay the consequences," Blue Sun Stone insisted.

"But carefully," Eagle Fighter countered. "For once, we must be smarter than our enemy. You have now seen his force up close. We do not want all of his terrible weapons pointed at us." He glanced at Pearl Hand and me. "No, let us learn from those who offer wise counsel. If he betrays us, let us betray him."

"And how will we do this?"

"Separate a small force and overwhelm them." Eagle Fighter ran a hand over his scarred forearms. "It will be like eating a buffalo. You don't swallow the whole thing at once, just a bite at a time."

Here, I thought, was someone who finally understood the way to beat the Kristianos.

The following morning, a line of nearly two hundred women, older girls and boys, and some middle-aged men assembled under a cloud-puffy sky. We watched as they made their way to Uriutina town to carry de Soto's heavy packs — hostages to prove goodwill.

Accompanied by Blood Thorn, Pearl Hand and I climbed a live oak so that we could see out over the town fields to where the Kristianos were assembling their march.

True to expectations, we could both see and hear Holata Ahocalaquen line out his people. Ortiz stood beside him, giving instructions as to which burdens the people were to bear. Also according to the agreement, no chains, ropes, or other confinement was placed on them.

"So far, so good," Blood Thorn remarked, and then he stopped, pointing. "Look! There's Water Frond."

I squinted hard, seeing a young woman walking beside Holata Ahocalaquen. Long black hair streamed down her back. The fact that it looked clean indicated that at least she wasn't being treated like a captive. She wore a girdle, belted at the waist, and had a slim body with small pointed breasts. Over the distance I couldn't make out her features.

"She doesn't walk like someone who's been abused," Blood Thorn said with relief.

We watched the long procession wind along a western trail.

Climbing down, we found the dogs and started back toward camp. In order to allay any suspicions on the part of the Kristianos — and avoid any unintended clashes — Blue Sun Stone was leading his large war party in a parallel course just to the south.

From projections, de Soto would camp at a small village that night, proceeding a long day's march to Napetuca on the following.

In a show of confidence, women and children, young men and elders, had begun to appear, most carrying flutes to communicate their nonhostile status. The idea was to give the Kristianos no reason to believe that any but the most peaceful intentions was involved.

That entire day we walked along, mixing with people. Sometimes they were joyous, but when they danced too close, or sought to share their goodwill, the Kristianos replied by drawing weapons. Clearly, the trust only flowed one way. More than once Uzachile tempers flared, and only a last-minute appeal by Blood Thorn averted violence.

"This could go either way," Pearl Hand muttered as we stopped to drink from a creek. Blood Thorn slaked his thirst, wiped his mouth, and added, "Let's just hope the Kristianos are as good as their word. I just want Water Frond and the holata back. Then the Kristianos can leave and go where they will." He glanced at us. "If they do, you can stay with us. We'd make you welcome."

"I can't," I told him. "The wound they gave my souls is too deep."

Pearl Hand gave me a smile. "He's had Power dreams, Blood Thorn. While we wish you and your people well, we'll continue to dog their tracks, seeking a way to destroy them."

"Do you hate them that much?" Blood Thorn asked.

"You haven't seen the things I have." I shrugged. "Until you do, it's impossible to understand. But in the dreams, I went to places, saw things, talked to Spirit Beings. We're beginning a long battle. One not to be decided any time soon, but we're fighting for our world, our beliefs." I gestured out at the distant Kristianos. "If this de Soto wins, others will come licking at his heels. Should he fail, perhaps they will leave us alone."

"These dreams . . . ?" Blood Thorn asked suggestively.

"Three of them." I shrugged. "Power has chosen me for reasons beyond my understanding."

"Perhaps." Blood Thorn gave me an intent scrutiny. "But for you, we would have attacked them head-on. Many would be dead. At least this way there is a chance that de Soto will release his captives at Napetuca. Perhaps we can avoid the needless deaths of many of our people. And who knows what such a thing portends for the future?"

"There is that." I was remembering snatches of the Power dreams. Like the promise I had made to Water Panther.

"What?" Pearl Hand asked, reading my expression.

"Probably nothing. It's just that I haven't had a Power dream recently. My people believe that true Power dreams come in fours. I've had three."

"Maybe that's all that you need." Blood Thorn stood, watching the dogs resting in the shade.

"Maybe," I agreed, adopting a smile I didn't feel.

We lined out the pack dogs, and for most of the rest of the day Blood Thorn told us of the plans he and Water Frond had made. As the holata's niece, she would inherit his position upon his death, provided the clans agreed. Then, her son would follow her. In the process, Blood Thorn's prestige would rise in turn.

Who knew, maybe the Kristianos would actually honor their word, and he would live to see his dreams come true. For Pearl Hand and me, however, the future was a dark and uncertain place. Among the Uzachile we were learning valuable lessons, things we would need to know when dealing with other nations. Skills to influence their decisions regarding the Kristianos.

And then there was that fourth dream: *You reek of Horned Serpent. You are his creature.*

The only time Horned Serpent spoke to me, it hadn't turned out well.

The rain began in the middle of the night, blowing up from the gulf. Lightning lashed the clouds with such fury and intensity that a man could have gone about daytime activities were it not for the sheets of water that fell from the skies. The Thunderers were in deadly earnest war with the Spirit Beings of the Underworld.

Traders are used to camping in the open. Most of the Uzachile Timucua, unfortunately, were not so well prepared, having hurried to join the procession accompanying the Kristianos. Under my shelter — only damp and not soaked through — I snuggled closer to Pearl Hand. The dogs were huddled in soggy balls, noses buried in their tails.

"Soon."

I heard the voice as clearly as if it were spoken but inches from my ear. In the next instant a lightning flash illuminated the clearing just beyond the opening of our lean-to.

I saw him standing there, impervious to the

rain. Water Panther's snake tail was undulating, his yellow eyes fixed on mine.

When the next bolt of lightning glared whitely, he was gone. Only silver streaks of rain gleamed in the light.

What will be soon? I wondered.

When I finally managed to get back to sleep, my dreams were troubled. In them, I kept drowning over and over, sinking down, desperate to escape some terrible disaster that awaited me above the surface.

I thought I heard Water Panther laugh. When I blinked awake and stared into the blackness beyond the lean-to, flashes of lightning showed the clearing empty but for shining puddles of rain.

TWENTY-FIVE

Pearl Hand and I breakfasted on cold corn gruel traded from the stores that had been evacuated from Uriutina before the Kristianos arrived. The dogs got cold smoked venison, barely enough among them. Sometimes, if they were lucky, they snapped up a meadow vole that leaped from underfoot, or some unsuspecting lizard that scampered by at the last moment.

All but Bark had given up on grabbing frogs, and even he was starting to learn that sometimes they excreted a poison that made the mouth foam.

We were finishing up when Blood Thorn approached from the drizzle. "Could we see the two of you?"

"That depends," Pearl Hand replied as she stowed the gruel pot. "Have any of you had bouts of blindness recently?"

"You know what I mean." Blood Thorn was evidently too preoccupied for witty exchanges.

We shrugged. I grabbed Antonio's helmet and placed it atop my head. Raindrops made an interesting, almost musical pattering on the metal, but it was a wonder at shedding water.

Together we sloshed over to a cobbled-up ramada, roofed with branches and cane over which baskets of dirt had been poured. They hadn't anticipated this kind of downpour. The people beneath were strategically located to avoid dripping gobs of mud.

Blue Sun Stone, Eagle Fighter, Bit Woman, Holata Uriutina, and a new man were waiting for us. The newcomer was muscular, scarred along his arms and breasts. His chest was decorated by star tattoos. The shaven sides of his head were painted in red, while his central shock of hair was tied to stand straight from the top of his head. I wondered how he'd kept it from sagging in the rain. If he wasn't a high-ranking paracusi from Uzachile, I'd eat the copper-bladed war club that hung from his side. He kept glancing at the Kristiano helmet atop my head, his curiosity barely controlled.

"We have a proposition for the two of you," Blue Sun Stone began.

I met the paracusi's eyes. "I am Black Shell, a trader of the Chicaza. This is Pearl Hand, of the Chicora, my wife."

He studied me through stony eyes. "I am called Paracusi Rattlesnake, son of Cloud Woman, of the Panther Clan. I serve the Holata Uzachile."

"Your reputation is known far and wide, great war chief. The Apalachee, the Potano, and the Pensacola speak of you with great respect." I gave him a slight bow of the head, water dripping off Antonio's helmet.

"Forgive me," Blue Sun Stone said softly. "I have too much weighing on my souls. I forgot my manners."

"What proposition?" Pearl Hand asked bluntly. She always had a way of getting right to the core of the matter.

"Tomorrow, if the rain lets up, we are sending another delegation to the Kristianos." Blue Sun Stone raised his hands helplessly. "What we need to determine is if they have any intention of keeping their word. We were thinking that if the two of you accompanied us, perhaps you could discover their true intent."

"We will pay you," Eagle Fighter added. "Ask what you will of us in trade."

"Why?" Pearl Hand made a curious gesture. "Why tomorrow morning?"

"So that we have enough time to act accordingly," Rattlesnake said grimly. "If they are planning on tricking us, we can take certain measures. If they mean to honor their word, we will stand down some of our warriors." His smile was as cold as the rain. "But not enough to encourage them to folly."

"How many warriors do you have?" I asked.

"We have enough, Black Shell of the Chicaza." With that Rattlesnake effectively told me it was none of a foreigner's business. Then he asked, "Why are you doing this? Traders serve only the Power of trade. They do not take sides. Yet I hear you have done nothing but help Holata Uzachile and his people."

I straightened. "Were you having trouble with the Apalachee, the Mos'kogee, or the Koasati, neither Pearl Hand nor I would offer more than our best wishes and most heartfelt neutrality. With the Kristianos, the rules have changed. Paracusi, they have no honor when it comes to our ways, and they have offended Power. Not just the Power of trade, but all Power. They come following a cruel and vengeful god, one beyond our understanding or comprehension. They march on our land, and with them marches a dark and terrible evil. Perhaps, according to our notions, they are polluted — but their terrible way of war gives them the feeling of invincibility, and with it an arrogance like I have never seen before."

"Your words about Power are moving," Rattlesnake said, curling down like his namesake. "But which Power supports you? The Power of trade? That Power does not meddle in war. The red Power of your Chicaza people? But that would leave you unbalanced and without composure or wisdom. Surely not the white Power, for you speak of violence and anger."

"All of them," I said simply. "I fight for this earth, for the Underworld, and the dead." I paused, watching him closely. "Some have said I am Horned Serpent's being."

"You have seen Horned Serpent?" he asked. The others had gone completely silent, watching with wide eyes. Red and white Power may not have been integral to Timucua beliefs, based as they were upon the sun, the ancestors, and Spirit Beings — but they still respected it.

"Once. To my regret. Recently it has been Water Panther, First Woman, and Corn Woman, oh, and one of the Winds. Unless you include the tie snake guarding the passage to the Underworld." I looked into his eyes, willing him to see my souls. "Horned Serpent waits for the fourth and final dream. I think I'll be tested first."

His gaze never wavered. "You expect me to believe this?"

I thought about it a moment. My own people had called me a liar. "I'm not even sure why I'm telling you, of all people. Truth be told, great Paracusi, I don't care if you believe or not. My relations with Power are my own. What I do know is that somehow the Kristianos must be defeated. Having studied them, I still don't know how, but I think it will take time . . . and a great deal of blood."

"Then you will go with our delegation tomorrow?" He waited for the answer, and somehow, I knew that this decision would be binding, forever altering my future.

"I will go," I said carefully. "But not my wife."

"I can speak for myself," Pearl Hand interjected. "They need me more than you. It won't be the first time I've walked among them."

Rattlesnake glanced at her, a subtle respect in his eyes. "She doesn't take your orders well, Trader."

"I don't have to." Pearl Hand propped a hand on her hip. "We have a partnership. Half and half."

At her mention of half and half, Rattlesnake gave me a look that was both amused and disbelieving before he turned his attention to her. "You are sure you won't become frightened?"

I laughed at the thought of it, but Pearl Hand surprised me when she said, "Only a fool walks among the Kristianos and is unafraid. I will do my best to overhear their private talk. But you, Paracusi, will you be smart enough to be scared?"

"I killed my fear years ago."

"Then you had better relearn it quickly." She was staring into his eyes, neither giving in the slightest.

"And if I don't?" he asked mildly.

"They will kill you . . . and all you hold dear." And with that Pearl Hand turned, walking away, head high, back arched, her long hair teased by the breeze.

Everyone stood in shocked silence, including me. I'd never seen her so. But then I'd been mostly delirious when she'd dragged me from Uzita town. Only now did I begin to realize what it had cost her to come after me.

Paracusi Rattlesnake burst out in laughter, glancing up at me. "That is one remarkable woman."

"The most remarkable ever," I said, staring after her in amazement.

"Tomorrow morning then," Eagle Fighter added after taking a deep breath. "Dress for the occasion, Trader. We want to make a good impression."

I started out after Pearl Hand, Blood Thorn hurrying to catch up with me. "What you said back there, is it true? I mean about Spirit Power, and seeing the Spirit Beings? You just told me you'd had Spirit dreams."

"I don't like to talk about it." Then, at his expression, I made a gesture of frustration. "Yes, all right? It is. That's why I'm in this. Well . . . along with hating Kristianos."

I glanced back, seeing the chiefs at the ramada looking after us. "And somehow, for some reason, it was almost as if Power was making me tell Rattlesnake those things. As if I made a decision, crossed a divide I can never recross."

Blood Thorn shot me suspicious glances from the corner of his eye. "I don't know who is more frightening, you or Pearl Hand."

As rain pattered and dripped off Antonio's hat, I didn't either.

Neither Pearl Hand nor I slept well that night, and it wasn't just the soggy blankets. We spent most of the sleepless hours anticipating what could go wrong. Each time we convinced ourselves of the worst, one of us reminded the other that previous peace delegations had been allowed to return. Well, all but Holata Ahocalaquen's when he offered himself in place of Water Frond and his people.

As false dawn brightened the cloudy east, I threw off the blanket and began rummaging through the packs. Pearl Hand chose various ornaments that I laid out, trying this one and that until she was decked out like a high minko's first niece at the Green Corn Ceremony.

Squirm watched, his white blaze damp. Bark kept standing up each time Pearl Hand straightened. He watched her with worshipful eyes, ready to go with her. Skipper and Gnaw, they just tried to catch any extra sleep they could get.

I picked a series of shell necklaces, wrapping them so they hid the whitening scars on my neck. I hung a huge gorget cut from a large whelk shell over the gleaming mica breastplate I'd put on. If the sun shone, it would almost be blinding. Finally I hung copper images of Long Nose God from my ears.

Pearl Hand used a shell comb to pull the knots out of my hair, and I finished by shuffling through my goods for a little pot of white clay. This I mixed with bear fat, and each of us painted our faces white, the color emblematic of peace.

When all was ready, we ordered the dogs to stay, Bark staring up at us with a terrible longing in his eyes. You'd have thought we were leaving him forever. I prayed he didn't know something we didn't.

I picked out my trader's staff and preened the white feathers at its crook. For the first time in months I almost felt normal. The staff would be no protection from the Kristianos, but holding it was comforting.

We walked to the ramada, where — because we were foreign traders — we avoided the smoking, skin scratching, formulaic prayers to ancestral ghosts, and other preparations. However, each of us took a turn at the pipe and managed a swig or two of black drink. I enjoyed the heady rush that came of the holly-leaf tea.

By the time the sun was shooting brilliant streamers of orange and purple beneath the clouds, we were on our way. People formed up on either side, singing, dancing, beating drums, and playing on their flutes.

Passing through the screen of trees, we proceeded headlong toward the village palisade. Blood Thorn walked beside us, while in front went Blue Sun Stone and Rattlesnake, then Eagle Fighter and Holata Uriutina. They'd dressed in their very best: brightly colored feathers fluttering in the breeze, shell and copper ornaments polished. Tattoos had been darkened with grease, and their faces were painted in striking designs.

The people closed in behind us and followed as far as the Kristiano pickets. There they stopped, still waving, dancing, and praying for our success.

We passed through a maze of sagging cloth tents inhabited by sodden Kristianos and open camps of porters who'd been sleeping in the mud. They all looked miserable, the chained captives most of all. Smoldering fires made of wet wood filled the air with choking blue smoke, and the whole place smelled of feces and urine. Mud squished between our toes and I hated to think what we slogged through.

Fortunately the accursed *puercos* were bunched out on the periphery near the forest.

Two lines of guards formed outside the village gates, just as they had for the entering body of the Kristiano army. While we didn't get any gaudy flags unfurled, I was happy to forego that in favor of not having thunder sticks pointed at us and discharged.

I felt my gut tighten as Juan Ortiz strode out, followed by two captives. Perhaps they were servants? Then I noticed that both men, each having tattoos reminiscent of Southern Timucua, had little wooden crosses hanging from their necks. Could these be some of the converts we'd heard about?

Ortiz had dressed in shining armor and a puffy-sleeved shirt. He stood, feet braced, his thumbs propped in a sword belt. For a moment I wished I'd worn Antonio's helmet. It would have matched his own.

Blue Sun Stone came to a stop before Ortiz, calling, "We come to have council with the *Adelantado*." Then he related his clan and ancestry, and listed many of the long praises associated with the name of Holata Uzachile. Next, Paracusi Rattlesnake stepped forward, relating his credentials and so on, until they came to me.

"I come under the Power of trade," I said.

"With me is my wife."

Ortiz shot me a skeptical look, and for one terrible moment I was afraid he would recognize me. But, as I was to learn later, white face paint is a wonderful disguise. And no doubt one *indio* looked pretty much like another to these people.

"The *Adelantado* Hernando de Soto, *gobernador de la Florida,* at the order of His Most Catholic Majesty, Carlos, will see you." Ortiz bowed slightly. Then he turned on his heel, spinning a little divot in the mud, and — his servants following — led us through the gate.

My heart was pounding. The sensation on my neck was as if the weight of the collar were already pressing down. Flashes of memory shot up from my souls: war dogs, teeth bared, leaping at me; the hideous rattle of the chains; the yawning pit of futility one feels when death seems the only escape.

I battled for courage, desperate to turn and run. As we passed between the rows of armored men, I glanced anxiously at Pearl Hand and saw her hard composure in defiance of the pulsing vein in her neck.

I tried to mimic her stalwart expression, but my souls screamed as I followed the holatas through that terrible gate.

Blessed gods, don't let this go wrong!

TWENTY-SIX

The village wasn't much to begin with, but crowded with soldiers splashing through ankle-deep mud puddles hadn't helped anything. We were led past a small burial mound and through the maze of thatched houses to the chief's house: a round building with cane walls and a conical roof. This, at least, had been built on a low mound out of the mud.

A crowd of Kristianos, their armor polished to a shine, helmeted, and looking disdainfully at us, milled about. The highest ranking — no doubt the ones on the side of the mound — avoided most of the mud. The colors of their shirts were amazing: blues, reds, yellows, and pinks. Here and there I saw a deep purple, the like of which I'd never seen even at Uzita.

Unlike when I was captive, this was the first time I'd seen such a collection of Kristianos up close. They came in all sizes, tall and short, muscular and thin. As at Uzita, I remained amazed at the ones with light brown and even yellow hair. I noticed a couple with red and wondered if they were the same ones I'd seen in Uzita.

Then I caught sight of one pushing his way through the crowd. Thin and young, he struggled to the side of a gray-haired man, saying something to him. I felt a tingle of fear run through me. *Antonio!* So, he'd made it after all.

I wondered where my collar was, and winced at the notion that it might have ended up around some other poor wretch's neck.

The gray-haired man gave Antonio a fatherly smile and slapped him on the back. So this was the rich father that Antonio had thought would pay us ransom for his son's release?

Don Luis had small black eyes that contrasted with the gray in his hair and beard. They reminded me of a weasel's. The thin and deeply lined face, hawkish nose, and sunken cheeks did nothing to diminish the resemblance.

He's a cold man with no soul. The words

echoed between my own souls. I glanced at Antonio, seeing now the kind of man he would be as he aged. That rapacious arrogance he had displayed back in camp would only expand, eating what was left of the youth who now stood trying to mimic his father's erect stance.

I should have cut your throat back at Ocale, I thought. I glanced sidelong at Pearl Hand, seeing that she, too, had recognized him; then she turned her attention forward.

Don Luis clapped his son on the back and said some parting word. Then he strode purposefully to the doorway, nodded at one of the guards, and ducked inside.

Moments later a well-dressed man stepped out onto the porch; others, Don Luis among them, followed in a precise order behind him. None of these had mud on their polished boots. Even though I had been a captive, I'd seen few of the leaders up close. The management of slaves was obviously above their concerns.

Ortiz left no doubt as to the leader's identity as he and his Timucua servants dropped to one knee, bowing their heads.

Ortiz said, *"Los indios han llegado aquí, Adelantado."*

"Qué quieren, Ortiz?" de Soto asked, giving us all a vacant stare.

De Soto had a thin face with a trimmed beard. His eyes almost looked sleepy under heavy lids. The hollow cheeks were deeply lined from the corner of his large protruding nose down to the sides of his hard mouth. The wide lips were thin and pinched, as though he'd drank of something bitter. But when I looked into his brown eyes, it was as if a soulless darkness inhabited them. We might have been blocks of wood for all that he cared.

"Los indios quieren un encuentro," Ortiz began.

"The indios want a meeting." I lost the rest of it as the rapid *español* exceeded my limited knowledge.

At a gesture from de Soto, Ortiz stood and addressed Blue Sun Stone. "The *Adelantado* would like to know how he can be of assistance."

The freed Timucua, I noticed, remained on their knees, heads bowed. Something about that man on the right . . . I'd swear I'd seen him before. But then, on my way south I'd been through most of the villages de Soto had raided.

Blue Sun Stone launched off on his speech, noting that the Uzachile had complied with each of the *Adelantado*'s requests. They had provided food and labor, and had offered no sign of hostility. Further, having shown the goodness in their hearts, when might they expect the return of the Holata Ahocalaquen and his original party?

The men behind de Soto listened intently as Ortiz translated. What Blue Sun Stone had said in a long discourse was condensed into a couple of sentences.

The men around de Soto — I assumed they were war chiefs of some sort — immediately began discussing this. De Soto listened, nodding occasionally, but I could barely catch a word or two. Pearl Hand, however was listening intently, no expression betrayed on her painted face.

The talk went on for considerably longer than Blue Sun Stone's initial request. All the while we waited, standing there like posts of wood. I could see Paracusi Rattlesnake beginning to fidget. "Careful," I whispered. "Much is at stake here."

Though I was behind him, I thought I saw his ears redden. Perhaps he wasn't used to being lectured by Chicaza traders?

De Soto made a lazy gesture with his hand and the conversation stopped. He turned to Ortiz and spoke in a clipped voice, the words having the tone of command, not suggestion. Maybe no one lectured him either?

I studied de Soto, intent on his long, thin head and the curly dark hair. Here was the one man on earth whose skull I most would have loved to crush with a jagged rock.

Ortiz bowed slightly to Blue Sun Stone again. "The *Adelantado* is pleased to inform you that he enjoys the company of your holata. They have been spending many pleasant times together." Ortiz made a curious gesture with his hands, placing the palms together. "It turns out that the *Adelantado* and your *cacique* have much in common, being so beloved by their *súbditos,* their followers. The *Adelantado* understands your concerns, and wishes you to understand that it would grieve him to forego the pleasure of your *cacique*'s company, at least until we arrive at the town of Napetuca."

"May we see our holata?" Blue Sun Stone asked.

Ortiz relayed the question.

De Soto gave the barest of smiles and flipped his hand.

Immediately an order was given, and a young man dashed off through the crowd toward one of the houses in back. From my higher position on the mound, I could see the place was guarded by at least five of the Kristiano *soldados,* each holding one of those long spear-axes.

Moments later Holata Ahocalaquen emerged, flanked on both sides by guards. He was a stout man, thickly muscled through the shoulders. His once-shaven head was growing out on the sides, his long roach hanging down like thin feathers. Holata Ahocalaquen had a broad and pleasant face, but his eyes could not hide a soul-eating worry.

He was brought up and led to one side of

de Soto. I could see Ahocalaquen's jaw muscles tensing as he nodded to Blue Sun Stone. Then he glanced at Rattlesnake and froze — as if caught between tremendous hope and a sudden and terrifying fear.

Ortiz missed the subtle hand signs Rattlesnake began to form, perhaps believing it to be no more than continued fidgeting. Standing behind the man, I couldn't make out the words he was signing. Whatever it was, Holata Ahocalaquen's expression tightened, and he gave a slight nod.

De Soto spoke. Ortiz turned his attention to Ahocalaquen and translated, "The *Adelantado* was just reassuring your people on the fine nature of our growing friendship, Great Holata."

Ortiz didn't realize he'd just offered a terrible affront to the real Great Holata, who was, of course, Uzachile. Ahocalaquen winced, as did Blue Sun Stone and Blood Thorn. Rattlesnake, however, remained as motionless as his namesake.

"My niece and I are being treated most respectfully," Holata Ahocalaquen addressed us graciously. "Please tell my people that I deeply appreciate their consent to carry some of the *Adelantado*'s supplies. That they do so without causing alarm brings me great pride."

At the same time his hands were working. Not one of the Kristianos noticed it, but even a half-blind Tequesta would have understood.

Ahocalaquen then added, "I have been asked by the *Adelantado* to accompany him at least as far as Napetuca. There I shall be returned to you, and we shall travel on to Uzachile. Tell the *Great* Holata that the Kristianos and I look forward to his hospitality. It is our understanding that a wonderful feast is being prepared, and gifts will be given."

At this, to my surprise, Holata Uriutina stepped forward. He began reciting his clan, kin, and status, all the while Ortiz was listening, a frown on his face.

Finally Ortiz could stand it no longer. "Why are you here?"

It irritated me that the two Kristiano Timucua smiled despite their lowered heads. Who was that fellow on the right? It lay just at the edge of my souls, but I had other concerns for the moment.

Holata Uriutina ceased his recitation, nodding slightly. "I have come to offer myself in place of Ahocalaquen to travel from Napetuca to Uzachile. If the stories that are told are true, I would like to enjoy the *Adelantado*'s company. Perhaps we, too, have much in common."

Ortiz turned back, explaining the offer to de Soto. The conference of Kristiano chiefs began again, sometimes growing heated. Ahocalaquen meanwhile signed to Uriutina, asking if this was so.

404

Uriutina signed back that it was a test of the Kristianos' intentions. I could see the strain building behind Ahocalaquen's desperately placid expression.

The Kristianos continued to talk, some gesturing. Even with a smattering of the language, I could feel the frustration among the others.

Finally de Soto fixed on Uriutina with his soulless eyes. For the life of me, I couldn't read the man. He might have been discussing the quality of cornbread. Then he spoke, that sharp ring of arrogant command filling his voice.

Ortiz translated, "We agree to your proposal. If you will come to our camp at Napetuca, the morning we leave for Uzachile, we will regretfully part company with *cacique Aguacaleyquen* and look forward to your company, great *cacique*." No one flinched this time.

"May we do it in the flats outside of Napetuca?" Uriutina waved around at the crowded Kristianos. "Perhaps in a place where all of my people and Ahocalaquen's" — he stressed the proper pronunciation — "can witness." He smiled. "That way, without so many of your warriors, there will be no misunderstandings."

Ortiz laid it all out, the Kristianos listening. Then they began to harangue each other, de Soto listening. Ten men huddled with de

405

Soto, each trying to get his say. For a moment I tried to work out the hierarchy, then gave it up as a lost cause. One thing was certain from the heated bickering: de Soto's chiefs were hardly of a unified opinion about anything. Don Luis, however, got as much attention as any of the others. He was arguing vehemently against something, ranting about an *"idea muy malo."* Something very bad. That, in itself, was interesting.

I glanced at Antonio, who seemed to swell with pride each time his father had de Soto's ear. Then his face would go hard and sullen when his father was shouted down.

The details took almost a full hand of time but were finally worked out. The exchange of the holatas would be done in the grassy fields just outside of Napetuca. De Soto would come with a small group of warriors, and the holatas would exchange places.

"I will, of course, be taking Water Frond with me," Ahocalaquen noted as the final details were agreed to.

"Of course," Ortiz replied.

Pleasantries were exchanged, and de Soto made a gesture with his hand, then turned. He marched straight back through the knot of his officers, the rest following in order of rank as they reentered the building.

Ahocalaquen gave a smile, then proceeded with his guards, headed back toward his house.

I'd forgotten Antonio. Without his father to admire, he was staring intently at Pearl Hand's breasts, that half-dreamy look on his face. Then a puzzled frown lined his forehead and he turned his attention to Pearl Hand's face. I could almost see him searching for what struck him as familiar. By the time his eyes turned to me, I was looking straight ahead, but I could feel his hot gaze.

We should have anticipated that he'd be here. And if he recognizes us? Will that get us all killed?

Avoiding his eyes, I started to follow as Ortiz and his two Timucua took the lead, escorting us down the sloping side of the mound and into the mud.

"Un momento!" Antonio cried, stepping forward from the knot of Kristianos. *"Quién es el hombre?"* He was pointing straight at me.

Ortiz stopped, staring first at Antonio, and then me. *"Es un indio."* He shrugged. At that moment, the familiar Timucua at his side stared, first at me, and then at Pearl Hand. He gave a barely stifled gasp of recognition.

Ears! But without his necklace! I bit off a curse. It figured. No wonder he'd gone over to the Kristianos.

Antonio was stomping forward, a frown deepening his forehead. I could see indecision gnawing at him as he called, *"Alto! Quiero*

407

este hombre!"

My heart leaped. *Alto* was "stop." *Quiero* meant "I want."

"Antonio! Silencio!" Don Luis bellowed, appearing at the door with several others. I could see de Soto in the shadows, watching with a cold detachment. Don Luis walked forward, eyes drilling into his son's like deerbone stilettos. The old man waved Ortiz to continue, and I missed the heated exchange between father and son.

Ortiz growled under his breath, leading the way. Ears kept shooting glances back over his shoulder, a barely smothered smile eating at his lips. The looks he gave Pearl Hand added to the frantic beat of my heart. It would be a flagrant abuse of the Power of trade, on my part, were I to beat him to death with a trader's staff.

As we slopped back through the muck, lines of Kristianos watched us, hands on their weapons. Some were grinning, others pointing. A few called what had to be insults, judging from the mocking tone of voice. Others laughed. Pearl Hand got her share of the attention, many of the leering Kristianos asking if she wanted *joder.*

I watched her back stiffen, anger betrayed by the clamped muscles of her jaw — and wondered what *joder* was.

I breathed an audible sigh of relief as we passed through the gates. Ortiz, his two tame *indios* standing behind him, bade us farewell. I couldn't read Ortiz's expression, but Ears had fixed both Pearl Hand and me with a cunning smirk. The other guy fingered his little wooden cross, smoldering eyes masking some conflict within.

I hoped he and Ears would be happy in *paraíso* with their new lords — then dismissed them from my thoughts. I had more to worry about, like the fact that Antonio might have actually recognized us. Still, his look of uncertainty boded well for us.

I hoped.

All around us, camp was being broken down, tents folded, and cookware packed in large fabric sacks. I couldn't help but look at the largest with a trader's eye. I was walking through a literal fortune in metal pots, cloth, and *hierro* tools.

"Antonio?" Pearl Hand asked through gritted teeth. "Did he recognize us?"

"He wasn't sure." I shot her a glance. "That was Ears kneeling beside Ortiz. Remember? The one who couldn't wait for Irriparacoxi to get tired of you?"

"I saw him."

"And he definitely saw you." I paused. "What's *joder?*"

"Remember that guard the night I rescued you? We were doing *joder* just before I sliced his throat open."

"Oh."

409

"And I'd do the same to each of those crawling maggots," she growled.

Only when we passed the last picket did Blue Sun Stone turn to Pearl Hand and me. "Could either of you understand them?"

Pearl Hand nodded. "Know this: No matter what you do, de Soto will not proceed without hostages. For the moment a chief, any chief — what they call a *cacique* — will do. They are only interested in getting to Uzachile to see what resources are there. Once they arrive, de Soto will decide where he wants to go next. He favors Apalachee. That argument they had? Many, remembering what happened to Narvaez, advise de Soto to turn back south. Still others think they should continue north, that going to Apalachee was the fatal mistake Narvaez made. They believe that infinite riches are inland . . . that Uzachile is like someplace called Panamá, where little gold was found near the coasts, but fabulous wealth was located in the interior."

Rattlesnake turned his hard eyes on her. "You said they insist on having hostages?"

Pearl Hand looked him straight in the eyes as she said, "They do. Uriutina here will do in place of Ahocalaquen. As long as they hold a chief, they do not believe they will be attacked, no matter what action they take. If they are attacked, the holata and the other Uzachile hostages die. The volunteer porters will be locked in the collars and kept until they convert or die. That's the final word."

The Uzachile just stared, stunned.

Pearl Hand took a breath, as if releasing all the tension that had built inside her. The Uzachile continued to stare in disbelief, as if all their hopes had been crushed.

"Meanwhile," Pearl Hand continued, "you had better prepare yourselves, because once they reach Uzachile town, the one hostage they will insist on will be the Great Holata himself. No less than de Soto himself is planning on it."

"You have no doubts?" Blue Sun Stone almost pleaded.

Pearl Hand gave him a wistful and knowing smile before she uttered a couple of sentences in rapid *español*. "I just repeated de Soto's own words: 'It matters not which of these filthy *indios* we take now. At their capital we will take the leader, just as we took the great Atahualpa at Cuzco town.' " She gave us a puzzled expression. "Whoever Atahualpa was, and wherever Cuzco is."

Blue Sun Stone appeared mystified. "Have they no clue of the insult they have given us? Do they understand nothing of decency and honor? There is no greater affront to our people, our ancestors, and our honor than taking Holata Uzachile hostage."

"They do not," Pearl Hand replied. "Not one of de Soto's subchiefs had any qualms about betraying our trust. To a man they

411

agree that they can destroy any force Uzachile marches against them at the capital. Their only concern is avoiding any unnecessary risk to cabayos or supplies, which sustained fighting would ultimately cost them."

The only sound was the cracking of Rattlesnake's knuckles as he clenched his fists.

I remembered the signs passed between the holatas and the paracusi. A cold chill ran down my spine. A great many things began to make sense: The exchange was to take place out in the open; with only a small number of Kristianos. Meanwhile a massive celebration was being planned to mark the event. Why did I suddenly believe that most of the celebrants would be Uzachile's warriors?

The hard glint in Rattlesnake's eyes left me with no doubt. De Soto thought he was deceiving the Uzachile. And now, through Pearl Hand's knowledge of *español,* Rattlesnake knew it. But was the element of surprise going to be enough? I couldn't help but remember the ambush at the creek outside of Ocale.

You have one chance, Paracusi. You had better get it right!

TWENTY-SEVEN

They questioned Pearl Hand and me for hours as we hurried westward along winding forest trails. Overhead we could occasionally see thick streamers of cloud blowing north from the gulf. A vigorous breeze pawed at the trees, sighing in the leaves, and loosening occasional nuts and twigs to filter down around us. Pearl Hand recited the conversations over and over, telling her listeners what the Kristiano commanders had discussed.

Meanwhile I wondered about Ears. That he'd found a worse master than Irriparacoxi was apparent, but what did it mean for us? The answer: Probably nothing. I'd been a slave, and knew how powerless he'd become.

Rattlesnake had disappeared for about a hand of time, and I knew exactly what he was up to: sending messages to his chief and orders to his warriors.

I thought about it. De Soto could have passed in peace. All he needed to do was abide by the deal. Holata Uzachile would have insisted that any agreement be enforced. The Great Holata was willing to accept the events at Ahocalaquen as the mistakes of foreigners, willing to forgive and forget just to have them long gone from his lands.

Instead de Soto was going to arrive happy and hearty at Uzachile town, eat all their food, accept their presents, gifts, and volunteer labor, and then take Holata Uzachile hostage in return. Maybe he'd free him at the Apalachee border? Or maybe, once Holata Uzachile's usefulness had run out, he'd order him killed and left along the trail like poor old Sabal and the others he'd discarded.

The memory of his oddly soulless eyes haunted me.

"De Soto is the key," I said suddenly.

All eyes turned on me.

"We heard his subchiefs. They are divided, some wishing to return south and leave. Others wish to go north, fearing the same fate as befell Narvaez among the Apalachee. Yet others, including de Soto, think that by continuing to the Apalachee, they will succeed where Narvaez failed."

"What is your point?" Blood Thorn asked as he picked up a thin branch and began thrashing the grass as he walked.

"My point is that de Soto makes the decisions. If you kill him, and kill a great many of his warriors in the process, the others will bicker among themselves. The resulting discord will tear the Kristianos apart. Who knows? It might even lead them to attack each other."

Rattlesnake considered that. "Kill him, and the rest fall upon each other? This we can do."

"Success will cost the Uzachile," Pearl Hand observed. "If you kill de Soto, the rest will exact a terrible vengeance on your people. You understand this, don't you? Only after avenging their dead chief will they turn on each other."

Rattlesnake nodded, his expression somber. "What choice do we have? If we do nothing, they will march into Uzachile and take our Great Holata. You yourself heard them say so. On the other hand, if we can kill de Soto and scatter our warriors after the battle, perhaps we can lead small parties of Kristianos seeking revenge into traps. We know the country; they do not." He shook his head. "Either way, it is a gamble. But one thing is sure: At Napetuca, for one moment, we shall have the advantage of surprise."

I said, "Renowned Paracusi, I understand

the opportunity and your reasons for taking it. I myself wish for nothing more than the destruction of the Kristianos. But . . ."

At my hesitation, Rattlesnake turned his hard eyes on mine. "But what, Trader?"

"If I were you, I would have an alternate plan."

"Such as?"

"A way to stop the attack if de Soto is not fooled by your charade of peace."

He was watching me, considering. "And how will I know this?"

"By the disposition of his forces. Granted, he will bring Holata Ahocalaquen out with a small force, but if he leaves his massed reserves close . . . somewhere within sight where they can rush to his relief, it will be a disaster from which you will never escape."

He thought about it, seeing the logic. "You really believe he could destroy such a large party of my warriors?"

"I don't just believe, I know," I said bitterly. "If you can't surround and destroy his small force immediately, his cabayeros will come on the gallop and destroy any stragglers within a half hand of time. Your only hope is to kill him quickly and run for the timber like a red wolf."

"And if we can see his massed forces in the distance?" Rattlesnake asked.

"Call off the attack," Pearl Hand urged. "Use the occasion as a means of allaying de

416

Soto's suspicions. Then, perhaps outside of Uzachile, you can try again, having gained his confidence."

Rattlesnake took a deep breath. "In that case their full wrath would fall on the capital. They would destroy it, and probably kill even more people."

"If it goes wrong at Napetuca," Blood Thorn added, "we would at least have time to evacuate the capital."

"If it goes wrong at Napetuca," I said, "You will lose a great many warriors for nothing. De Soto, if he survives, will never allow himself to be in a vulnerable position again."

Rattlesnake glanced at me and then Pearl Hand. "I hear your warning, and understand. As much as it pains me, yes, if the main body of his force is close, or if he comes with too much strength, I shall call off the attack. We will use it — as Pearl Hand suggests — to allay his suspicions and then try and kill him later."

"Let us pray this succeeds," I whispered fervently. "Because if you can kill de Soto, all peoples, everywhere, will owe the Uzachile an incredible debt of gratitude."

Blood Thorn asked, "Will you come with us, Black Shell?"

I nodded, remembering First Woman's warning: *It falls to people, not gods, to determine the ultimate victory.* "I'm hoping I will be

417

the one to drive an arrow through de Soto's eye."

Pearl Hand and I were packing up camp, stowing the jewelry we'd worn, carefully wrapping the copper and shell ornaments, when Blood Thorn arrived. He greeted the dogs as they ran out to meet him, dropping to his knees, roughing up their ears.

I laced Gnaw's pack closed and straightened. "Maybe you should have been a trader. You could spend the rest of your life playing with dogs."

He grinned, rising, and nodded to Pearl Hand, who gave him an amused smile. She finished lacing up Skipper's pack and asked, "What news, Blood Thorn?"

He sighed and shrugged. "The warriors are running on ahead. Paracusi Rattlesnake wants them at Napetuca by first light. I'm on the way as soon as I leave here. Will you be all right traveling on your own?"

Pearl Hand cocked an eyebrow, that expression that said "You're kidding, right?"

I chuckled. "Since when do a couple of traders need an escort to Napetuca? Believe it or not, we're used to traveling."

I could see from his pinched expression that he'd been anything but concerned about our ability to make it to Napetuca.

"What is it, Blood Thorn?" I propped my hands on my hips.

418

He sighed, scuffing the grass with a moccasin-clad toe. "When we were leaving, one of the Kristianos called out, pointing at you. He said something, would have caused a fuss. It was as if he thought he knew you."

"Antonio. Our escaped prisoner." I added, "He's the fool who used to own that armor you've been inspecting over the last week."

Pearl Hand nodded. "His father, the old man who interrupted him, is one of de Soto's *capitanos.* We left in a hurry, but old Don Luis was telling his son in no uncertain terms that he better not ever interrupt a council in that fashion again." She smile wryly. "I'd have liked to have stayed. You know, just long enough to see that spoiled little creature put in his place."

Blood Thorn had pursed his lips as he listened. "Do you think it could complicate our plans? I mean, if he recognized you?"

Pearl Hand glanced my way, brow thoughtful.

I shook my head, saying, "He's only the son of a subchief. De Soto gives the orders, makes the decisions. Back at the council, we were both painted, our hair up and pinned. From his expression, he wasn't really sure who we were. And, even if he had been, what could he do?" I glanced at Blood Thorn. "If you were in de Soto's position, would you stop everything to pursue some warrior's request for revenge?"

Blood Thorn chuckled grimly. "No, I suppose not, but it's worth keeping in mind for the future."

Pearl Hand turned to the last pack. "Antonio is a bitter young man. By now he's convinced he saw us, and once again, he was humiliated. That is going to burn inside him, eat at his souls."

"Soul," I corrected. "He claims to only have one."

She gave me one of her irritated looks.

I glanced at Blood Thorn. "Antonio wasn't the only one. One of Irriparacoxi's warriors was there, too. A man everyone called 'Ears' for the necklace he used to wear. He's the one who sat at Ortiz's right. Once upon a time, he had desires for Pearl Hand."

"He still does," she muttered. "The look in his eyes was bad enough, but when he finally stood up, it appeared that he was having problems with his breechcloth. It just wouldn't hang straight."

"Or he's trying to start a new fashion," I muttered. "Either way, I don't see any threat from them. Antonio may be a Kristiano, but Ears is only a slave. They won't be a problem for the Uzachile."

Pearl Hand had that distant expression in her eyes. "Only for the two of us, should either of us be captured again."

The way she said it sent a chill down my spine.

■ ■ ■ ■

The following morning, after arriving outside of Napetuca, we walked out to see what Rattlesnake had in mind. Leaving the forest, we found a great many warriors assembled around the paracusi, who was explaining the intricacies of his ambush.

To the north, Napetuca stood, its thatched roofs plainly visible above the palisade. Only a few people could be seen around the town. According to plan, all the corn, beans, and squash had been left to ensure the Kristianos were amply fed, and to maintain the illusion that all was well.

With the forest stretching to the east, cornfields surrounded the town for several bowshots in each direction. Rattlesnake had chosen a grassy flat maybe seven bowshots south of the town gate. Here he would meet de Soto and his hopefully small party.

"What do you think?" Pearl Hand asked as I ran my eyes over the ground.

"Having the forest behind them would be better. It gives any survivors a chance to escape if it goes wrong."

"That's a long run from there to here. Especially with cabayos in pursuit." She pointed at where Rattlesnake was surrounded by his warriors.

"Come on. Let's go see what the plan is."

I held my wife's hand as we walked through the thick grass, and began to realize why Rattlesnake had chosen the place. Not even the tallest Kristiano could see what a man had laying at his feet. I could feel humps in the irregular ground, and came to understand that this was all fallow cornfield, resting for a couple of years before being put back into production.

Rattlesnake was pointing at the line of trees we had just left, his voice barely audible as we approached. It was only as we joined the warriors that I discovered the lake just behind the high war chief's position. It was a pleasant body of water, perhaps four bowshots across. And just off to the south lay another, longer lake, its shores partially hidden by sedges and willows.

Such bodies of water occur in limestone country. For Napetuca, the lakes had been a boon. Not only did they provide a source of fish, but drew waterfowl and provided water for the corn during times of drought.

As I tried to take it all in, Blood Thorn saw us and came trotting over.

"This is where it will happen," he said in greeting. I could see the strain behind his eyes. His thoughts had to be on Water Frond and her fate if it should all go wrong.

"How does Rattlesnake see this unfolding?" Pearl Hand asked, her thoughtful eyes on the terrain.

"We meet the *Adelantado* where Rattlesnake is standing." Blood Thorn pointed. "Many of our warriors will be positioned around here, not in any kind of formation, just looking like small clusters of onlookers."

"With their weapons hidden in the grass at their feet," I said.

"Correct."

"And if de Soto's reinforcements are close?" Pearl Hand asked.

"No one will be the wiser if Rattlesnake decides not to attack. By ones and twos the warriors can pick up their weapons and walk away."

I frowned as I studied the approaches from the town. "Why here? Out in this flat? Why not closer to the forest?"

"Several reasons." Blood Thorn pointed at the lakes. "With the lakes behind us, they cannot circle on their fast cabayos and surprise us from behind. Where we will meet the Kristianos is far enough from the forest they won't fear ambush, but close enough to allow escape after we kill the *Adelantado*. It's the best compromise we can come up with."

For the first time I began to feel a glimmer of hope. With de Soto dead, the Uzachile could fade into the forests before a retaliatory strike could be organized. The frustration of the Uzachile escape would add to tensions in the Kristiano camp. The leadership would begin squabbling. With luck the Kristianos would come apart like an unfired clay pot in a rainstorm.

"It's a good plan," I agreed. "You have good visibility in all directions to ensure that de Soto is vulnerable. Rattlesnake can gauge the distance to any reinforcements and break off the attack with enough time to evacuate to the forest."

Blood Thorn pulled a blade of grass and absently chewed the sweet, pithy stem. "Everything hinges on if de Soto is fooled. As long as he expects nothing, he'll bring Water Frond and most of our people to exchange for Holata Uriutina. The rest of our people, those serving as porters, will have to take their chances. As soon as it is shouted out that we've attacked, most, I'm sure, will flee."

"Some won't make it," Pearl Hand reminded him.

Blood Thorn twirled the grass stem, his eyes on the distant village. "People are at risk no matter how this works out. If de Soto comes in strength, and we don't have the chance to kill him, he'll end up taking captives with him. No matter what he says he's going to do, the fact remains that someone has to carry his supplies. And we all know who that will be."

"At least your people aren't in chains." Pearl Hand's eyes had fixed on the distant trees marking the trail to Napetuca. Even now de Soto's army would be coming, only several hands of time distant.

"There's more," Blood Thorn said. "As a way of allaying suspicions, Blue Sun Stone has sent a delegation to de Soto. We have asked the Kristianos to consider joining us in an alliance against the Apalachee. Given Narvaez's experiences with our common enemy, de Soto might be willing to consider combining forces with the expectation that we can strike them together."

"That's crazy talk!" I cried.

Blood Thorn shrugged. "Perhaps, but there is a contingent among us who believes that such an alliance should be given a chance. Offering it to de Soto serves several purposes. First, it calms any fears the Kristianos might have about our intentions. Second, it eases concerns among the peace faction who disapprove of our plan to kill de Soto. Third, if de Soto comes in force to exchange the holatas, Rattlesnake's attack will be out of the question. Instead he will have another option to buy us time. He can dissemble, parade his warriors, as if in a demonstration of why joining to fight the Apalachee would be a good idea."

I could see the rationale for the misdirection, but glancing at Pearl Hand, it was obvious that she wasn't enthused either.

"Besides," Blood Thorn said softly, "it's not your concern. We know their plans, thanks to the two of you. In the end, the course will be decided by de Soto, and how he marches out to greet us. If he comes alone, or with a small party of his warriors, he will not go back alive. If he marshals his forces for war, and there is no chance to kill him, talking peace will allow Rattlesnake to save a great many lives."

I nodded and sighed. The plan made sense, and the Uzachile were no one's fools.

Pearl Hand asked, "And if de Soto comes prepared for an attack and the battle is called off, how will this work?"

Blood Thorn rubbed the back of his neck. "If Rattlesnake decides not to attack, Holata Uriutina will trade places with Holata Ahocalaquen. Water Frond will be freed with her uncle. Holata Uriutina will travel to Uzachile town, and from there, hopefully on to fight the Apalachee. Meanwhile Holata Uzachile will evacuate the capital in advance of the Kristianos' arrival, and let de Soto have the town. As proposed, our forces will march alongside the Kristianos, and meetings will be arranged in a way that Holata Uzachile can't be taken hostage."

"Uriutina knows the risks he's taking?" I asked.

Blood Thorn gave a sober nod. "We all do, Trader. Since the Kristianos have arrived, the only thing we have left is risk."

"You look unsure," Pearl Hand noted, reading Blood Thorn's expression.

The burly warrior grunted uncomfortably and gave her a guilty squint. "I'm a poor excuse for a man. I should be hoping for the greatest good for my people. Instead, I can't seem to see past obtaining Water Frond's release. It makes me ashamed."

I placed a hand on his shoulder. "Don't be. There is no shame in being who Breath Giver made us. If making the choice didn't bring tears to our souls, it would ring as hollow as a rotten log. And I think you, my friend, have a heart as solid as a forest oak."

His smile was a fleeting thing. "I just want her back."

"I know." I paused, meeting his eyes. "Were it me, I'd let the world burn if it meant saving Pearl Hand."

A weak smile curled Blood Thorn's lips. "Then we are both fools, you and I."

Later that day we watched as de Soto's army emerged along the forest trail and marched to occupy Napetuca. The cabayos were tended to, camps pitched, and troops occupied every building within the town. The *puercos,* under the watchful eye of their tenders, immediately began snuffling through the cornfields, crashing down the stalks, rooting through the bean and squash plants.

De Soto's fate lay in how he emerged on the following morning. One way, he was a corpse by nightfall. And the other . . . ? Who knew?

TWENTY-EIGHT

We camped that night in the forest outside Napetuca. Pearl Hand fed wood to the fire after we'd finished a quick meal of smoked turkey that Blood Thorn had seen fit to provide. Around us, in every direction, low fires marked the camps of warriors.

While we sat in silence, the lilting songs of the warriors could be heard. Most were singing to their ancestors, asking for courage and cunning in battle.

The dogs were sprawled about, and we'd spent a finger of time picking ticks off them, pinching fleas, and just generally petting. In times of stress, the simple act of touching a dog can bring a remarkable serenity to the souls. Bark had been so happy he'd tried to go to sleep with his big scarred head in Pearl Hand's lap.

As I watched the fire burn down to embers, I wondered at myself. As a Chicaza, going into battle, I should have fasted for four days, avoided any contact with women, drank button snakeroot — a purgative — and smoked the pipe, sending my prayers up to encourage the red Power to fill me during the battle. Finally, I should have been purified by the hopaye, drank my fill of black drink, and painted myself for battle.

Instead I sat beside the woman I loved, stuffed from a full meal, and contemplated how I would enjoy lying in her arms after depleting my loins. Such a situation would have left a blooded Chicaza warrior in abject terror. Perhaps it was right that I was *akeohoosa.* Whatever Power willed for me, it wasn't going to be affected by following the time-honored rituals of my people, and believe me, the Chicaza had rituals for everything. Even brushing one's teeth with a frayed willow stick had to be done just so. Otherwise Power might be offended.

Given my dereliction, why had Power chosen me? I could think of hundreds of pious and dedicated warriors who would better serve the purpose of fighting the Kristianos. And among the hopaye, any number of them were more charismatic and eloquent.

But Horned Serpent called to me that long-ago day, setting me onto this path. Why?

"I want to take the dogs with us." Pearl Hand interrupted my thoughts.

"If things go right, it's going to be a fight. Why would you want to endanger the dogs?"

She was staring thoughtfully into the coals, the red light bathing her perfect face. She had her long hair pulled back over her shoulders, and the way it hung accented her cheeks. "They'll have war dogs with them."

"I don't follow your logic."

She glanced sidelong to where the dogs lay, lost in sleep, their paws twitching in dreams as their souls chased soul rabbits in another world. "The Kristiano war dogs are trained to bring down men."

"So I've noticed."

"Our dogs fight other dogs." She smiled wistfully. "Even though you do your best to keep them apart, they've been scrapping all their lives."

I began to see her point. All of my dogs were big and muscular; that was the first requirement for a trader's dog. Second, they'd survived numerous scraps with local dog packs. Bark might not have had much in the way of smarts, but he was lethal in a dog fight.

"It's not their fight," I said softly.

"What if we're killed? What happens to them? Slow starvation? Who takes care of them? Don't they just become some nuisance hanging around whatever is left of Napetuca?"

She was right about that. Most likely they'd end up in some starving Uzachile's stew pot since the Kristianos had eaten everything else.

Then she added, "Black Shell . . . you forget: It became their fight the day Antonio killed Fetch."

She had me there.

"I've got a better idea," I said, going back to the argument we'd had earlier. "Why don't you stay with the dogs? That way, no matter what happens, they'll have you to take care of them."

She gave me her "don't start this again" look.

I spread my hands in despair. "I know you think you have to be there. But I'd really prefer if you would —"

"Who will understand the orders called out by Kristianos in the middle of the fight? You?" She rattled off something in *español,* adding, "You can relay that to Paracusi Rattlesnake, right? Tell him to change the disposition of his warriors in the middle of the battle?"

"We've been through this before."

"And, since apparently it wasn't solved before dinner — although I thought it had been — we'll solve it again."

I hated it when she used that tone of voice. "What if something happens to you?"

She gave me that penetrating look, the one that said I was being an idiot. "How many men have you killed, Black Shell?"

"That's got nothing to do with —"

"I've killed three."

I straightened. "Three?"

"All of them up close . . . like that guard the night I brought you out of Uzita. But for his armor, I would have killed that Kristiano on the trail south of Ahocalaquen, too." She placed her slim hands together, glancing up at the tree above us. "Perhaps I should start introducing myself as 'Pearl Hand Mankiller.' " Mankiller was the honorific given to a blooded warrior among the Nations to the north.

I sighed. "Very well. The dogs can come."

She nodded, a resolute expression on her face. "This will be decided in the opening moments. My crossbow could make all the difference. If I can kill one of the *capitanos* with the first shot, it might demoralize them. They're not used to seeing their fellows killed by the likes of us."

"We'll be close. I'll shoot for their faces."

She nodded. "And don't forget the cabayos. Kill or disable them, and the rider has to fight on foot. Especially the lancers. They can be surrounded, closed with, and easily slaughtered."

The way she said it, so cool and composed, seemed a little eerie.

"You just remember," I countered, "once de Soto is dead, we run. Rattlesnake can carry this thing on as long as he likes, but you and I leave. When the Kristianos find out their chief is dead, they're going to come with a vengeance. We don't want to be there when that happens."

She nodded, lips pursed, eyes vacant, as if seeing it in her head.

I stared anxiously at the low coals. "I just hope de Soto falls for this. If we don't get him this time, he'll never be this gullible again."

"We serve the ghosts of the dead," she said softly. "All those people he's killed, the ones left by the side of the trail, they have no one to mourn for them, to send their souls to the afterlife."

I rubbed the scars on my throat. I had my own reasons for wanting to be there when the end came for de Soto. Not that I wasn't as compassionate as Pearl Hand, but the ghosts of the dead could fend for themselves.

I glanced at her, wondering at the woman she was. I knew she was hiding her own fears beneath that calm exterior, but when it came to keeping her out of the fight, it just wasn't going to happen.

I watch the Uzachile warriors surge forward in a great mass, the effect like following a wave of brown bodies as they wash onto the even ranks

433

of Kristianos. The valiant ululations of charging warriors communicates their courage — and changes in an instant as the Kristianos unleash carnage. Screams, like liquid agony, burst from a hundred lungs as crossbow bolts blow through wicker shields, skin, muscle, and bone. Thunder sticks pop and crackle, spitting smoke and death through disbelieving bodies — and leave them broken and oozing blood, torn tissue, and bits of splintered bone.

I hear the eerie whistle of the crossbow arrows as they streak past my ear and watch leaping and twisting Uzachile warriors as they engage metal-clad opponents. Sunlight on greased skin gives the warriors a surreal glint, as if to counter the sheen of their adversaries' polished metal.

Those in front fall first — no more than pegs flattened by the Kristiano gale. Now, unhesitant, the killing sweeps toward me, charging warriors are knocked over and bowled flat by a mighty wave. Those few who crouch, brace their feet, and withstand the onslaught of arrows, drive futilely against a prickling wall of metal men who pierce them, as though Uzachile muscle were no more than soft clay.

The shining silver ranks of the enemy respond as one, advancing, bearded men half hidden behind round shields as they hack and slash with silver-thorn swords. I cringe as hands, arms, and heads are lopped off with the same ease as a boy might slash flowers from their stems with a cane switch.

The blood is stunning — not just the profusion of it, but the color: a vivid, living red, squirting from severed stumps. I watch it jet brilliantly onto spring-green grass. Where crimson spatters polished Kristiano armor, it thins and smears in sheets that turn the metal coppery in the sunlight.

And on they come, bearded faces alight with a bloodlust that seduces the combatants, so firmly swaddled with invincibility.

I have been standing, rooted, my bow held before me like a winter-dry reed. In horror I watch the approaching Kristianos slash life out of the last of the fallen warriors.

Unable to run, I feel only numbing fear as the metal ranks widen, the flanks stepping out, jutting spears crimson and dripping in the sunlight as their deadly points center on me. The ranks stretch until I am encircled by a ring of clanking, hissing men, their faces framed by helmets and shields.

The ranks part and Ortiz steps forward, a slave collar clattering and dangling from its chain . . .

I jerked awake and gasped as adrenaline charged my body. Careful not to wake Pearl Hand, I eased out from under the blanket and dropped my head into my hands.

In the quiet of night, I shook my head to rid it of the horrible dream. I stared up thankfully at the inky forest overhead. The smell of living trees, woodsmoke, and the musk of old leaf mat filled my nostrils.

Bark and Gnaw raised their heads from where they slept to stare at me in the darkness. I made a flat motion with my hand and both dogs lowered their heads, each puffing out a sigh, as though irritated that I'd awakened them.

I pulled on my loincloth and draped a fabric cape over my shoulders before I stood. All four of the dogs were watching now, and I motioned them to come as I made my way through the inky shadows under the trees. The presence of the dogs reassured me. A man is never alone when accompanied by his dogs. And their senses are so much keener than mine.

I wound through sleeping camps of warriors. Where all should have been quiet, I heard men shifting under their blankets. Occasionally, soft murmuring reached my ears as anxious souls who should have been asleep asked for reassurance from their fellows.

Several paces farther on I heard the melodic rise and fall of a man's voice as he offered prayers to his ancestors, begging for luck and courage.

Turns out I was far from the only soul in the world with worries about the coming morning.

Stepping out from the trees I found a clear

sky, frosted with stars in all but the west, where moonglow from beneath the horizon paled the sky. The constellation of Horned Serpent had sunk into the west, leaving me with a slight sense of relief. I wasn't sure I wanted my supposed Spirit Helper staring down at me on this night. Instead only the upper portion of the Spirit Road that led to the Land of the Dead was visible in the northwest.

I stared at the hazy band, seeing where the two roads forked near the star that marked Eagle Man kept guard. My Chicaza, and most other Mos'Kogeans, believed that he quizzed the dead as they traveled up the foggy band of stars. Depending upon a person's answers, they might be directed on toward the Land of the Dead, or the other way, to the blind end. It was to that latter destination that those who had excelled only in mediocrity were directed.

Staring up at the night sky, I wondered if that was where I might eventually wind up.

"What do you think you're doing?" Uncle's voice haunted my memory. *"One day you will be made high minko of all the Chicaza. And when that day comes, though I am dead and buried, my souls shall be looking down, watching you. I expect to see a great man as he walks out of the Tchkofa, proud, dressed in his finest, with a shining copper hairpiece gleaming in the sun. On that day the man you will become*

will finally be measured."

Of course I would never know that day. Not after Horned Serpent whispered to my souls. Not after I was declared akeohoosa.

Grass hissed as the dogs and I waded through it to the place where Rattlesnake expected to meet de Soto at high-sun tomorrow. The spot had been beaten flat by many feet as Rattlesnake rehearsed his warriors during the day. I could smell the dank odor of the two lakes as the breeze shifted.

Turning, I stared at the dark shape of Napetuca town. The faint glow of fires outlined houses against the backdrop of the palisade. Off to the east, along the trail, were the camps full of exhausted captives. I could make out the tents housing the *soldados,* their angular shapes silhouetted by firelight. In the distance a cabayo herder sang to the horses. Once I'd been amazed at the sound; now I wondered if I'd be lucky enough to kill the man whose throat produced such soft strains.

Perhaps. But only after de Soto's accursed soul had been dispatched to his *paraíso.* He was the first and most important target. Kill him and, depending on the circumstances, perhaps we could hunt the rest of them down, one by one.

"Beat this into your silly head, boy. War is the ultimate experience of red Power. Assuming you have prepared yourself for the Power, fasted for four days, kept your peg out of a

438

woman, purged your body with button snake-root, and drank sufficient black drink, you will feel the red Power as you've never felt anything in your life!"

I narrowed an eye as I heard Uncle's voice thunder from the past. From the time I could hold a bow, he'd made me repeat countless drills. He'd given me my first war club when I turned seven and begun teaching me to use it. As to when I touched my first stickball racquet . . . well, I'd been so young the moment remains lost to memory. Nor can I recall the first time Uncle took me to sit at the feet of the war chiefs, the tishu minko, and the noted warriors, all wearing miniature white arrows in their hair. Those little white arrows were among the highest of war honors that could be bestowed upon a man. Uncle had six.

At their feet I was forced to listen; the hope had been that I would pick up the roots of knowledge. That I would grow to think like a warrior — that it would become part of my bones and blood.

Perhaps it had. During my wanderings, I had spent a lot of time among the warriors of various nations. Being Chicaza, I had been grilled by war chiefs, minkos, and warriors. Everyone was interested in Chicaza tactics. To my amusement, I'd found that most foreign war chiefs would listen intently and then proceed to elaborate on why Chicaza tactics wouldn't work.

Someone should have told the Chicaza. Maybe they would have realized they were winning all those victories by accident and stupidity.

At first I'd been indignant, arguing vehemently and for long hours into the night. It didn't take long to figure out that I was arguing against the wind. People will believe what they will — and few foreign warriors were willing to dedicate themselves to such harsh discipline, training, and ascetic beliefs.

The fact is that there is only one way to judge a nation's military: Does it win?

I'd seen the Kristianos in action and followed their wake of wreckage north. If de Soto didn't fall for Rattlesnake's ruse, tomorrow was going to be a very bloody day.

Assuming de Soto walked blindly into the trap, the Timucua would kill him and flee before the Kristianos could retaliate. Then, hopefully, the invaders would turn on each other, and we could destroy them piecemeal, or they would march south in force and leave our land altogether.

And if de Soto managed to save himself at the last moment? Ah, that would throw the back-fat straight into the flames. In the ensuing fight, he and his small force would face overwhelming numbers of real warriors for the first time. The Uzachile weren't Southern Timucua. They regularly mixed it up with

Apalachee, Koasati, and Mos'kogee and held their own. De Soto's men hadn't faced disciplined warriors like these.

"It will all hinge on the numbers," I said absently to the dogs. "If the Kristianos come massed, we can only pray that Rattlesnake has sense enough to call off the attack."

If he didn't, Kristiano retaliation would be brutal and swift. Images from the massacre at Tapolaholata rose to haunt my souls. I remembered the corpses laid out in a line, and how one brave young man, the "false" holata, had been mutilated, his decapitated head thrust down into his pelvis to stare out of the gaping hole where his anus should have been.

Then fragments of the dream I'd had earlier resurfaced. I hunched down, reassured to wrap my arms around my dogs.

TWENTY-NINE

Trees hid the faint glow of dawn when the dogs and I made our way back to the small camp we shared with Pearl Hand. I can't say that I was surprised to see her up, moving about, feeding sticks to a small fire.

"I thought about going with you," she said, not even looking up from her tasks, "but there are times a person needs to be alone with his souls."

"I didn't sleep well."

"Smart man." She poured the last of our water into our brownware cooking bowl. Setting the empty water gourd to one side, Pearl Hand shot me an evaluative glance through tangles of sleep-disheveled hair.

I thought she looked absolutely feral as she crouched there, hands smudged, lips in a pout, tight brown nipples jutting from full breasts.

I gestured for the dogs to stay and dropped to my haunches, meeting her questioning gaze across the fire. "I love you more than anything."

She smiled, white teeth flashing in the dusky light. "Maybe you should go walking in the night more often."

"No. I don't think so. The thoughts weren't pleasant."

"Then perhaps —"

"Perhaps we will slip back under the blanket while the stew you're making comes to a boil."

Eyes locked with mine, she reached out, taking my hand. She pulled me to the blanket, hooked her thumbs into the breechcloth, and smoothly slid it off my hips. As I undid the cape I was wearing, I watched her peel off her skirt, the fabric fluttering down her long legs.

She pushed me to the ground, settling the smooth softness of her buttocks onto my hips. As she braced herself on my shoulders, I reached up, cupping the wealth of her breasts. She stared into my eyes as the wild fall of her hair draped us in darkness.

"We may only have this one morning left," she whispered. "Let's make it memorable."

"Oh, yes."

We kept glancing at each other as we strode out from under the shelter of the trees. Pearl Hand walked on my right, her left hand held in mine, as though neither of us could get enough of the other. The dogs read our unease, an alert set to their heads as they coursed back and forth, sniffing here and there. They kept watching us, as if for some clue of what to expect.

My bow and war arrows rode in the alligator quiver strapped to my back. Pearl Hand carried her crossbow in her right, a waist quiver of iron-tipped short arrows swung at her hip. She'd polished her weapon's wood with hickory oil, and it glistened in the sunlight.

I should have been preoccupied with a hundred thoughts, but I kept sticking on one nagging question: Why did Power insist that Pearl Hand and I participate in this madness?

It seemed insane. De Soto had crossed oceans looking for gold. Now he was looting and killing his way across the peninsula, searching for a metal that I knew for a fact wasn't here. His army carried more gold with it than could be found throughout the great northern Nations.

In his ignorance, he had marched north, taking what he wanted by force, bribes, and intimidation. He had kidnapped people from

444

their homes, destroyed whole peoples, looted their foodstuffs, and imprisoned chiefs and their families. The man had smiled as unimaginable cruelties had been inflicted on innocents, and even his dogs had been turned into creatures of evil.

All for delusions of gold?

What was it about Creation and the makeup of the world that people like de Soto were permitted to exist? What flaw in the Beginning Times had allowed such perversions of intelligence to flourish?

One by one, I tried to recall the endless line of rotting corpses along the Kristianos' march, only to give up, overwhelmed by the number.

I glanced up at the low sun, hanging like a molten orange ball over the trees. *Breath Giver, can't you bring this madness to a halt?*

In that moment I wanted nothing more than to tighten my grip on Pearl Hand and lead her away, back to where we'd hidden the packs. I wanted to repack the dogs and turn east, following the morning sun to the ocean, and from there we'd head north, taking the high-country trails around the swamps and inlets. Somewhere, in an open glade, close to water, we could find good sandy loam that would grow corn. Weirs and fish traps would supply enough catfish, bass, and trout. The nut trees and the animals that fed off them would keep our stomachs full.

It wasn't much to ask of life. Certainly nothing like asking for gold, empire, and dominion over all. Why then was Power refusing my longing for so little, yet granting this maggot, de Soto, the possibility of so much?

Where was the justice?

"I can't read your expression." Pearl Hand cast a glance from under the hanging wealth of her hair. I caught a glimpse of a flashing eye and the soft curve of her cheek.

"I'm searching for understanding." I resettled my bow and quiver on my back. "Oh, and wishing we were headed east as fast as our legs could carry us."

That old wry smile bent her full lips. "All men seek answers, Black Shell. Only fools believe they'll ever really find them."

"That's depressing."

"No, people are depressing. The world is what it is. Only people are truly cruel, or remarkably noble, as the case may be. White Power verses red Power, forever seeking a balance that, once found, can never be maintained: De Soto and his Kristianos against us and the Uzachile. It's the way of things."

"But why?" I cried, balling my left fist.

"Because living the white Power of peace, order, and tranquility is stagnant; while the red Power's chaos, warfare, and strife are unsustainable." She gave me that mocking arch of her eyebrow. "Come on, lover, what do you expect? That life should be easy? Cheap?"

446

"Absolutely. Especially today. Come on. Let's go pack the dogs and run like a pair of swamp bunnies." I almost meant it.

She shook her hand loose from mine. "And your Spirit dreams?"

"They'll have to find me before they can punish me for running out on them."

I caught the amusement in her eyes. "Your secret is safe with me."

"That's just it," I muttered, growing serious as we approached the assembling warriors. "I really do wish we were anywhere but here."

Her subtle smile told me she probably wished for the same.

Clumps of warriors had assembled, all wearing their finest regalia. Faces were painted in bright colors. Like most Timucua peoples, the Uzachile favored a hair pom that rose up straight from the top of the head, and each warrior had decorated his with feathers, bright beads, and bits of crushed shell. Greased skin made their bodies shine and emphasized striking tattoos that covered arms, breasts, and shoulders.

As we passed, each group nodded respectfully. I could see the stress hidden in their stiff expressions and the fidgeting movements of hands and feet. Hard glances were fixed first on Napetuca town, and then on Rattlesnake, Blue Sun Stone, and Holata Uriutina where they had taken a position on the trampled flat. There they expected to meet de Soto.

Pearl Hand and I stopped a respectful distance from the chiefs, and both of us carefully placed our weapons on the ground. Kicking a bit of grass over them, I motioned the dogs to lie down and finally turned my attention to Napetuca.

The first thing I noticed was that the cabayo herd was smaller, the animals held out of view behind the town. Then came the wavering, squealing calls the creatures made when separated from their fellows. Through the palisade I could see some of the beasts inside the enclosure.

Blood Thorn detached himself from the others and came striding over, as though powered by a nervous energy.

"They've split up their cabayos," I called by way of greeting.

Blood Thorn had painted his face in red and white stripes. His pom of hair had been riddled with white heron feathers accented by a multitude of iridescent blues, reds, and yellows taken from painted buntings. Thick shell necklaces hung over his muscular breast, and he carried a wicker-cane shield on his back.

He propped his hands on his hips as he turned and studied the town. "We don't know what that means, but take it as a positive sign: De Soto hasn't massed his cabayeros. In addition, spies that we've sent close inform us that most of the *soldados* are still inside their tents just outside the palisade."

I exhaled some of the tension that had been building inside. "Then it looks as if the *Adelantado* doesn't suspect a thing?"

Blood Thorn grinned. "He still has a hand of time before the council is supposed to take place, but no. As far as we can tell, he hasn't placed any of his forces in formation."

I glanced at Pearl Hand, seeing her thoughtful frown as she studied Napetuca. "What about the tents?" she asked. "Don't they normally take them down in the morning?"

I turned to study the line of off-white canvas shelters. I could see a few of the *soldados* walking about. The handful that were visible wore shirts and pants, not armor.

Blood Thorn shrugged. "It seems they are planning on staying here for a couple of days before moving on to Uzachile." He made a face. "We left them at least a week's worth of food."

"And Kristianos don't leave until all the food is eaten," Pearl Hand said sourly.

"Well," I mused, "everything looks peaceful." A glance at the sun told me we still had to wait. "Let us pray that by high sun today, de Soto is dead and we are all running for our lives through the forest."

"So we pray," Blood Thorn agreed. "When the Kristianos come, we ask that the two of you approach so that you can hear what they say." He hesitated. "Assuming there are any but the most cursory of discussions."

"We'll be there."

I looked back at the town, seeing barely a hint of activity. The few Kristianos visible weren't even carrying weapons. Sometimes, in ones and twos, they would walk up to the palisade and stare out at us. And no wonder; Uzachile warriors were dribbling in by fours and fives, all taking positions in the tall grass surrounding the council area. Some were playing flutes, others clapping and singing, calling to their ancestors for courage and valor.

After Blood Thorn returned to the chief's council, Pearl Hand gave me one of her serious looks, asking, "How do you think Power will react to this?"

"What?"

"We have called de Soto to a peace council. If he comes expecting peace, we are going to kill him. It's an abuse, you know."

I shrugged. "After the atrocities committed at the hands of the Kristianos, Power will sigh with relief when we've killed the last one."

She nodded, turning her impassive face back toward Napetuca.

The long wait started, and it was all I could do to keep from replaying scenes from my nightmare. Images of blood and death lay just below my consciousness. It took a concerted effort to block them out.

Please, Breath Giver, I prayed, *blind this foul de Soto to our plans. Just give me one good shot.*

THIRTY

Mother Sun was high in the sky when the clattering of arms and movement of men gave us the first clue that de Soto was coming.

Around us, warriors rose to their feet, all eyes on the activity that could be seen through the palisade. We watched as armored guards paraded out the gate, unfurling their colorful cloth banners to hang over the route the *Adelantado* would take. Between the palisade posts we could discern the slow procession of men. Meanwhile, in the Kristiano tent-camp to the east, a few white-shirted men stood watch. Apparently the fools thought the meeting was going to be so uneventful it wasn't worth getting their fellows out of their tents to follow the festivities.

Then de Soto emerged — sunlight gleaming on his polished armor as he walked side by side with Holata Ahocalaquen. Two of the terrible war dogs marched on either side, their long lean heads turning our way as they sniffed the morning for our scent. A young woman who I took to be Water Frond followed in the ranks behind Ortiz. Behind them came armored men leading four cabayos. Six of the thunder-stick warriors strode out, the heavy weapons braced on their shoulders. I counted as the rest passed through the gate, coming up with twenty-five individuals — four of them captives.

A sense of elation rose in my breast as I figured the odds: Four or five hundred against twenty-five? I couldn't help but glance at Rattlesnake. The great paracusi stood as if he were carved of wood, hawkish eyes on the approaching party.

"Come on," Pearl Hand's voice was tense. "We'd better walk over where we can overhear the Kristianos. It might be the only warning Rattlesnake gets."

We picked up our weapons, carrying them against our bodies, the dogs following curiously, tails waving lazily in the air. Blood Thorn gave us a slight nod, motioning us close to the rear. I wasn't pleased to do it, but I laid my bow and quiver down in the mashed grass. If Rattlesnake ordered the attack, I'd have to shoot through the whole Uzachile delegation to kill de Soto.

Pearl Hand used the opportunity to cock her crossbow and place one of the stubby arrows into its rail.

My mouth had gone dry. A prickling sensation — like ants running across my skin — and sweaty palms reflected the tension inside my souls. I'd strung my bow earlier; now it seemed to mock me from where it lay in the grass.

I stepped around so that I could see de Soto and his party as they came walking slowly forward. Across the shortening distance I could see the man; he actually held Ahocalaquen's arm, talking to the holata with great animation. The Timucuan chief seemed to be nodding as Ortiz walked close behind, translating.

"Ready," came Rattlesnake's order.

Blood Thorn gave a hand signal, and I watched the surrounding warriors tense, many in a partial crouch, ready to reach down for their weapons.

My heart had begun to hammer in my chest and sweat tickled its way down my cheeks.

"Let him walk right up to us and stop," Rattlesnake reminded firmly. "If any man moves before my order, I will personally tie him in the square and cut him apart piece by piece."

His subchiefs gave the hand signal for the surrounding warriors to hold. I could see them giving their companions sharp glances as the tension built.

I kept clenching my hands, rubbing my fingers. Pearl Hand, however, stood like an oak, not a muscle moving, her left eye in a slight squint as she watched de Soto's party approach.

Her controlled voice caught me by surprise. "Antonio and his father are just behind de Soto."

I craned my neck, spotting them both in shining silver armor. Antonio's didn't fit so well. Obviously he'd taken it from a larger man to replace what he had lost to us.

"Easy," Rattlesnake commanded. "Everyone hold and await my signal."

I shot a glance at Napetuca, seeing movement behind the palisade, but couldn't make out the meaning of it. The soldiers' camp looked half deserted.

"This is going to work," I declared.

The dogs were poised beside us, picking up on the tension that seemed to sing in the very air. They'd fixed on the war dogs walking at de Soto's side. Bark's ears pricked forward, and he tensed.

"Steady," Rattlesnake called.

De Soto's party was no more than a half bowshot away, proceeding as if on a casual morning's march. He was still holding Ho-

455

lata Ahocalaquen's arm, but now his eyes were on us. Over the narrowing distance I could see a slight smile on his thin lips. His once soulless eyes seemed animated, as if delighted by something beyond our understanding.

I saw de Soto turn, speaking to one of the young men who followed just behind Antonio. The man lifted a yellow horn to his lips and took a breath.

At that moment the men with thunder sticks rolled them off their shoulders, and de Soto raised a hand. The party stopped, perhaps a half bowshot away.

I heard the word across the suddenly still clearing: *"Ahora!"*

What?

The shrill blare of the horn carried on the morning, lilting and rising, as though a call from some great raptorial bird.

I saw the confusion on Holata Ahocalaquen's face, could see de Soto's delighted smile as Ortiz grasped the holata from behind. Then de Soto was vaulting up onto a great spotted gray cabayo, while one of his men handed him a lance.

"We are betrayed!" Rattlesnake cried. "It is an attack!"

The thunder of hooves barely preceded the emergence of armored cabayeros as they burst through Napetuca's gate. Off to the side, the tents were being thrown back like

456

blankets, exposing small squads of armed men who leaped to their feet, rushing forward to form ranks.

We all stood, stunned, watching the impossible. Ortiz was dragging Holata Ahocalaquen back, and stopped only long enough to grab Water Frond. I could see total surprise on Ahocalaquen's face, his mouth working like a rebuked infant's.

"Attack!" Rattlesnake bellowed, raising his arms. "Forward and kill them all!"

"Blood and pus," I cried. "This is going to be a disaster."

Pearl Hand was already reaching for her crossbow. The dogs were alternately looking up at me, then back at where de Soto's little party was lining out, the thunder sticks being leveled in our direction.

Blood Thorn's cry broke the confusion, unhindered rage echoing as he started forward. He'd shifted his wicker shield to his left arm, a war club in his right hand.

One of the thunder sticks discharged, blue smoke following the ugly pop of the weapon. Simultaneously Blue Sun Stone's body jolted in time with a loud meaty slap, and something spattered on my skin. I watched the man stagger, a bloody wound gaping to the right of his spine, just below the shoulder blade. Blue Sun Stone's knees gave and he fell onto his back, body bouncing at the impact. Blue Sun Stone's eyes were already glassy, and the round red hole in his ribs bubbled blood.

Dumbly I noticed the bits of bone and tissue that stuck to my skin. *Pieces of Blue Sun Stone, blown right out of his body by the thunder stick!*

I wiped at the gore, a sudden shiver icing my souls.

"Forward!" Rattlesnake cried, waving his warriors in.

"You coming?" Pearl Hand called. "We've got this one chance to kill de Soto!" And she was sprinting — dogs baying at her heels — after Rattlesnake, Blood Thorn, Uriutina, and the other war chiefs.

In growing panic I fished for my bow, slung my war arrows over my back, and took one last look at Blue Sun Stone. Flies were already landing on his sightless eyes. Then I nocked an arrow as I charged off after Pearl Hand and the rest.

The staccato of banging thunder sticks reminded me of wooden hammers pounding on resilient wood. I heard and felt the whoosh of something invisible past my left ear. Old Crane — who had once called for peace — slammed face-first into the ground. The entire top of his head was blown open; blood gushed, washing bits of pink brain matter into the grass.

At the sight of it, I wanted to stop, turn, and run. But Pearl Hand and the dogs were just ahead. I watched as Rattlesnake shouted a command, and his warriors slowed, drawing arrows back.

I pelted to a stop beside Pearl Hand, panting as if I'd run a full hand of time instead of less than a bowshot.

De Soto was charging headlong for the center of us, and ahead of him, both of the war dogs came like streaking javelins.

"Get them!" Pearl Hand cried, dropping to her knees, pointing at the war dogs.

I watched Skipper, Squirm, and Gnaw leap forward, fixing on the closing dogs. Bark gave me a stupid look, as if he didn't quite understand. I gave him a "go" command, and as soon as it settled behind his thick skull, he uttered a mournful howl and launched after the others.

The dogs came together ten paces before us. Kristiano dogs may know how to kill a human, but against a trader's dogs? I had a brief moment of sheer joy as my pack body-slammed into the lighter war dogs. But the real fury was unloosed when Bark finally arrived. Skipper wisely ducked away, leaving Bark to bowl one of the war dogs onto its back. Before the startled war dog could even squeal, Bark had it by the throat.

The dogs gave us our break. De Soto's great gray cabayo didn't expect the shrieks of abject pain and terror let loose by the war dogs. The gray beast jerked sideways, shying from the snarling, screaming dogs. The

Adelantado was pulling at the control straps, bellowing curses at his beast in *español.*

"Get de Soto!" I shouted, having finally found my voice.

"Shoot the cabayo!" Pearl Hand cried. "On foot, he is ours!"

"Shoot!" Rattlesnake bellowed. "Kill them all!"

I drew, finding my mark as de Soto's cabayo wheeled. I watched my shaft fly true, driving itself to the fletching just behind the beast's right front leg, ahead of de Soto's armored shin. Heart shot!

As I pulled another arrow from my quiver, I caught sight of Pearl Hand. She stepped forward, the crossbow raised. Her head was lowered to the stock as she squinted, taking her time.

When she released, she was staring de Soto right in the face. He would have died then, but for the sudden bucking of his cabayo. As it was, de Soto almost lost his seat. Pearl Hand's short arrow hissed through empty air as the man was jerked sideways.

Arrows were thudding into the cabayo from all sides, and de Soto — demon that he was — realized it. He turned the animal, hammering it with his spurred feet, goading it back toward his Kristianos. Wonder of wonders, he made it. I watched the man step off the beast as it slowed and sank onto its belly.

Then we were after them, running in pursuit, ecstatic at the sight of de Soto afoot. But no sooner did his horse fall than the man who had sounded the horn led another forward. De Soto literally leaped onto the beast, jerked it cruelly around, and came charging back, his lance lowered.

Fool! Did he think he could take us single-handedly?

Apparently.

I watched him duck the arrows shot his way; others clattered off his armor. And then he was upon us.

I reached out at the last instant and tugged an oblivious Blood Thorn to the side. He stumbled back, unbalanced, as the wicked metal point of de Soto's lance slashed the spot where he'd been but a moment before.

"Thanks," he whispered.

"What were you doing? Didn't you see that coming?"

"Looking for Water Frond," he told me, pulling himself upright. "Did she run as the rest of the cabayeros passed? Did she get away?"

"Ortiz has her and Holata Ahocalaquen." I pointed to a place behind the approaching cabayeros. "They're almost back to the gates."

Blood Thorn gripped his war club and bellowed his anger.

There wasn't time for more. De Soto had wheeled his mount, scattering Uzachile warriors and chiefs the way a bobcat did a covey

461

of quail. The man's feet were pounding the cabayo's flanks, and the creature leaped forward, allowing de Soto to drive his lance clear through a confused warrior.

I watched in amazement. De Soto neatly twisted and rolled the long lance as his mount passed, the slim shaft slipping out of the victim's body with as little resistance as it had gone in.

Meanwhile the rest of his cabayeros were thundering toward our warriors. They came lined out abreast, leaning over the necks of their beasts, lances forward. In response, the Uzachile paracusi barked orders, forming ranks. These formations, literal squares of warriors, had withstood Apalachee and Tuskaloosa assaults and won the respect of war chiefs far and wide.

Breaking into little bunches, the cabayeros set upon the squared ranks of battle-disciplined Uzachile. And the effect? The Kristianos drove their cabayos right through the formations as though they were no more substantial than smoke. Slashing and hacking the riders lent to the chaos as the beasts physically sent warriors flying. Within a couple of heartbeats, all formation integrity had been broken, warriors fleeing in panic, throwing down their shields, screaming, running into each other, clambering over the fallen. By then the cabayeros had wheeled about, and were charging through again. The

Uzachile tried to flee before them like schools of fish before an alligator.

Screams in the hundreds could be heard over the clatter of arrows on armor. Dying cabayos shrieked like tortured women, and horns blared. I heard hideous laughter, crying, and the popping of thunder sticks. The odors of trampled grass, sweaty cabayo, blood, and severed intestines carried on the breeze. Everywhere I looked, men were running, cabayeros flitting through them like hawks piercing a flood of pigeons.

How long did it last? I can't tell you. It seemed like an eternity of sheer terror as Blood Thorn and I dodged the cabayeros and their deadly lances. When the opportunity occurred, I'd wait till the last second to drive an arrow at a lancer's head, or perhaps into his cabayo. Doing so saved our lives at least twice.

I had no opportunity to look for Pearl Hand.

Through the chaos of shouts, screams, pounding hooves, and squealing cabayos, Blood Thorn and I alternately ran, threw ourselves to the ground, or leaped sideways at the last minute.

Pearl Hand? Blessed gods, where are you? I tried to remember when I'd seen her last. And couldn't. I twirled on my feet, desperate to locate her. Everywhere I looked we were surrounded by death, movement, and panic.

"The trees!" Blood Thorn cried. "Make for the trees!"

Among the sights of that day, I remember a flashed image: that of a Kristiano war dog, his once-sleek hide ripped, an ear shredded. He raced past on three legs. His impotent paw dangled by a few tendons and flopped with each step. Behind him came Bark, fired with fury as he leaped to sink teeth into the fleeing dog's flanks.

Pearl Hand? Where is Pearl Hand?

Running after Blood Thorn, I kept searching the battle. Rattlesnake, Bit Woman, and the others had vanished in the meleé.

Tell me Pearl Hand's not dead.

Riders blocked us. We both pulled up, panting, staring wildly this way and that. That was the moment I first began to understand what was happening. Parties of Rattlesnake's warriors were formed up in bunches, desperate to maintain some kind of integrity as they launched arrows at the racing cabayeros.

But no sooner did a war chief, or deputy, get his fellows half organized than the cabayeros noticed. The massed cabayos — guided by armored men — would plow right through the nascent formation, sending individuals flying in panic. Then the sport began, riders following along behind, picking off routed warriors one by one.

After the cabayeros came the *soldados*, a solid line of them, trotting forward behind a wall of shining metal shields. As they advanced, they covered crossbow men and thunder-stick shooters. The few collections of Timucua warriors that rushed to meet them seemed to melt away like back fat on a red-hot stone. The popping of the thunder sticks seemed so paltry at first, but warriors fell, and the stinging smoke blew over us, reeking of sulpher and death.

The forest, and escape, blocked by Kristianos, seemed ever more distant.

I watched the pride of Holata Uzachile's military might disintegrate. His warriors reminded me of songbirds kicked out of a bush: They flew in every direction, bleating their fear. The number of brown painted bodies lying still or writhing in the grass began to hit home.

Pearl Hand?

I didn't see her, but caught sight of Antonio as he led a party of *soldados* in our direction. He was shouting orders, pointing with a sword.

"Come on," I called to Blood Thorn. "Steal a bow and some arrows from one of the dead. These, we can deal with."

I nocked an arrow as Antonio's Kristianos came thudding forward. These carried those long spear-axes and huddled behind round shields, eyeing us with anticipation.

"As long as they can't reach us, we can shoot," I told Blood Thorn, and then called out, "Antonio! You are a maggot from *el diablo.*"

He stared at me in surprise, then squinted, calling, "Black Shell?" Then he grinned. *"¡Bienvenidos al infierno!"*

I drew, took aim, and let fly with an arrow as he ordered his men to charge us. To my delight he tried to bat the arrow away at the last instant. It entered his wrist, slicing up through his arm. Antonio's scream of pain and fear was a delight to the ears.

"That one's for Fetch!" I cried, nocking another arrow and driving it at his head. Just as I released, he dropped to his knees, my arrow clanging harmlessly off his helmet.

"Ayúdame!" Antonio screamed at the top of his lungs. *"Papá! ¿Dónde estás?"*

Blood Thorn's newly acquired bow twanged beside me, and I watched one of the spear-ax men's cloth batting stop the arrow fast. The spear-ax men were now surrounding the wounded Antonio. Blood Thorn was giving the bow distasteful looks. "Cactus thorns against a turtle's shell."

Then I followed where Antonio's men were pointing.

Off to the left, five of the cabayeros were pulling lances from their latest victims. One, an older man with a graying beard, fixed us with his hard eyes. Oh yes, I knew him: Antonio's father.

"Antonio?" the old man cried, standing in his stirrups for a better view.

"We've got to run," I called, turning and sprinting for all I was worth. The promise of safety in the trees was choked by a group of thunder-stick men, surrounded by crossbows, and a hedge of those accursed spear-axes. I watched and listened as several of the long tubes popped and banged, smoke billowing from the muzzles.

"To the lakes!" Blood Thorn cried, grabbing my arm to slow my headlong rush.

"What?"

"The cabayos can't follow us into the water. We can swim across and get away on the other side."

It made a heap more sense than the forest. I ran my heart out for the lakes. All around us, it was apparent that things were not going well for the Uzachile. We passed men lying on the ground, their backs ripped open. Some were dead, others groaning, clutching at grass, struggling to drag themselves along while lengths of intestines trailed behind. Others, cut partially through from sword strikes, bled out in large pools of crimson. Most of the wounds — some disengaged part of me noticed — were in the back. Kristianos loved to kill people who were trying to escape.

As the depth of the disaster became apparent, I suffered the sickening realization that our little fight with Antonio had doomed us.

We'd lost too much time. But for the number of fleeing Uzachile, we should have already been run down.

I threw a glance over my shoulder, seeing Antonio's father as he bent low over his horse, shield and spear gleaming in the sunlight. He looked up from where the Kristiano footmen hovered around Antonio. The old man caught sight of us and turned his cabayo. It was only a matter of time.

I threw another look over my shoulder, fearful of being speared by Antonio's father. But four confused warriors spilled into the old man's path. One of them ended up on the Kristiano's lance.

When I tore my gaze away, Fetch was running several paces ahead of me. To this day I swear it: I saw him, clear as sunset on a cloudless day.

He shot a single glance over his shoulder, pink tongue lolling from his panting mouth. His eyes met mine, shining with that old delight. Then he took off. I followed, running as fast as I could. I ducked right when Fetch did, speeded up, slowed, and dodged, following his flying paws.

For that moment my souls were singing, and a sensation of pure joy seemed to flow up from my old friend. A warmth filled my heart and lungs. I faintly recall crossbow arrows hissing past my head. A brown and white cabayo — as if stuck in time — cut slowly in front of me, the deadly lance tip whispering a hand's length beyond my breast. An instant later it disappeared with a pounding of hooves.

Fetch led me past the first lake where two Kristiano cabayos were already working the bank. Fire had started in my lungs, and my throat was dry. Then Fetch was leaping full tilt into the tall willows surrounding the second lake. I plowed in after him, slapping the green wall aside, splashing into water.

Thirty-One

"Fetch?" I cried, sloshing out into the muddy depths. "Where are you?"

"Who?" Blood Thorn panted behind me. "Who . . . are you . . . calling?"

"My dog!" I bucked my way deeper into the water, stopping, cocking my head to listen for Fetch's splashing.

"What dog?" Blood Thorn dropped to his knees in the reeds and mud, water up to his chest.

"You saw him! He led the way. He was right in front of me."

Blood Thorn shot a worried glance over his shoulder as someone screamed on the other side of the willow screen. Then he squinted

470

up at me. "Fetch? Isn't that the dog you said the Kristiano killed?"

"I saw him!" I insisted, grabbing reeds, yanking them back so I could search along the bank. "He jumped in here just in front of me."

Blood Thorn cupped his hands, splashing muddy water over his sweat-hot face. "I saw no dog, Black Shell. I just followed you, and I thought you were going to get us killed time after time. . . . Only to see the place where I would have run suddenly fill with a squad of Kristianos."

Water dripping from his smudged face paint, lungs heaving, he gave me a sober stare. "If you say you saw your Spirit dog, I believe you. Nothing else explains our survival."

I kept pulling the thick reeds and rushes back, splashing around. Gods, it really had been Fetch, hadn't it? I'd never been as positive of anything in my life.

Blood Thorn and I froze as someone crashed into the cattails half a bowshot off to the left, followed by the huffing snort of a cabayo and a larger splash. From beyond our screen of willows, I could see a man strike out, swimming for the center of the lake. He kept throwing glances behind him, never slowing his rapid pace. A crossbow arrow flashed out, sailed across, and made a chug sound as it whisked past the swimmer's head into the water.

Blood Thorn gestured for silence as I carefully reached into my quiver. My questing fingers found only a single arrow left. I withdrew it and nocked it.

Distant shouts, the rattling pops of thunder sticks, and occasional screams were the only sounds. Overhead a V of ducks circled the lake, thought better of it, and winged away.

The cabayo crashed and splashed back to solid footing and we heard the clopping hooves as it passed just beyond our screen. Taking a breath, I slogged further out to where the willow thinned. In the middle of the lake, the swimmer had slowed, treading water. He kept looking back, fear in his eyes.

We had followed Fetch to the eastern and larger of the two lakes. Grimly I remembered that this body of water was supposed to keep Rattlesnake's forces from being surprised from behind. Other than the forest, it now seemed to be the only remaining place to hide.

Further down, we could see others swimming out. Within a finger's time, the water was bobbing with heads and ripples were washing over where Blood Thorn and I hid.

At the sound of a winded cabayo, I peered through a gap in the leaves, seeing Antonio's father ride impatiently past, his bloody lance held high. The expression on his face was one of black rage. He looked back and down, barking curtly in *español. Soldados* must have been in accompaniment, for I heard a respectful answer.

"We can't stay here," I noted. "Sooner or later they're going to search all along the shore."

Blood Thorn nodded, then reached up, taking a sight on the sun and moving his hand, palm width by palm width, to the western horizon. "Three hands' time until dark. If we can last that long, we'll be able to slip out come nightfall and make our escape."

I nodded. "I wonder how many are in the other lake?"

I'd actually have headed to that one instead, but for Fetch.

"Closer to the fighting," Blood Thorn shrugged. "It's probably filled. I thought I caught a glimpse of Holata Uriutina and his party headed that way."

"I wish them all luck." I paused. "Did you see my wife?"

He gave me a knowing look. "No, Black Shell."

I winced, crouching down in the water.

Pearl Hand, are you there?

I heard the stems bending ever so softly and gestured for silence. Pulling my arrow back, I waited. A hand parted the willows and pulled them back. I stared right down the shaft of my arrow . . . and into a black-bearded face. The Kristiano threw himself

473

back just as I released. A terrified scream tore the air, and I heard thrashing as he made his escape back toward the bank.

An explosion of Kristiano voices followed, and I recognized Antonio's father's among them.

"Come on," I said, slipping my bow into the empty quiver. I carefully hung them in branches of the willow, safe should I ever be able to retrieve them. "It's just luck that we've avoided discovery this long. Time to swim."

Blood Thorn and I struck out for open water, tossing glances over our shoulders. Antonio's father sawed at the straps controlling his horse. He was pointing at us with the bloody lance, calling orders.

From the middle of the lake we could see other cabayeros riding just beyond the cattails, rushes, and stands of willows. Every now and then, one would point. They were seeing places where the vegetation was crushed, and sent crossbow men in to flush the fugitives. But for my last arrow, either Blood Thorn or I would have been shot.

We watched other fugitives — driven from concealment — swim out to join the rest of us. Now riders were sweeping the opposite shore, driving anyone who swam across back into the center.

"Why do I get the feeling we're in a trap?" Blood Thorn asked as we struggled, chin deep, to find footing in the slippery mud. Any farther out and the water would be over our heads.

"All we have to do is wait until dark," I assured him. "It's a big lake. They can't be everywhere."

"No." Blood Thorn sighed, and I realized he had a bitter smile on his face. "You know, hot as we are, the water feels good. But it's going to be pretty cold by the time night falls."

I nodded. "Even warm water like this takes a toll." The cool feeling had already eaten into my skin.

"We're tough," Blood Thorn replied, watching another cabayo patrol trot along the far bank.

Antonio's father was still pointing at us, shouting orders as some of the footmen left and others appeared.

"Definitely tough," I agreed, staring back at the bank we'd just fled. A couple of Kristianos with thunder sticks had set up on the shore beside our adversary's pacing cabayo.

Blood Thorn and I watched as they poured something into the muzzle, then used hammers and a rod to pound a ball down the long tube. One of the men raised the thunder stick and pointed it. Even across the distance, I could tell we were the targets.

Antonio's father's voice came rolling across the water. Just one word: *"Fuego!"*

I cried, "Look out! They're shooting at —"

475

A geyser of water sprayed us an instant before I heard the weapon's bark. A *pat-pat* sounded behind us as the ball skipped and sank.

"Hey! Black Shell!" a cry came from shore. "Is that you?"

"It's our language," Blood Thorn noted.

"Southern dialect. One of Irriparacoxi's traitors."

"Who wants to know?" I bellowed back.

"Your sorcery didn't serve you as well as it did at White Bird Lake town."

"Ears? Is that you?"

"I am Stalks the Mist, you foul piece of shit. After accepting the blessing of *Jesucristo,* I am a servant of the true god."

"What do you want, Ears?"

"Don Luis Ruiz is willing to spare your lives. If you will come in, he will place you under his protection. He says that you spared his son's life once, and though you wounded him today, it was done honorably as part of battle."

"The answer is no!" I shouted back.

"Come in and get us!" Blood Thorn bellowed in rage.

"The *Adelantado* will have you in the end. Just as he foiled your planned attack today."

"Oh?" I shouted. "How?"

"I read your sign language when you had council with the *Adelantado* at Uriutina town. I told Ortiz. But the great chief of the

476

Kristianos, like his god, is merciful. We are told to tell those who fought so boldly against overwhelming odds that if they surrender, they will be fed, offered shelter, and forgiven for plotting against the *Adelantado*."

"May your mother's sheath be filled with pus and maggots, traitor," Blood Thorn shouted back.

"Your threats are the empty gestures of a man hiding in the middle of a lake. Mine are of a victor, fresh from the battle."

"They knew all along," I muttered under my breath. A hollow sense of futility began in the pit of my stomach.

Ears cupped his hands to his mouth. "You can surrender, or take your chances. The other lake, like this one, is fully surrounded. There is no escape. All you need to do is call out this word: *'Rendirse.'* Then swim to shore." He paused. "Do you *rendir?*"

"Why don't you go see if you can't stuff that mushy-soft penis of yours into one of your polluted *puercos!*" Blood Thorn roared.

Ears said something to Don Luis, who said something to the thunder-stick men. One of the long weapons was leveled onto a kind of brace. I could see the black hole in the muzzle seeking us out. As smoke gushed, I grabbed Blood Thorn and dragged us both beneath the surface. Water gurgled in my ears, and I could feel Blood Thorn thrashing in panic. Something slapped just over our heads. I felt the thing bounce off my shoulder. As it sank, I grabbed it.

Breaking water, I watched Blood Thorn claw his way up. He whipped water from his head, violence in his eyes. "Why'd you do that?"

"Saving your life." I glanced back at shore. One of the thunder-stick men was busy banging away with his hammer and rod, seating another of the projectiles, no doubt. The second thunder-stick man looked on, resting the butt of his weapon. Ears was yelling that we should *"rendir"* ourselves.

I stared at the ugly round ball. So that's what the accursed things shot? The lump of lead would have been perfect used with a sling. Thunder sticks, however, shot the murderous lead balls so fast a person couldn't see them coming.

Blood Thorn took it from my hand, rolling it in his fingers. "You caught that?"

"The water slowed it, same as it does with arrows."

Don Luis said something to the thunder-stick men and turned his horse, trotting back and forth as if enraged. Across the distance I could feel the heat of his stare.

"Where's Pearl Hand?" Ears called.

"Do you think I'd bring my wife into the middle of a battle, you limp-shafted wonder?"

"Wife?" I could imagine, more than see, his smile across the distance. "I shall remember

478

that when I finally drive my hard rod into her. Each time she moans, I shall delight in the knowledge that I can bring her the kind of joyous abandon that your pathetic and shriveled penis never did."

I slapped the water with an angry fist.

Blood Thorn gave me a worried look. I gave a brief shake of the head. "If he ever managed to catch her, she'd slip a knife between his ribs at the first opportunity. She's more woman than he could ever handle."

Blood Thorn's expression of amusement almost came as a relief after what we'd been through that day. He looked silly, the red and white stripes of his face paint smeared pink and dripping from his chin.

Ears bellowed: "Remember the word, Black Shell: *Rendirse!*" I saw him chuckling as he turned and talked to Don Luis. Antonio's father just sat on his cabayo, bent forward, arms resting on the front of his saddle. Then, after a finger's time, he straightened, pulled the straps, and walked the cabayo out of our sight.

"You know, Black Shell," Blood Thorn turned to me, trickles of pink water streaking down his face, "I think we're in real trouble."

I shrugged, creating ripples. "Come nightfall, we'll slip over to shore and find a way to escape."

"The moon is almost full. They'll be able to see us as if it were daylight," Blood Thorn

479

reminded. "But that wasn't what I was talking about."

"Oh?" I looked at him; the few war feathers that weren't missing from his hair were partially afloat in the water around his head. But the look in his eyes was of pure misery.

"Today I watched the might of my people broken and shattered like an old pot. From here on, there's nothing standing in de Soto's way. Not even the accursed Apalachee have a chance against him."

"No, they don't." I bit off sudden tears of frustration, a sense of futility rising within, and realized just how cold the water was starting to feel.

THIRTY-TWO

We waited in silence, watching as the Kristianos patrolled the shores. One by one, those
of us who had made it into the water swam
together, only to learn that any accumulation
of heads immediately earned us a shot from
the bank. Either a thunderstick ball or crossbow arrow would whiz out to splat or chug
into the water.

For safety's sake, we would work our way
into talking distance, and keep separated.

"What word of the holatas?" Blood Thorn
asked.

"Nothing," another returned.

"I saw them running for the small lake,"
yet a third voice called. "As far as I know,
they all made it."

"How many dead?" still another called.

"Too many," Blood Thorn whispered.

I wrapped my arms around my chest — a futile measure at keeping warm. The sun now hung a hand above the northwestern horizon. The first shivers had come a hand of time ago.

"I saw Ahocalaquen dragged back into Napetuca," someone shouted. "As to the others? I don't know."

"The entire war party from Uriutina is dead," another called. "With great bravery they charged the Kristiano foot warriors and were mowed down to a man."

I listened to the mixed horror and desperation in their voices and pulled my knees up, allowing myself to bob gently in the water.

Eyes squeezed shut, I worried about Pearl Hand. The cabayeros couldn't have cared less if it were a man, woman, or child fleeing before them. They'd have run one of their slim lances through Pearl Hand's back, giggling gleefully the whole time. Was her body lying in the trampled grass, flies already crawling through the blood-caked wounds?

I remembered the unlucky wretches I'd seen trying to crawl away.

Please, Breath Giver above, tell me she didn't suffer that way.

Or worse? She might have been captured. Perhaps even now some filthy Kristiano, covered with Timucuan blood, had pried her legs apart and jammed himself inside her.

She will kill him in the end. This was Pearl Hand, after all. Her captor had better enjoy what he slipped into her, because what she finally slipped into him would be long, metal, and deadly.

Nor could I keep from thinking about the dogs. The fact that any of us remained alive was because Gnaw, Squirm, Skipper, and Bark had stopped the Kristiano war dogs in those first critical moments.

I slipped my feet down into the soft mud, muscles knotted against the nagging cold. Pearl Hand had been right to include them. We'd have never managed to concentrate our fire enough to shoot the gray cabayo out from under de Soto with both of the dogs leaping among us.

I remembered Pearl Hand's shot, how de Soto's horse had jerked him sideways, accidentally saving the man's life. It had been so close, and the dogs had bought us that moment.

My teeth began to chatter as I remembered the sight of Bark chasing that wounded war dog.

"What are you thinking?" Blood Thorn asked. He was standing, water just below his chin.

"In the middle of the fight I saw Bark."

"Yes." Blood Thorn smiled thinly. "He was after that Kristiano dog. Do you think he caught him?"

I tensed the muscles in my jaw to keep my teeth from clicking as I talked. "Either a Kristiano killed Bark, or Bark killed the war dog. Once he's in a fight, there's no other outcome."

"In that case, I hope your dog lives to be a hundred, and meets a new Kristiano dog every day." A pause. "How long can a man stay in cold water?"

"This temperature?" I splashed absently at the surface. "I don't know. Maybe a day. It probably depends on how much food a man has had, on how fat he is." I halfheartedly pushed a wave his way. "You're built thick as a hickory stump so you'll last longer than I will. Me, I'm too skinny to hold heat."

"It's only a hand of time until sunset."

I looked up, seeing the moon a couple of hands above the horizon to the southeast. "It's been raining for days. Why does tonight have to be crystal clear?"

"Because our Power has deserted us, Black Shell." He lifted his water-logged hand, rubbing the puffy and swollen pads of his fingers. "For whatever reason, the Kristianos' Power is stronger than ours. Maybe their god really is the greater."

"That's goose crap," I growled.

"Really?" Blood Thorn sounded bitter. "I just watched the might of Uzachile swept aside as if we were children playing at war.

We've *beaten* the Apalachee! We've *defeated* the Albaamaha and Koasati! We're not fools!"

I raised a hand in mollification. "You heard Ears. They knew your plans in advance. I was there that day, watching Rattlesnake and Holata Ahocalaquen signing back and forth to each other. Who'd think one of our own would give us away?"

Blood Thorn rubbed his face, smearing the pitiful remains of his war paint. "And that wasn't Power working against us?"

"No, my friend. It was the stupidity of men. Especially my own. But mostly it was that pus-sucking Ears." I slapped the water in irritation. "And I'm not sure I can blame him. By reporting our plans, Ears has risen in status. Chances are that he'll never have to wear a collar again." A pause. "In his place I might have done the same."

I fought off another bout of shivers, wondering when I had ever felt this cold. My thoughts kept dredging up memories of hot fires and lying with my body warmly entwined with Pearl Hand's.

I forced them away, concentrating, and saying, "This fight with the Kristianos, it's different than anything we've ever done before."

"Spoken truly, Black Shell. In combat, it seems they can't be killed."

"It's not them. It's their weapons and armor that are the problem."

"And who makes their armor?"

"They do."

Blood Thorn gave me a strained grin. "That's my point."

"And then there's the accursed cabayos. I'd think they were Spirit Beasts from the Underworld, but they seem to shy away from water. Maybe we need to tame Water Panthers, ride them off to war with the Kristianos. Now that would really give us an advantage."

He hugged himself and stared at where the thunder-stick men remained, keeping watch on us. If we paddled along the shoreline, they kept pace with us. Apparently Don Luis had given them specific orders. The old man wanted us, and I knew why. By now Antonio's arm was swelling like a sun-rotten fish. And even if they'd cut my arrow out, Antonio must have been in excruciating pain.

"Any revelations?" Blood Thorn asked. "From that look on your face, I'm hoping you've just figured a way out of here."

"I wish." I knotted a fist and hammered the water. "No, we're just going to have to wait until dark and take our chances."

Blood Thorn watched the Kristianos on shore who were watching us. Occasionally they would call out: *"¡Indios! Queréis vos rendir?"*

I lifted my hands, inspecting the swollen white ridges on my palms and fingers. "Tonight. We'll make our escape."

"We will." Blood Thorn paused. "But what

then? Do we have a plan?"

"We've got to make the forest. See if we can find others. Once we know who's alive and how many we have to work with, we can begin to plan."

He swallowed hard, barely nodding as he stared wistfully at the shore. "How, in the name of the blessed ancestors, can I ever get Water Frond away from them now?"

"I don't know, my friend. But if we can get out of this bone-numbing water, we'll find a way."

I ground my teeth, partially from anger but mostly to keep them from chattering like sleet on a hollow gourd.

At least Blood Thorn knew Water Frond was alive. My imagination kept spinning images of Pearl Hand, and flies were swarming all over her sightless dead eyes, crawling into her gaping mouth, and feasting on her drying blood.

Low in the western sky the sun hung like a shimmering orange ball. The cattails, willows, and rushes along shore stuck up like black fringe, marred only by the silhouettes of patrolling Kristianos. The water around us had turned inky and dark. Thick with cold, it pressed relentlessly against the numb, soft clay of our water-swollen skin.

My teeth now rattled away in my head, jarring my vision and teasing my wobbling brain with the notion that a thousand woodpeckers were hammering at my skull.

Thick and burly Blood Thorn had finally succumbed. His shivering flesh vibrated the water, buzzing little ripples out to meet my own. To my cold-dulled wits, watching the patterns they made in the gaudy orange light of sunset proved utterly fascinating.

The number of bobbing heads hadn't decreased. No one who had fled the battle wanted to *rendirse*. Images of the dead and dying remained too clear. All a man needed to do was close his eyes, and there arose — unbidden — a stark reminder of what lay just beyond the water.

And did we believe the claims made by the freed Southern Timucua? They kept assuring us that the *Adelantado* thought we'd fought bravely, and that he valued courage. They insisted that anyone who would *rendirse* would be fed, given blankets, and allowed to warm at a great fire.

"Do you think that is really true?" Blood Thorn finally asked as the sun imperceptibly merged with the horizon, flattening, widening, and then vanishing behind the inky willows.

I didn't reply, refusing to use the strength to find words. My thoughts had congealed into numbness. Instead I only pointed at the scars on my neck.

Blood Thorn stared at them, then nodded

his answer. The tissue must have looked particularly gruesome after having soaked for so many hands of time.

I twisted around, giving the three-quarter moon that hung high in the east a hateful look. Conditions could barely have been better for the Kristianos.

"The longer we wait, the better our chances," I remarked. "They'll be expecting us to drift in closer with darkness. They'll be wary."

"How much more of this cold can you stand?" Blood Thorn's voice almost broke.

"As much as I have to," I whispered.

"People die in water. Even when it's this warm."

I nodded. "I knew a trader who died when his canoe swamped in an ice-choked river. From the time his canoe tipped over, he managed to swim all of a bowshot toward where we were waiting on shore. We watched as his breath ceased to fog over the water, and his hair froze. We could hear his teeth clicking, and he just sank. From start to finish, he didn't last more than fifty heartbeats."

"This water will kill us, too. Eventually."

I nodded. "After the moon passes the highest point in the sky. Then we'll try," I promised.

I tried to huddle against myself, only to bob under as my stiff legs slipped on the mud. Coughing and hacking, I clawed my way back to the surface. Wiping water from my face, I heard the Kristianos on shore. They were pointing at me, calling, *"¿Te rindes?"*

Filling my lungs, I shouted back as best my quavering vocal chords would allow: *"Uti asurupa!"*

One of the traitor Timucua must have translated because a thunder stick discharged. Not even an instant later Blood Thorn and I floundered as one of the balls blasted water an arm's length off to our left.

"Next time," Blood Thorn said, panting, "when you tell them to eat shit, I'd appreciate it if you would use the polite honorific."

WORRY

The old woman watched from her position of honor, high on the Tchkofa mound as the line of warriors passed before her. The day was bright and sunny, reminding her of Napetuca.

Why? she wondered, looking up at the sun. Was it the angle of the light? The time of the year? Or just the happenstance of an old woman's mind?

Beside her, the matron stood tall, her sleek black hair combed and polished, shell necklaces draped about her neck. Even her red skirt, donned for its appeal to the Powers of war, hung perfectly from the woman's hips.

"Your son is the pakacha thlakko, isn't he?" Pearl Hand asked, her faded vision picking out the red-and-black-painted warrior in the lead.

"Yes," the matron told her. "He leads this raid against the Chahta. He has prayed, fasted, and drank of the sacred root. Power walks with him."

Pearl Hand nodded, hearing the foolish pride in the woman's voice.

Power, Matron? Oh no, not with your son, not

on this day. And she thought back to Napetuca and the feeling of wretched despair she'd felt the night after the battle. How she'd run like a panicked rabbit, chased by cabayeros, darting through the trees. Twice she'd eluded pursuit by a quick dash to the side, using a tree trunk for shelter.

As night fell, she'd made her way to their camp, finding two of the dogs, Gnaw and Squirm, waiting, tails wagging, glad of her return. Each had borne wounds that she had cleaned and tended, all the time shooting anxious glances at the darkening trees.

Torn by indecision, she'd tried to balance her fear of Kristianos against that of packing and fleeing deeper into the forest.

But where would Black Shell think to look for her? With each breath she weighed fear of discovery against the desperate hope that Black Shell would come staggering out of the night.

Pray you never suffer what I did outside Napetuca, Matron. It bleeds the souls, and squeezes the moisture of pain from your heart.

Near midnight Bark's dark form came slinking in, and she'd thrown herself on him, sobbing into his blood-sticky fur. Skipper had appeared just before dawn, and with his arrival, the reality of Black Shell's absence came crashing down.

Only one explanation remained.

She steeled herself, gesturing the dogs to stay and guard. In the false dawn she had slipped away, ghosting from tree to tree, headed back to the battlefield. Somehow she had to find him, to recover his corpse.

Black Shell, I won't let the puercos *find you first.*

She shot a sidelong glance at the matron, aware of the woman's stiff posture. "There are worse things than death, great lady. Oh, yes. Worse things indeed."

THIRTY-THREE

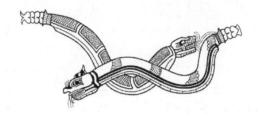

The moon stood three hands above the horizon when the first of the Uzachile fugitives finally cried out, *"Rendirse,"* in a weak and shivering voice.

Across the moon-silvered lake we watched the man slog his way into shallow water. Unable to drag himself over the willows, traitors waded out, pulled him over the vegetation, and onto shore. The rest of us waited, wondering if screams were going to be next.

Instead one of the Southern Timucua asked, "Anyone else ready for a hot meal, a dry warm blanket, and a spot next to the fire?"

We waited in silence, shivering, water lapping at our chins.

"The *Adelantado* knows it was Holata Aho-calaquen who led you to this. He does not hold a people responsible for the actions of its leaders."

"He's such a peaceful and . . . and . . ." I struggled to find the word.

"Pious man?" Blood Thorn asked.

"P-Pious man," I chattered under my breath.

Blood Thorn was watching me closely in the moonlight. Whether he really found it funny, or if unarguably bad humor was our only means of maintaining, I'll never know.

Less than a hand of time later, another of us cried out *"Rendirse!"* and started the bouncing, swimming, walk toward the shore. He, too, was pulled out by willing hands.

"Any others?" the Timucua called.

"Sure!" Blood Thorn cupped his hands, voice box squeaky with cold and fatigue. "Just as soon as you and your stinking Kristianos go off to squeeze each others' penises, we'll be right out of here."

The hiss of a crossbow arrow followed by the characteristic chug of the point lancing water was our only reply.

"You'd think they held a . . . a . . ."

"Grudge?" Blood Thorn offered.

"Grudge," I muttered, fighting a thick fog in my brain. Blood Thorn kept asking me questions, listening as I struggled to answer. Gods, I just wasn't thinking well.

Tired, that's what I decided.

Two others, down at the end of the lake, gave up. I shot a look up at the cold-white face of the moon. I couldn't feel my feet anymore, and my hands were as awkward as thick elk-hide mittens. Putting together any kind of thought was like pawing through buffalo wool: thick and stiff.

"Come on." Blood Thorn watched me with solicitous eyes. "It's time, Black Shell. Split up. Keep your head as low in the water as you can and still breathe. If they shoot at one of us, he has to draw back, screaming and splashing as if hit. Maybe that way they'll be so distracted they won't see the other one making for shore."

I frowned, nodding, realizing for the first time that the water had grown warmer. I wondered when my shivering had stopped. "Yes, we can . . . g-go . . . now." My voice sounded oddly thick, and I had trouble forming the Timucua words.

Blood Thorn slapped a clublike hand onto my shoulder. "Just to know you, Black Shell, of the Chicaza, makes me humble. If this doesn't work out, I will be honored to introduce you to my sacred ancestors."

"I think . . . think I'll just . . ." I fought through the fog in my head. "Um . . . a hot . . . what's the word in your language? Haunch? Yes, a hot haunch of venison . . . and a . . . a roaring fire. With you . . . and

Pearl Hand." I frowned. "What are we doing?"

"Heading for shore, Black Shell. Carefully. Remember that the Kristianos are hunting us?"

"Oh . . . the Kristianos." Odd, I'd forgotten.

"You must be quiet, Black Shell. You can't stay in the water any longer. The cold is getting to you, do you understand?"

"I . . . yes."

I saw white teeth flash in his face, then he ducked low in the water, slowly working his way off to the east.

I lay back, trying to find just the right depth where my body would float, my nostrils barely breaking the surface. Using my arms for balance, I began to slowly drift in toward the willows.

The Kristianos are hunting me. Got to be quiet.

Periodically I heard a shout from the guards, probably calling for us to surrender. Beyond the willows I could see a cabayero atop his mount, the helmet shining whitely. The man would pause, stare out at the water, and kick his mount onward. How many were left?

All I had to do was reach the shore, slither through like a snake, and get my legs back. Then, as soon as a gap opened in the line, I had to wiggle out into the grass. I needed to

be in the forest by first light. I needed . . .
what?

My head had gone foggy, floating, thoughts
lost.

It's the cold. That's why I can't think.

The hollow boom of a thunder stick carried across the water. I hoped it hadn't been
aimed at Blood Thorn.

For perhaps a hand of time I'd worked my
way toward the screen of vegetation, having
covered maybe half the distance. My heart
continued to beat slowly against my ribs. My
fear had gone, drained away into the wool-
thick confusion in my head. Gods, if I made
it to shore, could I even stand?

Does it matter?

I continued to drift, delightfully warm. I
thanked the sacred Spirits that the shivering
had ceased. I lay back, floating so easily in
the water.

When had I ever felt so tired? *What am I
doing here?* Something . . . something important. If only I could remember . . .

The water buoyed my souls, rocking them
ever so slightly. I closed my eyes, waves lapping at my cheeks. This wasn't so bad, floating in a warm haze.

All the hideous memories of war and violence began to fade, and I found myself running along behind Fetch again. Sunlight
gleamed from the dark black hair along his
back and shone golden in the brown along

his sides. His thick fur undulated with each leap. He kept looking back, his tail waving like a thick flag.

Lead the way, old friend. Show me the way.

The rocking of my body matched each step as I followed Fetch. His tail was wagging . . . wagging . . . drifting. It, too, faded into the rocking gray mist . . .

So tired . . . easing off into a gentle sleep . . .

Something grasped my right ankle. No sense of panic or worry built as I was pulled into the depths. My arms were out, my head back, and I could see moonlight dancing in shifting dapples as the surface grew ever more distant.

With each passing moment I expected to settle gently onto the thick mud. Instead the flickering moonlight grew ever dimmer as I dropped down, caressed by the warm waters.

Music began so faintly the origin couldn't be placed. Had it come spinning out of my hazy souls, or was someone singing? I gently hummed the melody, heart matching the beat of a pot drum, hands moving in time.

A soft golden glow rose from beneath me.

Like a falling leaf, I easily flipped over and stared down, trying to determine what was wrapped around my ankle. I was dropping into the Underworld, settling, arms outspread.

Finally I got a good look at the giant claw that clutched my ankle. Twisting, I stared straight into Water Panther's gleaming yellow eyes, my image reflected in his large black pupils. The Sprit Beast's upper lip was raised, the long ivory fangs curving as if in anticipation.

"Has any man ever lived a life as pathetic as yours?" the *Piasa* asked, and a terrible fear broke loose in my breast. Relief at my escape from the Kristianos died as I stared eyeball to eyeball with death.

"You should be dead, Black Shell. Your gutted corpse should be crawling with fly larvae at this very moment. But the Kristiano chief still lives, our world teeters, and the only thing you managed to save was your own foul and miserable skin."

Fear, in bright pulses, flowed with each frantic beat of my heart.

"Well?" Water Panther demanded.

I opened my mouth and uttered a faint squeak — like air squeezed from an inflated bladder.

"You are mine," Water Panther whispered softly. "Anything I wish, your body, souls, or life. Mine on a whim. A smart man would have avoided your fate. He would have thrown himself onto a Kristiano lance. Or, if he didn't have the guts for that — for instance, if he were a miserable worm like you — he might have just let the invaders snap their collar around his neck. You could have lived a bit longer that way, Black Shell. Isn't that your usual habit?"

"Wha . . . what?"

"You know, cling to life . . . no matter how demeaning it might be? Sell your honor, barter

500

any pride you might have? Anything for another sunset? That's your way, isn't it?"

I stared at him, a wretched hollow forming in my gut. Was that me? Really?

"Even your own people cast you out as a coward."

I saw truth reflected in those fathomless black pupils, like midnight simmering in a lake of molten yellow.

"No." It sounded weak, as though I didn't believe it myself.

"I might as well take you now." A second raptorial foot closed around my throat. I could feel it — cool, birdlike pads conforming to the curve of my neck. Each of the talons, sharp as obsidian, pricked my skin. "If I kill you slowly, I'll have to endure your pitiful wailing and pleading. No, better make it fast."

The pressure on my neck increased. I could feel my blood jetting, vibrant life pulsing against the tightening grip.

As incongruous as a midsummer snowflake, the memory of Fetch returning to save me during the battle popped up. In that instant I found myself refusing to believe the reflection in Water Panther's engulfing eyes.

Fetch had come for me. No matter what an Underworld Spirit Beast might think of me, a dog didn't come all the way back from the Land of the Dead just to save an unworthy. And believe me, a dog knows the quality of a person's soul better than Breath Giver himself.

Rage and indignation surged within me. Through the stranglehold, I croaked, "Eat your own shit and die in pain, you mismatched abomination."

How long did we glare into each other's eyes? I have no idea. The Underworld runs on Beginning Time, ancient time. The rules are different.

I felt the pressure lessen; then the great taloned foot released me.

"You still owe me whatever I decide. Assuming the Power of trade isn't another of your sleights and feints." Water Panther hissed in irritation.

"I am bound by the Power of trade," I managed hoarsely, rubbing my throat. "And by invoking the Power, you yourself are bound. You have asked for nothing, yet you would have killed me before I could have fulfilled any trade you asked for?"

"What of your life, human? You offered to trade 'anything.' Maybe I want your life."

"In exchange for what?" I countered, and in that moment I was myself again. "The Power of trade is about exchange. Killing me without providing something in exchange is an abuse. Or are you above the rules of Power?"

At that the yellow eyes narrowed, the black pupils seeming to sizzle. The lip curled back, exposing the long canines; those stiff whiskers actually vibrated.

I had him. I could see it in the swelling anger.

"Not everyone binds the *Piasa* in his own

trap," a slow voice came from the side.

I glanced over, seeing Snapping Turtle, his back covered with grassy moss. The pointed nose was turned our direction, the great beast's small round eyes inspecting first me, and then Water Panther.

"Enjoy it," Water Panther growled, stalking slowly around me, his four feet sinking into the mud. "Other times will come. Power is churning, twisting, bending around like currents in a mighty flood. Who knows where we're being carried, or to what fate?"

"Even you are afraid," Snapping Turtle declared, snapping his great curved jaws shut in emphasis.

"I fear nothing," Water Panther hissed as he continued to circle me, the blunt nose inches from my body.

"Not even oblivion?" Snapping Turtle asked.

Water Panther stopped short, stiffening, his snakelike tail rising straight.

I saw it ever so briefly: the panicked flaring of the eyes, the quiver of the whiskers, the little curl at the tip of the upright tail.

And then the terrible beast was gone. Like a trout, he seemed to flip, wiggle, and shimmer away into the gloom. The effect was as if he merged, as well as moved, becoming one with the weaving grasses, strands of moss, and the eerie golden light.

"Surprised?" Snapping Turtle asked. "Don't be. From the moment you could conceive of death, it was real to you. For the *Piasas,* Horned Serpent, Eagle Man, Long Nosed God, and the great Spirit Beings, there was only Creation and existence until the arrival of the Kristianos."

"I don't understand," I replied, stepping over, wary of that giant head.

"Water Panther has finally discovered an inconceivable destiny."

"Spirit Beings can't die," I insisted.

"No, but they can be forgotten."

"How could Water Panther and Horned Serpent be forgotten? They're Spirit Beings."

Snapping Turtle's small round eyes regarded me, as if pondering. I watched long strands of moss on his shell waver with the slight current. "Do you see images of the *Piasas,* the Horned Serpent, Eagle Man, or the Hero Twins on Kristiano armor?"

"No. Just their cross of wood."

"Ah. And if they should win?" Snapping Turtle extended his long neck, turning his huge head my way. "If they should convert all people to their cross? What if no one believes in Water Panther anymore? What then?"

THIRTY-FOUR

How could any person understand the impact of oblivion on the Spirit Beasts? To be born, live, and die? Humans, animals, and plants, we did that all the time. And for people, after death there was the road to the Land of the Dead. We had the jump from the western edge of the earth, through the Seeing Hand. Beyond that were the trials, judgments, and tribulations a person's souls must endure to reach the worthy ancestors.

But for Spirit Beasts and Power, what happened when people began to place faith in other beliefs?

Lost in confusion, I slowly shook my head.

Anhinga caught my eye as he gracefully flew down from above and cut a quick circle around my head. I gave the bird a wary nod.

"Alive, I see." Anhinga dropped onto Snapping Turtle's back, crushing the moss. "Now there's a small miracle."

"What do you want?" I asked. Unlike Spirit Beings like Water Panther, Horned Serpent, Eagle Man, and the rest, Anhinga, Snapping Turtle, and the other Spirit Helpers would survive as long as the animals they resembled continued to exist.

"It's time." Anhinga cocked his head, resettling his wings as the gentle current changed.

"Time for what?"

"For your final test," Snapping Turtle answered.

"What final test?"

The voice came from behind. "Me."

I had the briefest sense of movement, and then something huge hit me: the effect like hammering a deer-hide ball with a war club. I was bent backward, twisted, legs and arms flailing as I was literally punched away.

I couldn't move, pinned in place by the force of water. It tore at my body as I was rushed forward. Long passages, water-polished rock, thick tree roots, and waving fronds barely registered as they flashed past. Rock whizzed by no more than a hand's breadth beyond my head. The sensation was sickening, like spinning around too fast for too long — but I couldn't stop.

As quick as a slap, I shot out from a constricting tube into nothingness, the universe expanding around me in a black void. The pressure against my body vanished, and I reached up, wiping my eyes. Only to stare in amazement at the starry heavens. I knew the constellation that seemed to swell before me: the Seeing Hand.

The faint star in the great palm flared, growing bright . . . and then I was through.

I tried to squirm, realizing for the first time that I was being held about the middle. Blessed gods, not Water Panther again! Two thick and slippery bars pressed me back into a soft contour, one around my breast, the other over my belly. Looking down, they seemed opalescent, narrowing to points at one end.

A ridge of scale-clad bone restricted my left side. Then I looked up at my right, finding the two bars extending down from an even larger scaled jaw. Gods! I was in some monstrous mouth!

I threw my head back, craning my neck. A great wing — body-length feathers shimmering with rainbow colors — flapped across my vision. A long tail, vivid in hues of violet, vibrant red, burning yellow, and dotted with inky black spots, flashed into view. Parallel rows of rattles remained silent as the tail whipped back out of sight.

Bending even farther, I stifled a cry of horror. A crystalline eye — as big around as my head — was staring right through to my souls.

The voice actually echoed inside my skull.

"Black Shell, you've come full circle. You are my chosen."

I couldn't even cry out. The last time I'd heard Horned Serpent's voice, it had cost me everything. What would the price be this time?

"Your future, Black Shell." The answer sounded hollow, as if whispered into an empty gourd.

"What do you want from me?"

"A way to avoid oblivion." A pause. "You understand, don't you? Snapping Turtle gave you the key."

"But how can I . . . ?"

"You're fighting for your world. All of it, and in ways you cannot yet comprehend. You are my warrior, chosen long ago."

"Me? You could have chosen a great hopaye, a man familiar with the ways of Power, Spirit dreams, poisons, and magic. Or the high minko of some great nation who could sway an entire population to your will. Why not some great war chief, like Rattlesnake, capable of commanding warriors?"

Horned Serpent's voice echoed in my souls. "Had I chosen a priest, he would have been blinded by the Spirit World — and this fight is between men, not Spirits and gods. A great high minko can rarely see beyond the needs of his nation. Like a man viewing the world through a length of hollow cane, all to the sides is blocked. A warrior would feel honor bound to serve his own people before the needs of others. He knows only the raid, the battlefield, and the use of arms."

"But, me?" I repeated.

"I gambled that you would survive and learn."

"My Chicaza cast me out because of you. They called me a liar and a coward."

"And since that day you have traveled among all peoples. You have come to know them for who they are, learned and appreciated their ways. You see the whole of the world, Black Shell. You value the lives of the Mos'kogee, the Yuchi, the Albaamaha, and Timucua. You, alone, of all men, know the stakes."

"If Water Panther doesn't call in my trade and kill me first." I shivered at the thought of how close the *Piasa* had come to ending everything.

"Like you, the *Piasa* is afraid. Also like you, he is anything but a coward. Meanwhile, he is bound by the Power of trade. That you restricted him so reaffirms my reasons for picking you. My warrior must be keen of mind and clever."

"How can I destroy the Kristianos? They just defeated the Uzachile. Swept them away as if they were chaff."

"Time and guile, Black Shell. The struggle will be hard, and long. And after you, the battle will continue for generations. You are but the beginning."

A blur of images swept past. I was seeing the Sky World, aware of souls and creatures as they flashed by. I could see houses among the campfires that made the stars.

When I looked down, the surface of the earth lay far below. Land and sea glowed in the moonlight. Forests appeared as dark patches, and I could make out rivers, like threads of silver. Placing the peninsula, I located the approximate location of Napetuca.

"Is Pearl Hand alive?"

"Yes."

"Blood Thorn?"

"Even now he is shivering his way into the forest."

"Will I see them again?"

"That depends on your will, Black Shell."

I was suddenly released, the great fangs slipping from around my torso. I stumbled to my feet, glancing around. I could see the Path of the Dead, glowing before me. Just down there was the way to my ancestors, provided I could pass the junction where Eagle Man guarded the fork that split the great star road. One way, and I would eventually find welcome among my worthy ancestors. But, were I found wanting, Eagle Man would send me down the dead end, to wander lost among other lesser souls.

"You could go, Black Shell. I have brought you this far. The choice is yours."

"I didn't ask for this," I reminded him.

"The great ones never do."

I glanced back down at the distant earth. Pearl Hand lived. "There will be pain and suffering?"

"Yes. And if you go back, there are no guarantees . . . even if you should win. A great force lies across the ocean to the east: mighty peoples on a choking land, longing to bring their ways here."

"And if I destroy de Soto?"

"You buy time for yourself, for the people and the land. Even for Water Panther. If de Soto survives, his stories will be told across the ocean. Others will see our land for what it is: rich in soils, forests, and game. They will not come for gold, Black Shell. They will come to conquer our world."

"How do I destroy de Soto?"

"By offering yourself."

"To whom? To what?"

"To me."

I turned, truly seeing him for the first time. He rested in a shimmering coil, a fantastic great winged snake. Crystalline eyes, the size of bark plates, glittered in the moonlight like a thousand frost crystals. The scales around that massive square head glowed in purple, crimson, yellow, and green. Massive red antlers rose from the skull and forked into glistening points. Patterns of black chevrons and squares ran the length of his sinuous body, each surrounding a midnight black dot that seemed depthless, the effect as if each were a gateway to an infinite distance. The mighty rattles at the tip were the size of pumpkins.

I could feel heat radiating from behind his crystal eyes, and they glowed as if backlit by sunshine.

Tearing my gaze from Horned Serpent's magnificence, I glanced back down the Path of the Dead. It pulled me, called to my souls, as if to drag me away from where I stood on the stony roof of the sky.

"Your choice, Black Shell?"

I swallowed hard. Below me, the world seemed so peaceful in the moonlight. Down there, where Napetuca should be, Pearl Hand was alive. Was she even now staring up at the sky, wondering if my dead souls were on the way here?

I closed my eyes, seeing her face. She smiled at me, that quirk at the corner of her lips. Her hair was hanging in glossy waves, her arms out to enfold me. An ache built in my heart.

"I'll fight," I whispered. "For her . . . and for our world."

"You will not call out to me when things become too bleak? This bargain, you will not take it back? Even when the future seems futile and hollow?"

"I am bound by the Power of trade. A bargain is a bargain."

"Then you will surrender yourself to me?"

From the corner of my eye, I caught a glimpse of Fetch. He was standing in the moonlight, ears pricked, eyes gleaming. Like a feather wand, his tail swished in encouragement. He believed in me. That was enough.

"I am yours. Do with me what you will."

"No matter the cost?"

"No matter the cost."

I barely caught the blur of movement as Horned Serpent struck. I had the image of a great open mouth, fangs extending, the forked tongue lashing out. I put my hands out, as if to fend off the attack. Somehow I grabbed one of the antler tips, clinging desperately to save myself. Then the impact of that great mass seemed to shatter the world. The antler snapped under the strain.

I felt the mighty jaws tighten, crushing air from my lungs. Blind terror, like nothing I had ever known, seized me. Then pain, followed by the sickening feeling of my bones snapping and crackling. I felt, more than heard, my neck bones separate with a pop as my head was shoved down against my chest.

Gods! I'm being eaten alive!

Blood gushed into my mouth, driving a numb horror through my screaming souls. My ribs snapped like twigs as my skull broke through my breastbone. I was crushed ever smaller, my guts spewing through stretched skin.

A glittering blackness grew at the edge of my vision, expanding, closing down around a tiny little dot of light that finally vanished into midnight . . .

THIRTY-FIVE

Cold.

I tried to shrink back.

And couldn't.

In all the universe, only cold existed.

And darkness.

Cold and black. I struggled to move, unable to feel so much as the breath in my lungs. Breathing? Yes.

Did one breathe when dead?

I didn't know.

Had I ever felt this exhausted?

When I won the battle to open my eyes, moments passed before I could make sense of the images: Night. Moonlight on stems, grass, and mud.

Drawing a breath I savored the scent of rot, water, and mud. I knew that odor: a shoreline.

Again I tried to move, panicked that I couldn't feel my body. Lifting my head, I could look back, seeing the length of myself partially crushing the thick cattails. Water — unfelt — lapped at my legs.

Numb with cold. The words formed down somewhere in my souls.

I tried to move.

Nothing happened, as if my limbs were disconnected from my body. I stared at my right arm and found it entwined in stalks and mud. But how did . . . ?

Terror, like a lightning bolt, charged my blood and bones. The memory of Horned Serpent — and being eaten alive — came washing up through crystalline fear. I tried to scream, but only a gargling rasp broke from my throat.

Horror overwhelmed the terrible cold.

I lost track of time, sobbing, tears running down my face. Gods, I was scared. Afraid like I'd never been. All I could think of was being crushed in that hideous mouth, my bones snapping, and being swallowed alive.

But I *was* alive. Sort of. At least I could think.

Shaking from the effort, I managed to extricate my left arm from the sticky mud. The fingers slowly flexed and straightened on command, though I had no feeling in them.

None of the bones were broken. And, oh, I remembered the feeling of bones breaking . . . remembered so clearly that it had to have been but an instant ago.

A nightjar called in the distance, and I heard the breeze rattling the leaves around me.

Blood and pus! What happened to me?

Dream or reality? The images of the Underworld and Water Panther remained so clear. I could see Horned Serpent as if he'd just slipped away a moment ago.

Terror ran liquid in my gut.

But I am alive! I clung to that.

Where?

As if in answer, a distant voice called out in *español*.

Napetuca!

The lake. I was still in the lake. And out there in the darkness, Kristianos and their Southern Timucua allies were hunting me.

Pearl Hand lives!

I struggled to get my elbows under my chest, as if relearning my own body. Something warm was clutched in my right fist. I drew on it, as if the warmth spread through my hand, arm, and into my heart.

Then, like an oversized worm, I fought my way forward. Parting the thick cattails, I noticed a dim tunnel in the vegetation.

Muskrat trail.

I advanced another hand's length, but just

that effort left me sagging and exhausted. Numbly, I focused on following the trail, pulling myself forward, legs like dead wood behind me.

My shoulders are a good bit wider than a muskrat's, but I managed to muscle my way along the tiny trail.

Sometime I went to sleep, only to awaken in daylight. From the shadows cast by the reeds and cattails, it was either early morning or late afternoon. Which? And how long had it been since parting with Blood Thorn?

You've been in the Spirit World.

Time was different there. I'd seen a Koasati shaman lie for a whole seven days in one of their temples. The elders had finally decided he was dead, that his souls had been killed in the Spirit World. The shaman was carried with great ceremony to the charnel house, where, while being washed, he promptly sat up and opened his eyes.

The holy men had cracked the doorframe as they jammed through it in a mob escape. Moments later the shaman emerged, irritated that he'd been pronounced dead when he'd only been gone for a couple of hands of time. Or so it had seemed to him. Last I heard he still refused to believe his souls had been gone for seven days.

Had mine?

The distant boom of a Kristiano thunder stick reminded me that no matter how long it

517

had been, danger still awaited me just past the screen of vegetation.

Pearl Hand lives!

Gripping the root of a willow with my left hand, I pulled myself deeper into the plant's shadow and found the muskrat's house: a pile of reeds, grass, and other vegetation. With numb fingers I pulled it apart, and was pleased to hear squealing as I uncovered the pups. Small and blind, they squirmed around, obviously afraid.

Food. How long had it been since I'd eaten?

Once I'd have just choked them down. After what I'd been through with Horned Serpent, I mercifully snapped their necks before swallowing them whole. If you've never been truly hungry, you won't understand. Food is food, and I'd eaten worse. But all the while I wished for that hot haunch of venison I'd been discussing with Blood Thorn.

Pulling the remains of the muskrat house over my filthy skin, I dropped my head and slept. Thankfully, no Spirit Beings haunted me.

A sound brought me awake. I froze, realizing that for the first time, I really felt warm, and a high sun was shining down, baking my body.

Just off to my left, the willows crackled, and a voice called out in Southern Timucua. "I don't see anyone. But the brush is thick in here."

"They're a tricky bunch," another called.

I recognized Ears's voice and swallowed drily, tensing, aware that I could at least feel my body. The sensation of warmth grew in my clenched right fist, though my hand ached and cramped.

Turning my head ever so slowly, I could just see the man's face through a screen of willow stems. He was looking right at where I lay, filthy, caked with mud, and covered with leaves. Then his gaze passed over me and he cocked his head as he carefully scanned the surrounding brush.

"Nothing here."

"All right," Ears called. "Come back and we'll check the next place."

Through slitted eyes I watched the man back away, using his arms to make a way through the tall grass, cattails, and willows.

Sighing, I slumped onto the damp ground, thankful that I was so covered with filth and muskrat leaves.

Only after the sounds of his passage faded did I try and pull my legs under me. My stomach was growling. Having made the best of the muskrat pups, now it wanted more.

Carefully I uprooted one of the cattails and used my teeth to peel the skin from the root. Chewy raw cattail wasn't one of my favorites, but for the moment it was marvelous.

Bit by bit I slithered my way through the mess. Movement betrayed a water moccasin as he glided through the roots. I froze, watching. Unthreatened, he crossed no more than an arm's length from my nose, and we stared into each other's eyes. Perhaps he recognized me for one of Horned Serpent's creatures, or maybe he didn't care what I was, so long as I let him pass in peace.

By evening I had meticulously worked my way to the edge, carefully pulling up any of the reeds I'd crushed to hide my trail.

Using a leafy branch to obscure the outline of my head, I could lift high enough to see that no one was near. In fact, it looked as if the place were deserted; but what to do? Chance it and make for the distant forest? Or wait until the fall of darkness?

Wait.

With my left hand I fingered the scars on my neck. Patience could be learned in the most enduring of ways.

I settled back into the shadows cast by the willows, reminding myself of Horned Serpent's belief that I could be smart and learn.

The wait gave me ample time to reflect. Not just anyone gets himself eaten by his Spirit Being — and among my people, Horned Serpent is one of the most Powerful. In the Sky World, he sits just a notch below Breath Giver himself.

Why had he chosen me?

Or was it delusion, Black Shell? You were in cold water; your thoughts had turned to cotton-wood fluff. Men lose their senses when suffering from exposure.

I shook my head, suddenly unsure.

Then, as if prodded by something way down deep between my souls, I stared down at my clenched right fist. Frowning, I lifted it, aware that I continued to clutch something warm and throbbing. Making a face, I managed to straighten my cramped fingers, staring in disbelief. Perhaps as long as my pointing finger, and possessed of a translucent and unearthly red, one of Horned Serpent's brow tines rested across my muddy palm.

I swallowed hard, rubbing my thumb down the length of it, feeling the waxy surface.

Only the greatest shamans ever brought pieces of Spirit Beasts back from the Spirit World. We called such a thing a Sepaya.

Maybe Power really was with me, for as night fell clouds came rolling in from the west. They obscured the moon as I finally rose to a half crouch, peering through my disguising branch. I could see no one, hear no one. It had been hands of time since the last voices had called.

Straightening, I wavered slightly and made my way through the last of the brush. In the darkness I turned my steps for the forest.

Skirting the field where the battle had taken

place, a soft breeze carried the stench of rotting corpses. To the north I could see the faint glow of Kristiano fires behind the palisade.

How many dead? I wondered. *And where is Pearl Hand?*

I was staggering by the time I made it into the trees. I knew the general direction of our camp and forced one leg ahead of the other. All of my concentration went into keeping my trembling legs from collapsing under me. In desperation, I clutched Horned Serpent's brow tine to my chest, drawing from that tingling warmth.

I missed most of the corpses, detecting the smell before I tripped over them. As I veered around the rotting carcasses, night animals scurried away from the feast, their feet pattering on the leaves.

Why weren't these poor people being picked up by relatives? It should have been the first order of business after the battle. That the dead still lay unattended, even here among the trees, spoke ominously of the fate of Napetuca.

I was starting to feel dizzy and had to concentrate to keep my direction. How many days since I'd had a real meal? First there had been the exertion of the battle, and then the chilling waters of the lake. Cold took a lot out of a man, sapping his strength. That I'd been in bad condition was an understatement. Now, with the fall of darkness, my dirty skin was chilled, and beyond that I was so thirsty I could barely stand it.

I blinked, confused by the thought that not so long ago I'd been so surrounded by water that my skin had swollen like a loose glove.

"Who comes?" a soft voice hissed from the darkness.

I stopped, weaving on my feet. "Black Shell of the Chicaza."

Dark forms moved among even darker shadows. I dropped to my knees as they approached and said, "I was camped somewhere east with Pearl Hand and my dogs. I've been in the lake."

Strong hands pulled me to my feet, and someone draped my arm over his shoulder. I barely heard the whispers, and another man took my other arm. Together they supported my weight as we wound through the trees. At a small fire I was lowered onto brush matting.

In the dim light I couldn't place my rescuers. Three of them crouched around the fire, studying my filthy appearance through hard eyes. One had a poultice on an upper arm wound.

"Hungry?" one asked, offering dried venison.

"And thirsty . . . even after all that time in the water."

The man produced a gourd and said nothing as I emptied it and wiped my lips. Then I attacked the dried venison, relishing the taste as my mouth watered.

"Go find the Chicaza's camp," one ordered as he took his place across the fire from me. To the other he said, "Go back on guard before your eyes are night-blinded by the fire."

Both men nodded, and vanished into the night.

My remaining companion was muscular, tattooed with starbursts on his cheeks and breasts. His hair was up in a warrior's roach, and his face looked haggard.

"I am Wide Antler, of the Deer Clan," he offered. "I come from a village up north. We arrived here just before the fight." He smiled sadly. "Thirty of us came. I think only I am left. Long Arrow, who found you, is from Uriutina. Corn Thrower, the muscular fellow gone in search of your camp, is one of Rattlesnake's seconds."

"And Rattlesnake?" I asked softly.

"Captive. Or so we're told." He gestured to a pack. "You are welcome to share our food since the others are not here to eat it."

"I thank you." Then I studied his strained eyes. "How bad is it?"

He rubbed his hands together thoughtfully, and I could sense his hesitation at trusting a stranger. "Maybe two hundred dead that I have seen with my own eyes. More when you count those who are dying from infected wounds. They chased us from the fight, cutting down any they could catch. Then they surrounded the lakes . . . which you obviously know. For the first day they waited, letting the water wear the survivors down. You were in the small lake?"

"The large one."

He nodded. "That is why you avoided capture. They've taken all the survivors from the little lake. When those who refused to surrender became disoriented from the cold, they sent the Southerners in to drag them out by the hair. The same with those who surrendered in the big lake. They have all been taken into Napetuca."

"De Soto will make slaves of them," I muttered through a mouthful of venison. "I was with Blood Thorn. Have you heard word of him?"

"He's safe. He made it out last night after almost being caught. A Kristiano saw him heading for the forest and called an alarm. Blood Thorn was far enough away that he dove into the grass and crawled. He saved himself by pulling one of the corpses over his body."

"I would send him word that I'm alive."

"We will see to it."

I watched defeat settle in Wide Antler's expression.

"It's not over," I declared.

"How?" he asked. "They have all the holatas. Paracusi Rattlesnake is captive . . . and so many others. Word came that Uzachile is being evacuated even as we speak."

"The Paracusi Rattlesnake I have come to know isn't beaten just because he's a captive."

"It's those accursed Southerners." Wide Antler spat, turning his head to the side to avoid hitting the fire. Not even an angry Timucua would pollute sacred fire with his spit. "They betrayed us."

"I know. I was there at the meetings with de Soto. The Southerners read the sign language we used to communicate with Holata Ahocalaquen. The traitors bragged about it to those of us in the lake." I shook my head. "Who would have thought that they'd turn on their own people?"

"They're Southerners," Wide Antler said, as if that explained everything. "No better than the Kristianos."

"We have to stop thinking that way," I countered. "We are all the same now. We must come together, Wide Antler. If we don't, they will destroy us by using us against each other."

I saw no change in Wide Antler's expression. My words might have been like leaves in the wind, for the meaning completely eluded him as he insisted, "When this is over, I shall hunt them down and kill them all. Their corpses shall be left as our people's were — for animal food."

"To do that, you'll have to follow the Kristianos. The Southerners have become willing allies, even to the point of accepting the Kristiano god."

"All the more reason to kill them." He glanced at me. "I've heard of you, Chicaza. You were a Kristiano prisoner once. You were at the council with the holatas and de Soto. The holatas trust you."

I nodded, ripping off another piece of deer. As I chewed I said, "But for the traitors, we might have killed de Soto. Even at the cost of our lives, it would have been worth it."

He glanced at my right hand, firelight glinting on crimson. "Are you injured?"

Maybe I was just exhausted. Before I could think, I muttered, "Horned Serpent saved me. I broke a piece of his brow tine off . . ." I shook my head. "Nothing. It's nothing."

Wide Antler's eyes widened, and the tip of horn caught the light in a ruby flicker as I tucked it into my lap.

At that moment, we both heard rustling out in the forest, and I barely had time to brace myself before Squirm, his white blaze and bib gleaming, broke from the trees. Bark followed, Gnaw and Skipper right behind him. Then they were on me, bowling me flat, licking at my face. Tucking my head into my arms in defense, I was covered by delighted wiggling dog bodies.

Wide Antler was scrambling back, reaching for his weapons, when a stern voice ordered, "Down!"

My dogs promptly dropped to their bellies, tails swishing as they watched me with worshipful eyes. Rising from the overjoyed dogs, I struggled to my feet as Pearl Hand strode into the firelight. Until I die, I shall remember the tears streaking down her face, the relief in her eyes, and how she was panting from the run.

She rushed forward, wrapped her strong arms around me, and hugged the very breath out of my body.

Thirty-Six

Food, a bath, and a half a pot of sassafras tea can make all the difference. I reflected on that as the morning fire crackled and spat sparks. To be back in our small camp, just Pearl Hand and me, was the best healer of all. The dogs, once the joy of welcome had worn off, were giving us bored looks, or — in the case of Bark and Gnaw — were asleep. Pearl Hand sat beside me, one hand holding mine, the other gesturing as she spoke.

"When the charge came, I took aim and fired." She gestured her futility. "I *had* the shot. De Soto didn't even see it coming. He just moved wrong, and I swear, it clanged off his helmet. I was so close!

"Then the rest came. There was no standing against them. I broke off with Rattlesnake and ran back. Just the time it took to string the crossbow and set another arrow was time enough to become separated. One of the riders picked me out and came charging. He had only a sword, and had drawn it back to take my head off. At the last moment he realized I was a woman. I saw it in his eyes — that jolt of recognition. For only an instant did he hesitate, but I knew he had decided to kill me anyway.

"That moment of hesitation was enough. I got the crossbow up and shot as he started his swing. The impact of the arrow on his chest threw his arm off. I ducked. Just enough that the sword cut air a finger's length above my head. Then he was past."

She frowned and made a fist. "If I had to do it again, I'd have shot the cabayo instead. The animal might have bucked him off, and I could have used my knife on him before he got back to his feet."

"Did you kill any of them?"

She gave me a narrow-eyed glare. "I waited while you told me about being in the lake with Blood Thorn. I didn't interrupt while you told about your Spirit dream, Water Panther, and Horned Serpent. Let me finish."

I made an apologetic face.

"I managed to get the crossbow reloaded

530

and looked around." She grimaced. "We've been through enough of these things to know when all is lost. Instead of killing more Kristianos, I thought saving my skin was more important. I turned and ran for the forest. Somehow, shooting from behind the protection of a tree seemed a better bet than dodging cabayos in the open.

"I was one of the first into the trees, darting this way and that. Somehow, one of the riders managed to follow. He was about to run me down when I ducked behind a thick hickory. By the time he turned his cabayo, I was ready. He came slowly, carrying a lance. He kept calling, 'Come out, little flower. You can't hide. I have a new stem for you.'

" 'Come and get me, *pene muy blando*' I shouted back."

"What's a *pene muy blando?*"

"A very soft penis," she muttered. "It was enough to goad him. He charged forward and I managed to shoot an arrow into his cabayo's guts. Then I ducked behind the tree and ran off to the next. He knew his mount was wounded badly and pulled the animal around with the straps before he charged off back toward Napetuca. By that time women, children, and warriors were fleeing through the forest. I kept shouting for you, but everyone was screaming." She paused. "It was a confused mess."

For long moments we stared at the fire, lost

in thought.

Finally she asked, "You really went there, didn't you?"

"To the Spirit World?" I nodded. "It was so real, Pearl Hand. As real as this world. If I close my eyes, I'll see it again just as clearly."

Even as I said it, the terror of Horned Serpent's attack sent shivers through my body, and I was being crushed again.

Pearl Hand's voice brought me back. "It's all right. You're here, with me."

I sucked a breath, forcing my heart to slow. Meeting her eyes, I saw my own fear reflected there. "Sorry."

She ran her fingers along the side of my face. "You know, don't you, that only the greatest of priests and holy men are eaten by their Spirit Helpers."

I shook myself to be rid of the sensation. "But what does it mean? Gods, that final moment will fill my nightmares. It's unnerving, right down to the bones. To know you're being eaten alive . . ." I swallowed hard.

"You must talk to a hopaye. To someone who knows."

"There's more." I glanced around, ensuring that we were alone. Reverently I reached into my belt pouch, removed and handed her the finger-long tine from Horned Serpent. She stared at it, turning it carefully in her long fingers. I watched sunlight gleaming in its translucent red depths, as though it captured and played with the light.

"It's so warm to the touch, almost as if it vibrates."

"It's a piece of Horned Serpent's brow tine, a Sepaya. I broke it off as he . . ." I was suddenly unsure. Would she believe me?

Pearl Hand's brow furrowed; then she met my gaze, stunned. Her mouth opened, and then she managed to say, "You *brought* this from the Sky World?"

"It wasn't just a dream," I said cautiously, still uncertain about her reaction.

She continued to frown down at the red piece of tine. Then she shivered, quickly handing it back. After I took it, she rubbed her hands on her skirt, whispering, "I can still feel it, as if the thing's Power entered my hand." She stared up in disbelief. "You really went there, didn't you? I mean, in your body, not just your souls."

I nodded numbly, my thoughts as disorganized as the contents of a stirred pot. "But how does it help us fight the Kristianos? What was I supposed to learn?"

She shivered, staring into the fire. "That's the difference in you. Something more than just surviving the lake."

"Difference? What difference?"

Any further consideration evaporated as the dogs stood, making soft barks of alert.

I followed their gaze to a party of five warriors approaching through the leaf-dappled shadows. In the front I recognized Blood Thorn. I dropped the Sepaya into my pouch.

As our eyes met, he gave me a slow smile that belied the despair on his face.

Pearl Hand helped me to my feet and I stepped forward to clasp him to my breast. "By the sun and ancestors, I'm glad to see you."

He pushed me to arm's length, studying my face. "You, too, my friend. I've been worried sick about you. The news just came that you survived. Given your condition last time I saw you, it can only be a miracle that you made it. Have any trouble getting out of the water?"

I pulled him off to the side, whispering, "I had that fourth Spirit dream. But that's a story for later." I glanced nervously at the four warriors who stood respectfully behind Blood Thorn. Wide Antler, Long Arrow, and Corn Thrower were among them. "What is the news?"

"Bad, all of it." He took a moment to clap a hand to Pearl Hand's shoulder before she gave him a warm hug. "No, not all bad. The two of you are alive. At least that knowledge lightens my day."

He stepped back, turning his worried attention to me. "How are you? Really?"

"Still weak as a newborn fox pup. Nothing that food and rest can't cure."

"And Horned Serpent?"

"Where did you hear . . ." I saw Wide Antler drop his gaze, but I couldn't read his expression. "Later, Blood Thorn. When I'm rested. I don't want this thing to get out of hand, and we have other concerns for the moment."

He glanced back at the warriors behind him. "Let us not speak more of this until I have heard Black Shell's story. That is my wish." The warriors each nodded before Blood Thorn turned back to me. "Meanwhile, I will need your counsel. You've heard about our leaders?"

"All prisoners."

He took a weary breath. "Great Holata Uzachile has abandoned his city and fled to the forest. All through the country people are in confusion, hiding food, seeking to escape the path of the Kristianos. The stories told remind me of the Beginning Times when monsters roamed the earth and hunted people."

Pearl Hand turned away, averting her expression. I experienced a chill of premonition.

Blood Thorn lowered his voice. "I'm not sure I'm the one to deal with it, but the choice has been made. One of our scouts got close enough in the night to speak with the captives. Rattlesnake and the holatas have come to a decision. They will not be made into slaves. They will revolt. I *need* both of you at my side."

"Of course." I slapped him on his muscular shoulder. "You're a wise man, my friend." In a lower voice I asked, "Any word on Water Frond?"

He shook his head sadly. "I've spent the night organizing scouts. It was difficult enough to sneak even one scout close to the palisade. The Kristianos ride regular patrols around Napetuca. My man slipped in through the cornfields and lay in a ditch. He couldn't see much, and he doesn't speak Kristiano. He barely made it out undiscovered before daybreak and could only tell me the barest details of Rattlesnake's plan."

"I'm sorry, my friend."

Blood Thorn's weary smile vanished just as quickly as it came. "We must plan on how to help Rattlesnake's revolt."

We never had the chance. A runner came bolting through the trees, spied Blood Thorn, and turned his direction. The young man was streaked with sweat, his chest rising and falling.

"Iniha," he cried. "There is something happening in Napetuca! It sounds like fighting!"

"Gather all the warriors you can find!" Blood Thorn turned to his followers. "Have them assemble at the Lightning Tree. If Rattlesnake is making his move, we might be needed."

The four men left at a run. Pearl Hand had plucked up her crossbow as Blood Thorn spoke. I saw only three arrows in her quiver. And my own weapons? Blood and thunder, when had I lost them? Then I remembered: I could see them hanging from a willow back at the lake.

"Come on," Blood Thorn called, starting off after the runners.

I gave the dogs the order to stay and, forcing my weak body into compliance, followed at a trot. If there was a fight, I had no doubt that I'd find weapons aplenty.

The run to Napetuca wasn't more than a hand's time, but it left me winded. Nearing the fringe of the forest we could hear the shouts, the clanging of metal, and screams.

One of Blood Thorn's scouts appeared from the screen of trees, shouting, "I saw it start. Holata Uriutina smashed de Soto in the face with a club! It was the signal. All over the town our warriors grabbed up whatever they could and attacked!"

"And de Soto?" I cried. "Is he dead?"

"No," the scout answered, "but for the quick work of his guard, he would have been."

I stood gasping, one hand to my chest. For some reason I looked at the towering pine that stood behind the fringe of trees. Pines came in first after a fire, and this one was old.

I grabbed a branch, swinging up, and made my way toward the top. As I'd hoped, the old giant crested the younger oaks, hickory, and maples that had sprung up at the clearing edge. From my vantage, I could see over the palisade.

Beneath me, Blood Thorn and Pearl Hand were climbing.

My attention, however, was fixed on Napetuca. The place looked like a kicked anthill. There was no logic to the fighting. Here and there, scattered through the houses and raised granaries, rings of Kristianos surrounded bunched warriors. The Uzachile clutched Kristiano lances, sticks of wood, or the occasional sword. The most common weapons, to my surprise, were lengths of burning firewood! Obviously they'd picked up anything at hand. One or two had even donned chance bits of metal armor.

Even over the distance, I recognized de Soto. He stood at the foot of the chief's mound, surrounded by a bristling hive of guards. The *Adelantado* kept wiping at his bloody face. From his posture and the way he hunched, the man was seriously hurt, even dazed. His men were crowding around, acting solicitous.

By Breath Maker's will, tell me de Soto is dying.

"Should we attack?" Blood Thorn called up.

I was on the point of agreeing when the Kristianos made a major assault. Massed, they rolled forward on all fronts, weapons gleaming. For the first time I got a real idea of what those spear-ax weapons could do in the hands of a skilled man. They simply extended beyond the reach of swords and lances, chopping, spearing, and with a clever jerk, slicing a man's neck or shoulders. The formations of warriors broke, melting back only to be stopped by Kristianos rushing around behind them.

"No," I called down to Blood Thorn. "They're being crushed. By the time we could organize, it will be nothing more than a repeat of a couple of days ago."

A quick glance assured me of Blood Thorn's disappointment. I heard him calling orders down to the men below. Then he and Pearl Hand crawled up to my location, the branches bending and swaying.

In Napetuca, one warrior had managed to retreat to a granary placed high atop greased poles. The Timucua called them *barbacoas*. He stood above the ladder that led up to the doorway, brandishing a cabayero's lance. I watched helplessly as the Kristianos milled below him.

At another location, just below the charnel house mound, Kristianos closed in on a cluster of ten warriors armed with smoking lengths of firewood, and one who — oddly enough — brandished one of the heavy wooden chairs the Kristiano chiefs insisted on carrying with them.

At a shouted order, the Kristianos closed in, swords rising and falling. In no more than a couple of heartbeats it was over, but the raging Kristianos kept chopping away at the dead until only pieces remained.

The defiant warrior in the corn crib had resisted any attempt the Kristianos made at dislodging him. He still stood in the doorway, thumping his chest, shouting insults. One of the Kristianos had finally come to his senses enough to retrieve a crossbow. The others made room as he walked up and calmly took aim.

The warrior thumped his chest again and in one smooth move launched his lance at the crossbow man. Arrow and lance must have crossed paths in midair.

I craned my neck to see as the crossbow wielder went down. His fellows rushed to him, obscuring my vision.

Come on, tell me he's dead!

The warrior in the corn bin, however, had stopped shouting. He dropped to his knees and clutched something in his gut. The arrow had hit home. Even before the Kristianos could swarm up the ladder, the warrior flopped forward, one arm twitching where it protruded from the doorway.

The crossbow man was on his feet now, and I could just make out where the lance protruded from the ground at an angle. The warrior had missed.

Throughout Napetuca, those who had been overrun and the wounded were being slaughtered. Others, throwing down their weapons and calling out their surrender, were rounded up.

De Soto — surrounded by his guard — walked out, calling orders.

"What is this?" Blood Thorn asked from the branch just below me.

"Nothing good," Pearl Hand replied from her perch.

Captured and wounded warriors were herded into the plaza. The Kristianos only waited until de Soto had taken a commanding position on the chief's mound before they waded in, weapons flashing as they murdered their unarmed prisoners. From our high position, we could hear the screams, shouts of defiance, and the curses of the Kristianos.

In the midst of it I identified Antonio, gore streaked, gleefully flailing away. His right arm was in a sling, a sword in his left hand. Even over the distance, I caught a glimmering of blood as it was slung from his swinging blade. *If only I'd killed you that day, you two-legged maggot.*

Other survivors were led, dragged, or prodded to the plaza, where they, too, were cut to pieces.

I could just make out a little Kristiano — a small man barely chest high to his fellows — leading a captive warrior by his chain and collar. He made his way from the rear, raising a hand every now and then to still one of the angry Kristianos who made threatening gestures toward the captive. The little man was dressed well — one of their nobles, from the look of him.

When he reached the edge of the bleeding pile of bodies, he looked away, obviously distressed. One of the foot soldiers was reaching for the captive's chain when the warrior, instead of surrendering to his fate, grabbed up the little noble, raised him high overhead, and slammed the short man to the ground. Then the warrior was on him, beating the stunned noble with hands and fists, screaming like a wounded panther.

As the other Kristianos ran forward, the warrior ripped the little noble's sword from his belt and, with a howl, lunged to meet them.

We watched in amazement as the desperate warrior charged back and forth while a growing circle of Kristianos hemmed him in. Across the distance we could hear the clanging of swords as he beat back first one and then another of the assailants.

The warrior must have been a master of war club, for he was creating havoc with the unfamiliar weapon. His agility, courage, and desperation gave him a decided advantage.

Then the crowd parted, and five men with spear-axes arrived. In the time it takes to draw a deep breath and let it out, the valiant swordsman was laid low. One of the spear-axes reached out from behind, severing the man's leg. Another flashed down from one side and was drawn back, the sharp edge catching and cutting the warrior's neck. And then the rest were upon him.

With this, any will to resist crumbled. I watched, stunned, as one of de Soto's chiefs shouted orders.

Surviving captives, including the porters from Ahocalaquen — along with all the Uzachile women and children — were rounded up and dragged screaming to the palisade. We watched in silence as they were tied, one by one, to the palisade posts. Most just sagged in their bonds, broken of body and spirit.

"That's that," I murmured, remembering how I, too, was once bound to a palisade post. "Next will come the collars."

How wrong I was. To my amazement, the Southern Timucua were marched out in a long line. In growing consternation, I noticed that each of the freed Timucua carried a bow and arrows.

"They trust the Southerners enough to guard the prisoners?" Blood Thorn asked in amazement.

"Evidently," I said sourly. "Come on. Let's go. I guess we've seen enough." My stomach felt oddly unsettled, as if about to be sick.

"Wait," Pearl Hand called, and I looked back.

The Kristianos had formed a line behind the Southerners. These latter clutched their bows nervously, glancing uncertainly at their armed masters. Then they'd shoot wary looks at the bound captives hanging from the posts.

"Mátalos!" came a shouted order.

I heard it repeated by Ortiz, who stood to one side. He called it out in fluent Southern Timucua: "Kill them."

The archers shifted uneasily. I recognized Ears as he lifted his bow, nocked an arrow, and carefully drew back. Over the distance the shaft glistened silver in the sunlight. One of the bound captives stiffened, his heels gouging the dirt.

One by one the others followed. Drawing, aiming, shooting. After each shot they went forward, retrieving the arrows, stepping back, and shooting again. Through it all, screams and pleas rose in the air.

I stared in shocked disbelief. *Blessed Horned Serpent, tell me this isn't happening?*

"Why?" Blood Thorn asked in a pleading voice. "Why the women and children?"

"De Soto is teaching us a lesson," Pearl Hand said through clenched jaws. "And he's binding the Southerners to his bidding. Making them accomplices."

I wished to close my eyes, to turn away. *You owe it to these people to be a witness. To remember. And to carry the story to any who will listen.*

The screams had changed, those of desperation became those of victory, uttered from the throats of the Southern Timucua. Now the Southerners were dancing, slapping their thighs, calling on the sun to bless their valor and ferocity.

We watched for a while longer as the bodies were struck, hacked, urinated upon, and otherwise debased.

Blood Thorn's expression was unlike anything I had ever seen: It ached of grief, pain, and rage. His eyes had a glassy look that reflected the tortured and disbelieving souls that seethed and twisted within.

"Come on," Pearl Hand said hoarsely. "We'd better go. It won't take them long to remember to send out patrols. This, of all days, would not be one to be taken alive."

Climbing down, I felt soul-numb, as if some part of me had died along with the victims in Napetuca. The question *"Why?"* kept repeating in my head.

Still, I kept a close eye on Blood Thorn. I wouldn't have put it past him to simply let go and dive headfirst into the ground. As horrified and stunned as I was, this was his nation, his relatives and friends.

When we reached the forest floor, Blood Thorn remained in a shocked silence, his eyes locked on some distance only he could see.

I turned to one of the warriors, Walking Thunder, a somber man from Napetuca. "Pull the scouts back. Keep everyone away from Napetuca. Establish a perimeter well back in the forest. If the Kristianos come, we need enough warning to evade them."

Walking Thunder simply nodded, hardly aware that he'd just taken orders from a foreigner.

Pearl Hand gave me a knowing glance; then with a gentle hand on Blood Thorn's shoulder, she softly said, "Come. We have to plan."

As we walked back toward our camp, I couldn't help but glance at Blood Thorn's anguished face. The nightmare of what we'd just seen must have been replaying behind the man's eyes.

After this, nothing in our world will ever be the same.

THIRTY-SEVEN

We weren't the only witnesses, of course. Other scouts and warriors had had the same idea we had. Numerous eyes had been watching from various points of vantage.

That night, around a large fire, warriors came trickling in in ones and twos. Despite the cooking pots boiling with hominy and various cuts of meat, no one seemed to have an appetite.

Though I protested, Pearl Hand insisted I eat. Sitting beside me, she used a horn spoon and fed me one mouthful after another. I don't remember if I tasted anything.

All through the meal she kept turning uneasy eyes toward Blood Thorn. The man sat off to the side, his eyes still fixed on an eternity I dared not even guess at.

The dogs waited behind us, having picked up on the despair and grief that hung in a dark fog over the camp. They watched as warriors whispered to each other, like Pearl Hand and me, sharing details of the day's events.

Something dark and brooding lurked behind Blood Thorn's eyes. I'd seen him and Pearl Hand talking earlier. They'd been off to one side, Pearl Hand telling him something that, if only for a moment, seemed to ameliorate the tension in his expression.

Then she'd placed a hand on his shoulder, as though to emphasize what she was saying.

He'd frowned and nodded, then shot me a furtive glance before Pearl Hand walked back and squatted beside me. She used a stick to prod at the fire.

"What did you tell Blood Thorn?"

She pursed her lips before saying, "Things that might have reassured him. He's feeling lost right now, stunned. The only thing I could try and give him is hope."

"Hope? After what we've seen?" I asked. "What keeps you so strong?"

Her lips barely cracked a smile. "A weaker woman would never have made it this far."

"It will get worse." Horned Serpent's warning whispered between my souls.

"I know." She said it with such finality. "You should go. Before the end comes."

Her level gaze met mine. "We're committed, Black Shell. You by Power and your Spirit dreams." She shrugged. "Me, I'm driven by different Spirits — passions, if you will — but they're of my own making. Not the universe's."

"This will destroy us in the end."

"Maybe. But I know who I am now."

"But you could have a —"

She pressed her fingers to my lips, saying, "What? Go off and be a wife and mother? Fuss over a household, bear children, and grow old pounding corn, fleshing hides, and tailoring clothing? Do you see me sitting in the sun, growing old while I gossip with other old women? Becoming . . . ordinary?"

"Compared to ending up as a maggot-infested corpse rotting in that same sun? Becoming an *ordinary* old woman has a lot to be said for it."

She chuckled softly and fixed me with those knowing eyes. "Will you ever become *ordinary*, Black Shell? Not a chance. We were born different."

I reached out and took her hand. "I had to make one last attempt."

"I know." She dismissed the topic and gave Blood Thorn a thoughtful look. "I'm worried about him."

"His world died today. Uprooted like a great tree in a storm."

"He hasn't spoken a word."

549

"There are no words. There never will be."

"Napetuca. That word is enough."

I nodded, thinking of the Nations in the interior. How many were there? Apalachee, Coosa, Tuskaloosa, Ockmulgee, Chicaza, Mabila, and so many more. A list of names too long to be recited. How many of them would end up burned into my memory like Napetuca?

I felt Pearl Hand's gaze as I stared desolately into the fire. Her hand tightened on mine.

She leaned close, whispering, "You're falling into the pit, Black Shell. If you do, it will be nearly impossible to get you out."

"The pit is all that's left to us."

She rose, tugging me to my feet, a serious intensity in her eyes. "Come on. Let's go to our robes."

"I'm not in the mood."

"We're alive, Partner. Your bloody Chicaza spend their entire lives trying to maintain balance between order and chaos. Right now, you *need* to celebrate life. And so do I."

I had the urge to tell her that lying with a woman was anything but white Power. Warriors avoided women and their red-laced bodies, fearing they would be polluted, somehow corrupted, before a battle. Pearl Hand was obviously confused, or making some sort of joke at Chicaza expense. But the look in her eyes dissuaded me. Could it be that I was learning to trust her, no matter how absurd her urge at the moment?

I let her tug me to my feet. No one paid much attention as we walked off into the night.

Perhaps that's why Power had brought Pearl Hand into my life. No matter who or what she had been, we needed each other. I had given her a purpose, and that night she gave me balance.

I would never question her sanity for following me into this mess again.

De Soto, his men, freed and captive porters, cabayos, and the muddled herd of *puercos* pulled out of Napetuca the next morning. Scouts came to inform us. To my surprise, Blood Thorn remained at the fire, seated in the same position as when Pearl Hand had pulled me away the night before. His gaze was still locked on eternity.

I didn't need Pearl Hand's insistence to eat my fill, and it was midday before the remaining Uzachile tentatively left the safety of the forest and walked cautiously past the bloated dead and up to Napetuca. As we proceeded, the buzzards squawked and rose like a great dark spiral to circle in the sky. Their shadows floated like dots across the trampled and cropped grass. Emboldened crows continued to pick at the dead even as we passed, many too engorged to take wing.

I ignored the stench, but many of the warriors accompanying us bent to the side, retching.

At the Napetuca palisade gate, I hesitated, looking back to where Blood Thorn walked in the midst of his warriors. In total, I counted thirty-four: all that was left of Rattlesnake's great army. The others were dead, fled, or too wounded to travel.

As I led the way through the gate, the town stank of urine, feces, and decomposing humans. I held a piece of cloth over my face, ordering the dogs to wait outside. They seemed relieved to remain in the breeze.

Inside the town, the buildings looked forlorn, the doors gaping black holes. Broken pots and jars, ripped baskets, upended mortars, and broken pestles littered the passages between the houses. Above it all, the empty corn cribs seemed to stare down from their high poles, haunted. And over the entire town, an eerie silence lay, as if pressing down on the very air.

Fabric, much of it torn, lay here and there, and no one had bothered to cover the sun-blackened bloodstains. Bones could be seen — mostly from deer and *puercos.* Bits of shell jewelry glinted along with broken arrows and splintered bows. Pieces of wood and cane had been scattered about.

The bodies had been dragged to the plaza, blood and dried fluids marking the path.

There they'd been piled, as if to make a small and putrid mound. A fountain of buzzards and crows rose shrieking to the sky as we neared.

Even breathing through the cloth was difficult. I didn't try counting the corpses piled there. Suffice it to say, the pile was taller than I was. Until you've seen such a thing, you wouldn't believe it. The scavengers had taken the eyes first, leaving the slack-faced dead to stare at us from blood-dark pits. Sections of intestine, swollen from gas, protruded from sliced bellies. Here and there a severed arm or head had been tossed onto the heap. Pools of liquid oozed and dripped from the mess, all crawling with flies.

Blood Thorn stopped at my side, his eyes oddly unfocused. Then he turned and walked off through the garbage toward the palisade. Pearl Hand and I followed, aware of the horrified mutterings of the warriors who remained at the pile.

As if drawn, Blood Thorn wound through the houses, high granaries, and clan buildings. He walked like a man out of time — a living ghost passing through a world no longer his own.

The victims still hung from the palisade posts, left as they had died: limp and broken. Each body had its share of flies, but it seemed that the dead of Napetuca were so many that even the buzzing beasts were spread thin.

I thought of the ghosts, waiting, watching, and wailing in sorrow and injustice. As a good Chicaza, I should have been horrified at the wash of red Power, so out of balance with the white. The image remains locked in my souls, as if a distorted vision from another earth than ours.

This is what Horned Serpent was preparing me for.

Blood Thorn walked without hesitation, as if guided, to a young woman with long hair. She'd been stripped naked, and the arrow that killed her had left a vicious hole beneath her small left breast. Someone had ripped it out, pulling bits of lung through the puncture, leaving the wound puckering and black with dried blood.

"Water Frond," Blood Thorn whispered, uttering the first words since the massacre. She stared up at him through sunken gray eyes, her lips parted and dried.

"My heart bleeds with yours," I managed, despite nearly choking on the stench.

Blood Thorn turned, and without another word, walked away. Loath to leave him alone, I followed along behind, Pearl Hand at my side.

Blood Thorn led us straight to the gate. He didn't hesitate, didn't even slow. He just walked purposefully down the battered trail, following in the tracks of de Soto's animals and men.

I stopped beside the dogs, asking, "Should we follow him?"

"And do what?" Pearl Hand asked. "He's not sane right now. Nothing you could say or do would make a difference."

"If he catches up with the *Adelantado,* they'll just kill him." I started forward, and Pearl Hand placed a hand on my arm.

"Let him go, Black Shell. He follows his own Spirits. It's his way. He has to walk it. You can't do it for him."

"No. I suppose not." I glanced back at Napetuca. "Is there anything we can do here?"

She shot a dull look at the gates. "What's been done here is done. We have nothing left to offer."

"I do have one last thing. I think my bow may still be at the edge of the lake. I'd like to take a look. And then we'll be gone."

She nodded.

I started across the battlefield. Along the way I began picking up arrows that had been left behind. I only took the good ones, made by men now dead. Perhaps, Power granting, I could make better use of them than the men who had so carefully crafted them.

Where it rested against my breastbone — in a small leather sack, hung by a cord — Horned Serpent's Sepaya seemed to vibrate.

THIRTY-EIGHT

That I found my Caddo bow was a miracle, but it lay untouched in the willows, right where Fetch had led me into the lake.

That night Pearl Hand and I made camp by ourselves on a rise overlooking a cypress- and tupelo-filled marsh. The frogs were croaking, insects whirring, and for reasons of his own, a bull alligator was roaring, though the season was late for breeding.

I glanced at Pearl Hand as I greased the staves on my bow. She was seated across from me, Bark's head on her lap. I watched her long fingers stroking his thick head. Here and there scabs were rising on all the dogs, but Bark had the most.

"He saved me," she said softly. "They all did. The war dogs would have had me otherwise."

"I know." I told her about the war dog I'd seen trying to run on three legs. "The Kristianos corrupt everything, even the animals who serve them."

She glanced at me. "What about you?"

"Huh?"

"You're Chicaza. And you've just walked out of a town filled with the brutally murdered. According to your people's beliefs, your souls and body have been exposed to the shrieking souls of the dead. Death and violence have contaminated you. You're drenched in red Power, Black Shell. A good Chicaza would be desperate for a ritual cleansing. Most people would consider your body and souls polluted with war, death, and disharmony."

I set the bow aside and stared at my arm and hand. I made a fist, watching the muscles of my forearm ripple, the tendons standing from the skin.

"In Napetuca I wondered about that. I was swallowed alive by Horned Serpent. Perhaps I am a creature of the Underworld now, living under a different Power." I marveled at how my fingers wiggled, curled, and felt. "I've seen war and atrocity before. Once I watched a Tuskaloosa army destroy a Koasati town that refused them tribute. Men died; women and children were taken for slaves. I watched the Koasati mikkos hung in squares and tortured to death. One, a scarred warrior, endured the torture with such courage that the Tuskaloosa took him down, fed him, tended his wounds, and granted him his freedom. The ones who were made slaves were finally integrated into the households, made part of families. Many eventually ended up adopted into clans, marrying, becoming part of their new people."

She nodded, perhaps having witnessed similar events.

"The Kristianos," I continued, "are driven by something brutal and base. To them we are less than insects — beings without souls or feelings. They think of us as useful vermin to be tricked, used, abused, and discarded. To them the act of killing is nothing more than entertaining sport."

"I've known occasional chiefs and warriors who took enjoyment in butchery," she countered.

"But never an entire nation of them."

"No."

A deep-seated revulsion rose in my gut. "How can we ever make our people understand? Were we to walk into a Mos'kogee high minko's palace and try to explain, he wouldn't believe us. It would be like trying to convince him that Cannibal Turkey had come back, or that an army of Stone Men were coming. Our people can't think in terms of the Kristianos. Their very existence defies our understanding."

"The stories will travel, Black Shell."

"But will they be believed? Even after we saw the dead in Tapolaholata town, would you have imagined what happened at Napetuca?"

"Only in my nightmares."

"We have to make people think in a way they can't even conceive of."

Her fingers traced designs across Bark's skull. "You must trust Power, Black Shell."

"That doesn't reassure me."

"It shouldn't. Power is tricky. But you have no choice. The fact that Horned Serpent devoured you, and still you came back makes you something very special."

"Believe me, there was nothing reassuring about it."

She regarded me with level eyes. "The day Blood Thorn made it back, he told me about the last time he saw you. You were so cold you'd stopped shivering and felt warm. According to him, you couldn't talk, couldn't think from the cold. That if you'd somehow made it to shore, you were so disoriented you'd have stumbled into the Kristianos. And if your souls had fled from the cold, you'd have drowned. He said I should prepare myself to consider you dead."

"I would have been . . . if Water Panther

hadn't pulled me into the Underworld."

"And when it was all done," she insisted, "Horned Serpent deposited you on the bank. You've been granted a marvelous gift. I can feel it in you. So can others. A difference that even an Uzachile warrior can detect when you give an order."

"There was no one else to give it." My thoughts went to Blood Thorn. Where was he? Had he already caught up with the Kristianos? Had his sense of honor demanded that he attack them, alone and valiantly, hoping his death would free his souls to search the afterlife for Water Frond?

"Horned Serpent must have known what was coming." I flexed my fist again. "He asked me if I would fail him by crying out in desperation when things became bleak. Napetuca has changed the way I think of 'bleak.' "

I shivered, unable to shake the memory of those piled corpses. The gaping sockets of their eyes continued to stare in my direction, demanding to know why. Demanding an answer I didn't have.

"We know the stakes now, Black Shell."

I nodded, remembering everything that had befallen us since the day I was captured by the Kristianos. "There's no going back."

Pearl Hand traced her fingers through Bark's thick hair, her expression soft as she stroked his head.

I stared at the fire, wondering. In the old stories cannibals stalked the land, along with the terrible Stone Men, and great birds like Cannibal Turkey. Heroes, like the Orphan and Morning Star, had come to rid the world of their menace. But those heroes had been born of First Woman and Corn Mother.

With a terrible shock, I realized that I, myself, had lain with Corn Mother. And what Power had come of that joining? Only a corn plant growing up from her womb, or something else?

"What's wrong?" Pearl Hand asked.

I swallowed hard, my heart skipping. "Black Shell, the trader, died when Horned Serpent swallowed him. I am only beginning to see the man who was born of that death." A man beyond the white and red Power, a creature of the Underworld who existed only for a single purpose.

I could see the sudden uncertainty in her eyes, and then she gave me a brave smile. "That man tricked Water Panther. He eluded the Kristianos with the help of a Spirit dog. He stood face-to-face with Horned Serpent, and passed his judgment. You walk through death and war, unfrightened by the ghosts of the slain. Perhaps that's the kind of warrior we need now."

I felt a cold shiver run down my spine. In the stories told of the Beginning Times, the heroes are never frightened. But I was, way down deep in the marrow of my bones.

For two days we hurried westward, bypassing the town of Hapaluya and trading for river passage at a small farmstead. After landing on the far shore, we hurried toward Uzachile.

No more than a hand's time later, Skipper shot a worried look over his shoulder, ears pricked, tail rising. Bark turned his thick and scarred head toward our backtrail, a growl rising in his throat.

I gave a slash of the hand: the order for silence. Pearl Hand lowered her crossbow, stepped into the ring, and yanked the string back before nocking one of her last arrows. Squirm was already trying to weasel out of his pack.

In an instant, I had my bow strung and an arrow ready from my quiver.

A man appeared on the trail behind us, and I recognized Walking Thunder. Behind him came four more, all following along in our tracks. Each was painted for war, his hair bobbing in the characteristic pom tied atop the head.

"Black Shell?" Walking Thunder called. "Wait! We've been on your trail for a hard day."

"What's happened?"

He and the rest trotted up, chests rising and falling, sweat gleaming on their skins. Each man slowed, and I was surprised by the odd reverence in their eyes.

Walking Thunder then dropped to his knee, hands out, palms up. The gesture was that of a subordinate to his chief.

"What are you doing?" I asked nervously as the rest followed suit, dropping to a knee, hands out.

A mixture of desperation and hope lit Walking Thunder's eyes. "We come to offer ourselves to you."

I was about to protest when Pearl Hand stepped before me, demanding, "Why would Uzachile warriors seek to serve Black Shell?"

"Because Horned Serpent devoured Black Shell in the Land of the Dead and brought him back to life to fight the Kristianos."

"Where did you hear that?" I asked, dumbfounded.

"Blood Thorn told us just before we entered Napetuca." Walking Thunder lowered his head, eyes on the ground before him.

Wide Antler added, "I saw the piece of Horned Serpent's antler that you carry."

"I never told Blood Thorn about that," I insisted.

"I did," Pearl Hand said coolly. "The morning before the captives in Napetuca were killed. He asked how you survived the lake." She gave me one of those knowing looks. "You told him of the Spirit dreams. He knows, Black Shell. As I do. As Walking Thunder, Corn Thrower, and these others now know."

"I saw it, didn't I?" Wide Antler added. "That was what you clutched in your hand. Remember? When I asked if you'd been hurt? I saw the red gleam when you tried to hide it."

Before I could reply, Pearl Hand stepped before Walking Thunder, pointing at me. "This is Black Shell, once of the Chicaza. But before you join us, you must understand. He is akeohoosa, outcast. Black Shell serves no single people. He is not Chicaza, not Uzachile, not Apalachee. He fights for this world, and all peoples, regardless of who they might be." With great authority, she added, "He is Horned Serpent's chosen. Power walks in his tracks."

I stared at Pearl Hand in disbelief. What was she up to?

"I understand," Walking Thunder whispered softly.

I couldn't stand it any longer. "Why are you doing this?"

Walking Thunder kept his eyes carefully lowered. "My people died at Napetuca. Like you, I am an orphan."

An orphan? Did he mean the Orphan? The hero from the Beginning Times? Orphan was one of Corn Woman's two children. When Corn Woman's menstrual blood dripped onto the ground, she dug it up and placed it in a pot. Ten months later she was surprised to hear a baby crying. When she looked in the pot, she discovered the Orphan, and raised him along with her naturally conceived son, Morning Star. Equating me with him? Not to mention that I'd coupled most ardently with Corn Woman in that Spirit dream. By Breath Giver's knees, this was too much. I took a breath, ready to protest.

A sharp glance from Pearl Hand bade me still my tongue. In a low voice, she added, "Our fight will be long and hard. It will take us wherever the Kristianos go. We will not stop until they are defeated. Those who would join us must renounce everything but the struggle to destroy the invader. Like us, they must have no single people, but all peoples. They are not Uzachile, but of all nations. Can you do this?"

Walking Thunder swallowed hard, jerking a brief nod. "I can."

The others weren't looking so sure.

Pearl Hand pulled Walking Thunder to his feet. "Then join us."

"Walking Thunder?" Bear Paw, one of his companions, asked, plainly disturbed.

It was Wide Antler who turned to his friend. "Bear Paw, your nieces lie dead and unburied in Napetuca. They were only supposed to carry Kristiano baggage as far as Napetuca. Instead they were made to carry all day, and bed Kristianos — one after another — all night. You saw the bruises. You know they did not serve men willingly."

Bear Paw lowered his gaze as Walking Thunder said, "Holata Uzachile has abandoned the capital. His only goal is to encourage the Kristianos to pass through without further fighting. If you stay, Bear Paw, you will remain Uzachile, but is that how you want to live the rest of your life? What about your souls? How will you ever forget?"

Bear Paw took a deep breath and extended his hands even farther. "I will serve Black Shell. I am" — he winced — "no longer Uzachile."

I took Bear Paw's hand and pulled him to his feet. Long Arrow and Corn Thrower made their decisions, and I pulled them up, too.

My new warriors looked uneasy, nervous, as if these events had caught them off guard.

"Come," I said gently, "we've got to make time. We need to be ahead of de Soto for once. If Holata Uzachile has abandoned his town, the *Adelantado* will fortify it and send out raiding parties. He's low on captives. And this time, with your help, we're going to be ready for him."

I gestured to the dogs and took up the lead, taking a fast pace down the trail.

Behind the pack dogs, the warriors lined out, trotting along, their expressions anything but confident.

"So," Pearl Hand called from just behind

me, "it begins."

"What does?"

"The mighty storm. You're the tornado, Black Shell. Just as Horned Serpent intended. Do you have a plan?"

"Just the glimmerings of one."

"Good. Because if you can keep these men, inspire them, we have a chance."

I called out, "Are any of you from around the capital?"

"I am," Corn Thrower called back.

"Do you know of any swamps outside of the city?"

"Swamps? Yes, there are many."

"Good. When we get close, I want you to show me which ones are the closest to Uzachile town, and if there are any trails through them."

As we continued, Pearl Hand asked, "Thinking of something?"

"Oh, yes. It's time we started using what we know against the Kristianos."

"And just what might that be?"

"Their arrogance." I gave her a thin grin.

I could see it all happening in the eye of my souls. Now, if Corn Thrower could just show me the right place.

THIRTY-NINE

That afternoon we began encountering small bands of Uzachile fleeing southward. These were mostly composed of women and children, with some elders. Panic lived behind their eyes as they hunched under their loads, disbelief in their expressions. They confirmed that the capital was being evacuated in anticipation of de Soto's arrival.

"Holata Uzachile sent the Kristianos several deer," one man, his back bent under a heavy pack, told us. "He hopes that the invader will not treat us the same way he did those at Napetuca."

At the news, my Uzachile growled with displeasure. Rewarding the butchers of Napetuca affected them like a slap in the face.

"There is no appeasement," I told the fugitives. "The Kristianos have no honor. If Holata Uzachile has any sense, he's taken to the woods and ordered all of his people to stay as far away as they can."

"But it's harvest time," the man pleaded.

"The only harvest anywhere near the Kristianos is death," Pearl Hand told them coldly. "Going hungry, you can make do, even if it means eating roots and rodents. In Kristiano chains you'll starve as they work you to death."

"What of us?" Walking Thunder asked as we watched the small party head south. "What do we do?"

I glanced at the few remaining arrows Pearl Hand had for her crossbow. "Corn Thrower, draw me a map of the swamps."

He squatted in the trail like a burly toad, muscles bunched as he used a twig to illustrate. The man had a good head for terrain, or so I hoped.

"I've hunted all this country," Corn Thrower told me, and pointed to three lines of white scar on his shoulder. "That's how I got these. Killing a bear here" — he pointed — "in this swamp."

"You know it well?"

"Very. My uncle liked to hunt and fish there. He wasn't much of a warrior, and my mother did most of the farming. Uncle did his best to keep me out in the swamp as much as he could."

I thought about where de Soto might be. "They're probably building one of those heavy bridges back at the river. We should be at least a day ahead of them."

"It's a good day's march from the river to Uzachile town," Walking Thunder agreed. "If they make it in one march, they'll be exhausted. They'd have to rest an additional day after arriving at the capital."

"Which means?" Pearl Hand asked.

"That we can get a look at the land south of Uzachile. I was through there last fall. It's good country, mostly flat, and the farmsteads will be flush with corn. Given the way de Soto uses up his captives, he'll be wanting more. After all, he killed the ones Holata Ahocalaquen provided at Napetuca. The ones still alive will be getting worn down from double burdens."

"That means he's got to raid for more." Pearl Hand fingered her chin thoughtfully.

"That's right. Small parties. Perhaps ten men per group."

"But how do we know where they're headed?" Walking Thunder asked.

"We don't. But from past experience they fan out in all directions." I glanced up at Corn Thrower. "I need you to take me to a place in the swamp."

"Where?" he asked, almost eagerly.

"That, I'm hoping, you'll tell me." I bent down, using his stick to scratch in the dirt. "I want it to be something like this. Water here, land sticking out like a narrow finger into the swamp. A dead end."

He studied my drawing and nodded. "I know of such a place."

"Is there a good trail to it?"

"Yes."

"One passable to cabayos?"

"Very. The trees are old on the high ground, the way open."

"Then we may have work to do first." I looked up at Long Arrow, an affable man from Uriutina. "Meanwhile, after Corn Thrower leads us to this place, we may have a lot of hard work to do. Digging, chopping. Are the rest of you willing to sweat in the sun?"

"Yes, *Peliqua*." They'd taken to calling me the Orphan. The title bothered me; it sounded so final. But the reverence with which they said it bade me to hold my tongue.

"Good."

We followed Corn Thrower through the growing darkness, winding down a low ridge. He stopped at a confluence of trails.

"Uzachile town is there." Corn Thrower pointed to the north. "A little less than a day's run." He pointed along the trail to the east. "You can see the oaks and hickory here, but it falls off to either side. That's the way into the swamp."

"And there's a village or collection of farmsteads close?" I asked.

Corn Thrower pointed. "Follow that trail west. Maybe two hands of time at a trot. It will take you to the Squash Meadows. Kin of mine, Deer Clan people, live there."

I pointed to Long Arrow. "Go. See if anyone is there. Warn any women and children and the elders to flee. Then meet me here at dawn. Two days from now. Can you do that?"

"Yes, Peliqua." Long Arrow gave me a serious nod.

"May the Ancestors go with you."

I watched him disappear into the growing gloom. "We'll camp here for tonight. First thing in the morning, let's take a good look at your swamp, Corn Thrower." Then I asked, "Which one of you is the fastest runner? All of our lives might depend on it."

That night, in my dreams, restless fingers of worry pulled at my heart. I was about to take the fight to the Kristianos. So far all the others who had tried had failed. Would I be any better than a blooded war leader like Rattlesnake?

Other than the fact that Corn Thrower had been right about the ridgetop being wide open, the place was perfect. The long ridge protruded into the swamp like a skinny finger. At the end it tapered into a narrow dip, then rose like a knuckle before vanishing into the water. The swamp around it extended in three directions, studded with bald cypress, tupelo, and water oak. Hanging moss draped raggedly from the branches, and cypress knees rose like oddly shaped teeth. On firmer ground, grape, greenbriar, and honeysuckle vines gave the trees a webbed appearance.

I gathered my little band and walked the length of the skinny peninsula. "All right, here's where the work comes in. Dig out the packs and you'll find good greenstone celts. We need to start cutting vines. Back yonder was a fallen hickory. We'll need to drag it across the neck to make a barricade."

"We're going to fight from a barricade?" Walking Thunder asked. "Against Kristianos?"

"Of course not," I scoffed. "Do I look like a fool? We need it to block most of this neck, but leave the cabayos a way around. Do you see? Our task is to make an obstacle course that men can run straight through, but where the pursuing Kristianos have to zigzag back and forth. See where I'm headed with this?"

Walking Thunder nodded. "I understand. To the Kristianos it looks like they're chasing a man into a dead-end trap."

"Right," Pearl Hand agreed, propping her hands on her hips. "It's our job to figure out how to slow the cabayos down, spread them out, and knock them off one by one without them knowing."

When they got the idea, they pitched in. The air rang with the sound of chopping, punctuated periodically with the cracking of timber.

Meanwhile Pearl Hand and I walked down to the low marshy approach to the knuckle. The narrow neck of soil was saturated and the ground felt spongy under my feet. Probably firm enough to slow, but not stop, a cabayo. "We'll have to dig this out."

Pearl Hand gave me a skeptical look. "So far I haven't said anything, but if this goes wrong, there's no escape."

"That's what I'm counting on." I bent low, much to the dogs' interest. They came close, trying to discern what I was looking at as I speculated on how to build our trap. Make this low restriction even more mucky, and maybe throw in a couple of camouflaged logs?

I shoved Bark out of the way and, thinking about fields of fire, looked out at the water. Perhaps we could build some sort of blinds, or relocate cypress knees? "When the time comes, do you mind getting a little wet?"

Her eyebrow arched in reply. "Wet? Are you joking?"

"Me? Joke? Never." If this didn't work out, swimming would be our only escape.

"Ten cabayos?" Wide Antler asked that night as he sat by our fire. We'd made camp at the cross trails. "We can't get them all." He was staring at the map we'd sketched into the dirt.

I looked up at the firelight reflecting off the branches of the great hickory that arched over the small clearing. I could see the nuts ripening above. The air had a chill, reminding me that the sun was heading south, that the harvest was beginning, and that soon the leaves would fall.

"We don't need them all. Nor do we want them all. Just a few: the foolhardy ones who can't resist."

"I want them all," Walking Thunder said grimly where he squatted on his haunches, chewing on baked smilax root. "Napetuca burns in my souls."

"Mine, too." Wide Antler laid aside the shell knife he'd been sharpening on a small flat of sandstone. My dwindling trade had found a most utilitarian use. He looked around. "Most of my family died at Napetuca."

"I died at Napetuca," Corn Thrower admitted, wiping his thick hands on the flap of his loincloth. "I shall become someone else now." He shot a desperate look my way.

"Napetuca burns in all of our souls," Pearl Hand reminded. "But you saw what happens when Kristianos are massed. Even ten would be too many. The Peliqua is right. When the time comes, we take what we are offered. Power chose Black Shell for his wisdom and restraint."

"Patience is a difficult skill to learn," I agreed, sipping at a cup of sassafras tea. Draining it, I reached for my pipe and tamped it full of tobacco with a stick. A good Chicaza didn't touch tobacco with his finger. Odd, I was the Peliqua, yet I still clung to the customs of my people.

I lit the bowl with a burning stick, took a puff, and passed it to Pearl Hand. As I exhaled the smoke, I prayed, "Breath Giver, give us just a few. We are not overconfident. We only pray that the Kristianos are."

Pearl Hand placed the stem to her lips, inhaling. Blowing the smoke to the heavens, she prayed, "Steady my aim. I need only one Kristiano for now."

Corn Thrower studied the pipe she handed him as though it were something precious. I'd watched in amazement as he'd muscled heavy logs throughout the day. Now the pipe looked delicate in his thick-fingered hands.

Our construction of obstacles across the neck of land was coming along nicely. And we had taken great effort to disguise our work. My hopes were that the cabayeros would be too keen on the chase to notice any sign of human activity, but I'd been learning not to take things on chance.

The bowl glowed red as Corn Thrower took his turn. Bending his head back, he blew toward the sky, saying, "I, too, need but one. For now."

"But what if the Kristianos don't come?" Wide Antler asked as he took the pipe.

"Then we've worked ourselves sweaty for nothing," Bear Paw interjected.

Wide Antler drew and exhaled upward, praying, "I will take only those Kristianos that Power will give me. I, too, will learn patience."

"We're not getting sweaty for nothing." I watched Walking Thunder accept the pipe, offer a short prayer, and take a draw. "This is a learning process. A new way of war against a different kind of enemy."

"It would never work against trained warriors." Wide Antler hugged his knees, eyes on the fire. "They'd come cautiously."

"And someday," Pearl Hand noted, "the Kristianos may, too. But that time isn't now." She glanced at me. "Arrogance is their greatest weakness."

The others were giving us curious looks as I took the pipe and drew. I slowly blew the smoke toward the sky, adding my prayer. "May their arrogance lead them right into our hands."

Water swirled around my ankles as I wrestled with a length of log. Pearl Hand and I had elected to tackle the dirty job of levering up mud and building our trap in the marshy dip that separated the "knuckle" from the rest of the ridge. As we worked, we thought up additional modifications like laying logs in the muck we were creating.

Overhead, a breeze rattled the oak leaves, and throughout the day, pattering noises had mixed with the sound of chopping as the first of the acorns dropped. Among my distant Chicaza, the first such sounds would have been met with excitement. Proof that the fall harvest was coming.

The dogs lay on their sides just up the slope where the leaf mat provided a comfortable bed. They watched, bored, ears twitching as the occasional insect tickled them.

Skipper suddenly rolled to his belly, uttering a low woof.

"Quiet," I ordered, slogging out of the sticky mud.

I caught movement through the trees and wiped my dirty hands as I reached for my bow.

Long Arrow, my errant Uriutina, appeared, followed by two stringy young men in breechcloths. Their hair swung with each step, and they peered about cautiously.

"Peliqua!" Long Arrow cried and, smiling, trotted forward.

"You're early."

He kept grinning. "It wasn't as difficult as I thought. The people at Squash Meadows had already been warned by one of Holata Uzachile's runners. They've been hiding their food and valuables. These two boys are the fastest runners in the country, Peliqua. They have volunteered for a dangerous task." He lowered his voice. "And, of course, seek fame and glory in the process."

I immediately figured out Long Arrow's angle. "And you, instead of being bait, can help spring the trap, right?"

Long Arrow masked a smile. Then he went on to introduce the boys. Or perhaps young men. They were at that indeterminate age.

"Is there a canoe nearby that you can use?" I asked.

"My uncle has one hidden just over there." The boy called Fly pointed off to the north. "It's a good one, made of cypress wood. It will carry us, plus two large alligator carcasses."

"If you go get it, can you paddle back here, to this point, without getting lost?" I indicated the knuckle.

He looked at me like I was an idiot. "Of course."

"Then go. Beach the canoe at the end of the knuckle. Then come and find us."

Fly left at a jog-trot.

"What news?" I asked.

Long Arrow waved at a pesky mosquito. "The Kristianos are in Uzachile town as of last night. According to the rumors, they have been harassed the entire way. Anyone who strays too far from the main column is shot at. A couple of them have been killed while trying to pick corn from the fields. Shot from ambush."

I considered that. "Then they'll be angry. Ready to put us in our place as they did at Napetuca."

"But Holata Uzachile will not openly oppose them. Word is that the *Adelantado* has requested the Great Holata travel to the capital and have council."

"Uzachile has refused, I hope."

Long Arrow gave me a quick nod. "Lessons learned hardest are lessons learned best." He squinted at three logs half sunk in the muck. "What is this?"

I slicked mud from my thighs. "You're looking at the only route cabayeros can follow to capture two fleet-footed boys who've just fled onto the knuckle."

"They'll never try to cross that."

"It's not finished yet." I grinned with what I hoped was confidence. "When Pearl Hand and I are through, they won't even hesitate."

Then Long Arrow looked back at the haphazard barricades of branches, vines, logs, and brush that we'd built across the neck. From where we stood, Walking Thunder could be seen weaving grapevines between trees.

"Is Walking Thunder leaving a big enough gap? After all, the boys will be fleeing at a full run."

I followed his pointing finger to where we'd

roped a log slantwise between a narrow gap. "We'll try it out later and see. Now, since you and the boys are here, you can dig me a slit trench right there at the north end of the barricade. See that opening between the two trees and just up from the water? I need it to be narrow, not more than two hands across, with logs set longways along the lips of the trench."

"Like a narrow pit trap."

"Just so. And when it's finished, you need to carry the dirt off and scatter it. Then place twigs across the trench before you lay leaves over it."

He nodded, getting the idea, then frowned. "Shouldn't it be wider?"

"No," I told him. "The size is just right."

"Maybe for a rabbit," he muttered.

"And you," I turned to the remaining youth. "First off, I need you to go back to the trail crossing. We need to collect five piles of firewood. They must be spaced out roughly the same distance from each other as the fires in a small village. So that from a distance five pillars of smoke will be seen."

"Yes, Peliqua."

I studied him carefully, aware of his curiosity and unmasked anxiety. Would he hold when the time came? I was betting a great deal on the boys.

"By the time you've scrounged up enough wood, your friend Fly should be back with the canoe. When that happens, I'll walk you through and show you exactly what you have to do."

"Long Arrow said it was dangerous."

"What was your name again?"

He made a face. "I'm still called Toad. But I'll have a man's name soon."

I gave him my most serious expression. "Toad, if you and Fly do this correctly, you'll both have earned your man's names. On Horned Serpent's honor, I promise that."

At the sudden excitement in his eyes, I suffered a stab of worry. What if it all went wrong? Images from Napetuca, Tapolaholata, and all the other places came back to haunt me.

I had to ask myself, *How often has it gone right?*

FORTY

Slogging in mud up to my waist, I heaved. With Bear Paw's strength assisting me, I rolled the final heavy log into place, watching mud spatter as it settled beside its mate. We'd laid three logs longways, through the narrow marsh below the knuckle.

Hidden behind the knuckle's rise rested the canoe that Fly had brought. In every other direction stretched open swamp, shaded by cypress and tupelo, dotted here and there with water lily, duckweed, and clumps of grass in the occasional shallows.

I leaned my head back, hearing the buzzing of insects, the melodic birds chirping in song. Something made me glance to the right, and there, perched on a cypress knee, Anhinga watched me.

"Go tell Horned Serpent we're counting on him," I growled. "Tell him we're trying to do this smart for once."

The bird watched me for a heartbeat, then dove neatly into the water, rings widening where he'd disappeared.

Bear Paw was staring first at me, and then at the rings spreading where the anhinga had disappeared.

"You've got to watch those anhingas," I told him. "You never know which world they'll fly to, or to whom they'll say what."

"Yes, Peliqua."

I grinned, then slogged my way out of the muck, sluicing mud from my legs. "Are the fires set as I asked?"

Bear Paw glanced back up the ridge. "They should be."

I gestured to the logs. "Then let's add the finishing touches to this. I say we pull up grass by the roots and lay it over the ooze. Maybe add a couple of saplings, trees like hickory that wouldn't grow in muck. As soon as this dip looks like solid ground, we can light the fires."

"Bait for the trap," Bear Paw agreed. He waded out from where we'd been digging with sharpened sticks and sloshed water to wash the goo from his hide. "It's been a lot of work."

"Oh, yes." I couldn't help but admire the way my small band had pitched in. "Now let's just hope the Kristianos are so carried away with the chase that they don't realize what's happening."

Later, as I walked up the ridge, I double-checked everything. Here and there we'd hauled in logs and brush and left it in piles to break up the open spaces. Anything to make the raised ground look as if thirteen people hadn't been working like slaves to re-arrange it.

We were ready. Now all I had to do was rehearse my little band so that they understood exactly what I wanted. If it fell apart, the best outcome would be that the Kristianos simply turned tail and fled. The worst would come if they figured out what we were doing and came ahead slowly. Then, either we'd have to swim for it, or die.

I made a face as I stared out at the swamp. Did I have the courage to trust myself to the water again?

I absently fingered Horned Serpent's Sepaya where it rested in the pouch hanging from my neck. Nightmares lay in that direction.

The morning was calm, and I stood, my head back, as five columns of smoke rose above the trees. Periodically one of the youths would toss a juniper or pine branch on the blaze, and for a few moments a darker plume would rise. Then it was back to green branches that kept the smoke white and clearly visible from a distance.

The waiting had begun. And with it came indecision. Had we picked the right place? Were we close enough to Uzachile town? Was our trap too far for one of the patrols to investigate? Would the Kristianos really come?

With each passing finger of time I fretted, pacing up and down the jutting sliver of land, ensuring that everyone was in position. Being down near the knuckle, it took all of my will to keep from running back to check on Toad and Fly. They had the most critical job: keeping the fires going until the Kristianos arrived.

And what if the Kristianos brought war dogs with them? We'd planned for that eventuality, but I'd placed our dogs just above the slope that led down to the knuckle. At my call, they might be the difference between success and disaster. If I was wrong, the Uzachile boys would pay with their lives.

I spun around, staring down at the low spot that joined the knuckle to the main ridge. From here, it just didn't look right. Had we placed the logs sufficiently far apart? Would the Kristianos see the difference? Would they recognize the two blinds floating on either side of the trap? We'd tried to make them look like muskrat houses.

"Will you just sit?" Pearl Hand asked. "This may take a couple of days."

"If they come at all."

"I'm betting on the Southerners."

"Me, too." I slapped hands to my hips and glanced at where my bow and quiver waited. "The Kristianos will be exploiting their skills at woodcraft. Toad assures me that our fires should be visible all the way to Uzachile. If we're right, the traitors will tell de Soto it's a distant village." I began to pace again. "If cabayeros aren't here by tomorrow, they're not coming."

"Exactly," Pearl Hand agreed. She was sitting on the leaf mat, her crossbow and three iron-tipped arrows ready at hand.

"What if the boy tending the fires is caught by surprise? What if he doesn't blow the conch horn we gave him? What if —"

"What if you don't shut up?" she grumbled.

I smothered a smile. "So, the waiting is getting to you, too."

"No," she shot back. "You are. Trust the Kristianos to be themselves. The only way they won't come is if de Soto doesn't linger in Uzachile. But he will."

"Why?"

"Think, Black Shell. Use your head. Would the man you saw in Uriutina be in a hurry to leave a big, fortified town full of food while he's low on slaves? You saw him. He thinks this whole country is his. He broke any organized resistance at Napetuca."

"But Long Arrow also said that his men were being harassed, ambushed. He might —"

The hollow sound of a conch horn carried through the thick trees.

"Blood and pus," I muttered, my heart skipping. "They're here!"

Pearl Hand sprang to her feet, placing a foot in the loop and stringing the crossbow.

I scrambled for my bow, wrapping it around my leg and using my hip to string it. Then I grabbed my quiver.

Pearl Hand had her three arrows in her left hand. She paused long enough to say, "Shoot straight, my love. Don't miss."

"You either," I added, and trotted down to the low spot that joined the knuckle to the ridge. At the water's edge, I glanced back at where the dogs waited, alert now, watching.

"Stay!" I shouted and gave them the hand sign. "Down . . . and stay!" I watched as all but Bark dropped to their bellies. Oh, yes, if they were going to make a mess of it, Bark would be the one. He cocked his head, tail wagging.

I waded out into the soft muck. We'd placed each of the shooting blinds on a raft of branches no more than five paces from the bridge and back so that we wouldn't be shooting at each other. Squishing my way behind it, I laid my quiver on the logs that formed the base. The idea was that the floating wood would stop a crossbow arrow. Now I wished I'd taken another couple of hands of time to build it stouter.

My breath was coming fast, my heart pounding. I kept working my fingers, craning my neck to see through the tree boles and barricades that screened the ridge.

Shouts carried, softened as they bounced between the trees. I could hear birds crying their alarm. Then came the first faint clink of metal, followed by a shouted command.

Come on, boys. Run! Don't panic, just run for all you're worth.

I carefully nocked an arrow, testing the pull of my bow. The little mound of swamp grass before me seemed too small. They'd see me for sure.

I could just make out Pearl Hand's head where she waited on the opposite side, screened as I was, barely visible over the camouflaged logs laid in the low spot. Her crossbow would be resting on her screen, ready.

I almost jumped out of my skin when a fish began nibbling on my leg.

Careful, Black Shell.

When had my mouth gone so dry? Gods, why couldn't I still my banging heart or damp the sweat on my palms?

I caught movement, and true to form, Fly lived up to his name, feet pounding, arms pumping, his hair streaking out behind him. And on his heels came Toad. One after another they ducked, leaping through the small gaps we'd left in the barricades.

The sound of clanking metal, the thud of cabayo feet on unforgiving ground, seemed to shake the very earth. And then I could see them, a ragged line of cabayos rounding the end of one of the barricades. It was working! Our course had them zigging and zagging, running the cabayos back and forth in search of holes in the timber. The Kristianos were yipping and shouting, smacking their mounts, carried away by the pursuit.

I caught a glimpse as one of the cabayos seemed to stumble, going down, the rider thrown full onto his face ahead of the tumbling animal. The others barely hesitated, hammering their cabayos' sides in pursuit of the fleeing youths.

Fly ducked as he leaped through the last gap and led the way down the ridge, Toad on his heels. Fly slowed only to mince his way across the hidden logs. Toad only took a moment longer to pick his way across the leaf-strewn logs. Then they were sprinting, full out, over the rise of the knuckle to the canoe on the other side.

"Stay!" I bellowed at the dogs, all of whom were standing now, heads turned toward the approaching riders. "Stay!"

In shouting, I'd taken a chance, but the

Kristianos didn't seem to notice that my voice wasn't a youth's. Their leader had already picked out the gap we'd left at the water's edge and he drove his beast full for it. The cabayo leaped the gap, followed by two more. They obscured my view as the fourth mount dropped a foot in the slit-trench Long Arrow had placed dead center. The animal fell sideways, slamming its rider against one of the trees at the side of the gap. The impact could be heard over the shouting men, the huffing cabayos, and creaking leather.

I took a deep breath, watching as the remaining three galloped full-out down the ridge. Even then I couldn't help but marvel. I'd never had time to notice the grace with which they rode, how man and animal merged into one fluid motion.

Squatting low, I drew the arrow back to my ear. The lead rider never even hesitated. The great gray cabayo hit the grass-covered dip at full speed, making two steps before a hoof slipped through the scattering of leaves and twigs that masked the slippery logs. The beast went down, straddling the length of the log, sliding on its belly. To my amazement, the rider kept his seat, though his feet were dragging in the ooze.

The second cabayo went wide, sinking up to its belly in muck. Its rider fell, slamming into the rear of the first. In the confused tangle, men and animals thrashed. Men were shouting, the cabayos trying to buck their way out of the mess.

The final rider barely pulled up, his copper-colored mount sliding on all four feet, settling back on its haunches. When he turned his mount my arrow arced into the copper cabayo's underbelly. Then instinct from long practice took over. I drove shaft after shaft into the animal as it stood, wheeled, and began to sidestep. Meanwhile, the rider, feet forward in the stirrups, sawed at the straps, seeking control.

That was the moment the dogs arrived, barking and snapping, adding to the confusion.

The great copper-colored cabayo tried to bolt, bucking several times before it went down on its knees. The rider stumbled off, fell to one side. As he tried to climb to his feet, Skipper jumped full on his back, driving him face forward into the leaf mat.

The rider of the second horse — up to his waist in mud — was struggling with the straps with his left hand. His right, I noticed, was in a sling. The cabayo pulled free and turned. I took that moment to drive an arrow into the beast's unprotected side.

The first rider had stepped off, managing to find one of the now displaced logs. As he struggled with his mired cabayo, he lost his footing and fell. I had a momentary glimpse of Antonio's father, eyes wide, mouth open, the grizzled gray beard jutting up from his chin as he splashed backward into the ooze.

FORTY-ONE

"Papá," Antonio cried, starting forward.

Screams could be heard up the ridge where Bear Paw, Long Arrow, Wide Antler, and Corn Thrower had been hidden. Their job had been to wait as the riders passed, shooting into the rearmost cabayo as it rode by. If successful, we could hunt down the men on foot one by one.

The loud clang of a crossbow arrow on armor rang out, and Antonio staggered. He stared in horror. Fletching stuck out of his oversized armor, just below his breast.

The old man saw, screaming, *"Huyes! Afuera! Ahora! Salvate, Antonio!"*

"Papá?" Antonio looked up with disbelief.

The image of Antonio wading through dying men, his sword slinging blood, filled my memory. I turned, shooting too quickly. The arrow glanced off Antonio's helmet.

He wheeled, seeing me as I came sloshing through the water, my bow already bent. Recognition flashed in his eyes.

"For the dead at Napetuca," I shouted. "For their ghosts, and the ones you murdered like a coward." Then I remembered the word. *"Cobarde! Antonio, tú eres un cobarde!"*

The old man shouted something else and came wading through the mud. He reached for the muddy sword at his side and pulled it from the scabbard. Black mud clotted in his beard, and he'd lost his helmet.

"Cobarde?" he cried. *"Mi hijo? Nunca!"*

On impulse I turned, sighting down my arrow. It hit me. *He's only wearing a mail shirt!* That accursed armored carapace was missing. I loosed my arrow, watching the muddy silver shirt ripple as the point drove deep into the man's gut.

Don Luis staggered forward, almost tripped, and stumbled onto firm ground. His eyes were round, his mouth open. Glancing down, his left hand went to the shaft protruding just below his breastbone.

Antonio swallowed hard and started forward as I nocked another arrow. He ducked as I let fly, and it shattered on the rim of his helmet.

In one smooth motion, I drew another arrow, nocking it, drawing it smoothly back as I approached. Antonio had drawn his sword, thinking to close and kill me. Over the point of my arrow, I saw his eyes widen with the understanding that he was too late. The very instant I released, he spun, throwing his sword to the side. My arrow clanged off his armor an instant before he jumped onto his wounded cabayo. I ran after as he hammered the animal with his heels. The cabayo, panicked, raced straight for the brush fence, chased by Skipper and Squirm. I could see my arrow deep in its side. With a leap, the great beast crashed through our matting of vines and branches.

The third man had regained his feet and was now swinging a sword as he chased Bark and Gnaw. They were game, barking, leaping, tails swishing as they avoided his angry swings. But it was only a matter of time before he'd manage to kill one.

"Aquí!" I bellowed, drawing another arrow. "Here, you fool!"

He turned, no more than five paces away, and I was looking into his face as I drove my arrow through his right eye. His head jerked at the impact, and he staggered backward. Like a hewn tree he dropped heavily onto his butt. This time the dogs were on him for real.

"Black Shell! Behind you!"

I leaped and pivoted on one foot as air

hissed through the space I'd been in.

Don Luis staggered, recovered his balance, and lifted the sword for another swing. His dark eyes were fired with a desperate resolve, his lips twisted to partially expose his irregular brown teeth. Mud dripped from his beard and mixed with the dark red gut blood leaking around the arrow shaft in his belly.

"Indio sucio!"

I was pawing for another arrow as he took another wobbling step toward me. That was when Bark, carried away with his own attack on the man I'd killed, thudded into the back of my legs. My knees went out from under me, and I landed flat on my back.

Rolling, I barely avoided Don Luis's vicious slice, his silver blade slashing through the leaf mat where I'd been but a moment before.

The strap of my quiver pulled tight against my arm, trapping it, and stopping any further scrambling. A tingling sensation rolled through my guts and bones, anticipating the keen blade.

Don Luis saw my plight, and he grinned. *"Te mato!"* he sneered as he raised the blade again, eyes burning.

His body jolted, his belly jutting oddly forward, and his mouth opened to a puzzled O. I watched in fascination as he lurched forward, as if shoved from behind. Kicking up with my feet, I kept him from falling on me and managed to slither sideways, breaking my quiver strap.

The man's shirt of interlinked metal jutted out wierdly, pulling oddly at the embedded arrow shaft. When he spun and dropped to his knees, I saw why. Antonio's sword had been driven clear through his body. The force of the blow had pierced the armor in back, but hadn't the energy to break the links in front.

"Eres una puta," he rasped as he stared at Pearl Hand. *"Deseo que el Adelantado te matarías. Coño enfermo."*

Pearl Hand set her feet, grasping the handle, and wrenched the sword free. Don Luis uttered a wracking gasp, staring up in disbelief.

"Enjoy *paraíso*," she cried.

He was still staring as Pearl Hand braced herself and slashed his throat open.

FORTY-TWO

Pearl Hand, efficient as always, stepped over to the copper-colored cabayo and stripped a quiver of crossbow arrows from the animal. The owner's weapon remained lashed to the saddle.

"There's still more of them." I pointed up the ridge where shouts could be heard.

She nodded, then indicated the cabayo as it floundered sideways off the log, almost rolling in the churned mud and water. "What about that?"

"Later. Come on." I paused long enough to pick up the man's sword, thankful it wasn't covered with dog blood. After a hand command, Bark and Gnaw fell in behind us.

At the first gap, the cabayo who'd stepped into the trap was four paces uphill, its right front leg hung and flopped with each step. The man who'd hit the tree lay flat on his back, his face scraped and bleeding. He must have still been dazed because there was no recognition in his eyes as we approached. I lifted the sword, feeling its heft and balance. I owned two now.

He never knew what hit him.

At the next trap both cabayo and rider were dead, the latter with an arrow driven through his throat. The cabayo had been dispatched with a sword.

Walking Thunder, followed by Bear Paw and Wide Antler, came trotting in our direction, each carrying a sword or lance matted with crimson.

"Three got away," Walking Thunder announced by way of greeting. "How are the boys?"

"Alive." I waved out at the swamp. "They made it safely to the canoe. They're out there, some —"

"No, we're not!" Toad called as they came trotting up the slope. "And we've got our men's names now."

"Yes," I mused. "You do."

Corn Thrower appeared between the trees, a grin splitting his wide face. "How many did we get?"

"Seven out of the ten," Wide Antler cried,

then he shook a fist at the ridge. "And those three are running like rabbits from a fox!"

"Antonio's cabayo was gut shot," I added. "It won't make it far. They'll have to double up, or one will have to walk."

"What next, Peliqua?" Bear Paw asked in wonder.

"Three got away?" I grounded the sword tip, staring up the ridge where another of the Kristianos lay spread-eagle under one of the shagbark hickories. "By the time they make it to Uzachile, it will be dark. But that's no guarantee. Provided they don't get lost in the night, they could be back before dawn."

"Agreed," Wide Antler said. "So, we should strip the dead and be gone?"

I nodded, oddly tired. Where was the elation I had anticipated? "Take anything that seems worthwhile for trade or our own use. Sink the rest of it in the swamp where they can't find it."

Walking Thunder dropped to his knee, palms up. "You've done it, Peliqua. You've found a way to beat them. The dead at Napetuca are cheering."

The others, too, had dropped, offering their hands, eyes worshipful.

"It's only seven out of a thousand," I said softly.

"But it's a start," Corn Thrower answered. "And this time we didn't lose a single man. Not even wounded."

"We were lucky," Pearl Hand snapped, stepping forward to pull them up. "Come on, we've got work to do. And may Horned Serpent help us if a second party is anywhere close."

"She's right," I agreed. "The sooner we're off this point, the safer we'll be. If they catch us here, we'll all end up out in the swamp. Having survived the lake at Napetuca, that's one place you'd rather not be."

"What of that stuck cabayo down at the bridge?" Toad asked.

I handed him the sword. "Make it so that no Kristiano can use it to ride down another of our people."

Toad took the sword, awe in his eyes. Then he headed back down the ridge.

Something sharp and angry lay behind Pearl Hand's eyes as she said, "I want to leave a message for the Kristianos. Something they will remember this day by."

"And that is?" I asked.

"I'll show you," she told me through a bitter smile.

Within a hand's time, we had attended to the tasks at hand. Skipper and Squirm emerged from the forest as we were packing up. Both were filthy, and Skipper had a patch of hair missing from his side. Though obviously bruised, he seemed unusually pleased with himself.

"Come on," I ordered. "Hurry up. We've

bloodied them. I've looked into de Soto's eyes, and the man I saw will unleash his full fury when he finds out."

Oh yes, they'd be coming for us, and I didn't want to be found.

As the fire crackled and spat, I poked my finger through the hole in Don Luis's curious metal shirt and studied my companions. The momentary joy of our victory had faded against the memories of Napetuca. Long Arrow's expression had grown pensive, his eyes vacant, as if seeing the souls of friends who had been butchered. Walking Thunder had taken it the hardest; it had been his town, after all. Bear Paw's pinched lips barely hid the pain in his heart. Wide Antler sat cross-legged, poking at the fire with a long stick, fleeting memories sending brief and bitter smiles to die on his lips. Corn Thrower's eyes communicated a grimness of purpose, and his hands twitched as if he were strangling something imaginary.

I watched firelight ripple across the polished metal links. The sense of loss was palpable, if beyond identification. How could a person feel the loss of something he'd never really known he had? And with such poignancy?

I glanced down at the ring-coat. The garment amazed me. Relatively light compared to the armor worn by *soldados* — and even that sported by Antonio when we first captured him — this was a masterpiece of craftsmanship. It had been composed of thousands of small interlocking rings of metal.

"To make something like this?" I shook my head. "It must be worth a fortune."

Corn Thrower gave me a skeptical look. "Maybe this Don Luis didn't expect to fight today. Perhaps we are even luckier than we thought."

Pearl Hand took the shirt of rings, studying it. "There are few of these, and they are only worn by the nobles. See how the *hierro* is so polished that it shines?"

"Maybe it's pretty, but wouldn't they have tested the effectiveness of these? Why wear such a thing when an armored breastplate over batting provides better protection?"

She ran the pliant metal over her fingers and glanced at my bow. "They've been in the south, Black Shell. Your bow is of northern manufacture, and takes a much stronger pull than the average Timucuan hunting bow with its cane-tipped arrows."

"But even my bow can't penetrate the average *soldado*'s armor."

She held up the fine ring-shirt. "Well, let's hope all the nobles wear such things in the future."

I nodded. "Think Antonio made it back to Uzachile? Your shot partially penetrated his armor."

Pearl Hand shrugged. "Maybe. His armor was oversized to start with, and perhaps half the length of the arrow was sticking out. I don't think it would have been enough to kill him."

"We'd best assume he lived." I reached for my pipe. "One way or another, he knows his father is dead. And that we killed him."

Long Arrow leaned forward, his face hawkish in the firelight. "This Antonio, he is a Kristiano subchief? Like an iniha?"

"More like an Apalachee clan chief," I said as I packed tobacco into the pipe bowl. "With his father dead, I assume he's now Don Antonio." I thought about the way he'd tried to imitate his father that day at the council. And I remembered how Don Luis had rebuked him for trying to have us detained. "I wonder if he's up to it? Or if de Soto is going to wish the old man were still alive to keep the brat out of trouble?"

Pearl Hand smiled grimly as she bent to the fire and retrieved a burning stick. She held it as I drew on the stem and filled my lungs with smoke. Exhaling, I called, "Thank you for the small victory we won over the Kristianos. Tell the dead at Napetuca, Tapolaholata, and elsewhere that the Orphans have begun to strike back."

I passed the pipe to Pearl Hand. She drew, offering her own prayer to Power. The pipe was passed among our warriors, one by one.

I listened as they called out to dead family, assuring them that Napetuca, and their deaths, were not forgotten.

"What did Don Luis say before you killed him?" I shot a glance at Pearl Hand. "I couldn't follow much of it."

"It doesn't translate exactly, but he said my sheath is diseased, and that I would lie with any man."

I studied her. "Is that why you were so adamant that we leave him hanging naked and upside down from a tree?"

She gave me a half-lidded appraisal.

I thought about how the mortal remains of Don Luis had looked, his pale white skin shining like a beacon against the greens and browns of the swamp. "Antonio will be very annoyed with us."

She stared absently at the fire. "Good. Men who are enraged lose any sense of danger. As time passes — and we grow more proficient at killing them — we must encourage wild rage that overcomes any sense of caution among them."

"That blade cuts in two directions," I reminded. "Remember Blood Thorn."

"I never forget him," she said softly. "And pray that he is alive, safe, and back in his normal senses."

As if any of us were. I needed but look inside at the curious hollow place that had been ripped open under my heart. Or remember the way we'd left Don Luis and the dead Kristianos. Each had been stripped and hung upside down from one of the trees, arms dangling, a reminder to the relief party that Napetuca wasn't forgotten.

That night as the fire burned low around our small camp, I lay under the stars and tried to understand what was happening to us. The Kristianos were bringing a fetid darkness into our world, changing the dynamic that had been established by Breath Giver in the Beginning Times. What we'd seen at Napetuca had hollowed out something fundamental in our souls. Before we had only hated the Kristianos, but after Napetuca something ugly and terrible burned within us.

I stared longingly at the Path of the Dead where it banded the sky in a white, hazy bar. When this was all over, would I ever find my way back to the balance between red and white that made a man whole? Or would the terrible ugliness have burned any chance of redemption into ashes? Could a man, once driven by such a twisted hatred, ever make the leap through the Seeing Hand? Could he pass the tests of Old-Woman-Who-Never-Dies where she waited just past the Seeing Hand? And if I did — even though Horned Serpent had chosen me — would he allow me to follow the Path of the Dead? Would Eagle Man direct me to the dead end? Or pass me on to join my ancestors? Would those worthy ancestors take me in? Or would they shun me as something warped and maimed?

De Soto's image lurked between my souls. I could see his long face, the thin beard, and those detached and empty eyes. What wretched sickness of Spirit had he brought among us?

Even if we destroyed him, would we, ourselves, be destroyed in the process?

FORTY-THREE

A half day's walk west of Uzachile lies a band of forest and swamp. The country is wild, uninhabited, thickly overgrown, and in many places nearly impenetrable. Over the years any old growth forest that was easily passable had been purposefully burned to encourage the growth of brush, briars, and young trees. Both the Uzachile and Apalachee contributed to maintaining the relentless tangle. By its very nature, the thicket provided an easily defensible boundary zone between these longstanding enemies.

Crossing this contested territory was actually easy, provided that a person took one of the three main trails that wound through the mess. With good weather the journey could be made in three days.

We had rain.

De Soto, as we later learned, had rain and constant ambushes.

When I'd come east I'd taken the main trail that led more or less straight between Apalachee and Uzachile. This time we would take the southern trail since de Soto and his army were effectively choking the main route.

On the fifth day we were breaking camp on the northern edge of one of the swamps. The place was shadowed by mighty bald cypress, many of the trunks as thick around as a corn crib. Hanging moss draped from the branches, and white herons glided above the calm waters, their wings like pointed triangles.

Pearl Hand used sand to wash out our cooking bowl as our Timucua warriors attended to their weapons. She kept giving me a suspicious look from under lowered brows.

"What?" I finally asked as I set about packing up the dogs.

"That's what I was about to ask you," she answered. "You didn't sleep well last night."

"I had odd dreams. Fragments that made no sense. I saw Blood Thorn, a collar about his neck, and blood trickling down his skin." I fingered the piece of Horned Serpent's horn where it lay in the pouch about my neck. The thing had an oddly warm feeling, and it had been vibrating through most of the night.

She noticed my fiddling. "Is it trying to tell you something?"

I glanced warily at the warriors. "I don't know."

"It was a gift from Power," she replied. "Don't ignore it."

I strapped the last of our plunder onto the dogs and checked my bow as I slung my quiver onto my back. Squirm was looking up at me, his tail waving slowly. Bark was trying to scratch through his pack to get at an itch on his shoulder. Not even years of fruitless effort had managed to dissuade him from the folly.

Three trails entered the clearing: the one from the east that we'd arrived on, one heading north toward the Apalachee town of Agila, and the final being the route I intended to take. That route, according to Uzachile sources, wound through the swamps to the west. I had taken no more than three steps before the pouch containing Horned Serpent's Sepaya literally swung out and thumped me on the chest.

I frowned, trying to see what might have snagged the cord. Nothing. I took another step, and it thumped me again. At each step it seemed to hammer my breastbone with greater urgency.

I stopped.

Behind me, Pearl Hand asked, "What's wrong?"

611

I stepped back, crowding Skipper and Gnaw. The pouch remained calm. As I stepped forward, it seemed to swing of its own volition and thumped me again, as if urging me backward.

"I think we need to go back," I said uncertainly, watching as I backtracked into the clearing, dogs, wife, and warriors crowding around. I waved down their questions, turning slowly. The pouch slipped sideways on my chest, as if leaning toward the northern trail.

I sidestepped south, feeling the weighted pouch pull against my chest. When I took a step in the direction of the western trail, it thumped on my breast.

"Is the Sepaya moving?" Corn Thrower asked in dismay. "Or are you doing that, Peliqua?"

"I'm doing nothing," I muttered. "It feels like it's pulling toward the northern trail."

"But that leads toward de Soto." Pearl Hand frowned at the pouch.

I took a step toward the trail, and the pouch seemed to float, as if all weight had vanished. "I don't understand," I kept repeating.

"Let's try north." Pearl Hand slapped a hand to her crossbow. "But we've got to beware." She glanced distastefully at the thick underbrush lining the trail. "If we run into Kristianos, all we can do is stand and fight."

The pouch seemed to be pulling me. I

slowed, taking a step back, only to have it thump me on the breast. Moving forward, it grew feathery again.

"All right, we go north. But everyone, keep your ears open."

Behind me, the dogs lined out, and I heard mutterings among the Timucua about Power, the Peliqua, and Horned Serpent.

Throughout the morning, the Sepaya led me. We wound along the dim trace, pressing through brush, following a faint path beneath stands of pine, or walking on partially rotted logs that had been placed for footing in swampy areas. When fresh deer trails would have misled me, the pouch would swing to the left or right.

"Is this right?" Pearl Hand asked as we pushed through vines and clambered over a section of deadfalls. A tornado must have blown through sometime, cutting a swath through the older stands of oak, hickory, and maple.

I ducked under a thorny stem of greenbriar, watching the pouch swing forward, as if of its own volition. "It's not thumping on my chest."

The dogs scrambled along behind, the warriors following as they picked their way through honeysuckle and blackberries that were growing up to engulf the downed timber.

At the end of the swath, I used my bow to

brush poison ivy to one side and slipped my way through a crush of sumac. Weaving and twisting, I pressed ahead, parting the branches, and finally stumbled into a grassy clearing where fire had charred the downed timber. The faint trail, but rarely used, could be seen snaking its way north.

Pearl Hand, having struggled through with her crossbow, stopped to pull bits of spider-web and leaves from her hair. The pouch seemed to swing out, as if demanding I move.

The clearing couldn't have been more than four bowshots across, and I was almost to the stand of oaks at the far end when I heard the clinking of metal from ahead.

Without thinking, I slashed my hand for silence. The order was meant for the dogs, but immediately everyone froze. As if I were a youth, rehearsing combat command under my uncle's watchful eye, I pointed left with four fingers, right with three. I called the dogs to follow me as I slipped off through the waist-high grass, clambered over the burned trunk of a fallen tree, and motioned the dogs down.

Even as I strung my bow, the sound of metal clinking grew louder. Then a branch snapped.

Bark growled, and I gestured for silence. Moments later, I could hear panting and more clinking. I knew that sound: metal chain. Then came the irregular thump of feet, almost staggering. A branch whipped against skin. Raising my head, I saw a man break from the screen of oaks. He was muscular, thick of body — and ready to drop from fatigue. Sweat glistened on his smudged and filthy skin, and his lungs were heaving. The collar hanging from his neck stood out like an abomination, links of chain jumping and jerking with each hammered step.

From behind came another crack, and the clank of metal. The heavy sound of cabayos made the man glance over his shoulder, and I got a good look at his tortured face. He blinked, as if in agony, and tried to run, managing only to totter forward.

I gestured silence to the dogs, and nocked an arrow as the exhausted man tripped and blundered on down the trail.

I almost missed the war dog as it charged out, head down, sniffing along the man's trail. Then came the first of the cabayos, a brown beast bearing a rider splotched with forest detritus.

Behind him followed three more. I waited as they passed, then shouted, "Now!"

My arrow drove through the gap where a batted-cloth hanging covered the cabayo's side.

As my dogs went charging out, barking and growling, the cabayero's mount began bucking sideways into the obscured deadfall. Fouled by the rotting trees and branches, the animal careened onto its side, crushing its rider amid snapping timber.

Nocking another arrow, I started forward as the second rider tried to spin his cabayo and flee. The dogs, encumbered by their heavy packs, blocked the trail, barking and growling, causing the cabayo to rear. Clutching his crossbow with his left hand, the cabayero made the mistake of spurring his animal off into the grass. I saw him stiffen, rising from the stirrups, then his mount stumbled into a hole and pitched him off one side. The panicked cabayo bucked and clambered over the deadfall, breaking branches as it disappeared in the oaks.

As quickly as it had begun, it was over. The first cabayo had fallen to its knees in the trail, its rider laid out to one side. Walking Thunder and Long Arrow were creeping up, bows drawn. Pearl Hand had risen from the grass, stepping up to shoot point blank at the second rider. Bark and Gnaw were missing, but I heard the war dog squealing somewhere out in the grass.

Bow drawn, I crept up to the third rider, still trapped under his dying cabayo. Each time the beast kicked and lurched, it crushed the man against a great log. Taking a deep breath, I released the tension on my bow.

Wide Antler, a Kristiano sword in his hands, was stalking up from behind the man.

I silenced Skipper with a gesture, and took

a head count. We were all alive and un-wounded. Then I trotted back down the trail to where the escaped slave had dropped to his knees, gasping for breath.

"Thank the sun and the ancestors. I couldn't have gone any farther." He panted softly as I strode up.

"Thank Horned Serpent." I stared down at him. "Because of you, we can claim three more for the dead at Napetuca."

"Black Shell?" He seemed half dazed.

"It's all right, Iniha. You're safe now."

The others were gathering behind me, staring down in disbelief.

"How did you escape?" I asked.

"I used a piece of sandstone. One of the pieces you gave me. I was able to grind a notch in the chain . . . dabbing feces on it when they came checking. If they catch us grinding at the chains, we are killed outright as a lesson to the others. Man, woman, child, it doesn't matter. This morning when they overran Agila town, I escaped in the confusion."

"So they've attacked the Apalachee?"

Blood Thorn looked up. "Can you believe it? After fighting their way out of Uzachile, they caught the Apalachee completely by surprise. That's the only reason I was able to escape. The Kristianos were so obsessed with catching new slaves, they didn't keep watch on the ones they already had. I sawed a link in two, and slipped away. I thought maybe I could reach one of the southern trails, head home."

He swallowed hard. "Just bad luck . . . I was running. One of the cabayeros, searching for Apalachee, saw me and shouted. I . . . I thought I was going to be caught again."

I said, "You weren't. And we've some experience at taking collars off. And this time we can use metal to loosen the buttons."

"I was such a fool. I just wanted to die."

"If you're over that now," Pearl Hand said, "you're welcome to come with us. We're headed to Apalachee. There are Kristianos to kill there."

Still kneeling in the trail, Blood Thorn dropped his head into his hands and began to weep.

Epilogue

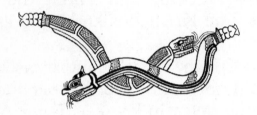

I fingered my pouch, wondering that it had led us to Blood Thorn, urging us to be at just the right place, at just the right time.

I watched my little band as they sat around the fire. The rich smell of cooking venison was borne on the night breeze as haunches crackled and hissed over a thick bed of glowing coals.

Pearl Hand sat to my right, Blood Thorn to the left. His neck was raw where the collar had been. Like me, he would have scars as a reminder.

The rest of the Orphans sat in a ring, listening as Blood Thorn told his tale. I knew the story. It had happened to me once upon a time.

"Yes, Antonio recovered Don Luis's body." Blood Thorn took the pipe Wide Antler offered him. He pulled on the stem, and blew the smoke up at the cloudy night. Then passed it to me.

As I drew and exhaled, he told us, "Believe me, they are upset. Perhaps infuriated is a better word. They know you now, Black Shell. Your story is being told among the Uzachile captives. The Kristianos know you as *el huérfano.*"

"The Orphan," Pearl Hand translated.

Blood Thorn shot me a sober look. "The traitor, the one you knew as Ears? Accompanied by Ortiz and Antonio, he looked me up the night before we reached Agila . . . seeking information about you."

"So, Antonio's alive?"

"And healing. Last I saw, his right arm was still in a sling, but the infection's subsiding. The puncture in his side is sore, but doesn't slow him down." Blood Thorn shook his head. "No matter what, neither of you must ever be captured by him. I saw it in Antonio's eyes. Death lay there."

"How did they discover that you knew the Peliqua?" Bear Paw asked.

"The traitors repeat anything Uzachile captives discuss." Blood Thorn rubbed his hands absently. "The Kristianos are learning, and that's something to consider. It will make the future a more difficult place for us all. Many

620

of the *soldados* are growing dissatisfied. All they have found is war and women. They want riches."

I handed the pipe to Pearl Hand. "Heading straight into the Apalachee? I think they're going to get a bellyful of war."

Blood Thorn turned his attention to me, and then Pearl Hand. "Antonio knows you're following de Soto. He kept quizzing me about your movements, habits, and so forth."

Pearl Hand crinkled her nose in disgust. "What did you tell him?"

Blood Thorn shrugged. "What could I? You are a well-known trader, a man of honor. He already knows you were a captive once, and that you've killed his father. Ears, however, has told him more. About the things you did at Irriparacoxi's town. From others they know that you advised our holatas, that you were part of the attempt to kill de Soto." His gaze grew serious. "Even de Soto knows who you are."

I fingered the Sepaya, feeling its outline through the pouch. "We were given no guarantees. We knew that from the beginning."

"Power is with us," Corn Thrower said earnestly. "Just like when it led us to you, Iniha."

"It must be used cautiously," I reminded. "We are but weapons in a great war. And sometimes, in battle, a weapon must serve a purpose, even if it's destroyed."

That sobered them.

I glanced from face to face, taking their measure. "As Horned Serpent told me, it will be long and hard. And as Old-Woman-Who-Never-Dies told me, this is a battle among men, for the hearts and souls of all peoples. We fight for our world. Perhaps it is up to fate to determine if any of us live to see the day the last Kristiano leaves our land. But until that day, we Orphans have a purpose greater and more compelling than anything we had before. No matter what the cost, let us not lose the future."

I felt Horned Serpent's horn warming under my touch, as if it came alive with the words.

All we had left to worry about were the Apalachee — and how I was going to explain the presence of a band of Uzachile warriors to High Mikko Cafakke and his thorny war chiefs.

I smiled at the thought. After all, I'm Black Shell, of the Chicaza. I've known Cafakke for years. He was one crafty — if crippled — character.

Despite his physical disabilities, he had a weakness for chunkey matches. In the game, two players rolled round stone disks down a flat clay strip. Then each cast a lance at the rolling stone. He whose lance landed closest to the disk when it finally stopped received a point. In the past — to his chagrin — he'd always bet against me. Perhaps I might lose by a point or two this time?

I felt Horned Serpent's brow tine vibrating under my fingers.

BIBLIOGRAPHY

Bense, Judith A.
1994 *Archaeology of the Southeastern United States: Paleoindian to World War I.* Academic Press: New York.

Brose, David S.
1984 "Mississippian Period Cultures in Northwestern Florida" in *Perspectives on Gulf Coast Prehistory,* edited by Dave D. Davis. University Press of Florida: Gainesville.

Brown, Robin C.
1994 *Florida's First People.* Pineapple Press: Sarasota.

Clayton, Lawrence A., Vernon James Knight, and Edward C. Moore, eds.
1993 *The De Soto Chronicles,* Vols. I and II. University of Alabama Press: Tuscaloosa.

Duncan, David Ewing
1995 *Hernando de Soto: A Savage Quest in the Americas.* Crown Publishers: New York.

Dye, David H.
1995 "Feasting with the Enemy: Mississippian Warfare and Prestige-Goods Circula-

tion" in *Native American: Interactions: Multi-scalar Analysis and Interpretations in the Eastern Woodlands* edited by Michael S. Nassaney, and Kenneth Sassaman. University of Tennessee Press: Knoxville.

De la Vega, Garcilaso
1998 *The Florida of the Inca.* Translated by John and Jeanette Varner. University of Texas Press: Austin.

Granberry, Julian
1993 *A Grammar and Dictionary of the Timucua Language.* University of Alabama Press: Tuscaloosa.

Grantham, Bill
2002 *Creation Myths and Legends of the Creek Indians.* University Press of Florida: Gainesville.

Hann, John H.
1988 *Apalachee: The Land Between the Rivers.* Ripley P. Bullen Monographs in Anthropology and History: No. 7. The Florida State Museum/University of Florida Press: Gainesville.

Hudson, Charles
1979 *Black Drink: A Native American Tea.* University of Georgia Press: Athens.
1976 *The Southeastern Indians.* University of Tennessee Press: Knoxville.

Hutchinson, Dale L.
2006 *Tatham Mound and the Bioarchaeology of European Contact.* University Press of

Florida: Gainesville.

Larson, Clark Spencer, Christopher B. Ruff, Margaret J. Schoeninger, and Dale L. Hutchinson.

1992 "Population Decline and Extinction in La Florida" in *Disease and Demography in the Americas* edited by John W. Verano and Douglas H. Ubelaker. Smithsonian Institution Press: Washington D.C.

Larson, Lewis H.

1980 *Aboriginal Subsistence Technology of the Southeastern Coastal Plain during the Late Prehistoric Period.* The University Presses of Florida: Gainesville.

Lankford, George E.

2008 *Looking for Lost Lore: Studies in Folklore, Ethnology, and Iconography.* The University of Alabama Press, Tuscaloosa.

Laudonniere, Rene

2001 *Three Voyages* translated by Charles E. Bennett. University of Alabama Press: Tuscaloosa.

Martin, Jack B., and Margaret Mauldin

2000 *A Dictionary of Creek Muskogee.* University of Nebraska Press: Lincoln.

Mckivergan, David A.

1995 "Balanced Reciprocity and Peer Polity Interaction in the Late Prehistoric Southeastern United States" in *Native American Interactions: Multiscalar Analysis and Interpretations in the Eastern Woodlands* edited by Michael S. Nassaney and Kenneth Sassaman. University of Tennessee Press: Knoxville.

Milanich, Jerald T.
1996 *The Timucua.* Blackwell Publishers: Cambridge.
1995 *Florida Indians and the Invasion from Europe.* University Press of Florida: Gainesville.

Milanch, Jerald T., and Charles Hudson
1993 *Hernando de Soto and the Indians of Florida.* University Press of Forida: Gainesville.

Myers, Ronald, and John J. Ewel
1990 *Ecosystems of Florida.* University of Central Florida Press: Orlando.

Nelson, Gil
1994 *The Trees of Florida.* Pineapple Press, Inc.: Sarasota.

Peregrine, Peter
1995 "Networks of Power: the Mississippian World System" in *Native American Interactions: Multiscalar Analysis and Interpretations in the Eastern Woodlands* edited by Michael Nassaney and Kenneth Sassaman. University of Tennessee Press: Knoxville.

Purdy, Barbara A.
1991 *The Art and Archaeology of Florida's Wetlands.* CRC Press: Boca Raton.

Reilly, F. Kent, and James F. Garber, eds.
2007 *Ancient Objects and Sacred Realms:*

Interpretations of Mississippian Iconography.
University of Texas Press: Austin.

Townsend, Richard F., ed.

2004 *Hero, Hawk, and Open Hand: American Indian Art of the Midwest and South.* Art Institute of Chicago in Association with Yale University Press: New Haven and London.

Scarry, John F.

1996 "Stability and Change in the Apalachee Chiefdom" in *Political Structure and Change in the Prehistoric Southeastern United States* edited by John Scarry. University Presses of Florida: Gainesville.

Swanton, John R.

2000 *Creek Religion and Medicine.* University of Nebraska Press: Lincoln.

1928a "Aboriginal Culture of the Southeast" *42nd Annual Report of the Bureau of American Ethnology,* pp. 673–726. United States Government Printing Office: Washington, D.C.

1928b "Social and Religious Beliefs and Usages of the Chickasaw Indians" *44th Annual Report of the Bureau of American Ethnology,* pp. 169–274. United States Government Printing Office: Washington, D.C.

Ubelaker, Douglas H.

1992 "North American Indian Population Size" in *Disease and Demography in the Americas* edited by John W. Verano and

Douglas H. Ubelaker. Smithsonian Institution Press: Washington, D.C.

ABOUT THE AUTHORS

W. Michael Gear and **Kathleen O'Neal Gear** are the authors of over twenty international bestsellers that have been translated into twenty-three languages. Their novel *People of the Raven* won the Golden Spur Award in 2005. In addition to writing both fiction and nonfiction together and separately, the Gears operate an anthropological research company called Wind River Archeological Consultants, and raise buffalo on their ranch in northern Wyoming.